JOSHUA'S Revenge

A NOVEL

Richard L. Wren

Poor Richard Publishers
Oakland, California

What readers are saying about Richard L. Wren

"I've been a biker all my life, and I really enjoyed CASEY'S SLIP. Mr. Wren told me that one of the lead characters in his book was modeled after me and I had a lot of fun recognizing myself. Casey's Slip was an entertaining read, with lots of unexpected twists and turns. I had a hard time putting it down and am looking forward to his next, JOSHUA'S REVENGE."

—Andy Kokot. Motorcycle enthusiast and antique car collector

"Really enjoyed this book, seemed to grab me right away. Of course, I love Yosemite anyway. Fast moving, interesting characters, good story development. This author's books just keep getting better.

—Karen Branin, Port Orchard, Washington.

Copyright © 2012 by Richard L. Wren
Poor Richard Publishers 1st Edition

CHAPTER 1

Half way down the four mile trail from Glacier point to the valley, Josh's cell phone interrupted the quietness of the afternoon. His first reaction was to ignore the call. He and Fern had been honeymooning for two weeks, hiking, exploring and camping in the high country behind Yosemite. The phone call was an intrusion into their last day before his going back to his work as a Yosemite Ranger.

They both stopped in mid-stride. Fern said, "it must be important, nobody would call if it wasn't."

"Maybe it's a wrong number." Josh replied. "Anyway, the darn phone's buried so deep in my back pack I don't know if I can find it."

The phone rang on and on as Josh shrugged his back pack off and rummaged through it, searching for the cell phone.

"Besides, who the heck'd be calling me now. Maybe I'll just ignore it."

Finally, deep at the bottom, he found it, still ringing. Holding it up, he drew his arm back as if he was going to throw it away. Fern grabbed him and said, "don't you dare. Quit kidding around and answer it."

Somewhat belligerently he clicked the phone on and answered. "Yeah, who's there?"

"Josh, where are you?" The Yosemite Park superintendent's voice was immediately recognizable.

"About half way down the Four Mile Trail. What's up?"

"Don't move, let me see if I can spot you with our binocs."

"Don't move?"

"Yeah, we've got an emergency. You may be in danger. Stay where you are— Okay, we've got you. Jesus Christ, Josh, you and Fern have to get the hell out of there. Keep your cell phone on and run as fast as you can to the switchback immediately uphill from you."

Josh looked around. He couldn't see anyone else on the trail and no sign of anything dangerous. "That doesn't make sense, I don't see any danger here at all," he replied.

"Josh, this is an order. Get going, fast! Take my word for it, it's life or death! I'll explain on the way."

Josh and Fern grabbed their packs and hiked quickly back to the last switchback, Josh kept his cell phone to his ear.

"Here's what's happening. Two teenagers decided to hike up to Glacier but they decided the trail was too tame for them. We've been keeping an eye on them with our 'scope. Now it looks like they're stuck a little over five hundred feet almost straight above where you were and one of them seems to be slightly injured. We've been watching them but haven't been able to reach them. Damn kids don't even have a cell phone."

"Okay, I'm trying to find them with my binocs, but don't see them so far."

"I don't think you're going to see them from where you are, they're in a little ravine. Where they've been climbing the rocks are so unstable it's a miracle that they haven't already started a slide. What's even worse, when they come out of the ravine the next stretch is even more unstable. We're almost positive they're going to start a slide and be carried away themselves. They have no idea of the danger they're in."

"Tell me where they are, I'll go after them."

"That's not why I called. You're way too far below to reach them in time. All you can do is stay out of the way. We thought about a helicopter but the rotors would probably start the slide. No, you and Fern need to get out of the way. If they trigger a rockslide it's going to take out part of your trail, right where you were. It'll go right down the middle of several of the switchbacks. For your own safety you need to stay at the switchback. Stay away from the middle section."

"I think I see where they must be. It's above us and about fifty yards to our left and there's a lone pine tree just above it?"

"Yeah, that's it. See what I mean about getting there? It's all dangerously loose shale between you and them, impossible to traverse. The only way there is they way they went, over the big boulders in the center. It'd take an hour of rock climbing to reach them. By that time anyone could reach them they'd either have gotten through the slide area or be dead and there's not a damn thing we can do about it."

While talking with the Superintendent, Josh had been making a quick assessment of the situation. Where they were standing they were over a hundred yards away from the ravine.

Just above them the trail was steep with a series of short switch-backs, gradually leading closer to the actual slide area. He estimated that the third switch-back was much closer to the boys, maybe even within shouting distance.

Josh cut the Superintendent off in mid-sentence. "Wait, I want to try something."

He switched the cell phone off to discourage any argument, handed it to Fern, and told her "wait here," then sprinted up the trail.

At the third switch-back he was very close to the edge of the slide area and within perhaps fifty yards of the boys. There was no sign of them. He thought that even deep in the ravine, they might hear him call.

"HALLOO, HALLOO," he called as loudly as he could, "IN THE RAVINE, CAN YOU HEAR ME?"

His voice echoed back to him in the silence.

Just as he was about to call again, he heard a thin and quavery, "WHERE ARE YOU?"

"ON THE TRAIL, JUST WEST OF YOU, CAN YOU SEE ME?" he answered.

In a moment he saw an arm waving at him and quickly issued some orders.

"I'M A PARK RANGER, DON'T MOVE FROM WHERE YOU ARE. THAT'S AN ORDER. YOU'RE IN IMMINENT SLIDE DANGER. WE'RE COMING TO GET YOU TO SAFETY. UNDERSTAND?"

"YES, SIR, WHAT DO WE DO?"

"JUST WAIT AND DON'T MOVE OUT OF THE RAVINE. OKAY?"

"YES, SIR."

The fifty or so yards between Josh and the boys was a particularly unstable looking section of the slide area, most of it composed of shale and small rocks. Josh thought it would be extremely slow and dangerous to try to reach the boys that way. He was afraid the boys might be afraid or full of false bravado and do something foolhardy if he didn't get to them soon.

He also knew that he could do something that perhaps he, and only he, could do to get to the boys quickly.

Quickly he raced down to Fern, telling her to get the Superintendent back on the phone.

"I'm going up!"

"Josh, be practical. It's physically impossible for you to reach them before they move again. I don't want to lose a Park Ranger. That rock slide's a killer. Stay on the trail; take care of Fern and yourself."

"I'm going up!"

"Josh, didn't I make myself clear? This is an order. Stay where you are!"

Josh didn't reply, simply turned off his cell phone, handed it to Fern and started barking succinct orders.

"Go up to where I was when I talked with the boys. Keep the cell phone out and stay hooked up with the Super, I'm going up."

"But, you can't. I heard what the superintendent said. It's almost straight up and covered with large boulders all the way. He said you couldn't possibly get there in time to stop them from going into the avalanche area. He said you'd be killed."

"I think I can. I know something he doesn't know. We're wasting time and I AM going."

Fern heard something in her husband's voice she had never heard before. Steel and decisiveness.

Josh took her hand. "So far everything's okay. No slide yet. The boy sounded a little panicked to me. I need to get there and take charge of the situation,---quickly."

"But----------," Fern started to say,

"Don't argue, there isn't time," Josh answered.

He stripped down to just his pants, shirt and shoes and started running back down the trail.

Fern thought to herself, "why is he running *down* the trail?"

CHAPTER 2

When he reached a spot about halfway to the next switchback, to Fern's complete amazement, Josh abruptly leaped off the trail and onto a large boulder just above the trail. She expected him to stop there but he didn't. He looked like he barely touched the boulder before leaping onto another and then another. It appeared as if he was flying up the hill. Each boulder was a little higher on the hill than the previous one. It was almost ballet like. He never stopped. Never slowed down. In a matter of moments he was at the ravine where the boys were stuck.

He disappeared into the ravine. Fern couldn't believe what she had just seen. A couple of minutes went by before he reappeared. She had been so surprised by what he had done she hadn't called the Superintendent.

Standing on the edge of the ravine, Josh called down to her. She could just barely make out his words.

"Fern," he called. "Get on your cell phone."

In a moment Fern had the Superintendents office on the phone.

"Tell him I've got them. One of them has a broken ankle, but the other one's okay. They're shaky, but okay. I'm going to carry one of them out and the other one can follow. Fern, stay where you are, I'll come to you. Don't leave the switchback. I'll be carrying one of the kids and traversing the slide area. The other kid's going to have to follow me across. The slide danger's going to be great, got it?"

He disappeared back into the ravine.

Fern was extremely apprehensive, but she had no choice. All she could do was watch and pray.

Josh carefully surveyed his possible escape routes. Directly above him, the slide had been diverted by a huge, totally impassable cliff. On either side the slide area extended for some 30 or 40 yards, and looked extremely unstable. Where they were was a grouping of large boulders, comparatively secure. Somehow he had to cross one of those unstable areas in order to reach the safety of the trail, carrying a 120 pound boy with a broken ankle. He couldn't go down, not with that added weight.

The obvious route was across the hill to his right which would take him back to the trail where his wife was waiting. It looked dangerous as hell. Studying the slide formation he was struck by it's similarity to a river. It wasn't just one jumble of rocks, it had dissimilar patterns to it, like the currents in a river. One section had a mixture of small and large rocks, another had areas of what looked like shale and would be extremely brittle and unstable. Another section had been diverted to one side of a large boulder, away from the trail and looked comparatively safe. Somehow or another, he had to cross all those areas in order to get these two boys to safety. He thought that if he could reach the boulder, the rest was passable.

In spite of his great strength and agility, he had only be able to carry one boy at a time. It might be possible that the second boy could make it on his own with Josh's help.

He tossed a good sized rock at the shale area which immediately caused a small slide. Very unstable and extremely dangerous. He would have to be very, very careful. He would have to test each step.

Josh slowly, step by careful step, started across the slide area. The center of the slide, where the boys had been climbing was made up of huge boulders, relatively stable. As he approached the edges of the ravine the rocks became smaller and smaller. Weighed down by the boy, unable to move quickly, testing every rock before he put weight on it, every step was a danger. There was no trail to follow, he could only slowly and delicately transfer his weight from rock to rock. The slide area was wide, almost as wide as the area between switchbacks. He could feel many of the rocks move ever so slightly under his feet as he gradually shifted his weight onto them. The slate crunched and rattled as it moved. He withdrew from a couple of them as he felt them start to slide. They were like jackstraws, if one moved they might all move. If they all moved, it would be a full scale rock slide, he and both the boys could be crushed under tons of rocks.

Watching him, holding her breath, Fern could only marvel at his progress. Suddenly, most of the way through, the whole section that he was standing on began to slide, the large piece Josh was standing on riding the crest. In a moment both he and the boy were cascading down the hill. Josh yelled "Hang on" and threw both his arms out to his side like a skier. The boy was welded to Josh's back like a back-pack. Fern's heart was in her mouth. The slide gained in momentum. She saw what he was attempting to do. He was riding the piece of shale like a snowboard. It couldn't go on, she expected the shale to break at any moment.

Suddenly she saw him crouch. A fraction of a second later he sprang toward the large boulder. Miraculously, covering several feet, carrying the boy on his back, he made it look easy.

The boulder was diverting the rock slide away from the switchback and once Josh had rested, he and the boy made the rest of the trip easily.

Looking back at how close he had come to disaster, he knew he couldn't risk that again. Maybe he couldn't save the other boy? Only he knew how close he had come to being killed and taking the first boy with him. He had to find another way.

First though, he needed to reassure the boy left in the ravine. He called to him, "did you see how dangerous that shale is? Whatever you do, don't move away from the ravine. We're going to figure another way to get you over safely. Understood?"

Josh had the germ of an idea, but he had to wait for help. He spoke to the Superintendent and asked for some specific supplies to be sent up with the rescue team.

He called over to the boy again. "Do you see that lone pine tree just above you?"

The boy had to climb up on one of the boulders to see it.
"Yes, sir."

"Can you reach it safely?"

"No problem."

"Okay, sit tight for now, got it?"

"Yes, sir."

Fern told him that the Superintendent said that a rescue crew was using small four wheel cross country vehicles to get to them as soon as possible, maybe ten to fifteen minutes. Maybe longer if the trail below them had been compromised. Over the diminishing sound of the sliding rocks, Josh could faintly hear them making their way up the trail.

It took over half an hour for the rescue crew to arrive. They said that the slide hadn't reached the trail but there had been lots of single rocks they had to clear.

The first question he asked them was, "did you bring the light line and the monkey fist I asked for?"

"Yeah, we got it, but that's sure a long throw, and what about the slide danger?"

"I'm not worried about making the throw and I'm going to aim at that tree just above the ravine. I can hit the tree and not touch the slide area at all."

The medic raised his eyebrows. Then, disbelievingly, asked. "Then what?"

"He ties the line around his waist, we go directly above him on the switch back, above the slide area and pull him out. He might start a slide on the way but with a couple of us on the other end we can pull him to safety."

"So you're going to throw the line to the tree, he climbs the tree, fastens the line around his waist and we pull him up?"

"That's it, unless you can think of a better idea. Personally, I don't think he'd make it if he tried to come across the way I did."

They did think about it, and after several minutes and climbing on up the trail to survey the route to pull him up, they finally agreed with Josh that it seemed not only the safest way, but perhaps the only way. "If you can make an accurate throw that far."

Once the decision was made, it turned out to be fairly easy. Josh made a perfect throw, the teen was able to retrieve it and tie it around his waist following Josh's instructions. The team placed themselves above him and were able to pull him up as he scrambled across the field of broken rocks. He set off a couple of small slides but they were able to pull him quickly out of the way. The rescue turned out to be simple and fast.

Fern hugged Josh and told him how scared she had been as she watched him carry the first boy to safety. The rescue squad largely ignored them as they packed the two boys on the four wheel vehicle they'd arrived in.

Josh thought his troubles over, having successfully engineered the rescue of the two boys, until Fern checked in with the Park Superintendent. She expected congratulations, but that was not what she got.

The Superintendent was spitting mad. "I want you both in my office first thing in the morning. It was a very brave thing Josh did and it came out okay, but he still disobeyed my direct order. I want to know what the hell went on up there this afternoon. Tell THAT to your new husband!"

That evening, after they were safely back in their quarters, Fern had some questions for Josh.

"What happened up there? I can hardly believe what I think I saw. You looked like you had wings."

Josh tried to keep his answer low key and casual. "Oh that. It's a variation of something the Germans dreamed up. The French do it, too. They call it *parkour* or *free-running*. The basic thought was that a lot of momentum and speed was lost each time a soldier stopped and rested, at least over short distances. By experimentation they found that if they could train their soldiers to have fast enough reflexes, they could leap from obstacle to obstacle at high speed and cover a lot of ground very quickly. I just took the idea a little farther. That's why I ran down the trail before I took off. Once I got my speed up, all I had to do was not stop. It's not supernormal or anything, it's just that I can do it a little better than most."

"Josh, you were almost flying! No matter the Germans or the French, nobody can do what you just did! Do the Germans go uphill the way you just did?"

"Probably not," he answered, hoping she would leave it at that.

This was what Josh feared. He knew he could do extraordinary things that, as far as he knew, no one else could do. He wanted to keep his prowess to himself even though he knew he would have to tell Fern someday. He didn't want publicity. He told Fern he was going to stay up for a while, maybe go over his notes for the meeting with the Super in the morning.

"Don't wake me up when you come to bed. I'm so looking forward to sleeping in a real bed." A kiss and she left him alone at his desk. Josh was glad she was tired and not too inquisitive. He didn't know what he would tell her.

Sitting alone, Josh reviewed the day. It had started early with Josh admiring the dawn breaking over Yosemite Valley. It had been a beautiful beginning.

CHAPTER 3

Like most mornings of their camping trip Josh was awake and out of his sleeping bag before sunrise, way before Fern. He had thought he would let her sleep in because it was the last morning of their honeymoon camping trip. Tomorrow would be business as usual at valley headquarters.

The morning had broken bright and clear. So, wanting to do one of his favorite things one more time, he had quietly slipped on his hiking shorts and boots and made his way to the cliff overlooking the valley. There he had carefully sat down on the edge, dangled his legs into space, and waited for the sun to creep across the campgrounds below him.

The view was magnificent. Almost the whole Yosemite Valley was visible. A view very few ever saw. Where they were camped was off limits to anyone but Rangers. The early morning chill was being offset by the sun shining on his back. His legs were icy cold while his back was warm. He had pulled his legs up to his chest and looked down between his boots at the hundreds of people doing whatever those people far below him did. They looked like ants scurrying from here to there. Some grouped together, some were hurrying someplace by themselves. Often they would disappear under some trees for a short time and then reappear on the other side. He had wondered what it would be like if he could listen in on their conversations as well as watch them from up here. Wisps of smoke were rising from early morning campfires.

His reverie was interrupted by his wife. "Josh, hotcakes are ready."

Carefully backing away from the cliff edge, he called out that he was coming and started for their campfire. She was standing with her back to him as he approached. He had paused for a moment to admire her. Slim, young, and brunette, wearing a blouse, shorts and huge hiking boots, she had looked beautiful to him. Josh knew how lucky he was to have found her.

At 27, he had almost given up hope of finding someone that could share his life style and what most people referred to as his peculiarities. Then she had come along.

One evening at a Ranger hosted party Josh heard talk about a young lady guest of the valley doctor, who made a habit of spending her winters alone in the Alaska wilderness.

Josh usually spent his off duty nights camping alone or with some Native Indians, learning the Indian way of living off the land and survival in the wilds. But, a young lady that spent her winters alone in the Alaska wilderness? That was intriguing. He had to meet her. She might understand his quirks.

She wasn't at all like what he had expected. Immediately the center of attention, she was tall, willowy, young, pretty and alone. He had expected a rather boyish appearing, extrovert. Instead she was the epitome of femininity and rather quiet.

As he was watching and studying her, trying think of a way to wangle an introduction, she suddenly made eye contact with him. Very deliberately, she eyed him up and down, then somewhat precipitously excused herself from her admirers and strode directly to him.

"You're Josh Rogan, aren't you?"

Josh, surprised, stammered that he was.

"I've heard so much about you and your studies of the martial arts and now I understand you're studying the American Indian?"

She continued, "I'm going to be here several days, can we spend some time together?"

Of course Josh agreed that'd be a great idea. That led to them spending much time together and that'd led to a whirlwind romance. They had so much in common, three weeks later they married.

Now, after a two-week long honeymoon backpacking into the high country behind Yosemite, this was to be their last day alone.

After breakfast, she asked him, "What's on for today?"

"First we clean up, then we warm up, then we pack up. Probably get to the four mile trailhead by noon and in the valley by mid-afternoon."

They'd policed the campground before warming up. Warming up had consisted of Fern practicing the Tae Kwon Do that Josh was teaching her.

The sun had warmed their campground by then and they both stripped to just shorts and boots. Fern had commented on his body.

"I hope you don't expect my muscles to look like yours someday."

He mimicked some of the poses you see in muscle magazines.

"That's it, you've got all the muscles those guys have, but somehow it's different. You're somehow," she had paused for a moment, "sleeker? And of course, much handsomer."

"Sleeker? Is there such a word?"

"Yeah," she had answered, "Like a panther."

"Okay," I'd replied. " I know what you're doing, you just want to get out of your morning practice session with flattery. No such luck."

Forty-five minutes later, they'd finished the ten exercise routines he had taught her. "Even though they're strenuous," she told Josh, " I really enjoy doing them with you." Then she had asked him, "Now that I'm so good on the ten-step program, how long will it take me to master Tae Kwon Do?"

Josh had laughed and said, "Forever."

CHAPTER 4

Josh was not exactly kidding when he said, "forever." He was the exception to the exception in martial arts. After only fourteen years of practice, he was considered one of the greatest grand masters of the art that had ever lived. A living legend at the tender age of twenty-seven, he was rarely recognized outside the relatively small world of Martial Arts, just the way he wanted it.

Josh had been born with a pair of unique assets and one unique liability. His assets were a superbly built body and a very high IQ. A body that allowed him to excel at any sport or activity he chose, and a mind that matched. His liability was that he had a pathological loathing of publicity and attention.

While he reveled in his prowess in sports, he came to hate the publicity and hoopla that went with it.

In high school, he first went out for the football team. An immediate starter, he became the backbone of the team quickly and led them to city and state championships. The more successful they were, the more he was sought after for publicity purposes. Josh hated it. In his senior year he refused to play, much to the chagrin of his coach and his school.

In college he went out for baseball, expecting it to be less of a big man on campus deal. It wasn't. He immediately became a star, and shortly thereafter quit.

For him it was a catch twenty-two situation. He craved the competition but hated the accompanying attention. He could have withdrawn from all sports and concentrated on school, but school was easy for him too.

In desperation, he joined the high school chess team. There again he was shortly the school champion. The school wanted to enter him in an open competition, but when he saw the publicity campaign they'd planned he revolted and quit that team as well.

Earlier, when he had just been starting high school he had been invited to a martial arts demonstration at the local YMCA. He had immediately been attracted to it and enrolled in a class. It was quickly apparent that he was a natural and rose rapidly through the lower belts.

As he studied karate, something immediately struck him. The Master where he studied was world famous in the martial arts, but hardly anyone knew of him outside the martial art world. It was a highly competitive, demanding sport that usually didn't create stardom. In short, it might be exactly what he was looking for, even though he didn't know he had been looking. He finally quit all college sports and concentrated on martial arts.

Progressing through the various age and experience stages, he devoted hours and hours to practice and study. He never lost a competition. Much of the learning wasn't competitive but some was. He went through all the belts in remarkable time and was shortly putting on exhibitions along with acknowledged masters.

He accompanied other students to many competitions and never lost. He became the one to beat in national and international meets and no one could. Eventually he went to China and studied with the best in the world, every form of martial arts taught.

Then, intrigued by the history of Ninja, he moved to Japan and intensively studied its history. Much different than the strict rules about honor in combat, the function of the Ninja included assassination, sabotage, infiltration and open combat. He quickly became expert in Ninja practice and art, and particularly enjoyed their fabled ability to make themselves invisible. Of course they couldn't actually do that, but he became extremely adept at blending into a background, especially at night.

He was without peer in the martial arts world. A legend at age 27. But still hounded by his dislike of publicity. As he gradually separated himself from the competitive world of martial arts he delved more and more into its history, studying its mysticism and practicing the more deadly forms that had been common practice hundreds of years before.

One other important thing separated him from others. Something he kept to himself. He felt that the strongest and most graceful athletes were often ballet dancers. The strength to lift and hold their partners in mid air combined with the grace and agility to perform with beauty. He trained secretly with ballet masters to maintain that grace and agility along with his other attributes. It was the combination of his naturally born advantages together with all other training that made many call his movements panther-like.

Now he was into something else. The American Indians had perfected the art of living and surviving off the land. They were at home in the forest and on the plains. Their tracking, hunting and fighting skills were incomparable. Their horsemanship had been often described as the finest cavalry in the world. He wanted to add their skills to his knowledge. It would be a combination of the greatest martial arts from all countries plus the survival knowledge of the American Indian. Something he could work on while at his job in Yosemite. And he had Fern to share it with.

CHAPTER 5

Next morning they appeared in the superintendent's office exactly on time.

"Josh, you've got some explaining to do. On the surface, you're exactly what we want in a Ranger. But little things keep popping up. Like that very strange thing you did yesterday afternoon. Would you like to explain that?"

Josh told him the same thing he had told Fern the previous night.

"The Germans? Can you get me some information on that program?"

"Sure."

"But that isn't everything. Your resume is really impressive. Not only degrees from Stanford, but advanced degrees from outstanding Asian schools. 'Most of them in Philosophy and Religious Study. Now I'm told that those degrees are quite probably euphemisms for martial arts programs. Is that true?"

"Partially."

"Can you explain that? Bear in mind, there's nothing wrong with taking martial arts courses. My concern is whether you misrepresented your education."

"There was no misrepresentation at all. If you'll check the curriculum at those Universities in China, you'll find all the courses I took are listed as part of their regular offerings. The problem is that in China, Oriental Philosophy, Religious Study and Martial Arts are inextricably intertwined. One of the most important requirements in all martial arts is finding your inner self. That requires lots of meditation and self analysis. The Chinese tradition of martial arts is thought to be over four thousand years old and a revered part of its history."

"I'm also told that you have a certain reputation in the field of martial arts as being pretty good, is that true?"

"Yes, it is. But I'd rather that information be kept between the three of us it at all possible."

"And why is that?"

"Putting it simply, I don't like publicity. Also, my training can make me dangerous. It's kind of like a boxer has dangerous hands. I'd rather keep that part of me to myself." He skirted around his personal fears.

"Would you be willing to teach a little of what you do to some of the other Rangers? Particularly that German Part?"

"I guess so. Actually I've already started teaching some to Fern and she'd like to continue."

"Okay! I'm still mystified about what you did yesterday, but no one can say you didn't do it. Can't quarrel with facts, can we? Anyway, you've got two grateful sets of parents waiting to see you at the hospital and they'd like you to talk to their kids and tell them exactly how much danger they were in, can you do that this morning?"

"Be glad to."

"Then go! Let me know if you need space for teaching or anything."

Josh felt like he had dodged a bullet. Maybe the Superintendent would keep his secret and he could be just a Park Ranger with a little martial arts sideline, while he worked on his private project.

CHAPTER 6

The next two weeks passed in a blur. Crowds of visitors kept the Rangers busy, year long. Winter, spring, summer and fall, the valley was hopping. Josh was fairly new to Yosemite, but not new to being a Park Ranger. He was assigned to the law enforcement part of the Park Rangers and given a partner, a newly appointed young Ranger named Timothy Park. Quite naturally, nobody referred to him as anything but "Park." Except Josh. To Josh he was Tim. Josh took him under his wing, giving him the benefit of his several years as a Ranger. They patrolled the whole valley plus the roads to Glacier Point and the two other park entrances. Most visitors were familiar with the park valley only. The whole park encompassed much more than that. They became familiar with it all. From the Northeastern area at Tuolumne Meadows near Nevada to the Southern entrance at Wawona. A large part of the job was enforcing speed limits, parking infringements, drunk driving violations, fairly routine stuff. The same type of law enforcement that any big city police department would do.

Josh took an immediate liking to Tim, inviting him over to have Fern prepare a home cooked meal for him numerous times. Tim flirted outrageously with Fern, while she shopped for a girl friend for him. At night, after Tim had left for his own rooms, they talked about what a nice kid he was and how much they enjoyed his company. Josh said he felt like he had a younger brother.

In addition to patrolling the roads and keeping them safe, there were some things peculiar to Yosemite they needed to keep an eye on. Harassment of animals was a big one. Drunk and disorderly campers was another. Fireworks was another. Occasionally they had to relieve a camper of guns as firearms of any sort were outlawed in the valley. Once in a while, there was a dispute between campers about who had the right to camp where. All camp spaces were reserved a year or so in advance and occasionally a camper didn't want to leave at the end of his reserved time.

Most of the disputes they were involved in were resolved quickly and easily. The arrival of armed Park Rangers tended to calm down most problems.

Fern got a job working at the general store in the Lodge. The store manager was very sympathetic about Fern's hours. He made it possible for her to work the same hours that Josh did.

Their time off was mostly spent exploring the valley. It was not entirely their idea although they loved doing it. Josh's boss had made a strong suggestion that Josh and Fern get familiar with the valley as soon as possible. Not just by car, but by doing a lot of hiking, just like the tourists.

"I love it here, Josh. Mirror Lake is spectacular. Is it true it almost disappears later in the year?"

'Unfortunately, yes."

"I wonder if all these tourists realize that"

"Unfortunately, no."

"What do we do now?"

"We tourist. Pretend you're on vacation. You're seeing Mirror Lake for the first and maybe the last time. You want to take it all in, take the perfect picture for your friends back home."

"Yesterday Happy Isles, today Mirror Lake, can't we use bicycles instead of hiking? Lots of tourists bike around."

"Maybe tomorrow"

Fern was getting used to Josh's somewhat terse use of the English language. She figured out that he didn't mean to be short with anyone, he was just impatient with wasted words.

"C'mon, Fern, there's a whole bunch of little trails we should take a look at. I want to know this area like the back of my hand. I think that's what the chief meant when he said to get familiar with the park." Often Tim enthusiastically went along, wherever they wanted to go.

If there was anything Fern learned about Josh, it was his attention to detail. He never did anything halfway. If he did it at all, he did it thoroughly. It was the same with his exploration of the valley and with his friendship with Tim.

That evening, when they got home, there was a phone message for Josh.

"Josh, report to me in my office at eight-thirty tomorrow morning." The call was from the Superintendents' office. "This is very serious. Tell Fern not to expect you home until tomorrow night, maybe longer."

CHAPTER 7

Josh entered the superintendent's offices promptly at eight-thirty the next morning. The secretary indicated that he was to go right in. Inside he found the superintendent and three regular Park Rangers.

"Men, if you haven't met him yet, this is Josh Rogan. He's in traffic right now but he has some special qualifications I think can help us."

"Josh, meet Rob, Chet and David. They've been up here for an average of about four years each. I wanted them here because they're young and in good shape. Like you!"

David spoke up, "Some young movie actresses need escorting around the park?"

"Stop right now. Like I told you last night, this is very serious. There's something going on in the Park that scares me and we have no idea how to handle."

"What's that?" Josh asked.

"Up in the high country, someone's slaughtering our bears. Chet's been up there and confirmed the killings."

"I know, it sounds preposterous but the evidence is overwhelming. We've had three bear carcasses found in the park within the last few days. Each one was reported to one of our Rangers and they in turn reported them to me. One was alarming enough, but three is frightening. No telling how many more we don't know about. We do not need wholesale slaughter of our bears ever, particularly not during summer."

"Someone's killing our bears?" David asked. "Why?"

"Killing them is disturbing enough. What's really scary is that it looks like body parts had been harvested from each bear!"

Joshua's ears perked up. "What parts?"

"As far as we could determine, the claws, the gall bladders and the teeth. Maybe more, but those for sure!"

"How about the testicles?" Josh asked.

He got a surprised look from the superintendent. "How did you know that?"

Josh asked the superintendent if he had any idea why those parts in particular may have been stolen.

"Not at first, but now I do and what I've learned scares me!"

"You're thinking Chinese or Japanese medicine?"

"On line I found that these parts are in demand all over the Orient. Evidently there's still traffic in bear parts for medicine there. The computer mentioned Indonesia, Singapore, Korea and Malaysia in particular. The article said that the Sun Bear was almost decimated by the demand. But the article doesn't say anything about American bears being killed for parts. I'm afraid that someone is killing our bears for the oriental medicine market. I just don't know what to do about it."

They were all silent for a moment, then Josh spoke up.

"Well, you're right. I've seen ground bear's claws and even ground bear's testicles in Chinese herb stores right here in the states, but I always thought they came from China."

"So it's possible that someone may be killing our bears for their organs?" Rob asked, and then continued, "Where did the killings take place?"

Chet answered."One of them was near Tenaya Lake on the Tioga Pass Road and two were up in Little Yosemite Valley."

"Were you able to determine how fresh the killings were?" Josh asked.

Chet replied again.

"I did! I've had a little necropsy training and I took deep body temperatures at two of the kills and looked carefully at the decomposition of tissue purposely to see if I could figure out when they were killed. As far as I could determine, all three were killed two or three days before we got on the scene."

"So the hikers that actually found the bodies, must have found them pretty soon after they were slaughtered?"

"You're right. Took them a day to find us and a day for us to get back there."

"I wonder why it was so easy for the hikers to find them. Seems like the killers could have hidden the body?"

"Did you ever try to drag a six or seven hundred pound bear?"

"I guess you're right. But if they were all killed in the same day or two, there must have been more than one killer. There's no way someone could get from Tioga Pass to Little Yosemite in a day or even two!"

The superintendent spoke up.

"That's what scares the hell out of me. It may be a gang! On top of what they're doing to our bears, think what might have happened to our campers if they had happened on them while they were butchering the animals! Besides, there's probably more, three is all we've found, so far."

Josh added to his worries. "If they're anything like some of the gangs I've met in the Orient, they can be merciless. We could end up with dead campers as well as dead bears."

CHAPTER 8

"Good Christ Josh, you're not helping. You honestly think they'd kill any of our campers?"

"If they got in their way? Yes, I do. These aren't individuals acting on their own, they're part of a criminal gang. Murder's part of their life."

"Well, that brings me to the purpose of this meeting. I've contacted the National Park headquarters, Fish and Game, plus several police and sheriff departments and they have absolutely no advice for me. They'll help with manpower if we want to organize a manhunt, but that's the last thing I want to do. We can't alarm the tourists!"

Continuing, he said, "So, at least temporarily, it's up to me. More accurately, it's going to be up to you four. You're going to be my task force. The problem is I don't know what to tell you to do! Josh, Do you think you could track these guys down before they get more dangerous?"

"I don't know, it's a lot of territory." Turning to the other three Rangers, he asked them, "What do you think?"

"Just the four of us? We can start where the kills were found and try to track them, but we're already several days behind."

The superintendent added, "And the two kill spots are widely separated. We've never had anything like this before, I don't know where to begin. You guys put your heads together and come up with a plan, but for God's sake, make it quick."

He was silent for a moment and then added, "Rob, Chet and David; you're going to report to Josh. Josh, you're going to take the lead on this. Guys, we may have had a stroke of luck in Josh. Josh has a lot of experience working with Asians, he's lived in both Japan and China. I forgot to ask you Josh, do you speak any Chinese or Japanese?"

"Just enough to order a decent meal and get a good hotel room," Josh replied.

Actually, Josh was fluent in several Chinese dialects but decided to keep that to himself.

"There's something else about Josh. He has some unique physical and education qualifications that make him the only person in the valley for this job. And, because of those unique abilities, I want you three to work with him as close as possible to find out whose doing these things and put a stop to them! Any questions?"

Josh spoke up, "Yeah, one. "What about our regular duties?"

"Already taken care of. As of this morning your supervisors have been notified that you're on special assignment to me for the next few weeks. None of them know what the assignment is and I don't want them to know. We can't start a panic or a lynch gang among the tourists."

"And one more thing. You're free to travel. If you have to go outside the park to trace these guys, do it! If you need park wheels, take them! Chet, I know you and Josh are married, are you okay with this assignment?"

Chet spoke up first. "Sure. Nancy's used to me being gone overnight, even a couple of days occasionally." He turned to Josh. "Did I tell you about our one year old? She's cute as can be."

"I think my wife told me there was a real cute new baby in the village. Congratulations. As far as Fern's concerned, after living in Alaska by herself for so long, she'll be okay."

"Okay, that's settled." He added one more thought. "By default, so far this whole thing's in our laps. No one else has any ideas. Josh, you're the only one that has had any experience dealing with gangs of this sort and any experience in the Orient. We have to keep a lid on the killings and catch these bastards as soon as possible. As far as the rest of the force is concerned, you're teaching a martial arts program to these guys, and that's it!"

CHAPTER 9

Josh took charge of the meeting as the superintendent had requested.

"Okay guys, Here's where I think we should start"

Chet interrupted him. "Hold on a minute. I know the Supe said you should be in charge, but I'm not so sure. You've only been in the valley for a few months and I've been here over six years, and spent a lot of time in the back country. Seems to me that my experience trumps your experience!"

"You are so right! All three of you have a hell of a lot more experience in the valley than I do. But I don't think that's the experience he was alluding to"

"What's more important than experience here in Yosemite?"

"For one thing I've lived in the Orient and probably know more about oriental uses of animal parts for medicine than all three of you put together. However, there's something else."

Chet again, "Okay, I'll bite, what is it?"

"Simply? Kung Fu."

Dave spoke up. "I've heard of Kung-Fu, why's that so important?"

Tersely, Josh explained. "The indications are that there's a Chinese gang involved. I've had experience with Chinese gangs. They're usually quite good at Kung Fu. They can and do kill with it. If you met up with one of them and didn't have any experience with Asian Martial Arts you'd be in a world of trouble."

"What about you?"

"I've trained a lot in China and even taught some Kung Fu. I could probably hold my own for at least a while."

Josh deliberately played down his expertise yet he wanted them to rely on him. They seemed okay with his explanation together with what the Superintendent had said.

Rob spoke up. "Okay, but there's no way the four of us can patrol the whole park, there's literally hundreds of square miles of backwoods country."

"Yeah, and there's still lots of snow still around," from Chet.

Rob continued, "they have to take the stuff somewhere, maybe we could figure out where they take it and find them there"

"Good idea," said Josh. "That'd be the place where they'd be the most vulnerable, too. The way I see it is they're selling them to underground or illegal markets in large Chinese communities. Places like San Francisco, or Sacramento or Fresno. Near enough to be easy to reach but large enough to make the sale profitable. I think the best thing we can do is to split up and go to each of those cities and see if the local police have any information that might help us. What do you think?"

"What about Los Angeles and San Diego?"

"We may end up there if the closer places don't pan out."

"So this is the plan we take to the super this afternoon?"

"Unless you've got a better one, yeah!"

"Then we head off for S.F. and the other cities tomorrow?"

"Let's see what the Super thinks."

They discussed his plan at length and drew straws to decide who would go to which city. All except for San Francisco. Josh took that for himself. He thought it was far more likely to be the market place for illegal bear parts than the other cities.

CHAPTER 10

Later that morning Josh had them meet him at the park gym.

"You guys are young and in good shape, right?" They all agreed. "You can take care of yourselves in a brawl if necessary?" They laughed and Chet said, "you bet!"

"Okay. I'm in charge of our little task force and I'm trying to keep you out of danger. The danger is that you think you can take care of yourself in a brawl, but you have no idea of what being up against a well trained Kung-Fu fighter is like, and that could kill you!"

"I think the fastest way to convince you that I can teach you something worth while is by a demonstration. I'll stand here in the middle of the mat and I want Chet to come at me from behind and knock me down."

"My pleasure," said Chet, raising his eyebrows and smiling at the other two Rangers.

Chet stood at the edge of the mat and Josh stood with his back to him in the center. To make it even more convincing, Josh closed his eyes.

Time after time, Chet tried to knock Josh down. Josh easily blocked his blows and swept his legs out from under him. Each time Chet ended up flat on the ground, winded but unhurt.

Next Josh had two of them try it at the same time with the same result. He let them come at him from behind, from both sides at the same time, all getting them nowhere.

Then they tried three at the same time, again, no luck.

Josh was able to spin, kick, twist, turn and use their momentum against them so easily, he hardly broke a sweat.

Finally he had them come at him with an axe handle. Again he handled them with ease.

Then he had them try to stop him from attacking them. They finally gave up. They couldn't defend against him, they couldn't evade him.

But—they were gutsy guys. Instead of getting mad, they got curious. They wanted to learn.

Josh wanted them to completely understand the potential danger of any of them going one-to-one with a trained Martial Arts student.

"Look guys, this is what the superintendent wanted me to impart to you. No matter how good you think you are, these guys are probably better. That's why he put me in charge. If we're up against Chinese Gang members, and you try to go one-on-one against them, you lose. And not just the fight, it may be your life. You saw how easily I handled you and I'm not even Asian. You probably didn't realize it, but I could have killed each of you very easily several times over."

Chet said, "Okay. I don't know about you other guys, but as far as I'm concerned you've convinced me, you're calling the shots. What's next?"

CHAPTER 11

The first surprise the group got that afternoon was when Josh drove them over to the start of the Four Mile Trail.

"We're going to hike up until we get to the part where the big rock slides are. I'm going to show you something the German Army's using to help their guys move over obstacle courses much, much faster than normal. I think if I demonstrate it, you might be able to pick it up pretty quickly, at least get the concept. Again, it's something that might come in handy anywhere. Later, the Superintendent wants me to set up a class in it for all the Rangers."

Being young, it only took them about forty-five minutes to reach the trail portion at the lower end of the ancient and huge rock slide.

Josh sat them down and said, "While this looks like it's purely physical, it really isn't. In order to do what I'm going to demonstrate you have to be in the perfect mind frame. Your concentration has to be pin-point or it won't work. I'm sure you've all had the experience where you slide downhill in your boots. You're moving real fast, jumping and sliding, jumping and sliding down the hill. Your eyes and your mind are several steps ahead of you, plotting where you're going to go. Have you had that experience?"

All three nodded yes.

"Well, this is the exact opposite of that. It's the same except you're not always going downhill. It allows you to use the same technique on level terrain or even uphill. Simply put, using your strength and agility plus tremendous concentration and momentum, you can move across level or uphill terrain almost as fast as if you were going downhill!"

"You've got to be kidding!"

"Nope. Again, the best way to convince you is to demonstrate. There are some tricks involved that you can pick up in a hurry. I've picked this portion of the slide because it has smaller boulders, instead of the huge boulders in the center of the slide. The first trick is to get a running start and build up speed. The second trick is to never, ever, lose that speed. It's learnable. The whole German Army's learning it! But the most important thing, the thing you must absolutely have, is complete concentration. Your whole being must be concentrated on the next and the next rock at all times. You'll see!"

With that Josh walked further uphill on the hill, saying, "This'll help me build up speed before I enter the rock field."

As he walked up, he reflected to himself as to whether he should put on a modified demo or go all out. He didn't want to discourage them by doing something they could never accomplish. It was a simple fact to him that he could perform physical things that most people could never imagine, let alone do. He decided to put on a somewhat modified exhibition.

Running down the trail, he picked up speed until he was almost out of control. At the very last minute, just before he reached his class, he launched himself uphill, onto the rock slide. He barely touched the first boulder, just used it as a launching pad to the next. Not losing any noticeable speed, he leaped from boulder to boulder with amazing agility. Before they could even comment, he was a hundred feet above them, sitting comfortably on a rock which would have taken them at least a half-hour to reach.

"Anyone want to try it?"

The three Rangers couldn't find their voices for several seconds. Finally one of them said, "Holy mackerel, was your dad a Gazelle or something? What you just did was impossible. No way am I going to try something like that!"

"I don't expect you to. What I think you CAN do is begin. Before today is over I'll bet you'll be able to jump from the trail to the first rock and then the second maybe even to the third. The German army learned, you can too!"

At the end of the day they were worn out but excited. Josh commiserated with them and added, "Grab a bite and meet me at seven-thirty for more, I have to report to the Supervisor."

CHAPTER 12

At seven-thirty, the four of them gathered in the gym.

"You guys deserve to know a little more about me. Specially since I've asked you to defer to me if any danger looms up. Unless you've actually experienced Kung-fu fighting you can't realize how dangerous it can be. If you've seen it on TV, you've seen it as a sport. But lots of the moves you see are really designed to kill if carried out to their full capacity.

You know about how I kept switching sports until I found Karate. Karate allowed me to compete on a world-wide basis without all the corresponding hoopla that goes with most sports. You could become a world champion yet still not be pestered by fans in your home town

I keep using the word Karate, but that isn't accurate. Karate was originally developed in Okinawa. It gradually emigrated to the Japanese mainland and was really popularized by the Japanese, even though it was mostly taught by Okinawans. Now most people call all forms of martial arts, Karate, but it's just one form of many.

What I've mostly practiced is a Chinese form, not Japanese. It's called Wushu. There're a whole bunch of variations of Wushu. I'm not going into all the various forms, you wouldn't appreciate the differences anyway. The one I've spent the most time with is Kung Fu. It combines a lot of powerful kicks and high jumps and rapid movement. Additionally, we use strong arms, fast footwork and weapons. There's more to it though, than just the physical side. The Chinese say, 'Train both Internal and External.'"

He paused for effect. "External training includes the hands, the eyes, the body and stances. Internal training includes the heart, the spirit, the mind, breathing and strength. A well trained Karate expert fights with his heart, his mind, his spirit, his strength and his training. He might be almost invincible in hand to hand combat."

He continued. "I can't overemphasize how dangerous these guys we're up against may be. They'll be trained in Kung-Fu and deadly."

By the end of the evening the four had bonded. Josh felt comfortable with them and was looking forward to meeting Chet's family. They broke up early complaining that Josh had worn them out completely and they needed a good nights sleep to recuperate. He hoped his warnings had taken root.

They agreed to meet at noon the next day as Chet had some unfinished work to do. Josh planned on meeting with the Park Superintendent and bringing him up to date on their plans.

At ten-thirty the next morning Josh got a call from a very agitated park superintendent that changed everything.

"Josh, they've escalated the hell out of this thing. The son's of bitches killed Tim!"

"Tim? Tim's dead? Where? What do you mean he was killed?"

"He was shot, near the Badger pass ski area. Was he doing something for you?"

"No. All he said was he'd take our run over to Wawona by himself while I was working with Chet and the other guys and he'd be back before noon. What the hell was he doing up there?"

"We can't figure it out. They found his empty car about a half mile above the Ranger station and his body in the bushes just off the road."

"And he was shot?"

"Yeah, something small like a 22, twice. Probably last night. You need to get over here as soon as you can. I'm afraid his shooting may have something to do with what you're investigating. We need to figure out how we're going to handle this."

"Who's investigating his murder?"

"We are, so far. That's why I need you all over here."

Josh hung up and was alone with his thoughts. "Jesus. Poor kid." His immediate reaction was disbelief. Tim couldn't be dead. He was only in his early twenties. Disbelief was followed by grief. Tears came. He had come to enjoy Tim's company so much. As he had told Fern, it was almost like having a younger brother. How was he going to tell Fern? His thoughts were jumbled and chaotic.

"Badger Pass. Why would Tim have gone to Badger Pass?" He asked himself. He and Tim had theorized about where the poachers might have been headquartered. Badger had been one of their theories, but they'd had no evidence to back it up. Tim must have found something? But if he had been killed at Badger it meant that their theory must have been correct. The poachers had been there. Gradually his grief turned to anger. He needed to do something. The Superintendent had said they were blocking all the roads to and from Badger Pass.

Josh thought about that. The killers must still be in the back country. They must be travelling by some sort of all terrain vehicle. Probably what he called a quad. Four wheel, rugged back country transportation for one or two people. He thought the road blocks would be useless. He needed to get over there quickly. He called the Superintendent.

"Sir, I'm going over to Badger. Maybe I can find the killers." Josh hung up quickly before the Superintendent could object.

Once Josh decided what he was going to do, he laid out a plan. Letting his thoughts roam, it occurred to him that the murder changed the ground rules dramatically.

The Park wouldn't be able to keep the murder quiet. The Feds' would move in. But they'd be relatively ineffective in the Yosemite back country, where he was beginning to think the killers would still be hiding. He, by himself, would have an advantage over the Feds. After the killing, they'd desperately be trying to get away. Gradually what he had to do became clear in his mind. He had no choice. He had to become an American Indian and a Ninja warrior.

In Japan he had mastered the art of the Ninja and in China the various practices of Karate. Since then his curiosity had been piqued by the American Indians' mastery of the forests and their ability to track animals and humans as well as their use of the bow and arrow.

Working with the very few American Indian survivors in the Yosemite area that still knew the old ways, Josh had learned how to track, both animals and humans. He had learned how to survive in summer and the dead of winter in deserts and forests. He had learned where to find dry wood for fire in wet or snowy weather. He had learned how to move noiselessly through bushy terrain.

As a Ninja he had previously learned the art of becoming invisible in plain sight. How to scale impossible walls and suddenly appear in surprising places. He had learned how to use a number of weapons unfamiliar to westerners. He had also learned one of the basic Ninja tricks, how to use the night as an advantage.

He said to himself, "forget the Feds', I need to track those killers down while they're still in the park". Josh was even more certain that the killers had to be using an all terrain vehicle of some sort. While the bears in the valley were too tame and could be approached too easily, the ones outside the valley were still wild and would have to be hunted down.

The Indians had confided many of their tribal secrets to Josh as he earned their confidence. Most of Yosemite National Park was outside the valley. The area where Tim had been killed was close to where he and Fern had been hiking. He tried to put himself in their shoes, how did they get there, how did they plan to get out. They would need a car to get into Yosemite, but they couldn't leave it near the Badger Pass Ski Area. A Ranger Station was right there and the car would be spotted right away.

Getting in and out of Yosemite by car was limited to three roads. The one Josh was fairly certain they would use would be the Wawona exit, the southernmost gate. It was less traveled. Looking at the topo map, he had a pretty good idea what they must have done.

If they left their car at Wawona, it wouldn't be noticed. Lots of cars parked for days at a time at the Wawona hotel. There was even a golf course there. In order to get in and back out with a load of animal parts they'd have to be using at least one all terrain vehicle. All terrain vehicles are fairly large, noticeable, noisy and not legal in Yosemite. They would have used something like a small van to conceal them in if they brought them through the entrance and up to Wawona. At the hotel there was a trail that led through the back country and ended at a campground a short ways up from Badger. It almost had to be what they had used. The killing had occurred near Badger, but they couldn't get past there by car, the road to Glacier Point hadn't been opened yet. The trail was the only logical way to get to that area.

The more he thought of it, the more convinced he became that the murderers were still in the mountains and they were on that trail to Wawona. There was almost no other way. More and more Josh was convinced in his mind that they were on all terrain vehicles, probably two of them. They could travel light, enough food for several days and a couple of ice chests with dry ice in the for the organs they harvested. But they'd be in a hurry now, because of Tim's killing.

How could he catch them? If he was right, their van would be sitting in the hotel parking lot.

He needed to hurry, not to Badger but to Wawona.

CHAPTER 13

The topo map indicated there was a public campground at Bridal Veil falls, a few miles above the Badger Pass ski area. From the campground the back country trail led directly to Wawona. It was the only way in or out of that area other than the main road. The trail was about 40 miles long and it looked like it could be navigated by a small all terrain vehicle. As the trail from Wawona ended at the Bridal Veil campgrounds, he theorized they might have been using the campgrounds as their headquarters. This early in spring, still lots of snow on the ground, neither the campground nor the road to it was open yet. No crowds to contend with. Now, trying to get out, it would be slow going for them with all terrain vehicles, carrying ice chests, over what was really a hiking trail. No question they'd still be on the trail. If his assumptions were right.

If they could negotiate the 40 miles and reach Wawona, it was a short drive to the southern entrance out of Yosemite Park, and they'd be home free. Josh was sure that by the time Federal authorities arrived the murderers would be long gone. It was up to him to get there first.

What Josh knew and no one else did, was that he was perhaps the only person in the world that could head them off and capture them. He could cover miles of trail on foot, easily. He could track as well as an Indian. He could use his abilities to overpower and bring them in.

When he had said to himself earlier that he had to become both an Indian warrior and a Ninja he meant just that. The few weeks he spent with local Indians had been an eye opener. He was amazed at the similarities between Indian and Ninja lore. Both required the ability to live off the land. Ninjas in the old days traveled by foot from town to town. They often foraged off the land to survive. Both had the ability to track, both animals and humans. Both taught stealth as a way to survive. Both employed weapons of silence as opposed to guns. Both were taught how to conquer pain.

There were some differences. Ninjas were taught how to wage individual warfare in towns, whereas Indians' lore was designed principally for living in the wild. Ninjas had easily concealed throwing weapons and cross-bows, where Indians had their bows and spears.

Josh had set out to become totally proficient in all areas of Indian warfare and succeeded. The Indians he worked with were astonished at his learning curve. Within a few weeks he was their equal or better. The difference was that the Indians had been brought up learning their various arts and it was part of their life. Josh brought a dedication to learning their skills, combined with a world class athletes body that made him ultimately superior to them in their own fields of expertise.

Now he could put that knowledge and experience to work. He would drive to Wawona, get on that trail and with any luck, meet them head on. He felt he would hear them approaching long before they saw him. With surprise on his side, using both Indian and Ninja techniques, he could disarm and capture them quickly.

CHAPTER 14

At false daylight, just before dawn, Josh was up. He had bunked in at the Wawona Ranger station and gotten about 5 hours of sleep.

His plan was to travel as fast and light as he could and catch the murderers before they ran into someone else and killed again. He disavowed the traditional American hiking boots and heavy back pack in favor of light moccasins, a small back pack, knife and, as a concession to modern clothing science, pants, shirt and jacket designed for cold weather survival, plus a few special Ninja and survival items. If the chase lasted more than one or two nights it would be a real test of his Indian and Ninja abilities.

The first thing he found turned out as had theorized. There was a small van parked in a back corner. Using a flashlight and peering through the windows, he saw that the interior had been gutted and that the doorway had been widened enough to accommodate a couple of small vehicles. Score one for his ideas.

At the trailhead he further vindicated his thinking. Four pair of footprints and wheel prints of two four wheeled cross country vehicles. The footprints were deep and Josh could see they'd pushed the vehicles by hand for some time to avoid being heard. All the footprints had been made by cleated boots. Not something an experienced woodsman would wear. Josh's first clue as to the caliber and experience of the men he was up against.

Josh set off---slowly. He estimated he should be able to average 3 to 4 miles per hour, 6 or 7 hours per day, even on the uneven trail, once he was warmed up. He knew his strengths and he knew his weaknesses. He would need to rest regularly, he would need food for strength and water. He planned to travel on foot quickly, the Indian way.

He needed to remain alert and spot or hear the murderers before they spotted him. That meant he would need to stop periodically and listen for them. His big advantage was that his progress was virtually soundless, while theirs was noisy.

Timing himself, trotting noiselessly, he stopped every fifteen minutes and listened. At the second stop he heard a stirring in the bushes and was rewarded with the sight of a young black bear. Doing as the Indians did, he addressed the bear in soft tones and told him how happy he was to see him and that he meant him no harm. The bear stared at him, cuffed the ground and wandered off. Josh knew it was spring and mama was nearby.

On and on he went. Because it was still early spring there was lots of snow on the ground to contend with. Most of the snow was in shady spots, only occasionally was there snow on the trail itself. But the trail was fairly steep, quite often over rocks where his quarry had obviously had to carry their transport. Their trail was easy to follow, struggling as they were with the vehicles.

By four in the afternoon he estimated he had covered about half the distance to the campground with no sightings at all. Josh decided to find a spot to spend the night before it got dark. He doubted they would travel after dark.

He needed a spot where he could keep warm, be out of sight of the trail, yet be close enough to hear any movement. He was looking forward to using some of his recently learned Indian lore.

There were many deadfalls just off the trail and there were lots of jumbled rocks providing small caves. He needed a small cave facing away from the trail, behind a deadfall, yet still close. It was a good thing he started early. It took the better part of an hour to find the perfect location. Off the trail about fifty yards, it was a cleft between two large boulders, located just above a bend in the trail. There was a large deadfall in front of it, making it almost invisible from the trail.

Next he had to make it habitable, which meant a fire to keep him warm. All the wood on the ground was soaked through, totally unfit for firewood. However there were lots of trees around with mostly small dead branches on their lower trunks. Easily reachable, totally dry, perfect for a fire. Using a commercial flint and striker he quickly had a small fire going. He purposely built the fire on an exposed slab of granite in the cave, intending to scrape it away later and sleep on the warmed up rock. Dried jerky, some bearberries, the stalk of a Burdock plant and a chocolate bar would provide strength and endurance for tomorrow.

The Indians had warned him about the Burdock plant as it resembled rhubarb. The Rhubarb tops were poisonous, the Burdock was safe and good. The stalk of the burdock plant was good raw or cooked and it roots could be boiled or baked like a potato. The bearberries were moist and sweet and he boiled some of its leaves in a collapsible pan to make tea. For lightness and comfort he had brought a light weight reflective blanket which would catch and reflect the heat from the stone and should keep him warm all night.

He was comfortable, warm, well fed and had an excellent view as well as being within listening distance of the trail.

He reviewed what he now knew about the foursome from tracking them all day. They were not woodsmen, they were struggling. They were not in top physical shape, they had to stop and rest too often. They were wasteful, carrying and discarding way too much food and equipment. They were careless with open fires and used gasoline as a starter. All in all, he felt he could use woodsmenship, Indian and Ninja lore to disable and capture them.

So far they had made one camp. Josh had passed it after about three hours of hiking. Today he had hiked six hours and estimated they had probably made another camp shortly ahead. Assuming they were coming out at the same rate, he would probably sight them tomorrow. Four against one, required a plan.

At daylight he climbed high above the trail and surveyed it as far ahead as he could see. No sign of his quarry yet. Back on the trail he looked for a long flat, fairly straight stretch, a spot where he could assume they would be riding their vehicles and trying to make good speed. Next he looked for and found a spot that was narrow and had a steep drop off beside the trail. Reading the tracks they had made on the way up, he could see they had been riding at that point and that their outside wheels had come perilously close to the edge. They'd be doing the same coming back. Perfect for his plan.

With his knife he dug around the rocks supporting the trail at that point. When he judged that the trail would collapse under the weight of two men and their transport he carefully covered his work with dirt and snow, leaving no telltale signs. A carefully concealed trap designed to incapacitate at least two of the men, one that wouldn't be recognized as a trap. Depending on how close they were to each other and how much attention the second driver was paying, he might get all four of them.

If his calculations were correct, his quarry would come to him. Further back down the trail he caused a small rock slide. If they got by the trap, he would have a second chance.

The Indians had drummed the value of patience into him. Patience when hunting wild animals was all important. The patience to track the animal for hours until you found him. The patience to lie in waiting for the animal to come to you. The patience to wait for the right shot with your bow and arrow.

CHAPTER 15

Josh didn't have a bow and arrow, but he did have a set of 4 ninja throwing stars and two double bladed throwing knives. He also had the ability to use them effectively in distances up to fifty feet. They could be used to disable or kill.

He needed a hiding place. A place high enough to be able to see up the trail as far as he could, yet near enough to be able to attack the four men quickly to take advantage of the confusion his trap would cause. Following a small stream uphill from where it crossed the trail, he found an uprooted tree lying across several boulders. It provided good shelter and was out of sight of the trail, yet by standing on the boulder he could see almost a half mile ahead. He could even build a small fire using very dry sticks to limit the smoke. Fresh water, warmth and a good view of the trail, he was ready. Now, patience.

It happened even better than he had hoped. He first heard the unmistakable sound of their engines about two hours after setting his trap. The forest had been almost soundless while he was waiting. A short while after he heard them, he caught sight of the first one as it rounded a curve close to a half mile up the trail. On the straight-a-way, both vehicles sped up. There was no way they would spot his trap, no way they could avoid it. Josh got ready to jump down to the trail.

As the first four wheeler hit the weakened spot, the trail collapsed under the weight. The handlebars were wrenched out of the drivers hands and both the men and the vehicle tumbled over and over some 30 feet to the bottom of the hill. The second driver skidded to a stop with one wheel hanging over the edge. The two riders quickly jumped off, pulled the vehicle back and rushed to the edge of the trail trying to figure out what had happened.

With their backs turned to him, Josh was able to quickly leap down the hill, unseen. In a moment he was behind them on the trail. Using a vicious Karate chop to the back of the neck, he totally incapacitated each of them immediately. Two down, two to go. He bound the two with plastic ties and made his way down to the wrecked 4 wheeler. One of the men had been thrown free and was lying next to a rock, groaning. The other was under the wreck, dead. It looked like his neck had been broken in the tumble. Ignoring the dead man, Josh tended to the injured one, who was incoherent.

Not surprising to Josh, all four were Chinese.

He decided to radio for help. He had captured the four murderers when they had an accident. One had been killed in a fall off the trail. He had the two vehicles they had used and he supposed the two ice chests filled with bear parts were there also. Too much for him to manage by himself all the way back to the trailhead, he needed help. He didn't think it was necessary to mention that he had caused the accident.

He called the Ranger station in Wawona, informed them of what he had and where he was and requested assistance. At first they didn't believe him, didn't believe that anyone could have used that trail without their knowledge. Didn't believe that one Ranger could capture four killers. Eventually, after calling the superintendent's office to verify Josh's existence, they dispatched a team to help him.

While waiting, Josh carried the injured man up to the trail, determined that he probably had broken his wrist and was in shock. He treated him, bound his legs together tightly and waited for help.

Not unexpectedly, he got a call from the superintendent.

"Now what in the heck have you done?"

"It was kind of an accident sir. I had a hunch that they might use that trail and thought I'd take a look. It was just luck that I ran into them right after they had an accident on the trail. One of them was dead when I got there and another was injured badly. The other two were slightly injured and dazed and easily caught. I just happened to be at the right place at the right time and got lucky."

"Are you sure these are the right guys?"

"Have to be. They're armed, came from where Tim was killed and have ice chests with them. I haven't opened the ice chests yet but I'll bet they're full of parts from the dead bears."

"All right, good work. Stay with them until you get help, I'll try to figure out what to do with them."

Josh turned his attention to the three Chinese. They were chattering to each other in Chinese, having no idea that Josh understood everything they said. He led them on by pretending to get upset by their not speaking English.

"Speak English! How can I help you if I can't understand you? Are you in pain?"

They continued to speak to each other in Chinese and Josh learned a few things.

"Don't speak any English. Play dumb. We say we're just trying to make a living. We don't know anything about the Ranger that got shot. And for God's sake, don't say anything about San Francisco."

Josh egged them on. "I heard you say San Francisco, what's that about?"

Again in Chinese they spoke to each other. "Be careful, he's smart and listening. Don't use any names." Then he lowered his voice and whispered. "When the other guys get to Emeryville and find out we've been caught maybe they'll do something."

Josh now knew their was at least one other team in the mountains in addition to these four and that they delivered their gory stuff somewhere in Emeryville. He doubted that anyone else would get that information. The big question was, what was he going to do with it?

As he had initially surmised, it looked like a Chinese gang operation. He had caught the murderers, but the killing of bears had not been stopped. There was at least one other gang killing them. Also, he knew from experience in China that these four were cheap labor for some other group. Whoever had sent these guys in and bankrolled them was just as much a murderer as they were. His job wasn't done. His anger at Tim's killing was still building. He still needed to avenge Tim's death. He needed to find out who was behind both the bear killings and who caused Tim to be killed.

He reasoned that the FBI and local police were notorious for not successfully infiltrating or controlling Chinese gangs, they would screw it up. He was also sure that the Park Rangers were not up to this type of job. Josh felt he had a big start on getting to the ringleaders and stopping the bear murders and avenging Tim's death. What to do? Could he get away to Emeryville and follow his nose? Would the Super let him? Should he even tell the Super he was going? And what about Fern?

Suddenly he realized he was just wasting time. Way down deep he already knew he was going to follow the lead, come Hell or high water.

CHAPTER 16

Based on the information he had gleaned from his captives, the superintendent and Josh decided it wasn't necessary to send the other two Rangers to different cities, they'd concentrate on San Francisco and Emeryville. The Superintendent thought all four of them should go.

Josh has his own ideas. "I think I can do better on my own. We don't need several Rangers in San Francisco. If you can arrange for me to work with the San Francisco Police I'll have all the back up I need, and Rangers don't have the experience needed to work in the Chinese community. Besides, they should stay here and try to catch the other gang."

"Absolutely not. No way am I going to let you go alone after these guys. That would be way too dangerous."

"I wouldn't be alone. I'd be working closely with the police department and they'd be more protection for me than our guys would. All you have to do is clear it with their chief."

The superintendent mulled it over for a few minutes.

"You'd work with the police department, not go off on your own?"

Josh crossed his fingers and said, "absolutely."

"Okay, on one condition. Before you leave I'll call and make an appointment for you with the SF police chief and you report directly and immediately to her."

"The chief's a woman?"

"Yes she is, and a damned good chief. I know her and without her blessing I wouldn't send you there. Okay, you can go but the very first thing you do is report to her. Right?"

"Right."

"The Chief's office was not feminine in the least nor was she, at least in dress. Probably in her late forties, she wore a military style pants suit and looked very official. Her hair was cut attractively short

46

and she wore no make up. Josh thought she was a very handsome woman, but dressed for work in a man's world.

"My assistant tells me that the Yosemite Park Superintendent's office called and arranged this appointment. There's something about bears being killed?"

"Yes Ma'am, your assistant's correct. The park superintendent sent me."

"Why San Francisco?"

"We caught some of the guys and they inadvertently mentioned San Francisco and Emeryville as their headquarters."

"Since your call I've read up on the use of bear organs being used for Chinese medicine, but I've never experienced anything like that. Tell me about it."

Josh recounted the Rangers finds in the back areas of the park and how Tim had been killed. Then he described his personal experience catching the four murderers. He also told her of his travel in China and Japan.

All business-like she said, "All right, I see the picture. Now what about you, what kind of police experience do you have.?"

Josh told her about his training and background and she seemed sufficiently impressed. He did not mention his other skills.

"If we work together, you work through me. Got it? No heroics, no guns, just on-the-ground police work. If you get a solid lead you come to me. Understood? Everything's through me or my assistant, here's my card, just ask for the chief's office."

Her name was on the card, but she didn't say he could use it. Just ask for the chief.

She continued, "Here is how we are going to play this. I've checked and we have no records at all about your type of problem. However, our Chinatown unit probably does, on a personal basis. I've been in touch with the commander of that unit and he is expecting a call from you. I have instructed him to cooperate thoroughly with you. I'm more concerned with potential gang activities than anything else. It seems to me, there is a potential for gangs in this scenario."

"That was my experience in China. It's the same the world over," Josh said. "In Africa, it's elephant tusks, in Asia it's tigers. People are killed on a daily basis over the harvesting of animal organs. Usually it's rival gangs, but sometimes it's innocent bystanders."

She replied, "That is what I want to avoid. And that is why I've set you up with lieutenant Chew. In view of your lack of big city police training. I want you to partner with him as long as you're here. He is city wise, and you're going to need him. What I hope you're going to get is something from their personal experiences with the Chinese community. One other thing, I've asked the lieutenant to put you in touch with some of the leading pharmacies in Chinatown. They may be even of more help to you."

"Good idea, I hadn't thought of that!"

She gave him the lieutenant's phone number and said he was expecting the call.

"Where are you staying?"

"I haven't made any arrangements yet.

"Stay at the Hilton. They'll give you professional rates, just show them your Ranger ID and tell them I sent you. It's centrally located and they'll treat you okay. When you're settled call my office and leave your phone number."

"Better than that, here's my cell phone number."

"Call Lieutenant Chew right away, you'll like him. One last thing. I talked to the park superintendent to double-check on you and he vouched for you in a big way. But, and this is a big but, you are not to work by yourself. He wants you working with my people full time and to report directly to me. Is that clear?"

Once more Josh crossed his fingers behind his back and agreed with her. "Absolutely."

As he left her office, Josh suddenly realized how she had played him. First she said her assistant had told her about him, but later she told him that she had talked to his Supervisor . She had tried to let him hang himself.

CHAPTER 17

"Mr. Rogan? I was expecting your call," the Lieutenant greeted him. "The Chief told me why you're down here from Yosemite. Did she tell you why she was so cooperative with you?"

"Just that she was concerned with potential gang warfare? And, by the way, I'm Josh, short for Joshua."

"Josh? Okay, and I'm Chew. There's only five of us here, including me, and we're pretty informal."

"It's a lot more than that. She was practically raised in Yosemite. Her family spent every summer there when she was in her teens. Back before it became so crowded, evidently families could rent camping spaces for weeks at a time. Her dad would drive them up, stay for the weekend and then drive back to Oakland to work. As soon as you said Yosemite you had her!"

"For me there's a lot more in it than the bear problem. Did she tell you about one of our Rangers being killed?"

"No, when was that?"

"Just two days ago. It looks like he stumbled on the gang and they shot him."

"So there's a lot more to this than just the bear thing."

"You got it. For me it's personal. Tim, the Ranger they killed, was my partner and a good friend. We got the four guys that shot him, but there's some one, or an organization, behind them that caused this to happen. Plus we're sure there's at least one other gang of guys hunting up there besides the four we caught."

"How about the four guys you caught, any info out of them?"

"Three guys. One of them was killed in an accident before we caught them. The only lead we got from them was a vague reference to San Francisco and Emeryville."

"Not much to go on, but I'll help all I can. Personally, I can't say I know of any place selling animal parts here, at least not in large amounts."

"But you do know of some?"

"Yeah, but they're little mom and pop places. Places that cater to the elders in town. Usually the only ones that go there are really old and were born and raised in China."

"I've been thinking about that. How can a gang make enough money selling the occasional bear parts to make the risks worthwhile. I came up with two possibilities. One is that there are lots and lots of small Chinese shops scattered among the Chinatowns like San Francisco and Oakland. In the Orient they make it into a powder and then cut the powder with talc or something and make a huge profit on small sales. Similar to Heroin dealers. I don't know if there's enough profit in all those small stores to make it worthwhile or not."

Chew quickly responded. " It may be possible. If every Chinese grocery or convenience or drug store is selling this stuff, maybe there's enough profit to make it worthwhile. I'll start my guys quietly sniffing around."

Josh was impressed by Chew's response. No nonsense. He immediately grasped the situation, formed a plan and implemented it. Josh studied him for a minute before continuing with his ideas. Chew was short, about five foot seven, maybe thirty-five and chunky. Short black hair, a round moon shaped face and quick, darting black eyes.

"The other idea is that San Francisco is just a shipping point. The parts are processed here and shipped somewhere else."

Chew paused for a moment. "That's going to be a tough one, unless we can find the processing plant. This stuff's small and could be shipped by plane, or even carried. It'd be like trying to stop the cocaine or heroin traffic, like you said."

"I don't know if your chief was told, but one of the main reasons the Park Superintendent assigned me to this case was because I've spent a number of years in China. I know how they use things like gall bladders and feet for medicine. We've had three bears killed that we know of and their organs harvested. Just the gall bladders alone, dried and ground up and diluted would provide hundreds of doses and be worth a small fortune. What's going on with our bears is much more than a mom and pop operation. There's got to be a market somewhere for that much stuff."

"You're probably right, but I don't know of anything like that. Tell you what I've done though, I've got my entire squad coming in this afternoon at shift time, five o'clock. Maybe they'll have a handle on the volume of Chinese medicine sales by then. You better be here. You can meet them and ask them as many questions as you like. By the way, do you speak Chinese?"

"Very little."

"Well, don't worry. My guys all speak English fluently."

For some reason, Josh didn't want to admit that his ability to speak and converse in Chinese was much better than average. He hadn't admitted either to the Park Superintendent or the S.F. police how fluent he was in Chinese. Neither had he told the police of his martial arts abilities. While Chew seemed more than interested and cooperative, Josh wondered how much of that came because he had been sent there by the chief and if it was all talk. He would know tomorrow.

Josh was waiting at the Chinatown substation well before five. As the guys came in they eyed him somewhat suspiciously. The Lieutenant briefed them on what Josh was looking for and told them about the Yosemite background. Then asked Josh to bring them up to date.

"We're sure these bears were killed to get their organs for Chinese medicinal purposes. Nothing else makes sense. We're checking every major city with a large Chinese population within a reasonable distance of Yosemite. That includes Sacramento, Fresno and Stockton. We caught some of the guys and found out that San Francisco or maybe Emeryville was their destination. I personally think that the parts come to the Bay area, are processed here and sold throughout the west coast, or maybe even shipped to the Orient."

I think there's either a large enough secret facility here in S.F. or the stuff is moving through the city on the way somewhere else. Either way, I think there's a lot of new money moving around in the Chinese community and also these guys must have left some record of their trips up and back to the valley. That's what I need from you guys. Someone must have heard something. Whispers, gossip, suspicions, whatever you can dig up, however small, I want it."

The entire squad consisted of four men, plus Lieutenant Chew. Only two of them were in the field at a time. On top of that, they were expected to help on cases throughout the whole city, not just Chinatown. They were spread pretty thin. Josh thought his chances of getting any useful information ranged from slim to none. He could only hope.

One of the guys spoke up. "Lieutenant Chew asked me to get an idea of how many places in San Francisco might be selling traditional

Chinese medicines. I checked with a friend of mine in the wholesale pharmacy trade and he estimated they'd be in the thousands. He said every Chinese grocery store, drugstore, restaurant and so on might be selling them. Some over the counter and some under the counter."

Another of the officers said he hadn't heard a sniff about any large market in animal parts or medicine.

The other three agreed.

In Chinese, talking to each other, one of them said, "How about your cousin, the one that owns that big pharmaceutical lab over in Emeryville?"

Josh's ears perked up. He remembered the guys he had caught had mentioned Emeryville. What he heard next was even more interesting.

"Don't bring him into this. He's got enough troubles as it is. Financial problems up his kazoo"

Josh spoke up. "I've got an idea. Instead of a small pharmacy, maybe there's a pharmaceutical lab in the area that could actually process the organs into medicine and even ship it out in quantities enough to make big money. Maybe a lab that's in some financial difficulties and thinks they've found a way to make that easy, under the table, no records cash. Probably not in San Francisco proper, maybe somewhere nearby like, for example Emeryville.?"

"Oh crap, he speaks Chinese!"

"Yeah, I do. And I think I better take a look into your cousin's lab, don't you?"

"My cousin's straight. He wouldn't do anything illegal. That's why I wanted to keep him out of it."

"We'll see. In the meantime, keep absolutely quiet about this. Don't talk to anyone, not your cousin, not anybody!"

Josh didn't know if this lead would lead anywhere, but he felt he should talk to the Chief the next morning about the Emeryville lab.

He needed to get back to his hotel. He wanted to get a good meal, and call Fern for a long talk just before he hit the sack.

He was worried about leaving Fern alone, but then remembered her history of living by herself for entire winters in Alaska. She had insisted to him that she was entirely self sufficient, used to being alone and taking care of herself. And if his job required him to be away for a time, she would survive quite well, thank you. He thought again to himself how lucky he was to have found her.

CHAPTER 18

Josh checked in with the Police Chief early the next morning. As before, she was curt and to the point.

"Did you make any headway with Lieutenant Chew?"

"Maybe. His guys are going to check around for anything unusual. Do you know anything about a pharmaceutical lab in Emeryville?"

"Never heard of it."

"One of Chew's officers mentioned it. I think he has a distant cousin or something that owns it. He said his cousin's in deep financial trouble. That's kind of the situation I was looking for. Last night I did some research on the web and got some interesting information. There're quite a few pharmaceutical labs in the greater Bay Area, but only one that has Chinese ownership."

"I imagine that officer would be Mitchell?"

"Mitchell?"

"Yes I know. His father was about as Irish as you could get. But he was killed shortly after Dan was born. Dan was raised entirely by his Chinese mother and family. He is much more Chinese than Irish and speaks Chinese fluently. I think he is the only one with roots here in the bay area, so I thought he had to be the one with a cousin in Emeryville. Am I right?"

"You sure are."

"What did he have to say about his cousin? Did he think he should be investigated?"

"Actually? No, he didn't. He vouched for him, said he's the very picture of honesty. But then a moment later he told how his cousin was facing bankruptcy. I'm going to look into everything I can while I'm here but I particularly want to look into the Emeryville thing."

"What do you need from me?"

"I think I'll start with the Emeryville connection, but I haven't decided how to start yet. Can you give me an introduction to the Emeryville police chief?"

"I think I agree with you. Emeryville seems logical. And sure, I can give you an intro to him. How soon do you think you might go over there?"

"Probably this morning, but I don't quite know what I'll do when I get there."

"Okay, I'll call over right away. Why don't you meet with Jim first? See if he has any ideas, before you try anything. Don't forget, if you run into any of the actual gang that's been killing your bears, I want you out of there. Don't do anything rash."

"Jim?"

"James J. Johnson. Jim is young, not much older than you, maybe thirty. He has been on the job about two years and is a very effective and popular Chief. You'll like him. I'll set it up for later this morning."

"That should work. I've got to report in to the Park Superintendent first and then I'll head on over there."

The Superintendent was agitated. "What's going on down there? We've found one more bear carcass up here and the Feds are all over the place. We're discouraging back packers going into the back country, telling them there's an outbreak of an animal virus that's temporary. Are you making any progress? All in one breath.

Josh tried to make his report upbeat and reassuring. "Not bad. The police chief is very cooperative and has assigned the whole Chinese department to help me. We've got a lead in Emeryville and I'm checking it out this morning. I'll keep you posted." He didn't tell him that he was doing it by himself.

"Sounds promising. But be careful. Be sure and work with those other policemen, okay? And one more thing, keep quiet about what your doing. I haven't told the Feds or anyone where you are."

"You bet," was Josh's reply, once more with his fingers crossed.

CHAPTER 19

Next morning Josh drove over the bridge to Emeryville, arriving almost an hour before his appointment with the Chief. He had been warned that the traffic hour rush over the bridge sometimes resulted in long waits. What he hadn't been told was that the long wait in the morning was East to West. Consequently, going West to East was a piece of cake.

He thought he would put the extra time to good use and set out to find the pharmaceutical lab. Coming off the bridge he turned north toward Sacramento, but immediately took the Emeryville exit and found himself immediately in a huge shopping area. Just beyond that was an industrial area that extended for miles. Fortunately a service station was able to give him directions to the right street and he found the lab without much trouble.

Its size impressed him. It took up a whole building and looked very modern. Behind it was a private parking lot for employees and guests. Josh parked on the street and watched people coming and going. Most of the people were quite young, many of them wearing short green smocks.

He thought they were probably lab workers, although so many non-hospital people wear hospital greens, he couldn't be sure. None of the arriving workers struck him as odd or out of the ordinary. So far, the place looked far from suspicious.

At the Emeryville police station, he was asked to wait, "The chief said to tell you he would only be a minute or two."

While waiting, Josh's attention was drawn to a yellowing piece of newspaper hanging on a bulletin board. It had a picture of the new police chief and was touting his appointment. He was nice looking, nothing outstanding, but nice. The article said he was only twenty-nine years old and added that he had been hired from the San Diego police department after a brilliant stint as assistant chief down there. The article mentioned his outstanding career but spent more time on his good looks and the fact that he was a bachelor. They mentioned his blond, boyish hair and his grayish eyes. They even mentioned the cleft in his chin. You had to read between the lines to find out how good a candidate he was for the position of Police Chief.

Josh wondered if he was still single. After two years, and with the ballyhoo about his looks and availability, maybe some lovely young "Emeryvillian" had snagged him. At the far end of the hall a door was yanked open, and the young chief's head appeared in the doorway.

"Ranger? Come on down."

Josh was startled. He had expected a secretary or a desk sergeant to lead him to the Chief's office, not this very informal greeting and invitation.

"Sorry to have kept you waiting. There's always something brewing. Usually it's with the city council. Today it was one policeman against another. C'est la vie!"

He looked just like his picture. Too good looking and too young to be a police chief. He had a very intent way of looking at you. Like he was trying to devour you with eyes. Some people had told Josh that he had that look also.

"Anne filled me in on your project. Do you really think there's a gang of Chinese that are killing your bears and stealing their organs for medicinal purposes? I find that hard to believe!"

It took a moment for Josh to realize the Anne he was talking about was the S.F. police chief.

"Not only do I believe it, one more bear was killed in the exactly the same way since I left the valley plus the same gang killed one of our Rangers.

Our park superintendent had our park doctor look at the bear remains and said that the organs had not only been removed but had been done pretty professionally"

Josh paused for a second. "Yeah, it's happening and it's serious. These guys came into the park intending to kill and eviscerate bears and they had the tools to do it with. They also had been taught how to do it pretty professionally. We think our guy stumbled on them accidently and they shot him. We caught the guys but they aren't admitting anything-------yet."

"But what's the connection to us? Anne said something about the pharmaceutical lab here?"

"First off, a little background. I lived in China for several years. I've observed first-hand the traffic in animal organs that goes on. In China it's a huge underground business and it's been going on for generations. Like so many underground and illegal businesses, people get filthy rich doing it. Gangs are organized, lives are lost, it becomes ruthless. The Sun Bear in China has almost become extinct because of the demand for its gall bladder and other parts."

"Do you think that a gang has set up an operation here like they have in China?"

" I'm beginning to think that with the Sun Bear becoming almost extinct, some of those gangs are trying to find more bears to kill. If I'm right, they're going on a killing spree that could wipe out most the bears in California. That's where your lab might come in. The gall bladder for instance, needs to be kept on ice or immediately dried in order for it to be useful. It'd be virtually impossible to transport an iced gall bladder to China, but dried and powdered, it would be a cinch. This lab or one like it could process the organs into dried powder and move it easily. I don't know, maybe medical labs can ship things pretty easily anyway."

"I'll have my staff look into the background of the lab for you. You said you'd found out that they might be facing bankruptcy?"

"Yeah, at least that's the rumor in the Chinese community."

"So what do you want of me?"

"I'm going to claim that I'm a writer doing an article about how successful Emeryville is and how successful some of your businesses are. So I'm interviewing a few of them and the lab was recommended. Can I say that I've cleared the project with you already?"

"You got it. Let me know what you find out, okay?"

He gave the chief his hotel address and also his cell phone number, thanked him for his ideas and his help and left.

CHAPTER 20

Rather than waste any time he called the pharmaceutical lab on his cell

"Do you have a public relations officer I can speak to?"

The young girl's voice that answered the phone responded with a long, hesitant, "uuuuhh" as if that question had never been asked before. Then, "I don't think so, can I help you?"

.He told her he was an author just passing through Emeryville on his way to San Francisco. "My next book's going to feature Emeryville and the Emeryville police chief told me about the lab."

She was a little reluctant at first but finally agreed when he mentioned the police chief. She set an appointment for nine-thirty, saying, "I haven't been here too long, I'm just the receptionist but I guess it'd be okay to show you around a little."

Promptly at nine-thirty a young lady emerged into the lobby of the pharmaceutical lab and headed for Josh. She was wearing a green smock down to her knees and had blue shoe covers on. Her hair was covered with a cap and she was wearing glasses. Josh estimated her at just a little over twenty.

"Mr. Rogan?"

"That's me. I'm sorry, I didn't get your name?"

"Ellen" Rather breathlessly she continued. "I checked with the floor manager and he said a short tour would be okay as long as you're okay with the dress code."

"Dress code?"

"To begin with, just to pass through those doors, you're need to go into the changing room over there. You'll find plastic wrapped packages of smocks, hats, gloves and shoe covers. That'll begin to give you something for your book. The floor manager told me to clue you in about our cleanliness standards.We're heavily regulated with all kinds of government restrictions and oversight."

Josh emerged, leaving his jacket in the cubbyhole provided, wearing a smock down to his knees and the required hat, and shoe covers, carrying the plastic gloves.

"You're going to have to wear the gloves and keep them on as long as we're in the lab."

In the lab, Josh was immediately struck by its starkness. Everything was white. Walls, stools, benches, machinery, all white. It was also very quiet. Ellen led him on to a catwalk that ran over the workplaces. From the catwalk she directed his view to various parts of the operation.

"There's not an awful lot to see. Some of the workers joke that it's an undercover operation. Actually it is. By design. Just about everything is done inside machines to protect against contamination. We manufacture several over the counter medications as a subcontractor. We receive the processed material from the manufacturer and process it into pills."

"Oh! So you don't actually get a plant from Africa, as an example, and process it?"

"No, we can do all that but mostly that's done before we get involved. We make them into the proper pill size and package them. That's all. Have you ever seen the book that has every pill sold in America pictured in it?"

"Never heard of it."

"When we get back to the office, I'll show it to you. It shows the shape, color, and special markings of every pill on the market. I think you'll get a kick out of it."

They continued their tour, but Ellen was right, there wasn't much to see. Just a lot of shiny, chromed tanks surrounded by all white machinery. Even the end result was completely mechanized with pills spilling automatically into bottles. The bottles were capped and labeled totally hands-free.

He noticed that a fairly large part of the building was sealed off from the part she was showing him.

"Is there more in there?"

"There used to be. Before we got this new contract we used to process the raw material but we don't do that anymore. That was before my time. Ever since I've been here that part of the lab has been in disuse."

Josh couldn't see how this operation could possibly be mixed up in the processing and distribution of illegal medication. Not since they'd quit the processing portion.

Back in the foyer, Ellen handed him a copy of the pill book and told him he could have it as a souvenir of his visit. He asked her to wait while he grabbed his jacket from the changing room.

"A couple of questions about the business side of the lab and I should be through, okay?"

Again a little hesitation before, "Okay."

He stripped off the smock and the shoe covers, grabbed his jacket and reached for his comb in the inside jacket pocket. It wasn't there. 'Neither was his Ranger I.D. Carefully patting all his pockets, he found them in his other inside pocket. Absolutely not where they had been before.

Someone had hurriedly rifled through his jacket while he was being toured through the plant. If they hadn't mistakenly put his papers back in the wrong pocket he would never have known about it. Now someone knew he was a Yosemite Park Ranger and where he was staying in San Francisco.

Ellen was waiting for him in the lobby. Somehow Josh didn't think she knew anything about his jacket. He reflected upon the small hesitation on her part when he asked about the business side of the operation and made a quick decision.

"That was awfully thoughtful of you! I really appreciate the tour. My wife would probably bawl me out if I didn't offer to repay your kindness. Can I buy you a cup of coffee? Is there someplace nearby where we can sit down for a few minutes? Can you get away for a short time?"

Glancing around the empty foyer, she hesitated for a moment and then, "I guess that would be okay. It's just about time for my coffee break. There's a nice coffee shop just around the corner. We can meet there, I'll have to change my shoes and get rid of my smock. See you in five minutes?"

Waiting, Josh grabbed a booth and wondered why would someone steal a look at his ID? Whoever saw his papers now knew he was a Yosemite Park Ranger. His suspicions about the lab took a huge leap upwards. Did Ellen know what was going on? Was anything going on? Maybe he could learn a little more over coffee. Remembering Tim and that Tim had been killed, was he in any danger? Should he keep on with the investigation?

He examined his own motives in defying the Superintendent and continuing his own investigation. It had started with a deep, underlying love and respect for Yosemite and the animal life in it. He had been outraged about the bear deaths. Then Tim got murdered. That had changed everything. Before that it'd been an assignment. An unusual assignment which affected him deeply. Tim's murder made it personal.

"The hell with quitting!" Josh said to himself.

CHAPTER 21

"I'm going to have a Latte and a scone, how about you?"

"Just a coffee, please. George knows what I want. I come over here almost every day just about this time."

"Great, I've got a booth, I'll get the coffees"

The booth was part of Josh's plan. He sensed a little reluctance on her part and wanted to put her at her ease. The booth should be more relaxing than a stool at the counter.

Josh opened, "I gathered from what you said you haven't been working at the lab too long?"

"Almost six months now"

"Are they a good company to work for?"

"Oh yeah. Pays okay and the benefits are good."

"So, all in all, you'd say it's a good company to work for. That's great. I think I heard from the chief that the company had some financial problems recently?"

"May be, I don't know. I had a little problem with a paycheck about three months ago but nothing since."

"The owner's Chinese isn't he?"

"They're all Chinese."

"All? I thought it was owned by only one person."

"Not any more. I think some others bought into the company about three months ago. They're Chinese too. They were around for a few days then but not much now. Once in a while late in the afternoon, just as I'm leaving I see them come in."

Josh thought Ellen didn't know anything more that could help him. But what she had told him raised his suspicions even more. He talked a little more in generalities to avoid suspicion before he said, "I better get you back before I get you fired."

As soon as he got rid of her, Josh drove around the block and parked. The only way he thought he could find out what really went on in the lab was to get inside and explore. Walking around the block he noticed that the building seemed larger on the outside than it had on the inside. He wondered how large the closed-off part was and if it was really closed off. There was a sloped driveway at the rear of the building, leading down to a truck size roll up door and another delivery dock on the side leading to the front lab.

Could he get in if he really wanted to? The answer to that was simple. Yeah, he could see several walls he could scale and several windows he could reach. Not on the ground floor, there were no windows there. But he could do it. But was it the best way? He needed to see the roof. The only building tall enough to give a view of the roof was a hotel about a block away. That should provide a quick solution.

The hotel problem was simple. The desk clerk was more than happy to have a porter show him a couple of rooms. One of them had an overview of the lab. It was as Josh had guessed, flat with a short concrete balustrade along its edges. Toward the front of the building there was a small square structure with a door in it. Josh surmised that it was a way up to the roof and it could also be a way into the lab. There were also four huge skylights. Often the best way to surreptitiously enter a building was from a place that no one thought could be reached. Like a roof two stories off the ground.

Do I or don't I?, he asked himself.

He knew the answer. He was going to do it. That night. By himself.

He had to hurry. He needed to get back to the hotel, grab a change of clothing suitable for what he had in mind and once more become a Ninja.

CHAPTER 22

At his hotel the hotel desk clerk told him that a group of Chinese gentlemen had been asking for him.

"Did they leave any message?"

"No sir, they just wanted to know if you were in or when you were expected."

Josh immediately phoned Lieutenant Chew, thinking the "gentlemen" might have been some of his squad. They weren't.

Obviously they come looking for him after getting the information out of his coat pocket. The plot was thickening!

Josh thought he had to start taking some chances. Time was running out. The Superintendent had ordered him home, the police chief had ordered him to just look and "don't touch", and the FBI was getting involved. He needed to verify his suspicions, like now.

Thinking to himself, he made his plan. "Tonight I'll break into the lab and find out if what I think is right. I'm betting the lab is processing the organs into illegal Chinese medicine. If I'm right, then I'll start planning the next step, by myself if necessary."

He followed his own well-established routine to get his mind and body ready for the night's activity. First he stripped naked, sat down crossed legged on the floor and meditated for a half-hour. Josh had the ability to achieve a deep state of meditation in a matter of seconds. At the end of the half-hour he was both mentally and physically refreshed. He was ready to become a Ninja and more. If you had been able to see the transformation you would have thought he was taller, slimmer, and stronger than he had been a half-hour before.

Opening his suitcase he dug down to the bottom and unlatched a false bottom. Neatly packed in the false compartment were a variety of weapons for him to choose from. He decided stealth was paramount that night. Stealth called for a Ninja-style entry. Ninja was one of his favorites as it called for not only bodily strength and agility, but also secrecy. A perfect Ninja operation would be to complete a planned event and have no one know anyone had been there. That's what he wanted to do tonight. Get in and get out, with no one being the wiser.

Sometimes, however, things didn't work out the way you expected. He had to be ready with weapons if necessary. His hands and feet were weapons, but his most important weapon was his mind. He decided that for tonight they'd be enough. All he needed from his Ninja gear was a grappling hook to scale the wall.

Ninjas took great pains not to be seen. They commonly operated under -cover of darkness and blended in with the surroundings. He was planning on the cover of night but was wondering how to blend in with the surroundings. The exterior of the building was off-white and the customary black Ninja outfit would stand out like a beacon! He finally decided on almost white denim pants and shirt and white ninja shoes.

The last thing he needed to do was to perform what he called a "death ritual." He needed to become a Ninja. He needed to be ready to kill with his hands and feet. He was now a warrior. He was now a fighting machine. He was now one of the most dangerous men on the face of the earth. With all his years of training plus his superior body strengths, he could outthink, outrun, outfight anyone. All of his senses were heightened. He was ready.

He left the hotel just as night was falling, wearing just a shirt, pants and shoes and carrying a small bag around his waist. Through the lobby and on the way to his car several people glanced at him and probably thought he was going jogging.

In a short time he was back over the bridge and in Emeryville. The building was completely dark. No cars in the parking lot. It was time to go!

CHAPTER 23

Staying as close as possible to the building, Josh first made a complete circumference of it. The building only had three doors. The larger front door which he entered through on his visit, the large rolling delivery door at the rear and a smaller delivery dock door at the side of the front lab. None were open and what few windows there were, were sealed tight. Just as he had expected.

Back where he had begun he dug into his bag and took out the grappling hook. Grappling hooks had a few disadvantages. One was that they had a limited throwing range. Another was they had to have something to catch on. The third was that they were noisy. Josh wasn't worried about noise, being in an industrial area meant that there were no next door home owners concerned about thumps in the night. The hook was padded and no one was home.

The front side of the building was much lower than the rear side, however the front side had the disadvantage of being on the street. There was still some occasional traffic and he might possibly be seen. Crouching in the shrubs, keeping an eye on the traffic, he estimated the roof to be about thirty feet above his head.

He mentally rehearsed his plan. "I've got to step out from the building far enough to swing the hook and gain momentum. Then I'll need to throw it far enough so that it'll land on the roof and I can snub it on the parapet. I need to do it quickly between cars and then duck back into the bushes ready for the next step."

His first throw was a complete success. He even had time to take up the slack and make sure the grappling hook was well seated before he had to duck behind the bushes. Next he waited until there was a long break between cars and in a much practiced move, walked up the wall using the grappling hook line until, in a matter of seconds, he was on the roof.

He pulled up the line behind him and started exploring the roof. The structure he had spotted before was locked and bolted from the inside. No way could he use that entrance without leaving evidence of a break in. The skylights looked much more promising. They also looked unused. They were closed tight and had been painted over with black paint. He theorized that the rearmost skylight would be over the unused lab. Carefully he scraped enough of the paint away so that he could see inside. The lab was completely dark.

The skylight opening was fastened with a catch on the inside. Josh could see where the handle was positioned and was able, using a small glass cutter, to make an inch square hole in the glass next to the handle. With a short piece of wire, opening the handle was a cinch and in a matter of moments the skylight was open and yawning before him.

His calculations had been correct. He was over the unused part of the building.

There were no lights, the place was deserted. Josh switched on a small flashlight. He could just make out the outlines of big machinery and a catwalk, all painted a glaring white. He used his grappling hook and line to snake his way down to the catwalk. The catwalk would allow someone to observe each of the huge machines without descending to the floor. Josh wanted to drop down and examine the truck door for recent usage before he did anything else.

CHAPTER 24

The metal door was designed to roll up almost to the ceiling. Obviously not new, there was no way to tell if it had been used recently. However all the chains and blocks used to raise and lower the door were freshly oiled. On the floor he found tire tracks which looked fresh. Examining them closely, he found that the tracks were very slightly damp.

Someone had driven a vehicle in here within the last twenty-four hours, he estimated. The mud from outside hadn't completely dried yet.

Off to one side he found some discarded foam type ice chests that could have been used to carry fresh animal organs. Or maybe not?

There were numerous large machines scattered throughout the lab, some large, some small. Most of them were connected with a roller type conveyer belt. Assuming there was some kind of order to the arrangement, Josh decided to look first at the machinery nearest the delivery entrance.

The lab floor was up a short flight of stairs from the delivery area. The nearest piece of machinery was all white and chrome, bolted heavily to the floor. It looked to be about ten by fourteen feet square and a little taller than Josh, maybe about seven feet. From the outside he had no idea of its function.

On one side he found the manufacturers name and information about the machine. The brand name was "SAM" and it was of Chinese origin. The label identified the machine as a "DRYING MACHINE MODEL DR-O."

Under that it listed the purposes for which it had been designed.

"OVEN, (DRYING MACHINE), (DEHYDRATE) IS SUITABLE FOR HEATING AND SOLIDIFYING, DRYING AND DEHYDRATING RAW MATERIALS."

Below that it continued, "APPLICATION. IT IS SUITABLE FOR HEATING AND SOLIDIFYING, DRYING AND DEHYDRATING RAW MATERIALS FOR PHARMACEUTICAL, CHEMICAL, FOOD, AGRICULTURAL. MATERIALS CAN BE MEDICINE RAW

MATERIALS, CHINESE TRADITIONAL MEDICINE, POWDER, GRANULE ETC."

"Chinese traditional medicine!!" Exactly what Josh was looking for. This machine was capable of making bear parts into thousands of doses of powder.

CHAPTER 25

Following the conveyer system around he checked out the rest of the machinery. One was a pill-making machine, another ground dehydrated material into powder, another bottled pills, yet another was a labeling machine, and so forth. Josh assumed the first machine dehydrated the bear parts, the second ground it into powder while the third packaged it.

The lab certainly had everything it needed to process the gall bladders. They could probably handle the teeth and the claws too. What he needed was actual proof that it was being done here. The machines were immaculately clean, no evidence there. Maybe in the front office, if he could get in there, he could find some paper records.

The door was locked and alarmed. He could pick the lock fairly easily, but the alarm was something else. There was nothing in sight to indicate the door was alarmed except the sign warning that the door was alarmed at closing time every night. He couldn't take the chance of setting it off.

Just as he was deciding there was nothing else of value he could do here tonight, he heard a metallic sound at the rear of the lab. It sounded like someone had pushed against the overhead door.

Josh had to make a quick decision. Go for his grappling hook and climb out of sight (he hoped), or hide down here and try to find out what was going down.

'No contest! He quickly leaped on top of the tallest machine and laid flat. No one could possibly see him unless they crawled on top of the machine or went up on the catwalk. The machine was over fifteen feet tall and almost room size.

In a few minutes the door started rolling up and Josh could see a small van parked outside. Once the door was open the car was quickly driven inside. All this was done in the dark. Even the car's headlights were off. It looked very clandestine to Josh.

The passenger door opened and someone stepped out. The driver said, "Check the window and the skylights, make sure they're closed and still blacked out."

One of the men snapped a flashlight on and beamed it at the windows and the skylights. "Yeah, I can see from here, they're tight and black."

Fortunately for Josh, his climbing rope was hidden behind a girder.

The driver turned on a light near the van.

With the light on Josh could see there were four of them, all Chinese. He could also see the license plate on the van. It was from North Dakota. What were they doing here?

"What now?"

"We put the ice chests into the reefer and leave them. I put a note on them with my name on it and that's it."

"When do we get the money?"

"You'll get the money when I'm good and ready to give it to you!"

"How can we screw around in San Francisco if we ain't got no money?"

"I'll give you an advance, but the big money comes next week. First thing we need to go someplace near and clean up. We gotta get rid of that North Dakota bear smell. Now that you've seen the lab, what d'ya think of it?"

"It's big. What do they do here?"

"Doesn't matter. They turn what we bring in into money for us, that's what they do."

"Okay, you guys get back in the van, I'll put the stuff in the reefer."

He carried three fairly large picnic-type freezers over to the reefer. Dumping dry ice out of each of them, he put the freezers into the reefer. Next he scribbled a note and put it inside also. When all was done he closed and locked the reefer door. Josh wondered how may bears had been killed to fill that many boxes.

Josh was beside himself. He desperately wanted to get into the reefer and get a sample of what was in there. Now it was locked. What could he do? In a moment the driver would go back to the van and drive off.

Quickly, Josh scaled quietly down the backside of his machine. On the floor he ghosted his way to the side of the van without being seen and waited. The driver approached the car and called out as Josh had expected,

"I'm going to turn out the lights before I open the garage door. Keep the car lights off. Josh noticed that the driver had dropped the reefer key in his pants pocket. He would have a moment or two to get next to the driver and get the key out of his pocket, without his knowing it.

Using a Ninja practice, Josh closed his eyes and relied entirely on his other senses. He needed to stay hidden until the lights were turned out. By feel he located a short piece of two by four and held it ready in his hands. As soon as he heard the light switch he opened his eyes and spotted the driver. The driver was momentarily blinded in the dark. Josh needed to get next to him in a hurry.

As the driver was cautiously feeling his way in the dark to the van, Josh slipped in beside him and maneuvered the two by four just in front of the drivers feet and held it firmly in place. The driver stumbled on the two by four and fell to his knees.

"Freakin hell, where'd that come from?"

From the car, "You okay?"

"Yeah, I stumbled on something, I'm okay."

In his efforts to break his fall and find what had tripped over, he never felt Josh extract the key from his pocket.

"Just a god damn piece of two by four," he mumbled to himself.

Josh faded away behind one of the machines and waited for them to leave.

CHAPTER 26

Josh expected the driver wouldn't miss the reefer keys until later and then he would assume he had dropped his keys when he stumbled and fell. In the meantime Josh had a way into the reefer. In the dark one of them opened the overhead door, backed the van out and rolled the door back down.

Josh was by himself with the keys to the reefer. He took out one of the picnic size ice chests to examine its' contents. Several bloody organs were stored in it.

Using his small pocket knife, Josh was able to quickly cut off a thin slice from the organs stored in the refrigerator. It was still fairly fresh and bloody. Searching through the lab he found some luncheon supplies with box full of wax paper bags. Enough so that he was able to wrap the slice up tightly and place it in his small bag.

If the sample proved to be a bear organ he had enough evidence to prove the lab was involved in the bear killings, at least to himself. He needed to get out and have the bloody sample tested at the police laboratory.

Scaling up the grappling hook line, he was soon at the skylight and back on the roof. He covered the small hole he had made in the window with a piece of black electricians tape. In all probability it'd be years before anyone spotted it.

Getting off the roof was easier than getting on. While the rear of the building was about ten feet higher than the front, all he had to do was wedge his grappling hook and slide down the line. A hard flip on the line and the grappling hook came loose and fell to his feet. His plan was to head back to his hotel, put the liver sample in the room refrigerator, get a good nights' sleep and have the sample tested first thing in the morning.

Approaching his room, Josh set his backpack down and opened his door. As he reached for the light switch he sensed movement behind him, started to crouch and whirl, then felt a crashing blow to the right side of his head. He fell to his knees.

CHAPTER 27

Josh's instinctive reaction was instantaneous. On his knees, ignoring the pain, moving so fast it seemed a blur, he totally incapacitated the man behind him with a rear kick to his solar plexus area, leaving him writhing on the floor, gasping for breath.

At the same time he located two other men in the room, poised to attack him. Never stopping, keeping an effortless flow of movement he leaped, cat-like, to his feet and whirled to meet them. They were totally confused. Nothing was going as they had expected. Josh wasn't on the floor out cold, he was facing them ready to do battle. They were both physically and mentally off balance.

Josh spun toward the nearest of the two and watched as the man started to draw a gun. His movements seemed to be in slow motion to Josh. As he began to straighten his gun arm, Josh grabbed it. He pulled the gunman toward him and drove the flat of his hand at the man's nose. A broken nose is pretty incapacitating. The gun dropped to the floor. At the same time Josh dropped his hands to the man's shoulders, pulled him viciously toward himself and kneed his groin. The man let out a groan and dropped to the floor. Maintaining the same movement Josh kicked the gun to the corner of the room, out of reach.

The third man was just beginning to move. He was about four steps away from Josh. Josh continued his twirling moving and transferred his weight to his left leg. As he whirled around he generated the momentum needed to launch a flying side kick to the intruder's head and knock him unconscious

The three guys hadn't known it, but the battle was over before it began and had only taken a few seconds. For Josh it had been all reaction. Something easily done thousands of times before. His mind and reflexes had taken over. He hadn't even worked up a sweat.

Walking into the bathroom, he tore a long towel into thin strips and used them to effectively tie the three men up. All three were

Chinese. In the bathroom he glanced at his head to see if he was bleeding. He wasn't, but his ear was angry, red and burning.

Using his martial arts training, he ignored the pain. As if it wasn't there. Evidently the blow had been a glancing one, sliding down the side of his head and bruising his ear.

The questions now were: "Who are these guys, who sent them, what were they going to do to me, how can I use them and what do I do with them?"

The first guy, the one that'd hit him, was beginning to come around and was gagging.

Josh picked him up and took him into the bedroom. Dumping him on the bed he removed the sash around the curtains and tied him up so that his legs were doubled behind him and the other end was in a loop around his neck. He couldn't straighten his legs without choking himself. Any movement at all would be extremely painful. In effect he was torturing himself. He wouldn't go anywhere.

Returning to the bathroom he got washcloths and gagged all three of the men. He still didn't know what he was going to do, but he had the time to plan something, now that he had them secured.

In the bedroom he removed the gag from the first guys' mouth after warning him about another slam to his gut if he made any outcry.

"I'm going to ask you a question. Don't answer it. Just nod your head yes or no, understood?"

He got an up and down nod.

"I hit you in your solar plexus and knocked your breath out. You're recovering now but your buddies aren't. They may be dead already. That gives you a chance to save your neck. So, Would you rather talk to me or die?"

A frantic up and down nod. Josh removed the gag.

CHAPTER 28

"Okay. Now I want answers! Who sent you here?"

The man started babbling in Chinese and saying, "no speak English, no speak English!!"

In perfect Chinese, Josh answered him.

"Fine! We speak in Chinese then, would you prefer Cantonese or Mandarin?"

The man visibly caved and started speaking fairly good English.

"I give you what you want, don't kill me!"

"Okay, One more chance. Who sent you?"

"Fong, Charley Fong"

"Who's Charley Fong?"

"Charley's a private detective, sort of. He's got offices in Chinatown."

"What do you mean, sort of?"

"Well, he ain't really licensed. He just does lots of things in the Chinese community, you know, favors!"

"And you were doing him a favor? What were you supposed to do?"

"Not much."

"You call hitting me over the head with sap not much? You call pulling a gun on me not much? You're going to have to do better than that or you're going to join your buddies in the other room!"

The more the guy spoke, the better his English became.

"Jesus, I don't have a prayer. If I tell you, Charley'll kill me, and if I don't tell, you'll kill me."

"Look at it this way. I'm here now! Don't tell me and you're done for! Charley isn't here. He may never know what you tell me. What he doesn't know won't hurt you. I'm not going to tell him, are you?"

"If I tell you, you'll let me go?"

"Why should I keep you?"

"What about the other two guys?"

"I don't know yet. I may need your help getting rid of the bodies. You better make up your mind, I'm running out of time."

"Okay, Okay! We were supposed to beat the living crap out of you and then leave a note in the room."

"A note? Where is it?"

"It's in the other guys' pocket. The short guy."

"Don't you know him?"

"Not really. I've seen him around, usually in pool rooms. Charley just hit on me a couple of days ago and asked if I wanted to earn a little money. Told me to pick up a couple more guys if I felt I needed 'em. I've done a few odds and ends jobs for Charley before, but nothing like this. He said it'd be easy. He got me a passkey and told me to hide inside the room and clobber you when you came in. 'A cinch,' he said."

Josh gagged him again, went back to the living room and rifled through the short guys pockets. He wasn't too happy about it, but couldn't do much being bound and gagged. Josh found the note in an inside jacket pocket.

All caps, it read: "CAUCASIANS DISAPPEAR IN CHINATOWN ALL THE TIME. IF YOU WANT TO LIVE, GET OUT OF TOWN"

CHAPTER 29

Josh knew he had hit a nerve. The lab in Emeryville was the key. That was where someone had rifled through his jacket and found his identification and where he was staying.

He also had four new problems. He had to get rid of the three guys and then he had to locate and debrief the illegal private detective, Charley Fong.

First things first, he called the hotel chief of security. He identified himself and reminded him that the Chief of Police had arranged for his room.

"Can you come up to my room, please. There's a situation up here that I think you and I can handle with a minimum of publicity for the hotel."

In a manner of minutes the security chief was in his room.

The 3 prisoners were in the bedroom but the living room showed evidence of the fight. One broken chair and a seriously bent floor lamp.

"What's the situation?"

"The situation is, I've got 3 professional robbers locked up in my bedroom. They chose the wrong room and I was able to subdue them pretty easily. I'm here on an undercover job and don't need any publicity and I'm sure the hotel doesn't either. Seems to me you can have these guys arrested on some other charge than room burglary and avoid some bad publicity."

"They were trying to break into your room?"

"Yeah. They must have thought I was out."

"Three to one? You were lucky."

"I don't think so. They weren't expecting anyone in the room and weren't ready for a fight, although one of them did have a gun on him."

"A gun? Well that changes things. You're right. We don't need this type of publicity. We don't need the public thinking it isn't safe to walk in our hallways. I think we just found these guys trying to break into one of the retail stores in the lower lobby , after hours."

"So this is just between us?"

"Sure, professional courtesy."

" Can you move me to another room?, this one's pretty well messed up."

"Of course." He checked with the front desk and ended up moving Josh to another room on the same floor.

Josh's real reason for moving was that someone knew his room number and he didn't want another unwelcome visitor. Once was enough.

That took care of the three guys, next he had to find Charley the unlicensed Chinese Private Eye. All he knew was that he had an office somewhere in Chinatown but he did most of his business at one of several local pool halls.

After the exertion, he was wide awake and resorted to meditation to calm himself down. Within a few minutes he dropped into a deep sleep and didn't wake up until the phone woke him at 5:30 the next morning.

"Where the hell you been? I had a hell of a time finding you. The front desk said you weren't in your room and they thought maybe you'd moved. Finally they found you'd changed rooms, what's going on?" It was Lieutenant Chew.

"Chew? Slow down. Nothing's going on. The hotel had a security problem and asked me if I'd mind moving to a different room. No problem. What's up?"

"The Chief, that's what's up. She wants to know what you're doing and how come you haven't been working with me. She says you're going over to Emeryville to look into Mitchell's cousin's place and I'm supposed to go with you."

"Oh hell, I've already been over there. She gave me the name of the police chief in Emeryville as a reference and I thought I was clear to go. Wasn't much there to see but something suspicious happened. We need to gct togcthcr. How about this morning?"

"We better. She chewed me out and said I'd better keep track of you or my rear-end would be in a sling. Her words! You know where I am, I'm waiting."

Josh showered, cleaned and stored his equipment from the night before, got dressed and headed toward the Chinatown Police Headquarters.

On the way he realized he now he had another problem. He didn't mind sharing his information about Charley Fong, maybe they could help him find the detective's office. But how could he explain having the bear sample? How could he get the specimen analyzed? Maybe a private lab? On top of that, deep down in his gut, he felt he had to face these guys by himself, maybe a little outside of the niceties of Law. After all, no one else could or would do what he had done last night. He had to meet with Chew but he didn't have to share everything with Chew.

He needed to keep the Chief in his corner. He was sure that the Superintendent was clamoring for him to get back to the Valley and then there was Fern. He thought that maybe, just maybe, the police chief wouldn't want him to leave. She knew what progress he had made, whereas the Super didn't. Everything pointed to San Francisco. Her city, her jurisdiction. Sooner or later, the FBI would follow the trail to San Francisco and take over the case. Josh knew from experience, police usually resented the FBI's presence in their cities.

If he could get the chief to intercede. Maybe she would request that he stay on a few days if he could convince her that he was making headway and cooperating with Chew. He thought the superintendent might accede to the Chief of Police of San Francisco. If he could convince her.

At the station, Josh made a big show of cooperation with Chew and apologized about going to Emeryville without him.

"I didn't get a lot of hard information. The Emeryville Chief said that they'd had no complaints about the company and he gave me an intro to the company. I had a quick tour of the facilities and nothing stood out. The receptionist let slip that they had evidently weathered some financial troubles a short time ago and there were some new owners involved. All Chinese."

"And that's it?"

"She did say there was a part of the lab that was not being used any more and it was completely closed off. And one more thing. They made me wear a smock and booties when I went on the tour and when I changed back I found that my jacket and wallet had been searched. I also found out that a Chinese Private Detective name Charley Fong is mixed up with the new owners."

"How'd that come up?"

Thinking fast, not wanting to mention the fracas in the hotel room, Josh said, "I'm not quite sure, it was just something she mentioned in passing."

Fortunately, Chew seemed to be satisfied with that "Charley Fong? A Chinese private detective? Never heard of him. Of course there's lots of these guys operating outside of the law, particularly in Chinatown. Maybe one of my guys'll know of him."

"I think that's a good idea. It's the only name we've got so far. You should be able to find him if he's well known as a private detective. Can't be that many in Chinatown. Do you mind if I talk with your detectives?"

The only detective in just then was Mitchell and Lieutenant Chew asked him to work with Josh.

"Mitch, you ever hear of a Chinese P.I. called Charley Fong?"

"Sounds familiar, is he licensed?"

"Probably not. See if you can help Josh here find him, okay?"

Josh joined Mitchell at his desk and asked, "Where do we begin?"

"One thing for sure, it won't be in the phone book. If he's not licensed, he'll keep a low profile. Probably does all his business by word of mouth. I'll just have to work some of my contacts. Sit tight, let me make a few phone calls."

Josh sat tight. He hoped that Mitchell wouldn't find out what he knew. That Charley Fong did most of his business at a pool hall.

Mitchell made phone call after phone call. Several calls confirmed that there was indeed a Charley Fong, but they had no idea how to contact him. A couple said they thought he had an office somewhere, but didn't know where. Mitchell didn't give up, just said he would have to dig deeper. Maybe find some underworld elements that would know of him.

Lieutenant Chew interrupted them. "Look, this is taking a lot of valuable time from other investigations. Don't you have any other leads to follow up on? Maybe you could search the department of records and see who bought into the company, that might be a help."

Josh eagerly agreed. Anything to get away and find Charley Fong his way. If he could find the pool hall, he could find the elusive private detective. They wouldn't be listed in the phone book, he would have to find them the hard way. On foot and asking questions.

CHAPTER 30

In his experience, there were usually many Chinese businesses that never made it into the phone book. Thriving businesses that derived their customers entirely from the comparatively small but very crowded Chinese community. They didn't need to advertise. Everybody knew everybody. Plus, in these days, they all used cell phones and didn't need to be listed.

The problem was that the guys that had way-laid him in his room said that Fong traveled from pool hall to pool hall, looking for business. Josh might have to visit several to find him.

All he could do was nose around. It was never easy for a non-Chinese to nose around in the Chinese community, particularly outside the tourist area. However, being fluent in several dialects would give him an advantage. A huge worry was they might have his picture. 'They had known his hotel room because they had seen his Room pass key. But they had also seen his Park Ranger ID with his picture. Could they have copied it in that short time?

After further thought, Josh decided it was highly unlikely he would be recognized. Nobody knew yet that the attack on him had failed. The only person he thought might have his picture was Charley Fong himself.

He walked to Chinatown and became a tourist. On the way he devised a story that might help him find other pool halls if the listed one wasn't the right one.

In Chinese, he talked to several merchants.

"I'm looking for a Chinese Merchant seaman friend of mine. I was supposed to meet him yesterday in front of the temple, but my ship was a day late. All I can remember is that he plays a lot of pool and said there were a couple of pool halls here that he liked. I found one but I don't think that's the right one. Do you know of any others?"

Mostly he got negative answers. Some said they thought there were some, but they didn't know where. As it got later into the evening, some of the stores started closing. He moved further into the heart of Chinatown and away from the tourist streets. Here the stores were different. Grocery stores, meat markets, small restaurants, liquor stores, all open. Almost one hundred percent Chinese customers.

In order to blend in, Josh started buying stuff. A few dollars worth of groceries or meats bought him the opportunity to jaw with the owner for a few minutes or so. Often, the only reason he was able to get any information at all, was because the merchants were surprised by his fluent Chinese. Eventually he got a couple of leads.

The problem was that the information was pretty vague. They all knew they were around just didn't know exactly where they were. "Over two blocks, in a basement." Or, "Across from park, in a basement."

Evidently, wherever it was, it was in a basement. It reminded Josh of what a Chinese friend of his had told him once, many years before, in Shanghai.

"You want the best Chinese restaurant in Shanghai? Find a disreputable old building. Walk up three flights of a dirty staircase and down a dingy hall to the very last door. Inside that door you'll find that best restaurant!"

Now it was dark but there were still lots of people walking, talking and shopping. He was still able to walk the streets somewhat unnoticed. The closest place he had heard of was two blocks away and he headed for it. "Over two blocks and in a basement."

In two blocks, Chinatown became residential. No stores, no bustling shoppers, few lights. Tenement type houses, side by side, and apartment buildings. Many of the larger buildings had small windows just above the sidewalk level, obviously opening into basements. By now it was quite dark and a number of the basement windows were beacons of light. Josh was able to quietly make his way down the streets, peering into the basement windows.

Rounding a corner, Josh came across a group of Chinese teens. Expecting them to be belligerent toward a white stranger, he was pleasantly surprised by their friendliness A couple of them were hastily trying to hide bottles wrapped in paper bags behind their backs. Josh thought they were worried that he was "The Man", and would arrest them.

"Relax guys, I'm just trying to hustle up a pool game. I heard there was a hall nearby?"

"Okay, man. Pool? How about right there?" one of them said and pointed to a stairwell about two doors away. "But you ain't gonna like it!" Then in Chinese to his neighbor, "They won't even let him in!"

Speaking in Chinese, Josh said, "Why won't they let me in? "

A moment of surprised silence, then: "You're not Chinese."

"Right. But I am a pool player, I'm going in."

"It's your neck! Don't say we didn't warn you. C'mon guys, we gotta see this!"

Followed by the teens, Josh walked to the stairwell and stepped down about eight very dark steps to an unlighted door. Glancing back at the teens, he saw one of them pantomiming for him to knock on the door. In the quiet of the stairwell he could hear muted sounds from inside.

Josh had two cards to play. One was that he spoke fluent Chinese. The other was that he was a superb eight ball player. He thought, if I can just get in and challenge someone to a game of pool, I'll have a chance to get the information I need.

On the way, Josh had found a two-piece billiard cue at a second hand store, complete with carrying case. He used it to knock on the door.

CHAPTER 31

Josh didn't expect any real trouble. After all, there was nothing illegal about a pool hall, unless they were operating without a city license or something. He thought all he would have to contend with was being a complete outsider.

The door opened just enough to see half of a Chinese face.

A rather belligerent "Who are you?" in English.

Josh answered in Chinese.

"I guess I'm what you might call a "pool shark", looking for a good game."

"You want to play pool here?"

"That's why I'm here!"

"It's a private club!"

"You got any really good players here? I'd be interested in playing against your best player, maybe for a hundred bucks?"

That got him in. The room was quite large and filled with eight regulation tables. Six in the front room and two toward the rear of the hall. It was more like a private club with pool tables than a hall. One side of the hall had a bar and what looked like a small restaurant.

Josh could smell Chinese food and cigarettes. The hall was thick with cigarette smoke. At first, no one took notice of him. Gradually, at the tables nearest to him, the play stopped and he was stared at.

The guy that had spoken to him at the door, called for attention and said;

"This guy wants to play pool. 'Says he'll take on anyone for a hundred bucks a game!"

Josh added quickly, in Chinese:

"I got tired of playing against the amateurs at the "Y". A Chinese guy there told me about you guys. I'm just looking for some real competition!"

Toward the side, sitting at a table near the bar, a heavy set, middle aged, gray haired Chinese man waved a hand in the air and called out, "Over here!"

"Sit!' he said. "Who are you?"

Josh told him his real name and that he worked for the U.S. parks and was on vacation. He crossed his fingers, hoping that his name wasn't already on somebody's list.

"You're pretty good?"

"I think so."

"Willing to play for money?"

"Yeah. Sure!"

"Okay, this is my joint. I handle all the bets. That okay with you?"

"Sure, that's fine."

"Okay, you'll play the winner at whichever table clears first. We usually play for twenty-five bucks a game, okay? Plus five that goes to me, Okay? Anything over twenty-five, it's put up or shut up and I hold the stakes. Okay?"

Josh was tempted to say "okay" right back at him but settled for, "Sounds fair to me!"

"Okay! Want something to eat?"

"Tea and rice?"

"Okay." Was the answer, accompanied by a snap of the fingers and an order placed with the resultant waiter.

In a short time a table came free. The owner called the winner over to his table. Turning to Josh he said, "I'm Chan. This is Henry Yu. Henry, this is Josh. Josh says he's pretty good and wants to play for money. Okay?"

"Eight ball?" Henry asked.

"Eight ball!" answered Josh.

"How much?"

"Chan said you guys usually play for twenty-five but I can play for more if you want."

"Twenty-five sounds okay to me, at least for the first game."

Josh had barely had enough time to watch his opponent play in his previous match. He thought he would be pretty easy to beat, but he couldn't afford to be over-confidant. He had to win in order to continue playing and have any chance to direct the conversation around to Charley Fong.

CHAPTER 32

They lagged the cue ball for the break and Josh intentionally lost. He had seen just enough of Yu's game to be sure he wouldn't be able to run all eight balls in one turn. Josh drew solids and Yu broke the rack.

Sure enough, Yu missed on his number three ball. Josh took his turn and pocketed all seven of his balls and then the eight to win the match.

By the time he got to the number six ball a small crowd had gathered. By the time he pocketed the eight ball, others were ready to play him.

Chan called him over. "Okay, you want to play more?"

"That's why I'm here, but don't you have some better players? Maybe willing to make the game a little more interesting, say a hundred bucks interesting?"

Chan called out, "Man wants to play for a hundred bucks. You saw him play, who wants to take him on?" Half a dozen hands went up.

Chan selected one of the volunteers, collected a hundred and five bucks from Josh and his opponent and they headed to Josh's table.

Josh took a chance and used the same idea he had used on the first game. He intentionally lost the lag. This time his opponent was only able to get his first ball in before missing. Josh didn't want to scare off the opposition so he purposely missed after four balls. This time his opponent got two balls in before missing.

Josh easily ran the rest of his balls to win. He told Chan to hold on to his winnings because he wanted to play some more.

"Okay, Okay, plenty more want to play you."

Josh congratulated the guy he had just beaten and asked if he could buy him a drink. Josh told him he needed to relax for a minute or two before playing again.

At the table with Chan and his opponent, Josh tried to steer the conversation to Charley Fong.

"I have a Chinese mother-in-law. Lives over in Oakland, needs help with some sort of legal stuff. Some lousy tenants are giving her a bad time. She doesn't speak much English. I told her I'd try to find a Chinese attorney that wasn't too pricey. You got any ideas?"

"Lots of Chinese attorneys around but they charge an arm and a leg just to meet with you."

"Wait, I've got a better idea. She doesn't really need an attorney all she needs is someone that knows enough about the law to convince these squatters to leave. Maybe a private detective firm? Do you know anyone like that?"

The guy he'd just beaten glanced at Chan and said, "Charley?"

Chan shrugged his shoulders and said "maybe."

Then Josh stopped. He figured he would let them stew on that for a while and see if it led anywhere.

Over the next forty minutes or so he played three more games, winning them all easily and decisively. So far he had won over four hundred dollars but hadn't gotten any leads to Charley Fong.

He had noticed a group of tables in the rear of the room, almost all by themselves. A number of young Chinese were gathered around them, not mixing with the ones Josh had been playing. They were all dressed in black and making a lot of noise. Now a couple of them wandered over to his table and watched the action. Nobody got in their way.

After a few minutes they walked back to the rear table, only to return with a tall, young Chinese carrying his cue stick. Probably in his early twenties he had a perpetual sneer on his face. It was obvious that he thought he was big stuff. Again, all dressed in black, he watched for a short time and then addressed Josh:

"You! You think you're pretty much a hot shot, taking money from these amateurs. How about you let us take a little money from you?"

"You want to play me for serious money?"

"That's what I'm saying!"

"How much?"

"How about five to start?"

"Okay, but I want to speak to Chan first." With that he walked over to Chan and asked in a low voice, "You hear that?"

"Yeah, it's okay!"

"Are they good for it?"

"Sure, they're okay, are you?"

"I'm okay, here's a thou. Will you hold the stakes?

"Okay, plus five dollars!"

On the way back to his table, one of the guys he had beaten earlier sidled beside him and whispered, "Be careful! These guys could be dangerous if you win too much!"

Before Josh could thank him, he whispered again, "Ask Chan about Charley, for your aunt, he's a detective," and was gone.

Maybe Chan was the lead he would needed to find Charley, but he couldn't corner Chan yet, he had to play these tough guys.

CHAPTER 33

Seven of the black-clad guys surrounded the pool table. Most of other players in the room, the one's Josh had been playing so far, moved a respectful distance away. The tall one, evidently the leader, asked him, "You willing to lose some real money.?"

"Sure, let's get at it!"

"Okay, it's your table. We'll rack, you break" With that he turned to one of the six and said, "Ty, you start."

A short, round faced guy strutted up to the table, grabbed a chalk, and said, "I'm Tyler. 'Can't wait to start spending your thousand bucks. Bruce is our best, I'm maybe third or fourth, but Bruce thinks I'll take you in a snap."

Evidently Bruce was the boss of the gang, the tall guy with the sneer.

Tyler racked the balls and Josh set up to break.

Josh set the cue ball in his favorite break position, slightly left of center and stroked the ball with a little top English.

The ball got the top spin he wanted, hit the one ball square and achieved a great distribution. Two balls dropped, one striped and one solid. Josh decided to play the solid as he thought he could see a run on solid from the beginning.

The first two balls were a little difficult, the rest were easy and Josh ran all the remaining six and the eight ball to win the game. He turned to Bruce and said, "Next?"

Bruce took his guys into a huddle before answering. Evidently he still thought Josh was beatable and chose another of his guys to play the second game.

This guy was almost as tall as Bruce and had a scar running down his cheek. He looked to be in his early twenties also. By the way he walked over to the table, you could see he fancied himself as a tough customer.

Before they could get started, Bruce got himself into Josh's face and said.

"You got real lucky on that one! This one's ours!"

"You think so?" Holding his ground Josh said, "then let's up the bet! How about three grand?" Josh had come equipped to play a lot of pool in order to find Charley Fong, to the extent of having a pocketful of travelers checks. He could really goad these punks and maybe find out something at the same time. Maybe Fong would show up during the match.

A slight hesitation then, "You got it!" He turned to Scarface and said, "Beat the shit out of him, you got it?"

Josh deposited his winnings and a couple of travelers checks with Chan and Chan assured him that Bruce was good for that large a bet. Josh could feel the tension building up. He sensed that Bruce wasn't accustomed to being beaten, let alone humbled on his own turf. All Josh wanted was information. He didn't want a fight. On the other hand he didn't like to lose either.

Scarface said, "Piece a cake!"

CHAPTER 34

Perhaps feeling a little overconfident, Josh relinquished the break to his opponent. His opponent sank the seven ball and two more solids before missing. Josh successfully ran all the balls on his turn, showing off a little by doing a couple of intricate bank shots. One of his shots was called a masse. The ball curved around his opponents ball and pocketed the eleven ball as he had planned.

The guy was pissed off and so was the gang. Bruce told Josh to "wait here" and took his gang over to talk to Chan. Josh watched them reluctantly hand over the three thousand bucks to Chan and Chan signaled to Josh that he had his winnings.

Josh walked over to the group and said, "You want a chance to get your money back?"

Bruce, suspicion in his voice, said: "Now what?"

"Simple. You pick your best player and I'll put all my winnings in the pot. You win, you get all your money back!"

"You want us to put up another four grand against what you've won?"

"Sure, if you've got confidence in your best player!"

Josh thought Bruce had a real problem. He was their best player. If he backed down, they were not only out the four grand, but it'd make him look like a coward. On the other hand, maybe they couldn't raise the four grand.

Josh went back to the table and idly racked up the balls, giving the gang time to think over his offer. Watching them, it looked like they were negotiating a loan from Chan. Enough to cover the bet. In a few minutes, Bruce came over and said.

"Okay, I'll play you and I'm going to whip your ass!"

This time Josh exercised his prerogative and made the break and a very unusual thing happened. The eight ball went in the pocket. Quickly, Josh called over to Chan.

"Are we playing Bar Pool?"

Chan went silent for a moment and then, reluctantly, agreed that was what they played all the time.

"Game's over!" Josh said.

"What the hell are you talking about"

"In bar pool, if the eight ball is sunk on the break the shooter wins! Look it up, or better yet, ask Chan."

Bruce yelled to Chan across the room, "Is that true?"

Chan looked stricken. He hemmed and hawed for a while and Josh said "Let's look it up on line." Finally Chan agreed that Josh was right and the gang had lost. This time he had to dig into his own pocket to pay Josh. While he was digging the money out, Josh asked him about the Chinese private eye named Charley.

"One of your guys said there's a Chinese private detective named Charley, comes in here a lot?"

"You mean Charley Fong? He isn't no Private detective! Charley would like you to think he is. He might do you a favor occasionally for a fee, but he isn't licensed as no private eye."

"Could he help my Aunt?"

"Maybe, why? You want to get in touch with him? He's here almost every afternoon about four or so. Or, I can give you his office address but he's never there."

Josh was keeping an eye on the gang members in the meantime. They had gathered together in the rear of the hall and were arguing among themselves. He remembered what one of the regulars had told him, "They might be dangerous if they lose money". Altogether, they'd lost eight thousand dollars. Four thousand paid to Josh and another four thousand they now owed Chan.

"If I can't find him by tomorrow afternoon I'll probably come by here, if that's okay with you?"

"It's okay with me, but I'd steer away from that gang if I was you. They're okay in here, but out in the streets? Unh, uh! And the tall one, Bruce? He's a knifer and probably carries a gun. Did you notice they've gone?"

Sure enough, the gang had disappeared from the rear of the hall. There must be a back door, Josh thought.

"Eight thousand bucks of their money in your jeans, walking through Chinatown close to midnight? I'd be awfully damn careful if I was you. You want me to call you a cab?"

Josh thanked him for his professionalism, told him not to worry, and took his leave. Out on the streets, it was almost pitch dark. He decided to carry his cue in one piece instead of separating it into its two pieces and carrying it in its bag. He had a hunch that he wasn't through with the Chinese gang tonight, not yet.

CHAPTER 35

Walking up the steps to the sidewalk level, Josh tried to scan both sides of the street in both directions. It was a little after two in the morning and the streets were empty and very dark. He took a moment or two to let his eyes adjust to the darkness and then started walking up the block. His hotel was about ten blocks away, most of it through Chinatown.

As he rounded the first corner he realized his expectations. Bruce and part of the gang were waiting for him. Not taking his eyes off Bruce, out of the corner of his eyes Josh counted an additional five facing him. Six against one. They quickly formed a loose circle around him. Each held a cue stick. Several were beating the heads of the sticks into their palms in a threatening manner.

"Hi guys, I kinda expected I'd meet you again tonight. I bet you think you're going to get your money back?"

"Hell yes, wise guy. Either you give it to us or we take it. If we take it you're gonna be hurt. Bad!"

"So I have a choice?"

"Yeah, you can hand over our money and live a little longer, or…."

Calmly, Josh replied, "Given a choice, I think I'll keep the money."

"Okay, you asked for it. Guys, take him!"

The six of them started tightening the circle about him, holding their cues as clubs, ready to overwhelm him.

Josh let them come. When they were within about five feet from him he started twirling his cue stick around in circles, holding it by the tip end. Something he would usually do with a staff. They were immediately frozen in place, no way could they approach him with the butt end of the cue stick whizzing past their heads every second or so.

Once they were frozen in place they were easy to handle. Pulling the stick back to himself, Josh grasped it in the middle and in one continuous motion, using both ends he was able to leap at the nearest two and take them out with cue blows to their heads before they realized what was happening.

A butt end cue stick blow to the head can kill. He had to be quick, decisive and delicate. All he wanted to do was knock them out. His blows were surgical and successful. With those two out of the fight, Josh shifted to the four others.

Josh felt the familiar body sensations he expected when in combat or intense competition. His body relaxed, his senses sharpened. Again, everything seemed to almost be happening in slow motion.

Accustomed to their fear tactics scaring their enemies, they were in no way ready for the sudden onslaught that Josh unleashed on them. The surprise momentarily froze them in place. Taking advantage of their ineptitude, Josh continued his movement. Dodging the two crumpled forms in front of him, Josh threw himself toward the side of the building. In mid-air he twisted his body landing against the building feet first with his knees flexed. His knees absorbed the shock and Josh used his momentum to push off in a different direction. It was a little like doing a double somersault except he did it against the side of a building. Using the building as a springboard he landed on his feet behind the remaining four.

As they attempted to twirl around and confront him they were in each other's way. It's what's called a closing movement. There was no way they could now counter attack. Then before they could react, using the same lightning fast move used before so effectively, he swept the legs out from under two of them with the cue stick. One of them had the wind knocked out of him with the butt end of Josh's cue stick, the other started crawling away, one leg bent awkwardly, out of the fight.

That left Bruce and one more. Josh had deliberately left Bruce to the last. That turned out to be a mistake. Anticipating that the two remaining would come at him with their cue sticks, he was unpleasantly surprised when he heard the unmistakable sound of a gun being cocked.

"That's enough you bastard. Now stand up and drop your cue stick. Slowly! And if you think I won't use the gun, think again. It won't be the first time."

Dropping the cue stick, Josh raised his arms and backed up against the building wall. He wasn't too worried about handling Bruce, even with a gun. Guns are noisy and he doubted that Bruce would actually use it. But he didn't want any of the other gang members coming up behind him while he had his arms raised.

One of the first guys he had dropped had regained his breath and his cue-stick. He started toward Josh and, keeping a respectful distance, started poking and hitting at Josh, using the butt end of his cue stick. All the time making sure that he didn't get between Josh and the gun. Shortly he was joined by a second. They seemed to get particular delight in hitting him in the chest and legs. Josh could take a lot but the butt end of a cue stick is heavy, hard and dangerous. He felt a rib crack and knew he had to do something quickly.

He started taunting the two. Bruce seemed inclined to let them beat up on him for a while. Maybe he could work that to his advantage. If he could get them to come closer and get between him and Bruce, maybe he would have the time he needed.

He sneered. "You're real brave now that I'm defenseless and there's a gun pointed at me, a couple of cowards. You're so damned tough, come up and hit me with your fists."

They continued to slug him with their cues. Josh could feel the strength ebbing out of him. They began raining blows on his head. Josh thought he could use the change to his advantage. Pretending to reel from the blows, he slowly sank to a squatting position, back against the wall and put his arms over his head as if to protect himself from the blows.

Bruce yelled, "get the money."

The guys closed in as if for the kill and for a moment they were between Josh and the gun. Josh quickly reached behind his neck and palmed a black, star shaped, ninja throwing device. Something most Ninjas would never be without. Something that Josh could kill with if necessary.

He continued to feign fear and cower, all the time keeping an eye on Bruce. Bruce obviously thought he had the situation well under control. He was relaxed and holding the gun rather casually, barrel pointed toward the ground. Was he careless enough?

When the two got close, Josh exploded. Leaping up, he drove one of his attackers into the other with his left shoulder so that they both fell over backwards and at the same time drew back his right arm and threw the throwing star at Bruce. Before Bruce could respond the star found its mark, hitting the middle of his forehead, stunning him. He fell to his knees, dropped the gun and sat there, shaking his head, blood dripping down his face. Josh thought he might have a broken nose. Josh scooped up the gun and tucked it into his belt.

He was hurt. He'd had cracked ribs before and was sure he had another. It hurt but he could stand it. He could even disguise the hurt so that his assailants had no idea. He stood up straight, wiped his forehead with his sleeve and determined there was no blood. Outwardly he showed no signs of having been attacked.

He stood over the fallen gang members, picked up his cue stick and calmly twirling it in his fingers, said; "You still want my money?"

All six were done for. Josh walked back around the corner to the pool hall and knocked on the door. Chan himself opened it.

"Mr. Chan, you better call an ambulance. There are six guys, including Bruce, lying in the street around the corner. A couple of them looked like they'd been in fight and Bruce is bleeding pretty badly. At a glance it looked to me like he probably has a broken nose."

He took particular pains not to show his own problems.

Chan was shocked. He had been prepared to see the gang swagger back in flashing the eight thousand dollars. "How the hell?" he began.

Josh cut him off. "Some other gang, maybe? I don't know. They're just lying there and they need help." He turned and left.

The ten-block walk to his hotel was uneventful, if a little painful. On the way he reflected on the day's happenings. Had he wasted the whole day? All he had for his efforts, was the office address of the Chinese PI, a severely bruised or cracked rib and an expectation of catching Charley Fong at Chan's place tomorrow afternoon.

What he needed to find out was the organization behind the killing of the bears. An organization that was willing to kill a Park Ranger. Maybe Charlie could take him there? It was the only lead he had.

CHAPTER 36

Josh had put the "do not disturb" sign on his door and also requested that his room not be made up during his absence. He did not want to be surprised again. He had also spit glued a hair across the outside edge of the door. If the door had been opened the hair would be gone. It wasn't.

The room was pitch dark except for the small red light flashing on his phone. He had expected that. Expected that Fern would have tried to reach him and return his call. She had left a 'call me' message and answered on his first ring.

As she answered his mind jumped. It occurred to him that if the people at the lab had seen his I.D. and tracked him to his hotel, they could also track him to Yosemite. Could Fern be in danger? They probably knew by now that their warning at the hotel had failed, would they try again? He had moved from his room, but what about Fern?

"It's about time you called. I was beginning to worry. Are you okay? Why didn't you return my calls? Are you on your way home?"

Josh laughed. "One at a time. Yeah I'm fine." Even though his ribs were burning, there was no way he was going to tell her about it. He immediately changed the subject.

"You should be jealous. The hotel room is swaaanky. You'd love it. About coming home. The Superintendent has ordered me home, but the police chief may want me to stay on for a couple of days. Are you okay?"

"Oh, I'm fine. We're organizing a service for poor Tim and I've been spending a lot of time with his parents. The Feds are here and talking to everyone trying to find out what went on. They've been holed up with the superintendent and he told me to keep quiet about where you are and what you're doing. I think the FBI is coming into it. What's going on?"

Josh thought fast. "Nothing unusual. The S.F. police chief thinks there's a gang here behind the killings. She wants to keep the investigation here and thinks I can help for a day or two." He quickly changed the subject again. "Have they got any leads on the other bear killing gang?"

"Not that I've heard of. When do you think you'll come home?"

"As soon as I can. I wish you could be here. It's lonely at night, but the Chief's sure keeping me busy during the days."

With that they sent kisses and hugs to each other, Josh promised to get home as quickly as possible and hung up.

Even though it was very late, even though he hadn't had much sleep, Josh decided he needed to exercise and do Yoga before sleeping. From long experience he knew that if he had a cracked rib, it would take a long time to heal. In the meantime he would just have to ignore it. At one-thirty in the morning the hotel's exercise room was completely empty. He was able to go through an intense half-hour of repetitive Kung Fu moves and then another half-hour of deep meditation. By the end he thought his rib was just bruised. During his meditation another idea occurred to him.

If he could get the chief to extend his stay, there were three possibilities to work on. One was Charley Fong's office. The second was to find the delivery guys that had been at the Emeryville lab, the third was to find Charley Fong at Chan's pool hall.

By two-thirty, he was in bed and asleep. Totally relaxed, he slept until seven-thirty. By eight-thirty he was in the Chief's office, filling out papers and suggesting that she request he stay on for a few days.

"The park superintendent has ordered me back because the FBI's taking over. They're treating it just as a murder of a government employee and ignoring the bear mutilations. Anyway, I guess it's completely out of your hands now. Once the FBI steps in, your hands are tied?"

A sharp, "Who said that? We don't take a back seat to the FBI or anyone else if something is going on in our jurisdiction!"

It was the hoped for response. She continued.

"it seems to me you're stirring up a hornet's nest. While the suspicious lab is over in Emeryville, the attack on you took place here. You have made more progress in twenty-four hours than I would have thought possible. I think you should stay on the case with one of my Chinese detectives. Do you think your superintendent might agree to that?"

"Probably, if the request came from the chief of the San Francisco Police Department."

"All right then, consider it done. What's your plan?"

He told her about Charley Fong, the fake private detective and how he was working with Lieutenant Chew to locate his office.

"You think he is a lead to the people behind all this?"

"Possibly. His name came up in a conversation about the lab in Emeryville and he's about all we got, except the Emeryville lab itself. I don't see how we can directly investigate the lab, all we've got is guesswork. If we can find this private eye fellow, maybe we can convince him to give us some names. Seems to me we should concentrate on him."

All right, work with Lieutenant Chew and report back to me."

CHAPTER 37

At the door, Josh asked for one more thing.

"I need to find four guys probably staying in a motel in San Francisco. They're driving a small white van with South Dakota license plates. Is there any way you can find them?"

"Maybe. Why do you need them?"

Josh didn't want to disclose his foray into the Emeryville lab so he said, "the receptionist said she liked the job because it was unpredictable. She said the boss sent her on unusual errands and really trusted her. I asked her what she meant and she said, 'like today. The boss left an envelope with lots of cash in it with me to be picked up today or tomorrow.'

She said the last time he did that a Chinese guy picked it up and bragged about the great time he'd had in the City the last couple of days. She had noticed the van because he had double-parked in front. If I can find them it'll be a big help." That sound pretty suspicious to me.

"One condition. If you find them you call us, right? Let us interrogate them. What I can do is send out an all points bulletin and see if anyone's noticed the plates. South Dakota plates are quite unusual. Wait around a half-hour or so and let's see what develops. Talk to the desk sergeant."

Three-quarters of an hour and four cups of coffee later, a call came in that the truck had been spotted. It was parked on a side street near a small hotel just below Chinatown. Josh had gotten a lucky break. The only reason the truck had been noticed was that there was a two-hour limit on parking before the car had to be moved or ticketed. The car had been spotted when the driver was moving it from one place to another.

On top of that he got another break. When the beat cop realized that the Chief was interested in the truck, he had the gumption to follow the guy back to his hotel. The desk sergeant gave the address to Josh.

Calling the building a hotel was really stretching it. It was a dump. On the lowest edge of Chinatown it was a narrow building, squeezed between two other narrow buildings in the same condition. Exterior paint peeling, windows painted over, it was anything but appetizing.

Josh sat across the street and watched the building. It was just after lunch, there wasn't much traffic on the street. In a little over a half-hour the only people that entered the building were two fairly young Chinese women. Josh was sure they were prostitutes. They were wearing short shorts and high heels and looked totally out of place. He decided to go in.

A teenager was sitting at a small desk with a phone and a stack of textbooks just inside the front door. That seemed to be the entire lobby.

Josh was flying blind. He wanted to put the fear of God into the guys from South Dakota, but didn't have the foggiest about how to get at them. He was pretty sure that the two ladies that had come in were prostitutes and they were entertaining his quarry. The young Chinese kid looked bluffable.

"The two prostitutes that just came in, which room?"

"Two prostitutes? No, you must be mistaken" The kid spoke English, and very well. Josh assumed he was a college kid on a part time job.

"Don't give me that crap. I've been sitting across the street for the last half-hour and I've got pictures of them coming in!"

"Look mister. Two ladies came in. Are they prostitutes? I don't know and I don't want to know. I just don't want any trouble."

Josh decided he could play tough with this kid. He switched to Chinese. "You want trouble? You'll get a lot of trouble from my boss. No one cuts in on his territory. Either those two whores are out of here or your face might get permanently rearranged. Get it?"

"Okay, okay! It's not that big a deal. They're with two guys in rooms 221 and 223. The guys've been there all night and haven't been out yet today except early on for breakfast. And these aren't the first two ladies to come in, either."

"How many?"

"Just two, there were two others with them last night when they registered but they didn't stay."

"I'm going up. Keep your eyes open and your mouth shut and you'll be okay, get me?"

"Yes sir!"

CHAPTER 38

The building was much deeper than Josh had thought. At the top of the stairs a long straight hall ran in both directions. To his right and toward the front of the building the rooms were all even numbered. To his left the room numbers were all odd numbered. So 221 and 223 would be adjacent to each other and at the end of the hall.

Smiling to himself he thought, "I've got them cornered."

Standing in the stairwell, deciding what to do next, he heard the sound of a door opening down the hall. Peeking around the corner he saw a woman wearing just panties and bra back out of room 221 and head down the hall towards him. She sing-songed back to the room, "I'll be right baaack."

There was no place for Josh to hide and luckily he didn't need to. Halfway to his hiding place she opened another door and stepped in. On the door was a sign, "Women." Opportunity was knocking on Josh's door.

He quietly raced down the hall to room 221 and put his ear to the door. He heard nothing. The door was slightly open. Pushing it slightly it creaked and a voice said in Chinese, "You back already?" Josh could tell by the sound of the voice that the man inside was far removed from the door. Walking in he found the man, completely naked, lying on the bed.

"Who the hell are you, where's Elaine?"

His clothes were over a chair at the foot of the bed. Josh grabbed them and threw them out in the hall. "Shut up or I'll beat the crap out of you!"

Most men, when naked, won't fight. This guy was no exception. In a moment his girl friend returned. Josh convinced her to get dressed and sit quietly in the corner of the room. For her, the party was over.

"You won't get away with this. I've got friends that'll take care of you!" Lying there naked, his bravado was almost laughable.

"I told you to shut up. When I want you to talk I'll tell you. Now open the door and tell your buddy next door you're coming in."

"He won't answer, he's got a babe in there and he thinks he's in love."

"Let's convince him. Tell him your girl passed out. Tell him she needs his girl friend." With that Josh put a pressure grip on his elbow and hustled him next door.

"Louie, I need help! Elaine passed out or something. Hurry up!"

"Oh, fuck! Just throw some water on her and leave us alone!"

"God damn it, I need you! She may be dead! Either you come out or I'm coming in!"

Reluctantly, "Okay, okay. Give me a minute."

A minute or so later the door opened and the girl came out first. Josh pulled her out of the way and grabbed the second man's arm. He was hobbling, trying to get his foot into his shoe. Using the guy's forward momentum, Josh twisted his arm and walked him down the hall and into the next room.

"What the hell's going on," the second guy asked.

Josh didn't give them a chance to talk to each other. Roughly, he pushed both of them onto the bed. In Chinese he told them "Keep your traps shut or you'll get hurt."

Turning he told both the girls to vamoose. They understood his Spanish and seemed happy to get out of the place.

Josh didn't expect to learn much from these guys about the lab or its ownership. He thought he might get some information about the operation in South Dakota. From what the Supe had told him and what he had overheard, the bear killings were happening in at least three western states.

As he closed the door behind the girls, one of the guys tried to roll off the bed and launch himself at Josh. Not surprised, Josh easily stepped into the attack and with a quick chop, knocked him back on the bed. "Like I said, shut up and listen!"

CHAPTER 39

"Let's see what we know so far. You're from South Dakota. You've been killing bears and stealing their gall bladders among other things. You drove here in a white van with South Dakota plates and it's parked about two blocks from here. You delivered the gall bladders to a pharmaceutical lab in Emeryville. They were put into a refrigerator under lock and key. You complained about not having any free time and your driver brought you over here for a little play time! How am I doing?"

"Who are you?"

Josh decided to try a bluff. "Doesn't matter. Can you figure out how I got all that information? Maybe from your driver?"

"You got Chang?"

"How else do you think I found you?"

Josh was fairly certain these two guys didn't know much. And they weren't too bright. The driver had treated them like underlings. He would find out what they knew, try to trick the driver's whereabouts from them and let them go. Plus, now he had a name. Chang.

"Do you know what the jail time is for killing bears? Let me tell you it's a long time and we got you two dead to rights. Chang'll be going in for sure, and maybe you guys, too. You got one thing going for you though, we think you're just employees. Chang's the boss. Right?"

Two heads nodded yes.

"Okay. You help us, we help you. Tell us where the fourth guy is, we go easy on you. Okay?"

"Didn't you catch Chang at the hotel?"

Josh had to think fast. "Nope, we'd staked out your truck and he turned up there."

The two looked at each other in some confusion and said, "How'd he know where truck is?"

"Maybe he's keeping an eye on you! So where's his partner?"

"Same hotel as Chang. Across from park. Lots of steps in front."

Josh immediately knew the place they meant. Across from Union Square, it was the only hotel with lots of steps in front. A pretty ritzy place. It made it even more clear that these two were at the bottom of the totem pole. The other two were living it up while these two were in this rat hole.

"Take all your money out and give me your wallets. I'm taking your wallets and all your I.D.'s with me. I'll return them to the kid downstairs later this afternoon. If you try to leave to make a phone call or anything, you'll never see your wallets again. If you're real good, we just might forget about you two! Chang tried to tell us that you two were the bear killers and he was just the driver, but we know better. He's the one we want, but outside of telling us where you were, he's playing hardball. I guess he doesn't think much of you two guys!"

Leaving them with that thought and all their money, Josh took off with their wallets. He wanted to copy their I.D.'s before he returned their wallets. He would be able to find them again, easily. The hotel where Chang was staying was about twelve blocks uphill right on Union Square. Only twelve blocks, but a huge change in atmosphere. From squalor to splendor in twelve blocks. He took a taxi.

At the desk, Josh showed his badge and asked if Mr. Chang was still registered. He also asked if Mr. Chang had requested two rooms. He was and he had. Rooms 566 and 568, adjoining. He used the house courtesy phone and dialed number 566. A woman's' voice answered.

CHAPTER 40

"Excuse me Ma'am, did Mr. Chang just try to order room service?"

"You're really mixed up. He's in the next room."

Lucky, lucky! One phone call and he had found out they were both in and who was in which room.

Now he had to break into their rooms, tie them both up, get rid of the lady that had answered the phone and then try to find out what kind of an organization they were part of. He wondered how he would possibly get rid of these two. Then he had to get back to the pool room and meet Charley Fong. It was going to be a busy day.

Knocking on Chang's door, he responded to the "Who's there" by saying, "I have an urgent message for a Mr. Chang from South Dakota!"

"What the fuck is that all about? Just a minute, I'll be right there."

In a short time the door was opened and Josh pushed his way into the room. Chang was still trying to stuff his shirt into his pants and was in no condition to ward Josh off. Josh quickly pulled Chang's shirt down over his elbows so that he was pretty much immobilized, at least temporarily. At the same time he put a knee into Chang's midriff, rendering him breathless and unable to speak.

He showed his badge to the young Chinese lady that was hurriedly trying to get dressed and said,"Don't say a word! Just get dressed and get out of here. You don't want to be involved in this guys trouble"

Chang was gasping on the floor, trying to regain his breath. Josh got a washcloth from the bathroom and stuffed it into Chang's mouth. He decided not to bother with the guy in the next room. Keep Chang quiet and find out what he knows. Using some curtain tie-backs, he bound Chang to a chair in the middle of the room and started questioning him.

"You better listen and listen carefully. Then you got a decision to make!"

"We know all about you and your bear killing operation. We know about South Dakota. We know about the Emeryville lab. We know about you and your partner here and the two idiots you've got stashed in the sleazy hotel. We know about your white truck. We just about know everything we need to send you to jail for the rest of your life!" The same line that had worked on the two others.

Then he added something else.

"But there's something you DON'T know! What you don't know is that part of your gang murdered a Park Ranger. That changes everything! Now the charges against you include murder! So now you gotta make a decision. Either you cooperate with us and get some leniency or you don't and get charged with murder. Which is it?"

"Murder? I don't know anything about no murder! All I did was drive a truck and deliver a package to an address in Emeryville. I don't even know what was in the package!"

For effect, Josh switched to Chinese. "Bullshit! You didn't arrive at the lab in the middle of the night and open the rear doors with your own keys? You didn't have your own keys to the refrigerator to store the bear organs? You have no idea how deep in shit you are and how much we already know about you!"

Chang was in shock. How could anyone know all that about him?

Josh continued in Chinese, "Who pays you? Who told you to take the gall bladders to Emeryville? How'd you get the keys to the lab.? We don't give a shit about you, but somebody's going to answer for the murder. I can't keep you from getting jail time for kiiling bears but I can keep you from being charged for murder. It's your choice. Cooperate now or face the consequences!"

"Who's going to arrest me? You?"

"Yep! The San Francisco police are working with me, I'll just turn you over to them. In fact, they know I'm here and are expecting you."

"Who's been rattin' us out?"

"Don't matter, you gonna talk or not?"

"Okay, okay! But I don't know much. I get paid in cash. An envelope filled with cash. Enough to pay my crew and me."

"Where do you get the envelope?"

"At the lab on the way back"

"Who gives it to you"

"It's just waiting for me at the front desk. Usually there's a young girl out there and she just hands me the sealed envelope."

"You just walk in and she hands it to you?"

"Well, I gotta identify myself. And then she gives me the envelope with my name on it."

"How many other envelopes are there?"

"I dunno, maybe four or five."

Josh was beginning to think that it sounded more and more that the lab was the center of the operation.

"Who hired you?"

"Some guy that searched me out in South Dakota. And no, I don't know his name."

"Was he from South Dakota?"

"No, I think he's from here. I saw him once at the lab when I picked up my money."

"What about the keys? Who gave them to you?"

"Some new guy at the lab. I'd been bringing the stuff in every couple of months and meeting some guy in back during the day. This new guy said he wanted us to bring it at night. He gave me the key last month. Last night was the first time I'd used it."

Josh thought about it. It fit in with what Ellen had told him about an infusion of money into the company. The owner was going broke when somebody came to him with money and an illegal plan to make his business whole again. That meant that the real people behind the bear killings and the murder were the investors. He doubted he would get any more out of Chang. It was time to get rid of him and his friend.

"You two are in a shitload of trouble. The lab's going to be taken down, maybe it already has. A lot of arrests are gonna be made, including for murder. My advice? Get your truck and clear out of here as fast as you can. Don't look back, don't even try to pick up your money in Emeryville. Go back to South Dakota and hope to hell your name doesn't come up."

Josh untied them and left, but waited in the lobby to see what happened. Ten minutes later the elevator doors opened and both Chang and his accomplice hurried out, carrying small suitcases. Josh followed them to their truck, saw them hastily jump in and take off. Satisfied that they were out of the picture he called the San Francisco police offices and asked for the Chief.

"I just have a moment, what's going on?"

"I'm making progress. First off, the Emeryville lab's definitely where the bear parts are going and being processed, and your detective's cousin's in it up to his ears. I also found out that there's big San Francisco money behind the lab, and I've got a lead on who they are."

"Okay, fast work. As soon as you think you know who they are, report back to me and we'll figure out what to do. By the way, how are you and Lieutenant Chew getting along?"

Taken by surprise he answered. "Just fine, why?"

"He tells me he hasn't seen much of you in the last day or so. I hope you're not going off by yourself against my orders," she responded dryly.

"No, no. Of course not. I'm planning on seeing him right now and getting his help." He fingers were getting tired from crossing them every time he talked to the Chief.

"You better. And Josh, be careful. There're some dangerous people in Chinatown."

"Yes, Ma'am."

"I'm not kidding. Why just last night someone beat up a whole gang of youths outside one of the Chinese pool halls. I don't suppose you know anything about that?"

Josh evaded a direct answer. "One guy beat up a whole gang? I'll be extra careful."

CHAPTER 41

Josh walked the few blocks to the pool hall. Chan wasn't too happy to see him.

"You make trouble for me. Police give me hard time about tourist getting beat up by gang from here"

"Are they your gang?"

"No, No. I make plain to police. They not MY gang, just hang out here."

In his agitation, Chang's English was becoming more and more difficult to understand. Josh switched to Chinese.

"So who was the tourist that got beat up?"

"You! You're the one!"

"Do I look like I got beat up? I don't have a scratch on me!"

Chang looked him over carefully and said: "How'd you do that?"

"My secret! Charley Fong in yet?"

"Too early, maybe few minutes?"

Josh said he would wait and grabbed a chair. A few minutes went by with no conversation between them. Chang seemed nervous, but Josh was cool as a cucumber. Finally the front door opened and dapper middle-aged Chinese man came in. Josh judged him to be about fifty, a bit out of shape and a little vain. He was wearing slacks and a sport coat over a bright yellow shirt unbuttoned and spread over the coat collar. He started glad-handing everyone he ran into. He was either a complete extrovert or an overcompensated introvert. On top of that, he was noisy. Everyone seemed to know him.

"Hi Charley, How's it going, Charley? Caught any one famous today, Charlie?" Everyone greeted him familiarly by name. So this was the guy who'd sicced the goons on him, thought Josh.

To Chang he said, "That's Charley Fong?"

"That's him, the one and only Charley Fong!"

"Introduce me!" he told Chang. "I want to ask him about my mother-in-law."

Chang called Charley Fong over and said, "Charley, This is the guy that's trying to get me arrested for molesting tourists. He wants to talk to you about his mother-in-law." He paused, looked at Josh questioningly, and said, "I don't even know your name?"

"Just call me Josh." He offered.

Charley Fong looked over carefully. "Why d'ya want a Chinese detective?"

"My mother in law's Chinese."

"Well she's probably too old for me, besides I'm engaged!" and he let out a huge belly laugh.

Josh laughed too, but quickly told him the same story he had told Chan the night before.

"She really needs someone local that speaks Chinese and knows his way around the legalities of her real estate. I can pay you for your time if you think you can help her."

"Did you say her property was in Emeryville?"

"Yeah, Emeryville and some in Oakland. Is there someplace nearby where we can talk?"

"Sure! My office is just down the street. You wanna talk now?"

"Yeah. It's already been a day since I heard about you and I gotta get back to my job. Now's good."

Once outside the pool hall and around the next corner, Josh whirled around and chopped the private investigators' legs out from under him. He landed on his oversized rear, breathless.

"What the hell?"

"That's for the beating your goons tried to give me in my hotel room last night!"

CHAPTER 42

Gone was the pudgy, happy go lucky, everybody's' friend, good old Charley.

"What the fuck are you talking about? I don't know nuthin about any beating," he snarled.

"You don't? Let's see if I can refresh your memory. Three guys supposed to waylay me in my hotel room and deliver a message about laying off the lab investigation over in Emeryville. Three guys that had a pass-key to my room that probably has your fingerprints all over it. Three guys that're in jail now and are singing their heads off. Still don't know anything?"

"What did I do? Some guy hired me to scare off a business competitor.That's all. I'm a private detective and I gotta right to do business!"

"First off, you're not a licensed private detective, you're on the fringes of the law. Secondly, how about the note threatening to kill me? Did you forget about that? I'd say the least that's going to happen to you is to lose your business, more likely some jail time. Right now you better worry more about me. I get really pissed at people that threaten me. Just now when I dropped you to the ground I could just as easily broken your kneecap, your leg or your arm, take your pick! That'll be next unless I start getting some answers!"

"Like what?"

"Who really hired you?"

"Honest to God, I don't know, I never met him in person."

"How'd he hire you?"

"By phone, he phoned me."

"What'd he say?"

"Just that he needed a strong arm, and told me about you."

"He must have said more than that!"

"Well, when I asked him what exactly he wanted me to do he said, 'Get rid the bastard!' I got a little suspicious of him then. What did get rid of him mean? I told him I wasn't into killing. He said, 'Why not?' I said I got ethics."

"Wonderful! Go on."

"He said, 'To hell with your ethics. This guys a nobody, wouldn't even be missed. Get rid of him! If his body ends up in the bay, I'll make it right for you money-wise,' that's what he said."

"That's all he said?"

"Yep! I told him I'd get you off his back, but I never agreed to no murder. I thought I could scare you away. Most Caucasians are afraid to be in Chinatown alone at night. I thought you'd be the same."

"So you don't know the guy, he offers you a contract over the phone to kill someone, and you take the job?"

"The money was right, and I told him no killin'."

"What else do you know about this guy? How'd he hear about you?"

"I don't know nuthin' about him, except what he said. He said one of my, uh, clients told him I was a Chinese strong arm. The idiot thought he was doing me a favor. The damn fool told him I'd do about anything for money. He wouldn't tell who the client was. He told me that he was in San Francisco and was going to keep an eye on me."

Josh was disappointed. He had hoped for more out of Fong.

Suddenly, Josh switched to Chinese. "Charley, you're a worthless piece of shit. Hardly worth my time."

He made Fong show him where his office was and got his cell-phone number.

"Charley, I'm not done with you. If I find you're holding out on me I'll break your legs. And if I call you, you better answer, got it?"

Now what? He asked himself. I know about the lab and it's owners, but I don't who they are. Worse, they know who I am and where I'm living. Even a bigger worry was that they knew where he worked, he hoped they did not know about Fern.

CHAPTER 43

Josh didn't have a description of the new owner of the lab. He had to find out who he was. He doubted there'd be any official record of the new partner's buy in.

Musing to himself, Josh thought he should see the San Francisco Police Chief and report in.

"Chief, I've stumbled on to something I think you need to know about. Can I come in and meet with you? Like right now?"

At the Chiefs' office, she was quite friendly.

Josh didn't feel it was necessary to tell her everything. The fights, the pool game, the prostitutes, the money he had won playing pool, it wasn't necessary to tell her all that. What he did tell he was what he had found out without telling her how he had done it.

"It's a lot bigger operation than we thought it was. They're spread out all over the western states as far as South Dakota. It looks like everything funnels through the lab in Emeryville, but there's another organization calling the shots there. Your detective's cousin is in way over his head. I think he was going broke for some reason and these other guys showed up with money and he jumped at the chance."

"All-right, that may be, but what do I do about it. I do not run the show in Emeryville, even though Jimmy and I work together well."

"Well, I've got an idea. So far I'm way ahead of the FBI, it doesn't make sense to lay all this in their lap. Also, I'm sure the money behind the lab is right here in San Francisco."

"Why do you say that?"

"Everything points to it. The one guy I have a lead to is in San Francisco. The receptionist at the lab said she thought the new people she had seen there were from San Francisco. Plus, the threats I've gotten came from San Francisco!"

"What threats?"

Josh remembered he hadn't told her about the written threat that'd been delivered by the goons that'd tried to beat him up. He fished in his pocket and showed it to her.

"It was obviously just a scare tactic, I forgot all about it."

"Nevertheless, it's evidence. I'll keep it in case it turns out to be important in the future. Let me think for a minute." Josh waited while she spun in her chair and gazed out the window.

"So it may be that the top echelon of this criminal activity is based here in San Francisco. What do you think you're going to do about it and why didn't you meet with Lieutenant Chew this afternoon?"

"I just forgot. I stopped for an early dinner and got so busy trying to figure this mess out I ran out of time."

"Josh, why don't I believe you? Somehow you're making progress all on your own. If you worked directly for me I'd probably put you undercover or fire you. How am I going to handle you?"

CHAPTER 44

"Well, chief, I do have a plan. But I need your help. First I need some time. I need to convince our Park Superintendent that I'm needed down here. I wouldn't ask you to do anything but tell the truth for me. But I think I can really help you break this case right here in San Francisco. If you can call him and tell him there's been a break in the case and you need my help for a few more days?"

"I'll give you one thing. I wish some of my detectives were as resourceful and enthusiastic as you are. If I made that call would you really work with my department? I mean as closely as if you were really one of my men?"

"Yes, I would! My plan is to first find out the exact name and location of the investing company. Chief, if I'm kind of a freelance agent working for and reporting to you, I'll be able to do things my way but you're not really responsible for my actions. I'd like to be able to use your resources like your computers and stuff but be on my own."

"None of my detectives work on their own. They all report to me regularly."

"Don't you have some that work undercover. Some that you don't see for several days at a time? You said if I was in your department you might put me undercover."

A reluctant yes was his answer.

"My idea is to borrow your Chinese cop, the one that's related to the lab owner. That'd give me someone to work with and give you a string on me."

"I thought you and he had a little misunderstanding about his cousin?"

"Oh no. Once he found out I spoke Chinese, he was very cooperative. He seemed spunky and sneaky to me, just what I need!"

"You speak Chinese? Fluently?

"Yes, I do. As a matter of fact, several dialects."

"You're just full of surprises, aren't you?

I'll tell you what I will do and what I won't do. I won't lie to your Superintendent. I will tell him I need you here for a few days because of your unique relationship with the investigation. IF, and I repeat if, you work closely with Mitchell. I want Mitchell to know where you are and what you are doing at all times, understood?"

Josh thought Mitchell might be a help. He knew Chinatown intimately, was young and seemed very bright.

"Chief, I totally understand."

CHAPTER 45

At the station Lieutenant Chew was less than happy to see him.

"How the hell'd you get the Chief to have Mitchell seconded to you? I'm already short-handed and you're taking one quarter of my office? I don't get it!"

"Lieutenant, all I can tell you is that there's an ongoing investigation involving a number of cases that are apparently headquartered here in San Francisco and we're a step ahead of the FBI. They're trying to keep it hush hush because of the National Parks sensitivity. I'm the lead officer because I've been on it since the beginning. Plus I found the S.F. relationship."

"That may make sense to some, but what can you do that we couldn't do better?"

"Several things. One is that my face isn't known around here and I can infiltrate better than your guys could. Secondly, I'm the only person that's seen the Emeryville operation and I've got a contact there. Thirdly, and maybe most important, I think it was the only way the chief could me out of her hair!"

That earned a grudging laugh and, "I can see that. You're sure one persistent bastard! So okay, what do you think you need?"

"All I need is Mitchell and an okay from you."

"Mitchell's on his way in. He already heard from the chief. He isn't happy about this either, but I can guarantee you his cooperation."

"Do I have to call you 'Sir'?" Mitchell had suddenly appeared behind Josh and those were his first words.

Josh laughed and said, "Who're you talking to? Certainly not me! My name's Josh!"

"Sounds good to me, mine's Mitch."

Josh liked Mitch's looks. Maybe thirty, he looked one hundred percent Chinese, even though Josh knew he was half occidental. Thick black hair, a long lean rather dark face gave him the appearance of a very serious cop indeed. Josh judged him to be about six feet, about two or three inches shorter than himself. He thought that Mitch's opening remark perhaps showed a sense of humor that his face somewhat belied.

"Is there some place we can talk? Someplace private?

"How about someplace to eat, not Chinese!"

"Sure, got a place in mind?"

"Yeah. I can get us a private booth at a great steak house not too far away, actually we can walk and talk, if that's okay with you."

They ended up at place named for a famous San Francisco baseball player just off of Union Square. Josh had heard of it but never been there. It was everything it was cracked up to be and Mitch must have had some pull. It was crowded but a booth was waiting for them. Josh continued his assessment of Mitch. Not only did he seem to have connections in town he looked and moved very athletically.

"Why me?" Mitch asked as they ordered lunch.

"Truth? I liked your gumption and I liked it that you didn't object to investigating your cousin."

"Well, he is my cousin but I don't really know him that well. Actually I've always thought of him as a little bit of a turd!"

"The other reason's a little bit of speculation on my part. I think you're trained in Chinese Martial arts. Am I right?"

"How in hell did you figure that out?"

"I could see it, the way you walked and a couple of remarks you made."

"Actually I am. I'm working on my green belt. You? -----Wait a minute. Rogan? Joshua Rogan? My god, is that you? You're a legend! A living legend! What in hell are you doing here? You're not really a Ranger, are you!"

Josh laughed. "One question at a time. Yeah, I'm that Joshua Rogan but you have to forget about that, and I really am a Ranger."

"Now I remember. You withdrew from that last international competition because of too much publicity about your private life, or something like that?"

"Yeah, something like that. If I could just compete against other athletes without all the attending hoopla, I'd love it. As it is, I hate the invasion of my privacy to the point of not wanting to compete any more, at least publicly. Privately I'm working on a combination of all the martial arts that'll revolutionize the whole field. That's another reason I'm working as a Ranger. Nobody recognizes me and I've got the whole Yosemite outdoors to practice in. So. Question! Can you keep my martial arts identity a secret if I make it worth your while?"

"Make it worth my while? What does that mean?"

"If you'll help me, I'll help you. You help me with the investigation and run interference between me and the chief and I'll work with you on your martial arts development."

Josh was taking advantage of the almost mystical adhesion that develops among true martial arts converts to their achievement of excellence. It was almost inevitable that some would become totally devoted to the sport, considering its total body and mind involvement. It almost became a religion.

Mitch didn't hesitate, "Wow! You'd help me get my brown belt? Absolutely, yes!" A moment's pause. "As long as it doesn't compromise my job?"

"I'm not going to ask you to do anything you wouldn't do on your own. The worst thing I might ask of you would be a crime of omission. There might be a few techniques I use that I'd rather not have anyone know about. That work for you?"

"I think I can live with that."

CHAPTER 46

"I need to know how good you are. Is there someplace nearby where we can work out?"

"How about the YMCA, there's one really near."

"Perfect, let's go."

At the Y, they both stripped down to just shirts and pants. Josh had Mitch do some warm up routines while he did the same. Josh watched Mitch out of the corner of his eye to judge his competence. He was fairly satisfied with what he saw. He thought that Mitch might be advanced enough to cover his back if necessary. He tried to think of a way he could compliment Mitch on his ability without allowing him to get overconfident. Probably by demonstration.

"Hey, you look pretty good! I think you're a lot closer to the next belt than you think you are!"

"Really?"

"Yeah, I do! Tell you what, come at me. Let's see what you got."

They squared off in the traditional opening stances and Mitch started attacking Josh. In no time at all, Mitch was completely frustrated. He never touched Josh. To him, Josh was like a ghost. He was never where Mitch expected him to be. Mitch would rush at him using the best technique he had been taught only to end up on the floor, time and time again.

Through it all, Josh kept explaining what he was doing, as if he was giving a lesson. Even though Mitch was completely frustrated, he was enjoying the bout, and hopefully learning.

After a half-hour Josh said, "that's enough for now. I know you're frustrated. Remember that I've been at this for years. You're doing really well but still have a long way to go. I think we can work together and you're good enough to help me. What do you think?"

"I've never sparred with a Master before. It's pretty scary, knowing how bad I am."

"Whoa! You're not bad at all. In fact you're pretty good! You're just not up to my level. I think you'd beat most people you challenged. Don't denigrate yourself!"

"Will we do some more?"

"We'll have to, as soon as possible."

"So okay, what's next?"

"Next we have to figure out what's next! But first I should bring you up to date on where I am as of now."

Josh proceeded to tell him almost everything that had happened over the last day or so. When he told him about entering the lab via the skylight, Mitch was awed and concerned.

"Jesus Josh, I can't be involved in anything like that. The Chief would have my badge in nothing flat."

"I'm not going to do anything like that with you. Whatever we do together will be within police procedure, okay? By the way, how do you feel about your cousin's involvement, is that going to be a problem?"

Josh was pleasantly surprised at Mitch's' response, "Like I told you before, I've never liked the guy, . All he could ever talk about was money. He made it obvious to me that my being a policeman was way below his social strata. If he's guilty, let's get him."

"I think your cousin's small potatoes. I bet he doesn't even know who he's dealing with. They made a big loan to him in order to have access to the lab. Hell, they might even have engineered his cash troubles just to get the lab."

"So how do we find these guys?"

"I remembered something Charley Fong said that maybe could help. He said that one of his clients had given his name to a guy that was looking for an enforcer. I think we should revisit old Charley and get his client's name."

"Can you find him again?"

"I'm pretty sure he'll answer his phone," Josh answered smugly. "Is there a coffee shop or something near his office?"

"Sure, a dim sum place just a block or so from him."

Not surprisingly to Josh, the Chinese pseudo detective answered on the first ring and agreed to meet them at the restaurant.

CHAPTER 47

Charley was sitting at the back of the small restaurant, by himself and with his back to the door. Josh and Mitch walked around his table, pulled out a couple of chairs and joined him.

To say he was startled to see Mitch with Josh was to put it mildly. Obviously he recognized Mitch as a policeman. He choked on his food, pushed his chair back and searched around the restaurant with his eyes as if he expected more police behind them. Mitch put a hand on Charley's arm and said, "Relax, we just want to talk!"

"The last time I talked with your friend here, he almost broke my leg!"

Josh spoke up. "Well, that could still happen, depends on what you talk to us about!"

"I told you everything I know."

"I don't think so. I think you know something you don't know you know!"

"What the hell are you talking about now?"

"The other night you told me that the business owner got your name from a client of yours."

"Yeah, so what? That's all I know."

"It was someone that knew you might do some strong arm stuff or might hire guys to do it, but you didn't know who it was."

A long pause. Then a cautious, "Yeah, so what." Accompanied by a worried look at Mitch.

"Okay. We need to get back to your office and talk about each and every contact you've had over the past couple of years. You're going to help us find the client that referred you. You ready?"

"Maybe, maybe not. Why should I cooperate with you guys?"

Mitch spoke up, "Several reasons. One is that you don't want to get on my bad side. With what I know about you I could put you away on a whim. Second, my friend here is quite capable of breaking that leg you referred to. And third, there's a probable murder rap involved in this and I don't think you want any part of that. Do you?"

"Okay, I get the message. Can I finish my dinner?"

Josh glanced at Mitch and said, "I'm hungry, how about you?"

CHAPTER 48

Charley's office was deep in the heart of Chinatown about two blocks from the Dim Sum restaurant. Between a meat market and a gift shop, they entered a narrow door. A flight of stairs immediately led them to the upper stories, which were filled with small individual offices. Insurance agents, stock brokers, a wholesale food company, all housed in tiny rooms. At the end of the hall was Charley's' office. It barely fit the three of them. Josh realized why Charley spent so little time there.

Pushing junk off one of the chairs, Josh asked Charley where his files were. Shrugging his shoulders, Charley said; "What files?"

"Records! Don't you keep records of your clients? How about records for the IRS?"

"No records and I don't pay any taxes, not enough income."

"Okay. Back at the restaurant, you said maybe, what'd that mean?"

"Well, I got a diary. With the diary I can dredge up every contact I've had for the last several years."

"Terrific, let's get at it. Where do we start?"

Mitch suggested, "I don't think this client was some guy you met recently, let's start about a year ago and work backward. See if we can refresh your memory."

Charley dug out a well-worn, leather covered diary and they got started. There were too many names in it. He had a habit of jotting down every name of every person he met each and every day. On some days there were twenty or more names casually entered, very few of them had any corresponding data, just a name. It was slow going. But Charley was right, he remembered almost all of them.

Unfortunately he remembered too much. He wanted to talk about each of them. Mitch kept egging him on. Kept saying, "For Christ's sake, Charlie, we don't give a fig about what you had for lunch with the guy. Does he have money? Could he be the guy we're looking for?"

Gradually they inched backwards in his diary. After about an hour Charley looked up from his diary and said, "Maybe?"

"Did you find him? Let's see." Mitch said.

"As I said, maybe! I met him several times a little over a year ago but I haven't seen him recently."

"What's his name?"

"Edgerly, Dan Edgerly."

"Doesn't sound Chinese to me," Mitch offered.

"He's not. He's a food broker over in the east bay."

"Why would he say you might be the guy to do a little strong arming?"

"I think he might broker a few things other than food?"

"Call him, find out who he gave your name to."

They got lucky, Edgerly was in and remembered the incident as well as the name. Charley put the call on the speaker phone.

"Yeah, I remember giving your name to a guy at a party, why? Was there a problem?"

Charley thought fast. "No, not really. He just owes me a little money and I've lost his name. Do you remember it?"

"Leung. Jack Leung."

"What do you know about him?"

"Not a lot. He was supposed to be a wheeler-dealer. Lots of money, kind of flashy, maybe connected. Somebody told me he lived down near Palo Alto but had offices in San Francisco."

"How'd you meet him?"

"At some fund raisers. I went with a lady friend to a number of them over the years, still do. I remember thinking about this guy, I thought he was a phony. Like he was trying to break into society by going to these events at the Opera and so on. A couple of weeks ago he came up to me at that party and said he needed a connection in Chinatown."

"Why you?"

"I guess he'd heard that I use a Chinese private eye to do some credit checking stuff for me and that the guy's cheap.

"You think Jack Leung's his real name?"

"Sure, why not? He wanted to be recognized, why would he use a phony name?"

Charley thanked him and hung up.

Mitch turned to Josh and asked, "What do you think? Do you think it could be our guy? Sounds like it to me!"

"Let's check him out!"

Just then Josh's cell phone rang. Thinking it was probably Chief Anne, he answered it with a perfunctory "Yes?"

To his surprise it was Fern. "I got your message and came right down."

"What message?"

"Your e-mail, silly."

"What e-mail? I didn't send any e-mail. What'd it say?"

"It said you were going to be in San Francisco a few more days and I should come on down. Said you'd moved to the Jamison Hotel and I should meet you here. Is something wrong?"

"I'll say. I didn't send it. Where are you now?"

"That's why I called. I'm here at the Jamison hotel and they don't have you registered."

"Fern, something's wrong! Stay in the lobby near the desk and don't leave, I'll be right there!"

CHAPTER 49

Josh jumped up from his chair, pulled Mitch to his feet and said, "Mitch, we need to get to the Jamison Hotel fast. Fern's in a trap!"

Mitch reacted quickly. They ran to his police car and raced to the hotel, siren blazing. In less than ten minutes they were there and into the lobby. No sign of Fern.

Josh shouldered an elderly couple aside and asked the clerk where the lady was that had been waiting in the lobby.

The desk clerk stood on his tiptoes, looked over Josh's shoulder at the empty lobby and said, "Sir, I don't know. She was there a moment ago when I started checking this couple in." He turned to the couple, "did you notice her?"

They hadn't but when Josh questioned them, they did remember two well dressed Chinese men immediately behind them as they came through the revolving doors into the lobby. Now the lobby was deserted. Josh ran out into the street and Mitch asked about additional exits. There was no sign of Fern in the street and Mitch determined that the emergency exit through the kitchen had not been used.

Back at the front desk Mitch identified himself and asked if two Chinese men had rented a room that day. None had. Also the desk clerk was quite sure he would have noticed if the three had tried to go up to the rooms.

Josh had to face the reality of the moment. Somehow Fern had been tricked into coming to San Francisco and captured. It had to be the gang he was investigating. He knew how vicious they could be.

"God damn it, now what do I do?"

"We" said Mitch, "you and me. You need to call the Chief, and quick."

"Maybe. Let me think for a minute." A long pause. "Jack Leung. The guy that Fong mentioned. We're the only ones with his name, aren't we?"

They were interrupted by Josh's cell phone. "Josh Rogan?"

Josh instantly recognized Fern's cell-phone number on his display. "Yes?"

"Your wife says to say hello."

"You son of a bitch, you hurt a single hair—"

The speaker interrupted him. "That's up to you. You pack up and get out of town and she can, too. If you don't then all bets are off. I'll call back at seven-thirty sharp, that gives you two hours to get packing." He hung up.

"That settles it. I'm not going to the Chief. There's not enough time for the police to do anything and there's no way I'm quitting. I've got an idea that might work but I have to do it myself. You can check out if you want to, maybe you should. To protect your career."

What's your plan?"

"I'm going all out against Jack Leung. He's the only lead we have and we've only got two hours to find him. Will your squad help us?"

Mitch made an instant decision. "They better!"

Back at the Chinatown squad office, Mitch explained the situation to the rest of the squad, without telling them about Fern's abduction.

"We got a hot lead on the gang leader. His name's Jack Leung. Anybody heard of him?"

"Pretty common name. I know two or three," one of the other detectives said

"This guy's wealthy, crooked and probably stays out of the limelight."

One detective spoke up. "There's one, I don't know much about him, he's supposed to be some sort of criminal boss, got his fingers in all kinds of criminal activities. But he's sure low profile."

"What else?"

"I don't know. He's rumored to live down the Peninsula, but others say he has a flat on Broadway, here in the city."

"Any way we can find out in a hurry?"

" We can check out the Broadway address. The way I heard it is that he remodeled the whole top two floors over a strip joint. I also heard that the whole remodel was illegal but he greased a lot of wheels. I guess he's connected pretty well."

"How could he remodel two whole floors without getting permits and stuff?"

"Money greases the wheels? And I also heard he owns that big parking garage on what used to be the International Settlement."

"You mean the street below Broadway?"

"Yeah, and if he does and if it backs up to the strip joint, he could go back and forth from inside the parking garage to the flat with truckloads of stuff and nobody'd be the wiser."

Mitch had a question. "If he's so big time, why would he hire Charley and how come nobody knows about him?"

Josh replied. "I thought about that. I think at first I was just a minor interruption, something to swat at. He thought I'd be easily scared away or maybe somebody under him made a wrong decision. And the reason nobody knows about him? I think it's because he's the money guy. He's the guy behind the guy. He's layered, and practically never gets his own hands dirty. He works hard at being an unknown, at least to the general public and the police. He's gotta be the guy that put up the money for the lab in Emeryville."

Somehow he needed to light a fire under these guys, he had a less than two hour deadline.

"Guys, we need this in a hurry. We heard there's something else going down tonight we may be able to stop."

The squad got on the phones and in a short time found that according to city tax records both properties were owned by "JL Inc.", a California corporation. A little research at state records determined that "JL Inc." was owned by Jack Leung. Bull's-eye!

One of the detectives leaned on a young Chinese parking attendant and asked if there was anything unusual about the garage.

"He told me there's a huge pickup sized door off the third floor at the rear of the place that was never used and late this afternoon something unusual happened."

"What'd he say?".

"He was a little long winded telling me what it was. He said he and the other drivers park and pick up all the cars. The customers drive in the front door and then they drive the cars up the ramp to a parking place upstairs. They put a mark on the ticket showing the slot they put the car in and take it down to the office. The garage never lets the customers park their own cars. They always tell the customer that the insurance company won't let them park their own cars."

"So what was unusual?"

"He said that late this afternoon a Lincoln sedan, you know, the ones with the huge trunks? Anyway the Lincoln drove up and the attendant waved him right through, didn't even charge him. He said he was on the way over to pick up the car from the driver when the attendant waved him off. He thought that was really strange but then it got stranger. A few minutes later he drove a car upstairs to park it and he saw the Lincoln parked next to that third floor door at the rear of the building. You know, the one he said he'd never seen used. The big truck-sized door with a little door cut into it. The cars trunk lid was standing open and the small door in the wall was slightly ajar. It looked like something had been delivered through the door and they hadn't come back yet to park the car. When he came back downstairs, the Lincoln was gone and the door was locked again."

Mitch looked at Josh and said, "Got 'em!!"

Josh said, "I've got a plan, but we have to get an idea of the layout of Leung's place. Do you know anything about the strip joint under his flats.?"

"Never been inside, but I've been past the front lots of times. It's open to the public, not a private club. We can go in and see the general layout, should be a snap."

"Okay, but we should be paying customers and we need to do it fast and clean. I don't want to alert them with a police presence."

CHAPTER 50

The front of the building was gaudy, with glass encased posters on either side of the canopied entrance. Posters were prominently placed displaying semi naked women in provocative poses. A doorman stood under the canopy, encouraging people to take a tour. At the far right end of the building was a small, rather ornate door, marked private. Josh surmised it might lead to the upper floors.

Inside, the rooms were dark and almost empty. They were encouraged to buy a beer and roam around. A large stage dominated the main room. A young, attractive girl was rather lethargically doing a pole dance. The walls of the room were covered with draperies, probably for sound control.

They were devising a plan to explore the place when Mitch's cell phone rang. It was Lieutenant Chew. Mitch quickly walked to the front door and took the call. He apologized to the doorman for using his cell phone, but shouldn't have worried. The doorman told him it happened all the time. He said the calls were usually the same. He could hear the guys telling their wives they were still in their office.

Mitch hurried back to Josh. "You'll never guess what happened. Fong's been murdered."

"Murdered?" A short pause. "Do you think it was because of us?"

"Chew said it looked like a gang murder. A shot in the back of his neck. They found him dead in his chair in his office. Somebody got behind him and executed him. The doc said it was probably a 22 at very close range. Very professional."

" I didn't expect that. We need to be careful and we gotta be fast, these guys are really dangerous. I'll scout out the place and see if there's a way upstairs."

Josh was able to slip behind the drapes and quietly make his way backstage without being noticed. The backstage area consisted of a small dressing room, a toilet and two doors. One led outside and the other, heavily barred, led upstairs. No way to use it.

He slipped back to Mitch and said, "time to go, nothing here that'll help us get in upstairs. I want to get on top of the building next door and then we need to get back to the hotel room before the next phone call comes."

He had a plan. Getting into the building next door was easy, and so was getting onto the roof. It was one floor lower than Leung's building. Perfect.

They just had time to get back to Josh's hotel room before the threatened call.

As the phone rang exactly on time Josh warned Mitchell, "whatever you hear, don't make any noise."

" I'm here, Jack."

A long pause. "Jack? Why did you call me Jack?"

"Cause that's your name, Jack. And Jack, did you know there's a strip joint in your basement?"

A longer pause. "Who are you?"

"Somebody you're going to wish you never met up with. Somebody that's not leaving town. And I'm telling you now, you hurt my wife in any way and you're dead," and he hung up.

"For Christ's sake Josh, what've you done, you're gonna get Fern killed!"

CHAPTER 51

"I'll tell you what I've done. I've let him know that his cover's burned. He won't be used to being in the front lines, he'll panic. And I warned him again about hurting Fern. I bought us some time."

"What good does that do?"

" It gives me time to execute my plan, that's what. Come on, we're leaving. We need to hurry. We need to get back to Leung's flat before he flips his lid. We're going to bring some hell down on Jack Leung."

"What's the plan?"

" We're going to drop in on Leung from his neighbors roof. Come on, we can't waste time talking, we need to get going."

Josh dug into his hidden stash under the false bottom of his suitcase and put together a backpack full of what he deemed necessary for their raid. He explained his plan to Mitch as he packed.

"I'm going to break into his place and rescue Fern before they harm her. There's no time for the police to get involved, I have to do it myself. The thing is, I can do it. I've got some assets and abilities you don't know about. You're just going to have to take my word that I can do it. The question is, do you want to get involved? I'm going to break at least a couple of minor laws, like breaking and entering and unlawful detention, but we'll rescue a kidnap victim."

"You're not going to kill anybody, are you?"

"Not unless they try to kill me or Fern."

"And me?"

"If you decide to come along, of course."

"So what're we wasting time for? Let's get at it."

They piled into Mitch's unmarked police car, raced back to Broadway and parked in the alley next to the strip joint. It was now dark. Josh grabbed his back pack and they walked into the apartment building next door. Nobody challenged them as they made their way to the roof.

Josh could see the whole side of Leung's building. Five stories tall, the bottom three stories had windows that had been blacked out with very little light showing through them. The neon lights on the front of the building lit up a little of the alley between their roof and Leung's building. The top two floors had lots of windows with a few lights showing. The alley between the buildings was about ten feet wide. Just barely wide enough to accommodate their car. Other than the windows, the wall facing them was vertical and bare. The same was true of the building that Mitch and Josh were on. Their building was four stories tall making it a good twelve feet below the other.

Mitch threw up his hands in resignation. "Josh, there's no way we can get over there from here. It's way too far to jump to their roof. I don't see your plan."

Josh didn't reply. He opened his backpack and handed Mitch a rolled up bundle of clothing. "That's my spare black Ninja outfit, put it on and quit asking questions."

As he donned his own Ninja suit, he took out the rest of his equipment. Grappling hooks, suction cups, several lines, some throwing stars and a few odds and ends.

"See the top row of windows just under the roof line?"

"Yeah, five of them, and they're all pretty dark."

"I think the last two are bedroom windows. They're completely dark like a bedroom window would be if the door was closed. The three others have a little light showing like maybe from a hall light and those doors are open."

"What good does that do us?"

"The floor below has lights showing in every window. The curtains are completely drawn but you can see there's light behind them. That means that whoever's there is on the fourth floor and nobody's on the fifth floor."

"You hope."

"My target's the second window from the back. I'm betting it's a bedroom and it's empty. That's my target."

Josh was certain that no one would expect an entry to be made through a window that high and that isolated.

"Wonderful. How do you plan to do that? Fly?"

"Watch me. Stand back." Josh had tied the line to the grappling hook and was twirling it, preparing to throw it onto the next roof. In a moment he threw the hook lightly and accurately so that it just barely cleared the railing, landing softly on the neighboring roof.

"Perfect" Mitch said. "Now what?"

"Watch me." Josh took up all the slack in the line and fashioned a middle of the line knot around his waist. He then handed the bitter end of the line to Mitch.

"You get the idea?" he asked Mitch. "If I jumped off our building right now I'd arc over to their building and smash into it. That's what we're going to do but your going to let me swing over there gently. All you have to do is brace yourself and let the line out slowly. Ready?"

"Got it" Mitch said and braced one foot against the wall. Josh slid over the side of the wall until he was hanging by his fingertips and the line to the grappling hook was taut. "Okay, now slowly let the line out."

Mitch slowly let the line out until Josh was hovering directly in front of the window. Josh signaled an okay with his thumb and forefinger and Mitch held him firmly there. In a few minutes he had taped the window and cut a circle large enough for his arm. He was then able to tap it lightly and quietly dislodge the circle of glass. He soaked the window edges with a small can of silicon spray, reached through the hole, unlatched the catch and ever so slowly and quietly raised the window. He parted the curtains and found he had been right. It was a bedroom, empty and dark.

Inside the room he untied his lines and leaning out the window, whispered to Mitch, "come on over." Mitch pulled the line back to himself, secured the loop to his waist and tied the end of the line to a pipe. In a short time, Mitch was nearing the window and Josh was able to reach out and pull him in.

"Neat!" was Mitch's comment. "Now what?"

"Tiptoe and follow me. I can't see any light under the door so I think the hallway's not lighted, agreed?"

"Yeah. Let's try it."

None the lights in the hall were lit and none of the other doors off the hall were open. There were two more bedrooms and two baths, all dark. The only light was dim and came up the staircase from the floor below. They quietly crept to the stairs and could hear voices.

"How many voices do you hear?" Mitch whispered.

Josh signaled him to wait and quietly eased his way down to the bottom stair. After a moment or two he held up four fingers and beckoned Mitch to come down beside him.

He whispered that there were at least four voices he could recognize, maybe more. They were all at the other end of the flat, he thought they were in a kitchen. He needed to get closer and hear what they were saying to determine if Fern was there.

"Can we make it to the front door hallway? Should be able to hear everything there and I don't think they'd see us."

"They're sure involved in the kitchen. I don't think they'd notice anything. Let's do it, fast and quiet."

They ghosted across the room, into the front door hallway and could immediately hear every word.

A male voice said, "Now what?"

A second voice answered, "She isn't telling us anything. Keeps insisting he's just a Ranger. If he's just a Ranger, I'm Santa Claus. He's gotta be FBI or CIA or some sort of a black operator. How in hell did he figure out who we are and where we live? I'd like to find him and kill him," He paused. "How the hell can we make her talk?"

"How about we torture her? Maybe we get rid of her and him both."

"Jack didn't say anything about torture."

"Jack wants results, but he doesn't get his hands dirty. That's why he went downstairs."

"Maybe. Let's see how she reacts to the threat of torture first. If the threat doesn't work, we'll see . Beverly, you're a woman and you got a sadistic nature, what can we do?"

A woman's voice replied. "You know what I think will scare the hell out of her, at least it would me?"

"I'm afraid to ask."

"Something every woman knows about and is a little scared of. We gradually lower her hand into the garbage disposer as it's running. She's ground up chicken bones and stuff and knows what it'll do to her fingers. They'd be mangled into crap in a matter of seconds. I don't think anyone could resist that a threat like that. And if that doesn't budge her, we just keep going. After she loses a finger or two, she'll talk."

CHAPTER 52

"Jesus, Beverly that's brilliant. Get her and bring her in." The kitchen door swung open and for the first time they saw Beverly. She was a tall, slim Chinese woman, heavily made up and her jet black hair upswept very stylishly. Josh could only see her face in profile as she walked clear across the room, past the staircase and opened another door. In profile Josh thought she looked to be at least sixty even though she dressed very young.

As she opened the door, Mitch whispered to Josh, "Dammit, if we'd known she was out there we could have grabbed her and gotten away."

"I think we wait until we see what kind of condition she's in"

In a moment she re-emerged pushing Fern in front of her. Fern's arms were tied behind her back and she was blindfolded and gagged.

Mitch whispered, "Does she look okay to you?"

Josh couldn't reply for a moment. His throat was choked up with relief that she looked unhurt.

"Let them take her into the kitchen, I've got an idea. As soon as she's in the kitchen, go over to the front door and pound on it. One of them will come out and I'll cold cock him as soon as turns the corner towards the door. That'll be one down and we'll surprise the others in the kitchen."

Mitch quietly walked over to the door and tried the knob. As they'd expected, it was locked. He knocked firmly and waited. No response. This time he pounded on the door.

The kitchen door opened partially and a woman's voice said, "Who the fuck can that be?"

Another voice answered, "How the hell should I know. Maybe it's Jack come back?"

An older, more mature voice said, "For Christ's sake, somebody answer it ."

Josh ducked back out of sight as the door swung open and he could hear someone approaching where they were hidden in the hall. One person, as expected. As the guy turned the corner, Josh gave him a hard chop across the back of his neck. He fell to the floor, soundlessly.

"Quick, pull him out of sight. They'll be expecting him back any second, instead they'll get us. I'll go in first and you right behind me, okay? There should be two guys and the old gal, what's her name?, oh yeah, Beverly. I'll take the two guys, you take old Beverly, Okay? We go in fast and noisy. By the time they figure out what's happening, it'll be all over. Let's go."

Josh ran over to the kitchen door, pulled it open and charged in. In a flash, he located Fern, the two men and Beverly. Fern was perched on a stool in front of the kitchen sink and Beverly was binding some tape around her wrist. The two guys were between Josh and the sink, watching Beverly. Expecting the third guy to be returning they turned around slowly and were no way ready for Josh. Without slowing down, freezing them with his speed and giving them no time to react, he leaped across the room and swept their legs out from under them with a spinning kick. As they fell he delivered an elbow to one's nose and vicious hand chop to the Adam's apple of the other. In a moment they both were on the floor, writhing. Continuing the spin he kicked Beverly away from Fern.

"Take care of the old lady," he called to Mitch. "I got these guys. They're out of it." He said and turned to Fern. Out of the corner of his eye he saw Mitch deliver a hard right to the old lady's jaw. She fell like a log. "That's for Fern," he said.

"You okay? He asked Fern, as he carefully took her gag and blindfold off. The moment she say Josh, she started crying. As he carefully removed the tape holding her gag in place, and then the rope around her wrists, she threw her arms around him and started swearing.

"Honey, what's the matter?"

"Dammit, dammit. I didn't cry once until you got here. Now I'm crying, after it's all over."

"Don't worry about it, they're probably tears of relief, not fear."

"They said they were going to shove my hand in the garbage disposer, would they really have done that?"

"No, no. They had to be bluffing. Anyway, you're okay now and this handsome guy straddling the old Chinese lady is Mitch. He's a cop and a good friend."

Mitch said with a twinkle in his eye, "So you're Fern. You sure caused us a heap of trouble."

"Geez, I'm really sorry to have caused you any trouble," she responded. "But what kind of a mess are you two in? Who're these people that kidnapped me? And who is this horrible woman? Come to think of it, you two probably caused all this, right?"

Properly chastised, Mitch changed the subject and turned to Josh. "Now what're we going to do? "

Josh answered. "Drag the guy in the hall in. Fern, find something and tie the witch's hands behind her back, I'll tie up the two guys."

"Josh, what's going on? Who are these people? Why did they kidnap me? What are you two mixed up in?", Fern asked again.

Josh was more interested in where Leung was. "Was there another guy here, a guy that seemed like the boss?"

"Yes there was. An older Chinese? He came in just long enough to look at me and talk to those idiots before he left."

"Dammit! That must've been Leung. I was hoping he was one of the guys in the kitchen. He's the mastermind behind the bear killings and indirectly responsible for Tim being killed. We were getting a pretty good line on him when he found out about Mitch and me and tried to stop us. Somehow he found out about you and thought he'd get at me through you. Mitch and I figured out where you had to be and rescued you. I was hoping we'd catch him and turn him over to the police."

"I thought you said Mitch was police?"

"Yeah, he is, but we put ourselves on temporary detachment when you got kidnapped."

Mitch chimed in. "Nobody knows you were kidnapped, nobody knows we were here, nobody even knows about this place except us and we better by hell keep it that way. Jesus, if the Chief ever hears about what really went down tonight, my careers shot."

"Okay," Josh said. "Mitch, you and Fern search this place. Keep it quiet, we don't want to wake up the guys downstairs. There must be records somewhere that'll burn Leung."

Josh checked the tape bindings Fern had used on Beverly to make sure she was really secure. She was. In fact, her bindings were much tighter than Josh would have done them. Probably in retaliation for the garbage disposer idea. She was awake and staring at Josh with hate filled eyes.

She swore at Josh. "You son of a bitch, you'll never get out of here alive."

CHAPTER 53

Josh answered in English, thinking he might inadvertently learn something if they thought he couldn't speak Chinese. "We got in, we'll get out."

Leaving the four of them securely tied, he led Fern out of the kitchen, across the living room and into the study where Fern had been tied up. Mitch was looking through a large desk.

"How's the search going?"

"Unbelievable. There's a lot here. Leung poured over a quarter million into the lab in Emeryville when he bailed out my cousin. There's a ton of records, it's pretty obvious he thought he was completely safe here. He's got his fingers in a lot of things besides your stuff."

"Keep looking, see if you can find some bags or something we can haul this stuff in. And keep talking pretty loud. I want them to think we're all out here, I'll sneak back to the door and listen in on them. They don't know I speak Chinese, maybe I'll overhear something important."

Fern said, "You speak Chinese?"

Josh looked blank. He had completely forgotten that Fern didn't know his linguistic abilities.

Mitch spoke up, "Does he ever. He sure tricked me."

Josh left Mitch explaining it to Fern while he tiptoed back to the kitchen door. Sure enough they were talking in Chinese.

"What happened? How'd they get in? Who the hell are they?" The questions were jumbled and seemed to be directed at the older guy.

"Quiet!, they may be listening." At which point they started whispering. Josh could still hear them.

"What about the gang downstairs, how'd they get past them?"

"Maybe they came in some other way?"

"There is no other way."

"Okay, so how'd they get past the guys downstairs?"

"How the hell do I know? Look, it's obvious they came to rescue the girl. Maybe they'll take her and go."

Josh thought that might be a good idea. They'd alluded to a gang downstairs and probably Leung's there too. He quickly returned to Mitch and Fern.

"We need to get out of here fast. They say there's a gang downstairs. I don't know what that means except we probably can't leave that way. And one of them might come up any time."

"I've got bags full of papers, we need to take them too." Mitch said.

"Okay, meet me by the window." He pointed to a window directly above the alley where their car was parked. "I'm going to get the grappling hooks and lines."

In a few minutes they had the window propped open and had lowered the bags to the alley. Josh fashioned a loop seat in the line to lower Fern and Mitch used his gloves to hand walk himself down. In the dark they were practically invisible.

Josh thought he could throw an additional curve at the gang and Leung. He carefully closed the bedroom window upstairs and doubted anyone would notice the window had been jimmied, at least for some time. Then he propped this window up with a yardstick from the kitchen. Next, Josh readjusted it so that he could pull it loose from the ground. If he could successfully detach the grappling hook and then drop the window there'd be almost no sign that they'd been there except the tied up gang in the kitchen and no Fern.

It worked just as they had hoped. The window slammed shut with a loud bang, but there was so much noise from the street no one noticed.

"Let's go." Mitch whispered. "I'm going to turn the lights on so we won't look like we're sneaking out. I think we'll be less noticed that way."

"God damn it, we missed Leung. Now we're right back where we started, except we got some of his papers."

Fern slugged Josh in the arm. "What about me? Don't I count? I thought you were rescuing me not grabbing what's his name."

Josh turned and hugged her. "Yeah, that was serendipitous, wasn't it." He laughed.

She slugged him again.

Back in Josh's hotel room they had a council of war. They ordered a late room service dinner and brought Fern up to date on what they'd discovered while rummaging through all the papers from Leung's flat.

Josh said, "I don't know what to do about Leung. Now they're talking about a gang. I wonder what that's about. I thought it'd just be him like a business, but a gang? Mitch, you know anything about a gang here in Chinatown?"

"You kidding? We got lots of them. Some old time Chinese gangs like Tongs and some just a bunch of kids. Both kinds can be dangerous. If Leung is mixed up with a Tong type of gang, we need to be extra careful."

Josh made a short reply. "I know about Tongs and I know about kids gangs"

Fern spoke up. "Josh, don't forget why you were sent here in the first place. You are supposed to stop the killing of the bears. It seems to me that with all the incriminating documents you have here, the police will be able to put the lab out of business and jail Leung if they can find him. Won't that pretty much stop the bear traffic?"

"I guess so. But what do you want me to do, just forget about Tim being killed?"

Fern thought for a minute. "If you had caught him tonight, what would you have done with him?"

"I'd like to beat the living shit out of him, but I suppose I'd have ended up turning him in to the Chief. I see where you're going. You think we should turn all this stuff to the chief and let matters take their course, right?"

"It makes sense to me and it'd get you back in good graces with the Chief and the Superintendent. The Superintendent wants you back. He said you broke the back of the gangs when you caught that gang near the south entrance. On top of that they're pretty sure that the guy that was killed by the ATV was the guy that pulled the trigger on poor Tim. They had rifles, but he was the only one with a pistol."

Reluctantly, Josh had to agree.

Josh turned to Mitch. "What do you think, is there enough stuff here to nail Leung?"

"Probably."

"And close down the lab, at least the back part of it?"

"Unfortunately for my cousin, yes."

"What about the teams in the mountains still hunting?"

Fern answered. "They're already on that. They finally figured out they'd never catch them in mountains, but they're vulnerable when they try to leave the park. They already caught one group of three guys and have identified the van of a third team. All they have to do is wait for them to show up at their van."

"So they're using the same idea I had but they're waiting in the parking lot for them?"

"That's it and it's working."

Mitch added, "One thing we have to do is figure out a cover story. If we tell my lieutenant or the Chief any of the downright illegal things we did tonight, my ass'll be in a sling forever."

Josh said, "I got it. We lie like hell. We'll tell them that we found out about Leung's flat and decided to confront him with some questions and see what happened. We went to the flat, rang the buzzer and someone buzzed us in. We walked up to the third floor and there was a big cardboard box , full of Leung's valuable papers ,sitting in front of the door there waiting for us. So we took it and left."

Mitch laughed and said, "you're nuts."

"No I'm not. Think about it. Who's going to call it a lie? Leung? The old lady? The guys we tied up? They're gonna be busy denying the stuff in the papers not how we got them. And in fact they don't know how we got in. Maybe we did come in the front door. Maybe somebody on the inside crossed them up and made the papers available to us. Besides, nobody's going to need those papers to go to court with. There's so much stuff at the lab and at Leung's place, that'll hang him. Mitch said so. Right Mitch?"

Josh was right. The incredulous looks they got when they told their story soon vanished when the contents of the two boxes of Leung's papers were exposed.

Bank accounts, pay receipts, notes about retail places that sold the illegal Chinese medicines, even records of the payments made to the Emeryville lab. Some of the papers were in Chinese and had to be translated. They turned out to be even more incriminating detailing actual sales of the bear organs. Leung was nailed, Mitch's cousin was nailed and a lot of the people working both for Leung and at the lab were nailed.

The police tried to arrest Leung but couldn't find him. The word was that he had fled the city and was nowhere to be found.

The Yosemite trade in bear killing was effectively stopped. Everyone thought they should call it a day and head for home. Except Josh.

Way down deep, Josh knew he wasn't through with Leung. He still had to avenge Tim's killing. He owed that to Tim's parents. Leung hadn't been caught. His time would come.

CHAPTER 54
(THREE MONTHS LATER)

Josh parked his Yosemite Police car near their home, got out and stretched. He had been driving most of the day, patrolling the many roads in and around the Valley, something he had been doing almost every day since returning from San Francisco.

As he stretched he deliberated, should he go home, shower and change? Or should he stop by the store where Fern was working first? Shower and change won. She would be home in less than an hour and he could be all done by then.

Approaching the apartment, he was startled to see the front door open and hear the sound of music. He had talked to Fern earlier in the day and knew she wasn't expecting to be home early. Cautiously, he pushed the door further open and looked into the living room. Empty. The music seemed to be coming from the kitchen. On tiptoe, revolver in hand, he edged toward the kitchen and peeked around the door frame.

"MITCH !," he yelled. "What the heck are you doing here, you scared the piss out of me."

"Fixing your dinner, you big jerk. Put your gun away and have a beer."

"Dinner? You're fixing dinner? Where's Fern?"

"She's at work where she's supposed to be. I stopped by the store this afternoon and took her out for coffee. I told her I'd just driven up on a whim and needed a place to stay. So guess what, buddy. I'm your sofa guest tonight, like it or not."

"Great with me. But what's the dinner thing?"

"Least I could do. I like to cook and offered to fix dinner, so she gave me the keys, we did a little shopping and here I am. Japanese okay?"

"Do I have time to take a shower and change? I've been driving all day."

"Sure thing, O lord and master. I suppose I'm supposed to bring your pipe and slippers too?"

"Cut it out, I don't even get that kind of treatment from Fern"

"Take your time, dinner won't be ready for at least an hour, we'll have time for a couple of beers or maybe some rice wine first. After dinner there's something important we need to talk about. You know we never did catch Leung."

By the time Josh finished his shower and put on some slacks and a cotton shirt Fern had arrived. As he joined them in the kitchen Mitch handed him a cold glass of beer.

"Pretty fancy Mitch, I usually drink them right out of the bottle."

"You didn't know you married a slob did you Fern," Mitch said. Then turned to Josh. "This beer, my dear friend, is Kirin. A top quality Japanese beer and deserves to be quaffed out of a glass. It will make a suitable accompaniment to your soon to be superb Japanese dinner."

"Good Lord, what's got into him?" Josh asked Fern.

"I think he's in love with Yosemite. He said he had never been here before."

"Quit quibbling you two" came the voice out of the kitchen. " It's time to eat. The table's set, dinner's ready, wine's on the table, let's do it."

In spite of Mitch's joking around, the dinner was delicious. They found out that Mitch had been promoted to sergeant and had seriously taken up Judo. Josh was delighted and couldn't wait to work out with him.

After dinner the conversation took a serious turn.

"I told you we hadn't been able to catch Leung?"

"Right."

"We've learned a lot about him, since you got us on his tail. It turns out he's joined forces with a Chinese gang. Kind of an outlaw Tong. We've got an informant on the inside of the gang and he's picked up some worrisome stuff about you. Seems that after laying low these last three months, Leung's getting back into the swing of things. He's obsessed with you and is making noises about taking you out. I, for one, take his threats seriously. And I think you and Fern should take him seriously too. That's one of the reasons I came up."

"You think he might come after us again?"

Fern broke in. "Do you think he could come up here?"

"Like our guy said, he's obsessed. Thinks you're to blame for losing his flat, let alone the Chinese medicine business. Come to think of it, you are to blame. Yeah, I suppose he could come up here, why?"

"It's probably nothing, but yesterday I was stocking the back shelves at the market and I saw this Chinese guy."

"Leung?" Josh demanded.

"I don't know, could be. I just got a glimpse for a minute. He was Chinese and acting strange, like he was watching me. I ducked down so he wouldn't see me and after that all I saw of him was his back and profile before he left the store. I asked around but nobody knew anything about him. I finally convinced myself that it was my imagination."

"He was watching you?"

"I'm not sure. It seemed like it at the time."

Josh turned to Mitch, "do you think it's possible?"

"Could be. If so, Fern's in danger. She'd be an easy target at the store or walking to and from. He attacked her once, he would probably do it again. We can't take any chances. We need to be sure."

CHAPTER 55

Josh thought for a second. "If he is trying to find me it should be pretty easy. Everybody knows everybody in the valley. He couldn't just ask around about us, we'd hear about it in a flash. In that case, he'd have to be a little surreptitious, maybe take a few days looking around. If it is him, I think he would have to be up here at least a couple of days trying to locate me before he tries anything."

Mitch said, "I tried to get a room up here in case you couldn't house me and there's nothing available. Where would he stay?"

"Sometimes you can get a cancellation at the last minute. He could only be at the Ahwahnee, Curry Village, the Lodge or Wawona."

"How do we find out?"

" I could call and have the registries checked for Leung at all four of the places, that should be pretty easy." Josh thought for a moment."But he might not be using his real name. I think we should personally check out all three of them and describe Leung to the employees. It's still early, we can do that right now."

They decided to save the Ahwahnee for last because it was almost impossible to get a room there without reserving it several months in advance.

Josh said, "We'll have to do Wawona by phone, it's way too far to drive tonight and I seriously doubt he would be staying there, it's too difficult to get from there to here in the valley. Both the Lodge and Curry Village are usually all reserved but like I said, they do have cancellations occasionally." They used Josh's official car and checked out all three. After extensive interviews with the staff at each they concluded that there were no Chinese staying at any of them fitting Leung's description. They were about ready to conclude that Fern must have been mistaken when Josh said, "there's one more possibility. He might be staying outside the park. There's a large hotel just at the gate that provides jitney transport to and from the hotel to the valley several times daily. It's convenient and recommended when people call in for rooms. Lots of people use it. I'm going to try them."

A few minutes later they had confirmation. A J. Leung had indeed registered there two days ago and was still occupying the room. He had a suite with two bedrooms, saying that he and a friend were sharing. They told Josh he was Chinese and so was his friend. That was all they knew.

Mitch said, "That's must be him and he brought someone with him. And he's gotta be here because of you. So now what?"

"If he's been here a couple of days, he's probably already located us. He's probably biding his time, waiting for the perfect opportunity. Last time he took Fern to get at me, so she's a target too."

Mitch had an idea. "Let's beat him to the punch. It's only seven-thirty. Can we find out if he's at the hotel right now?"

"Gotcha. Good idea."

Josh called the front desk at the hotel, identified himself, and after a few minutes the clerk said that the lights were on in that room and he could see movement through the blinds.

"Okay, they're there. Your thinking the same thing I am? We confront them right now, there, instead of waiting for them here?"

Mitch agreed. "That's what I had in mind. Fern should be safe here if they're there. We can come up with a plan on the way. What're we waiting for?"

Shortly after nine PM they parked in front of reception at the hotel. Alongside the highway to the park, the hotel consisted of a number of two-story buildings on about an acre or more of ground. It boasted a restaurant, still open, and playgrounds for children. They confirmed the room number, found it, and parked so that they could keep an eye on it.

On the way over they'd discussed what they might do.

"Is there a warrant out for him because of the kidnapping?" Josh asked.

"No, there isn't because the police were never involved." Then he added, "At least officially they were never involved."

"Do we have any official reason to detain him?"

"Not really. We still would like to question him as a person of interest in several cases, including Fong's murder and some gang activity plus the bear business. Nothing concrete. Nothing we can arrest him for"

Josh deliberated for a moment, "So officially, we're on pretty thin ice?"

"Yeah, we need to be sneaky."

"We can't arrest them, we can't even haul them in for questioning. We know he won't cooperate with the police. Like you said, he's been laying low since we busted his flat. Seems like the only thing we can do is scare them out of the Valley. At least that'll make it safer for Fern. I think if he knows the entire Yosemite police force's been alerted to his presence here and that the SF police are looking for him, he'll take off. If I'm going to take him out, I'd rather be doing it on his home turf."

"I agree, but how do we do that?" asked Mitch.

"How about we just tell him? We knock politely on his door, ask him if he's Jack Leung from San Francisco and tell him the Yosemite Park Police would like to talk to him in the morning. I bet they'd take off for home within an hour or so from when we knock on their door. What do you think?"

"Maybe. I don't trust this guy's instincts. Look how he kidnapped Fern in broad daylight. No telling what he might do."

"What can he do? Hundreds of people around. He'll agree and bolt."

"I guess we're stuck with that plan, I can't think of anything else. Let's give it a try."

Josh and Mitch walked to the room door and listened. They could hear the TV and somebody talking, although they couldn't distinguish the words. They'd already walked around the back of the unit and seen that all the lights were on. It looked like the two were inside and unaware they were about to have visitors.

As Josh walked up to the front door, he had second thoughts. The more he thought about what Jack Leung had done to Fern the madder he got. He didn't want to merely scare him, he wanted to beat the hell out of him. More than that, though, he wanted to put him away legally and permanently. Actually he wanted both. Could he put some hurt on the bastard without damaging their legal case? He remembered when he had overheard them planning how they were going to torture Fern. He decided to beat him up, scare him out of the Valley and the hell with the consequences. He would lure him out of the apartment and cold-cock him. He knocked on the door.

"Who's there?"

"Mr. Leung?"

"Who wants to know?"

" Mr. Leung, there's no problem. I'm with the Yosemite Police. Could you step out here on the porch for a moment?"

The moment he said Yosemite Police, the lights were turned off in the unit.

"No need for alarm, Mr. Leung. We just want to ask you a couple of questions."

His answer was total silence.

Josh stood to one side of the door and Mitch edged his way past the window so as to keep and eye on the back of the unit. The window was dark, no lights at all inside. Mitch must have been silhouetted momentarily. Suddenly there was the muted sound of a gun shot and broken glass. Mitch let out a yelp of pain, another bullet crashed through the door, narrowly missing Josh, and moments later they heard the back door slam.

Josh's first concern was for Mitch. "You okay?"

"Yeah, I'm okay. Got a scratch from the broken glass. Startled the hell out of me. Two shots, right? You okay?"

"I'm okay. Big hole in the door, but I'm okay .I think they took off through the back door."

Mitch quietly replied. "I heard. Which way are they going?"

"Parking lot. We got any idea which car is theirs?" Mitch didn't.

"Okay, they're running You grab our car, I'll try to cut them off at the highway exit."

Josh covered the distance to the parking lot exit in a matter of moments, there'd been no car activities yet. Shortly he saw the headlights of Mitch's car snap on and start to slowly approach. Still no other cars were moving. Where were those guys? It didn't make sense that they wouldn't try to get away. They'd been identified, their only chance was to put distance between the Yosemite Police and themselves. The only way out of the place was the highway. Where were they?

Suddenly, as Mitch's car approached him, a nearby car engine roared to life. The car, with no headlights, rammed forward and clipped the front end of Mitch's car sending it into a spin and crumpling the front fender. The car quickly reversed, flipped on its lights and headed towards Josh. Josh started to dodge the oncoming car but the car followed him, pinning him in its headlights. Josh was on a narrow bridge between the parking lot and the highway. The car was gaining on him. There was no way he could outrun the car and it was so dark he couldn't see what was in the ditches on either side of the bridge. At the last moment, unable to see the beyond the headlights, he turned and ran toward the car. Blinded by the headlights, he threw himself into a somersault over the lights, touched lightly on the hood of the car and then bounded up once more, this time over the rear of the car, landing lightly on his feet facing the rear of the car as it roared over the bridge and onto the highway.

"Shit, shit, shit," Mitch yelled "They crumpled the fender against the wheel, I can't move it."

By this time the front office people were showing up wanting to know what was going on.

Josh defused the situation. He identified himself as a Park Ranger and said they'd been trying to interrogate a couple of teenagers on a reckless driving complaint and the kids had fled. "Not to worry, we'll catch 'em down the road."

Nobody seemed to have heard the shots.

The office manager got their utility man away from his dinner, explained the situation and he was able to pry the fender away from the wheel so that they could return to the valley.

"Mitch had some glass cuts on his hands and Josh had a scraped elbow from throwing himself over the car."

Mitch let out a laugh. "Look at us, a couple of wounded warriors, returning home with our tails between our legs and a battered car. As least we got those two to get the hell out of the valley."

"Yeah. And that's what we set out to do. I feel better about Fern with them hightailing it back to San Francisco."

CHAPTER 56

In the car, on the way back to the Valley, Josh told Mitch about his change of plan. "Maybe it's best they got away. I'd planned on beating the crap out of Leung before we sent him on his way to SF. He's got a hell of a lot to answer for like what he did to Fern, the murder of Charley Fong and Tim. He's responsible for all that. Why can't we build a case against him?"

"Unfortunately, the answer's simple. No witnesses. We can't even prove that Fern was kidnapped and we haven't been able to prove his connection with the Chinese gangs or Fong's murder. That's why I need you in SF."

Josh was silent the rest of the way home. At the house he said, "You're staying the night with us, let's go in and talk it over with Fern."

Inside, they had coffee and dessert and filled Fern in on what had happened. They downplayed the gun shots. Josh had questions.

"Your guy on the inside, is he getting any details?"

"That's part of the problem. We think the gang's suspicious of him. They're locking him out of any policy stuff, just sending him on gofer errands. We know that Leung's wormed his way into the Tong and he's obsessed with you but we don't know any details."

"What do you think we should do?"

"That's the other reason I'm here. They made me sergeant because we cracked the bear gang and closed down Leung's operation. Now they want to crack down on this outlaw Tong group and put Leung away for good. They assigned the operation to our Chinese unit and our lieutenant put me in charge."

"Great, a feather in your cap."

"Yeah, but. And it's a great big but. You and I know I couldn't have done it without you. If you hadn't insisted on taking a back seat when we exposed Leung and the medical lab, I probably wouldn't have made sergeant."

"Bull! You would've figured it out some way or another."

"Look. Let me cut to the chase. I've got the damn job. I think you and Fern are in some danger if Leung's allowed to run loose. I've been tasked to break up the gang and finish Leung. It's in your interest for me to succeed as quickly as possible. Long and short?----I need your help "

"You mean like to brainstorm ideas?"

"No. I need your help in San Francisco. I need a partner that knows the Chinese mind, can speak Chinese fluently, and above all, can outsmart these guys at their own games. Plus, a lot of these guys are pretty expert at Kung-Fu, and I'm not. What I'm hoping is that you can get a week off and help me. Do you have any vacation time coming?"

"You want me to spend my vacation chasing Chinese gangsters?"

"Sure, why not. Doesn't everybody? Oh yeah, something else. You'd be my secret. The Chief doesn't know anything about this idea."

"I don't know. It's intriguing and I'd sure like to see Leung behind bars. Fern, what do you think?"

"How dangerous is it?"

"Yeah, Mitch. You've been as close to the Chinese gang as anyone, are they murderers or are they just into control and threatening stores and stuff?"

"I can't lie to you. I just don't know. I'd be damn careful around them and remember, we never solved Charley Fong's murder."

Fern asked, "who's Charley Fong?"

Josh answered her. "He was a Chinese private detective that turned up murdered just after he gave us some important information. We're pretty sure his death's related to the Leung thing."

Mitch was impatient. "Well, what do you think?"

Josh had another question. "How much freedom of action do we have? Are we going to have your Lieutenant looking over our shoulder all the time? We bent the hell out of some rules the last time, can we do that again?"

"Same rules as last time. No shooting and don't get caught," was Mitch's answer.

Josh turned to again to Fern, "What do you think?"

Fern surprised both of them. "I'm beginning to get the idea that as long as I'm married to you and you've got Mitch as a friend I might as well get used to danger. Do you think you can get a week off? I know I can."

"What? No way. I'm not even sure I should go, let alone you."

"Josh, don't be an idiot. We can't wait around worrying about him coming after me again. And don't forget, I've lived by myself in Alaska and survived. I've outwitted bear and wolves galore and I've got a score to settle with your Leung."

"But this is a lot different, isn't it, Mitch."

"I don't know, never been to Alaska," was Mitch's rejoinder.

"You're not much help."

Fern spoke up again. "And there's Tim. Another reason to go after Leung."

They were all silent for a moment. Finally Josh spoke. "I haven't forgotten about Tim." Another pause. "I suppose I could get a week off for a trip to San Francisco. I'll have to check with the Superintendent's office first thing in the morning."

Before he could continue Mitch spoke up. "Great, wonderful. And I've got a place for you two to stay, free!"

"Pretty sure of yourself weren't you. Wait a minute. Did you two cook this up this afternoon before I got home?"

"Well, we might have kicked the idea around a little. And when Fern said she was a little bored around here, it just kinda clicked."

CHAPTER 57

Josh had to convince the Park Superintendent that he deserved the time off and the force could spare him and had to convince the Yosemite Police garage that they should pound out Mitch's fender and make it safe before they could leave. The Super's office reluctantly agreed, only because of all the extra time Josh had been putting in training some of the Rangers in basic Judo. By eleven in the morning everything was done and they were on their way.

Mitch had a close friend who was on vacation and had made the mistake of asking Mitch to house-sit for two months. "You're gonna love the place. It's huge, it's quiet, it's got every convenience and nobody'll know you're there. It'll be a completely safe place for our headquarters."

"Our headquarters? "

Deliberately ignoring Josh's question Mitch continued. "I have to report in every day but basically I'm on detached service as long as I'm investigating the Tong, almost undercover. I'll be able to spend most of my time working with you."

As Mitch promised, the house was huge. Five bedrooms and three baths. Josh and Fern settled into a bedroom suite at the opposite end of the upstairs from where Mitch was staying.

"As soon as you're comfortable come on down to the kitchen, I'll have coffee on," Mitch called.

At the kitchen table, Josh wasted no time. "What've you got so far?"

"Not much, but I've got an idea. Something I need you to help me do. This group is really secretive. There are a number of Tongs here, most of them do good. They're benevolent, really exist for the good of the community. But not this group. In fact it's not really a Tong, at least it's not recognized by the other Tongs as being legitimate. We haven't been able to find out who's in it at the top. Our informant says they do all their enforcing and other dirty work through teenage gangs. We think they may be a secret splinter group of one of the larger Tongs, trying to usurp power."

"You think Leung's involved with them?"

"No question."

"So how do we get at them?"

"We're going to get at them through one of the teen gangs. I've spotted one of them and I think we can rough them up a little and get them to talk, okay?"

"So we'll start at the bottom and work our way up? Sounds like a plan!"

"And I'm almost positive we'll have some real leverage on the teen gang leader. A source told me that he was probably paid to kill Charley Fong."

Fern questioned. "A teenager? Shot and killed someone on order? How're you going to capture him if they're carrying guns?"

Josh directed his answer to both Fern and Mitch. "First of all they're not all teenagers. They started out as a teen gang years ago but now lots of them are in their early twenties. And you're right they're dangerous as hell. My plan is to catch them in the streets, unawares. A lot of what they do is sell protection to shop owners, protection from themselves. If the shop owner doesn't pay up, he gets a broken window or something worse. They're really flagrant about it, operating in broad daylight. I figure if we seem to be kind of accidentally in their way when they're hassling some merchant they won't pull guns on us, 'specially in broad daylight."

Mitch agreed. "I think you're probably right. You think we can take 'em out before they know what hit them. Like we did before. How big a gang are they."

"Usually five or six. They're not particularly big or well-trained in Karate or anything, just willing to be vicious. The two of us should be able to take them out easily."

"Then what"

"We convince the leader he should be cooperative with us."

"What about the rest of them?"

"We might be able to convict them on something or somehow break them up."

"So you have all the answers, just when do we do all this?"

"Right now. I got a tip that the gang is out doing their rounds. They go around collecting their bribes and dealing out their brand of

justice on a regular route. Everybody steers clear of them on the streets.
We can follow them until we get an opportunity to confront them."

"How many do you think?"

"In the gang? Usually five or six."

"How do we find them?"

"The tip said they were on Grant almost to Broadway. Should be
easy to find."

In a short time they were on the streets of Chinatown and had no
problem finding the teen gang. As they made their way down Grant
Street, Several merchants were more than willing to tell them that the
gang had been by that day and which way they were going. Once they
found them they surreptitiously followed the six gang members
swaggering their way from store to store.

Mitch said, "I think I recognize the tall guy. His name's Cho-Lai.
He's been around a long time and has a really bad reputation. Probably
in his mid-twenties. Usually he and his brother work together. They're
both vicious. Cho-Lai's the one rumored to have killed Fong."

They continued to follow the gang at a distance, looking for the
right opportunity. At the end of one block, a store had a banner on its
front proclaiming "Grand Opening."

The six members gathered in front of the store for a few minutes
and then the tall one, the one Mitch had identified as Cho-Lai went in.
He was inside for a few minutes then came out and conferred with his
gang. Suddenly, one of the gang pulled a short crow bar from his jacket,
strolled over the storefront window and smashed it to smithereens.

Cho-Lai re-entered the store just as the owner rushed into the
street. Cho-Lai grabbed his arm and hustled him back into the store. In
a short time he emerged waving a wad of bills. Josh and Mitch could
hear him say in Chinese, "Guess what, we got a new customer."

Laughing and sharing the money, they again started swaggering
up the street, taking up the whole sidewalk, only to be confronted by
two unarmed, plain-clothed men who refused to get out of their way.
Josh and Mitch.

"Get the fuck outa the way, asshole."

Mitch glanced a Josh. "What do you think? Should we move?"

"It wasn't a very nice request, was it? I think we should stay."

The two groups were separated by about twenty feet. Cho-Lai
stepped forward and the others followed as he said, "It's your neck,
asshole. We're comin through and we'll take you out if we need to."

Josh calmly stood his ground and replied, "I don't think so, Cho-Lai."

The use of his name stopped him in his tracks. "Who the fuck are you, police?" Then, answering his own question, "No, you ain't the police. You'd be flashing badges and calling for reinforcements. Some sort of do gooder? Whatever, it don't matter."

With that he started forward again and told the gang to follow him.

"Come on, let's get this garbage out of our way."

The gang surged toward Josh and Mitch, just as they'd anticipated. Josh glanced at Mitch. "Four and two?"

Mitch, without taking his eyes off the approaching gang said, "which two are mine?"

"I'll take Cho-Lai and the three next to him, the rest are yours, on my signal."

They waited until the gang was about five feet from them and then, on Josh's signal, they exploded.

Josh leaped to his left, covering the distance between himself and Cho-Lai in an instant. He was already in a twirling motion when he landed, and continuing it he swept both legs out from under Cho-Lai. As he fell Josh threw a crushing blow at his throat and knocked him retching to the ground. Continuing the motion and using his arm's momentum he chopped the edge of his hand to the nose of the teen standing next to Cho-Lai, breaking it. The kid sank to his knees, blood running profusely from his nose. He was out of the fray.

He paused for a second and glanced at Mitch. He had one out cold on the ground and an arm lock on the other, totally under control. The two remaining gang members of his four targets were just beginning to react, so fast had Josh's attack been. One of them lunged forward to attack him. Josh used his momentum against him. In a lightning fast move, he grabbed his wrist, dropped to his knee and flipped the teen over his head. He heard the kids arm crack as he landed. The remaining teen started to back away and reaching behind his back pulling a gun from his belt. Josh, from his kneeling position, launched himself toward the gunman. Before the kid could aim the gun, Josh disabled him with a hand chop to his forearm. The kid's arm was instantly paralyzed and the gun fell to the ground. Josh whirled and kicked the outside part of the kid's knee. He heard it snap.

CHAPTER 58

Josh turned back to Cho-Lai, who was writhing on the sidewalk. Everything had happened so fast, passerby's were just beginning to stop.

He asked Mitch, "Which one is Cho-Lai's brother?"

Mitch pointed to the tallest of the two he had pinned to the ground. "That's him."

"Okay. Grab him and I'll take Cho-Lai. Leave the others here. We need to get the heck out of here, before any uniforms show up." Josh surveyed the scene. Two teen's out could, another with a broken nose, one with a smashed knee and the last with a broken arm. They weren't going to be terrorizing any merchants again. Not for a long time. They left them there with a gathering audience.

With that they marched their two captives to the next corner, pushed them up the hill and shoved the still dazed pair into Mitch's car.

Mitch drove and Josh used the brothers' belts to lock their elbows together behind their backs, even though they were both still groggy. Mitch glanced at his watch.

"Jesus, that only took three minutes. Seems like a half-hour. Are they both still out of it?"

"They're okay, just coming around now. Put them face down on the seat, they don't need to know where we take them."

"Where shall we take them?," Mitch whispered. Can't use the house, too public." Mitch paused for a minute then: "Wait, I've got it. There's an abandoned warehouse on the embarcadero. It's got a lot of police yellow on it and we have to roust squatters out of it every so often, but we can use it and nobody'd be the wiser."

The warehouse was huge and on the bay. The front had an abandoned restaurant in it, the rear overhung the water. Mitch opened a truck-sized door and drove in.

"We've got the whole place to ourselves and there's some offices in the back that'll be really private for us."

As they unloaded the two from the car, Cho-Lai suddenly leaped forward and tried to butt Josh in the stomach.

Josh easily sidestepped the lunge and casually knocked him back to the ground.

"Not as out of it as you looked, huh?" Cho-Lai glared at him. Josh realized that he was indeed a pretty tough kid. In order to get the information they wanted he would have to play hard ball.

The offices must have been abandoned in a hurry. They were still furnished with desks, chairs and filing cabinets. All the desk and filing cabinet drawers were hanging open and empty. All the windows overlooked the bay and were boarded up on the outside, except one. One was open. Someone had opened it and pried off the boards, letting light into the room.

They quickly tied them to chairs with torn-up pieces of the kid's shirts. They were across the room and within eyesight of each other. As a further precaution Mitch suggested they tie each of them to adjoining radiators. Now they were tied and immobilized. It should seem pretty hopeless to them. Josh figured he had to convince one or the other how hopeless their situation was. So far Cho-Lai had been knocked down twice by Josh, rather easily. Josh planned to further intimidate Cho-Lai by demonstrating once and for all how much physical power he had over him.

Stepping out of the offices for a moment they cooked up a plan.

Back in the office Mitch approached the brother while Josh quietly walked up to Cho-Lai. Bending over him, he started untying the makeshift torn shirts they'd used as ropes. First he untied his ankles and then started untying his wrists which been tied to the radiator. As he loosened the fastenings he talked to Cho-Lai.

"You might as well get used to the place. No one knows where we are and this place's been empty for months." He wanted to destroy any hope Cho-Lai might have of his gang rescuing him. Mitch produced hand cuffs.

By untying his hands and feet Josh knew he would be giving Cho-Lai an opportunity to attack him. He attached a pair of cuffs to one of Cho-Lai's wrists. Pretending to be momentarily distracted by something Mitch was doing, he glanced away from Cho-Lai and gave him the opportunity he was waiting for. Using the arm to which the cuff was attached, Cho-Lai swung the cuffs at Josh's head with all his strength.

At the same time he lunged up from his knees and tried to knee Josh's groin. Josh was ready for it, and in fact had been counting on it.

With practiced ease, Josh toyed with Cho-Lai. He easily deflected the handcuff attack and turned away to deflect the knee jab. Purposely, he let Cho-Lai get to his feet and think he had a chance to escape. He charged Josh and tried to slash him with the cuff still attached to his right arm. Josh wasn't where Cho-Lai thought he would be. Superhumanly fast, Josh sidestepped the rush, and using Cho-Lai's momentum against him, grasped his arm and swung him head first against the radiator. Dazed, Cho-Lai picked himself up and, a little more carefully advanced a second time against Josh. This time he adopted a martial arts stance and said, "I'm going to kill you!"

Suddenly he launched a karate kick at Josh. Laughing, Josh easily sidestepped the kick and moved toward his opponent at the same time. As he slid into Cho-Lai he jabbed his elbow into Cho-Lai's neck, temporarily paralyzing it and knocking him to the floor again. Cho-Lai struggled to his knees and threw himself at Josh's legs, trying to wrestle him to the floor. Once again, Josh had anticipated the move and was so anchored to the floor, he was unmovable. Josh reached down, grabbed a handful of long black hair and lifted Cho-Lai up to his feet.

To Cho-Lai's dismay, Josh said, "This is fun, you enjoying it?" And sweeping his legs out from under him again, left him lying prostrate on the floor. Cho-Lai just curled up and lay there. To further make his point, Josh pointedly took his time cutting all his clothes off and cuffing him to the radiator.

Mitch had allowed the brother to witness Cho-Lai's humiliation while he was stripping and cuffing him.

Josh motioned Mitch over to the corner of the room and whispered, "I think we can talk to them now. They don't have a clue as to who we are. They may think we're thugs like they are. They don't know where they are, their gang's been beaten up, they gotta be worried. I'll play that part to the hilt and threaten to feed them to the sharks unless they tell us who they take orders from. Just follow my lead, okay?"

CHAPTER 59

"Cho-Lai! You don't know who we are, do you? Fact is, nobody knows *who and where we are!* Your gang's beat up, nobody's coming to save you. You're in a shit pot full of trouble. My orders are to get certain information out of you or feed you to the sharks. If I get the info I want, you'll go to the police, if not, it's shark bait for your brother."

"Go to Hell!"

"Okay by me." Turning to Mitch, Josh said, "Open the windows and get all the sash weights and cords. There're eight windows, that's sixteen sash weights, eight for each of them. That should be enough to keep their bodies down. We can use the sash cord to tie them better."

Hesitating only momentarily, Mitch started opening the windows and removing the sash cords and weights. After the fourth window he used the cords to tie the brother up more securely and attached all eight weights to his legs. The brother was staring at Cho-Lai.

Josh told him to lengthen the rope on the weights. "Use a longer piece of rope on the weights and drag him over to the open window. You can lay him on his back with his legs up to the window and drop the weights outside. Then we don't have to lift the weights and him together when we feed him to the sharks."

Cho-Lai's brother plaintively raised his voice, "Cho-Lai?"

Cho-Lai sneered, "don't worry, they're bluffing."

Josh turned to Mitch, "put him on the sill."

The brother once more called out, "Cho-Lai?" He was precariously balanced on the window sill, hands still tied, with eight sash weights hanging below him, trying to pull him off and into the bay.

Mitch was really into the game. He had one hand holding on to the brother's arm, keeping him from falling.

"I let go, he's gone."

"Okay, okay! You win! What d'ya wanna know?"

"Not much. You see, we know you shot Charley Fong!"

"Bullshit!"

Turning again to Mitch, Josh said, "See, that's the problem with these punks. When they deny something we know is the truth, how can we trust anything they say? I think we should just go ahead and get rid of them! What do you think?"

"Maybe you're right. How're we going to know if they're ever telling the truth? What'd the boss say?"

Josh took his time. Finally he answered. "He left it entirely up to us. 'Said we needed to do something to these punks to scare the hell out of the others. The last thing he said was he didn't think anybody'd miss 'em if they just disappeared. Like maybe into the bay?'."

Cho-Lai had been following their conversation. Suddenly he spoke up."I didn't shoot him, they wanted me to but I ain't no murderer."

"Ah Hah. I'm told that's not true. You've got a rep as a killer. Let's say I believe you. So who are they?"

"Christ, I can't tell you that. They'll kill me!"

"Let's see. What your saying is, if you tell us they might find out about it and maybe catch you and maybe they'll kill you. On the other hand, if you don't tell us what we want, we've already got you and we will kill you. Some choice!"

"But you don't understand. It's the gang. You don't know the Chinese gang. I'd have to move away, never see my family again. You're a round eye, you have no idea of how powerful these gangs are."

Josh abruptly switched to fluid Chinese. Both brothers and were astonished. "You can't tell me anything about the Tong I don't already know except which one ordered the killing! Now make the choice. Jail or death! Which is it?"

Cho-Lai caved. "All right, I'll tell you. But you gotta get us to jail safe!"

"We'll personally deliver you!"

Whispering, Cho-Lai said, "It's the On Sing Family Association."

Josh turned to Mitch and whispering, asked if he knew of them.

"Absolutely, but all good things. They're one of the oldest Tongs and really looked up to. I don't believe him. There's no way the On Sing family is mixed up in murder. He must be lying."

"Let's keep him on ice and find out."

Mitch asked Cho-Lai a question. "How do you know it was the On Sing family?"

"He said so."

"Who said so?"

"Mr. Lee. He said he was from the Tong and needed my help. Said it was a super secret favor I'd be doing for them and they'd make it worth my while. He said that that detective was blackmailing someone high up in the Tong and he needed to be eliminated. He promised me five grand to do it and keep quiet about it."

Josh pulled Mitch over to the corner of the room and whispered, "You know anyone named Lee in the Tong?"

"There's lot's of Lee's. The president's a Mr. Daniel Chinn. I know him and his family. I'd stake my life on his honesty. I think we should check out his confession with Mr. Chinn. Maybe there's something going on in the Tong we don't know about. Mr. Chinn's easy to see, I could arrange an appointment today."

Josh returned to Cho-Lai. "Okay, you've won yourself a little time while we check out your story and it better check out. You're sticking with your story?. Last chance."

Cho-Lai said it was all true and wrote a complete confession before Mitch removed the weights from the brother.

Mitch went back to his car and returned with an unopened roll of duct tape. They taped the brothers' legs and arms together and gagged each of them. Duct tape, when applied in several layers and then criss-crossed between their ankles and wrists is virtually impossible for even a superhumanly strong person to break. The brothers were secure. As an added precaution Josh used more of the tape to link their arms and legs together behind their backs and then to a radiator

CHAPTER 60

"So what do you know about the On Sing Association?," Josh asked Mitch.

. "First off, they have the whole third floor of a building on Grant Street, right in the heart of Chinatown. I think they own the whole building. Like I said, their current leader is a very respected businessman. His Name's Daniel Chinn. His reputation's terrific."

"So you think he's not involved in this? Maybe Cho-Lai lied to us?"

"No. I think he's right. I think the On Sing Association's involved, but maybe Chinn isn't. There was a Tong leader killed a while ago and the murder was never solved. That was one faction against another. That may be going on again. Right now the association's reputation is pretty much benevolent. Every once in a while a group of young hotshots want to turn it into a get rich quick scheme for themselves. Blackmail, protection rackets, intimidation, even murder. That may be the real reason for having Fong killed."

"You think there's a faction inside the Tong that wants to take it over and they'd murder to do it?"

"Don't kid yourself. It's just like the old time China Tongs. There's a struggle going on all the time for control. I wouldn't be surprised if that's what this is all about, a younger group within the Tong trying to take over."

"So you think Cho-Lai might have been truthful. There is a Mr. Lee claiming to represent the On Sing Tong and he paid for Fong to be killed? Makes sense if they were looking to Leung for capital. Fong snitched on Leung, they need to protect Leung 'cause they need his money to finance their fight against your Mr. Chinn."

"That sure fills in all the gaps, doesn't it."

"So can we talk to Chinn?"

It was still early and Mitch thought they could get in to see Chinn before the dinner hour. A phone call set up an appointment within the hour.

On the way Mitch filled Josh in on what little they knew about the On Sing Tong. It wasn't much. Rumors that there was friction between the older and younger members. Rumors that the younger members would like to get rid of the elders. But what was always true with the Chinese Associations, was that very little was actually known about them that the Chinese didn't want known. Even the Chinese detectives were kept in the dark.

The building that Mitch took Josh to was located in the heart of Chinatown, facing on Grant Street. The entire first floor of the building was occupied by Chinese merchants and took up a large part of the block. The front door was small and had a restaurant on one side and a gift shop on the other. An elevator took them up to the third floor.

It wasn't at all what Josh expected. Most of the entire third floor had been opened up into one large hall. Sitting and standing in lines snaking around the hall were about thirty-five to forty Chinese people. Josh and Mitch were directed to an office at the front of the building. Rather sparse, it contained four quite elderly Chinese men and one much younger that Josh judged to be about fifty. A large window gave a view of the activities going on in the hall. Josh noticed that every minute or two the first person in line out in the hall would be called into an office on the other side of the room. Shortly thereafter he or she would emerge carrying some papers and head back down the stairs, only to be replaced by a new one coming up the stairs.

His attention was snapped back to the group in the office when the younger one said, "What's this about a murder? You're trying to blame a murder on us?" Turning to Mitch he challenged him. "You know me better than that, don't you?"

Mitch had told Josh that he had once been introduced to Mr. Chinn. Evidently Mr. Chinn recognized and remembered him.

Mitch took control of the meeting in true police fashion. "Can we sit? And yes, I do know you better than that. But I think there may be something going on you don't know about. We think that some young hot heads in your Association are committing crimes in your name. Including maybe murder."

"What murder?"

"You probably didn't know him. He was an unlicensed Chinese private detective, kinda operating under the radar."

"Charley Fong? Of course I knew who he was. We were well aware of his illegal venture but he wasn't doing any harm, in fact he was sometimes productive for us. You think we had him killed? Preposterous!!"

While Mitch and Mr. Chinn were speaking, Josh studied Mr. Chinn's face. Josh revised his first impression, he now thought he might be in his early sixties, considering that many Chinese looked younger than they were. Well-dressed in a suit and tie with University of California colors, he looked the very model of a successful businessman. Josh noted that he was almost as tall as himself. He also noted that Mr. Chinn was lean and looked to be in very good shape physically. Like many Chinese he had a full head of black hair. Josh wondered what part of China his forebears came from as his face was lean also. Tall and lean, from northern China? He also seemed to be a very serious gentleman.

Mitch held up his hand. "Oh no, sir. We don't think you had anything to do with it. We think somebody used your Tong's name to hire the killer. We think a part of your association is responsible without your knowledge."

"No way! I would have heard about it! They're giving us a bit of trouble but nothing that serious." Turning to the four elders in the room and speaking in Chinese, he said, "I think Mitch's being manipulated into saying these things to satisfy this white cop." And still in Chinese, "Isn't that so Mitch?"

In very clear Cantonese, the language in which they'd been speaking, Josh took the lead. "If you'll sit down, Mitch and I can bring you up to date on what we've learned to date. Which, by the way, we've learned working together over the last day or so."

Obviously shocked and embarrassed by the faux pas he had just committed, Mr. Chinn apologized and invited them all to sit.

CHAPTER 61

Josh took over. In clear Chinese he said,"I'll let Mitch fill you in on what we've done to date. But, in a nutshell here's what we've found out. There is a young faction in your organization that's working behind your back to kick you out. Plus, we have a signed confession that they engineered the murder of Charley Fong."

"But there's more. They've allied themselves with a lot of money, you know Jack Leung?"

"They're getting backing from him?"

"He tried to set up an illegal Chinese drug business, killing and eviscerating wild bears for their organs. We broke that up. Now we think he's thrown in with the young faction in your Tong. They're trying to get enough money to topple you over. We heard that you denied them money some time ago?"

"You're right, we did. It was obvious they were going in a direction we didn't believe in so we said no to them."

"Maybe that's what triggered all this. The worst part though, is that they've enlisted the teen Chinese gangs to do their dirty work for them. The murder confession we got is from one of these leaders of the teen gang. He told us that your Tong had ordered the killing."

Mr. Chinn's outward demeanor didn't change upon hearing all this, but his tone of voice was agitated as he turned to the elders and asked in Chinese, "how could this happen without our knowing about it?"

One of them replied. "It has to be young Lee. Wasn't it he that tried to borrow money from us? He's an impatient young fool."

Mr. Chinn replied, "Yes, he did try to borrow money. Said something about building up the younger membership. But trying to overthrow me? I don't see it."

Another of the elders said, "The signs are there if you look for them. He's got a young clique around him. He's been avoiding our regular meetings and I've heard that he's been having clandestine meetings outside of our hall. He's certainly up to something."

"We've got to do something. If people think we're condoning murders or other gang activities of this sort, it'll ruin our reputation."

Josh interrupted. "That's why we came to you. We broke up Leung's gang of bear killers but we missed Leung. We're going to get Leung and to get him we need to break up your young turks. So if we work together it can be mutually beneficial. Like for example, we know your Tong's been identified as the source for at least one murder. You know that's not true and it's a group within your Tong that's turned bad. And you know the name of the probable leader."

"Mr. Chinn directed his attention to Mitch, "I don't know in what capacity you're working. Is this an official police investigation?"

"Yes and no. I've been officially tasked with identifying and breaking up the gang that caused the murders. But the way Josh and I are going about it is unofficial as hell."

Turning to Josh, Mr. Chinn asked, "And who are you, my Chinese-speaking Caucasian friend?"

Josh gave him a brief history of his Ranger duties and his experience working with the SF chief of police. He also mentioned his studies in China but didn't mention any of his martial arts experience. "I'm here mostly to help Mitch on a private basis."

"Okay, let's assume that what you've told us is correct. What can I do about it? Can't the police arrest Lee for murder?"

"All we've got so far is a confession mentioning the On Sing Tong. Nothing provable about Lee or Leung. We need your help in identifying who you think might be in the dissident group and a way to get at them. That'd be a beginning."

Mr. Chinn made a snap decision. "All right. Meet us here tomorrow morning at eight-thirty and we'll get started. But, not a word of this to anyone, right? Not your police chief, no one! We'll investigate first and then decide what to do. Agreed?"

They agreed. On the way back to their headquarters and Fern, Mitch asked Josh what he thought they'd accomplished.

"Lots. We got the probable identification of the faction within the On Sing Tong and it's leader's name. We got the consent of the Tong to help us. We found out that the actual Tong leadership isn't involved. Plus we're sure that Leung's involved with Lee. We get Lee, we'll get Leung. We're moving !"

"I hope Mr. Chinn comes through for us."

"He will. Tomorrow we're going big game hunting. We'll try to beard this guy Lee in his den. If he's the guy behind the teen gangs and Leung's tied in with him, we need to know that. I think we'll drop in on him."

"That could be dangerous. What if the guys we left in the street reported back to him and he knows about us. Hell, he might already have his teen gangs looking for us. We might be walking into a trap !"

"I've got an idea, if Mr. Chinn will help us."

They had an early night and agreed to have breakfast early enough to go over their case together before their meeting with Mr. Chinn.

CHAPTER 62

As it turned out, Mr. Chinn was more than eager to help them.

"Of course, I'll be happy to put you in touch with Lee. I don't know what good it will do, I'm certain he won't admit anything." Mr. Chinn spoke with almost an old world courtliness, and his English, while colloquial, was very good.

He continued. "We talked about this situation last night after you left. For some time we've been increasingly aware of and concerned about the rise in Chinese teenage gangs. They've expanded in size and become more and more dangerous. They're carrying knives and guns and are a threat to our community and to our visitors. Now it seems from what you've told us that these gangs are being recruited and organized against the better interests of our community."

The three elders behind him said nothing, but nodded in agreement to what he was saying.

Mitch added. "The police have been aware of the increasing incidents of teen gang activities and are worried about an all out war between the several gangs we're aware of."

"Yes." Replied Mr. Chinn. "And we have a proposition for you. We're not police nor are we experts on gang activities. However it seems to us that if the teen gangs were broken up it would solve most of the problems. It would make our streets safer. It would take Mr. Lee's power away and it would probably result in the capture of your Mr. Leung."

For a few minutes there was silence in the room. All eyes were on Josh.

Finally he answered. "In effect you're asking us to put the gangs out of business?" He turned to Mitch.

"What are we talking about here? How many gangs, how many teens?"

"We think three or four gangs of any size or consequence, maybe 30 or 40 kids total, including Cho-Lai's gang. And Josh, this is what I was supposed to be doing, remember? I was tasked to find and break up these Chinese gangs."

"So it would be the two of us against maybe 40 teenagers carrying guns and knives?" Josh wasn't sure.

"Actually it'd be the two of us against one gang at a time. Maybe two against ten or twelve? And Josh, we've already partly broken up one gang, remember Cho-Lai. I think we could do it. These kids are scary and unpredictable, but they're also untrained. Kind of a mob mentality. I think we could do it and as Mr. Chinn said, it'd help solve all our problems."

Josh had been thinking. "I think the best way would be to pit one gang against another. You already said there was a lot of bad blood between them. Maybe we can use that to our advantage."

"Then you'll do it?" Mr. Chinn eagerly asked. "We'll help all we can. We can be your eyes and ears."

"We don't want a lot of people knowing what we're doing, Mr. Chinn. The way I see this developing is that Mitch and I'll spy on at least two gang locations and try to set them against each other."

Josh had come up with idea on the spur of the moment as a response to Mr. Chinn's request.

"Mitch, what do you think? Can we make that idea work?"

"So you think we can take advantage of the gang rivalry and start a war between them?"

"Why not? They're hot-blooded teens, accustomed to bullying their way around. Should be a cinch! They'll be so busy attacking each other, they won't be of any use to Mr. Lee."

Mitch thought it over for a minute. "But what about breaking up the gangs for good?"

"We'll do the same number we did on Cho-Lai. We'll figure out who the leader is of each gang and neutralize them."

Mr. Chinn interrupted. "Wait a minute. We won't condone any killing."

Josh answered. "Neither will the police. We'll do the same as we did with Cho-Lai. We'll scare the hell out of him and embarrass him in front of his peers. The only kids that got hurt were ones that were attacking one of your merchants."

Mitch added. "And these so called kids had guns and were threatening us."

Mr. Chinn conferred with the three elders for a few minutes and then turned back to Josh and Mitch. "We asked around earlier and found that one of the gangs hangs out at a garage on O'Farrell near Van Ness."

Josh turned to Mitch. "You know where that is?"

"Of course."

"But." Mr. Chinn interjected, "they're not there all the time."

"Okay. It's a beginning," Josh replied. He and Mitch decided to check out the garage immediately.

It turned out to be body shop. Josh and Mitch parked in a two-story parking lot across the street and watched. It was midmorning and business was slow. A few cars in and out but they sighted no individuals. On the outside it looked very normal.

"I'll walk over and take a look-see." Mitch said.

In a few minutes he was back. "It's a pretty big place. A small office and counter on the right front as you enter. Then, there're a bunch of lifts on either side of the place and a pretty good size-room at the rear on the left. If the guys meet here that's the place."

"How many doors to the little room?"

"Three, but two of them are side by side way at the rear. I'm pretty sure they're labeled Men and Women. The door we're interested in is at the front, it's partly open and I could see at least two teens in there."

"What about the employees?"

"They're all Chinese and really busy working on the cars. I don't think they even knew I was there. I had to bang on a bell to get one of them to talk to me."

"Okay, I've got a plan. I think we should move right now if you're sure there're two of them in there now. You waltz in as if you belong there, I'll take them by surprise."

CHAPTER 63

"Won't work! Everyone in the neighborhood's Chinese. You'll stand out like a sore thumb."

"Not if they don't see me! And believe me, they won't! You go in first, casually walk to the back room, throw open the door and walk in big as life. They're probably just sitting around, maybe watching TV. Now, the next part's important. Walk clear across the room and stand there. With your back to them so they can't see your face. Their eyes'll be riveted on you with their backs to the door. Before they can say boo, I'll be through the door and have them on the ground. They'll never see me."

"What if there's three of them?"

"No problem, trust me. I can handle a lot more than that."

"What about the mechanics, they'll be able to identify you."

"They'll never see me, never know I've been there!"

"Then what?"

"Then we leave them. Hog-tied, gagged and blindfolded with a note from the other gang. Something simple, maybe scrawled on the wall. Something like, 'Get the fuck out of our On Sing business. Next time it'll be a lot worse. Do we know the name of the gangs?"

"Cho-Lai's gang calls themselves the Dragons, but they're kinda decimated. I think this one's the Tigers and one of the other big ones call themselves the Fire. There may be one more I don't know the name of."

"So we sign the Fire's name?"

"Yeah, and then tomorrow we'll strike back at the Fire and leave a note from the Tigers. We'll have them at each others throats in no time. Then we can pick them off when they're diverted against each other."

"Should make these guys madder'n hell, if we can make it work."

"It'll work! We'll make it work. We'll be like puppet masters. We'll keep pulling the strings until they blow up! Let's do it before any more show up. "

CHAPTER 64

Mitch hurried down the parking lot stairs, Josh right behind him and walking across the street, calmly walked into the body shop, past the owner, the mechanics and a customer and made his way to the rear of the shop. Only a couple of the mechanics even glanced at him. Mitch turned his face away and waved casually continuing toward the restrooms at the rear.

Pausing for a second at the door, he could hear a television program inside. He glanced behind him expecting to see Josh tailing him. Josh was nowhere to be seen.

"What the hell've I got myself into. Oh well, onward and upward." He opened the door.

While Mitch was distracting everyone's attention, Josh flitted through the shop, ghosting from car to car, not noticed by anyone.

Following Josh's instructions, Mitch quickly walked across the room and stood with his back to the room. As Josh had predicted, they turned to face Mitch, not noticing Josh's appearance in the doorway.

"Who the fuck do you think you are?" one of the gang asked as he drew a gun. "Get him!" another said.

In a flash Josh assessed the situation. Two teens with drawn guns, a small room made even smaller because of tables and chairs scattered around. And Mitch, unarmed, face against the wall, depending on Josh to save the day.

Because of the limited space, Josh used the walls as weapons. The teen's chairs had been overturned when they jumped up. Now they lay on the floor directly between Josh and the two teens, right in his way. Josh made a sideways leap, caromed off the wall, over the two chairs and landed lightly next to and slightly behind the nearest teen. He kept his momentum and using a powerful leg sweep, hit the kid in the upper arm, dislodged the gun from his hand, and knocked him to the floor. At the same time he delivered a hand chop to the forearm of the second gunman, paralyzing his arm and forcing his gun to drop. Before the two could turn and confront him he continued his momentum, performing a speed vault. He leaped sideways to his right, straightened his body using his hand on the desk and changed direction, coming at the two from a different angle. He pivoted on his left leg and swept both the teens to the ground with his right leg.

Quickly they were both on the floor, face down, never having gotten a glimpse of Josh. Suddenly, a shot rang out.

Josh's reaction was instantaneous! He spun and launched himself toward the doorway. With no conscious thought, he immediately known where the shot had come from. It had to have come from just outside the room, probably someone standing near the doorway. He assumed it was either from another punk just arriving or one of the mechanics. In mid-air he spotted the shooter, or at least part of him. Only a hand and arm were visible. Josh placed his right hand on the desk, made a one-handed vault and then propelled himself forward with his left arm. Spinning, he smashed his right arm onto the gun, knocking it loose. Like a flash he dropped to one knee, grabbed the shooters shirt front , dropped onto his back and with his other leg lifted and propelled the shooter over his head and across the room. He ended up next to Mitch and out cold.

Quickly, Josh swung the door open and checked the working mechanics. They evidently had heard nothing. Josh wasn't surprised. The ongoing noise of air guns and metal work made it hard to talk, let alone hear anything.

"Mitch, you okay?" Josh whispered as he closed the door quickly gathered up a total of three guns.

"I think so, Josh. I can't find any blood, but I think I got shot!"

"Let's take a look."

Mitch took off his jacket and Josh looked at his shoulder. "A big red angry looking welt, but no blood." Looking around, he said, "Are you a Buddhist?"

"Nope, maybe a Christian, why? Is it that bad?"

"Well you got dinged by a Buddha. This little statue looks like it got shot." Josh held up a small figure that'd fallen to the floor. "I bet it took the bullet and then banged into you hard enough to make you think you'd been shot. I think you're going to survive."

"Who the hell is that?" Mitch asked, pointing to the unconscious teen on the floor.

"That shot you?" Josh rolled him over. "Just another teen."

CHAPTER 65

"Now what?" asked Mitch.

"Blindfold and tie these guys up before they see me. Better gag them too. Then we'll scrawl our message on the wall. Find something to write with."

After tying them up they explored the drawers of the desks.

Mitch found what they needed. "How about a bright red wide-tipped Sharpie?"

"Perfect." Josh had to straddle the body of one of the teens to get to a clear section of the wall. He penned the message they'd agreed on in bold, bright red colors and signed it "Fire" with a broad flourish.

"Beautiful," commented Mitch. "Now you got any ideas how we get out of here without being seen and before another gang member shows up?"

"Yeah, there should be a window in the toilet. All we need to do is sneak a few feet from here to the men's room, pry the window open and disappear. Should be a piece of cake."

Mitch quietly inched the door open and ascertained that all the mechanics were totally absorbed in their work and not looking their way.

"It's clear. I don't think they pay much attention to these kids."

In a few minutes they were in the men's room. As Josh had predicted, there was a shoulder high window. It was filthy dirty and nailed shut. Josh produced an extremely small, tough and sharp piece of steel from his pocket. With it he was able to pry the nails loose and force the window open.

Mitch said, "Jesus, I bet that window hasn't been opened in years. Good thing you had that little doohickey with you."

"Never without it. It's a Ninja thing." He hoisted himself up on the window shelf. "It's a short drop to an alley and just a few feet to the street. Let's go."

They followed the alley to the street, turned away from the garage and walked around the block to get back to their car unobserved.

"Now what, how do we get the other gang involved?"

"First we have to find them. Did Mr. Chinn have any info on where the other gang hangs out?"

"Yeah. He said they hang out at a fast food place just below Chinatown. Said the owner's complained about them a whole bunch of times. Says they just hang out there and play the pinball machines. He complains that they scare his customers away."

"Did he say how many?"

"Yeah, but it varies. Sometimes one or two, sometimes a half dozen or more."

"Do you know where the place is? It's not even noon yet, let's take a look."

"Sure I know where the place is. But don't you think we should wait until the rest of the Tigers show up and find their buddies all tied up and gagged? And what about Fern? You should spend some time with her."

"Don't worry about Fern. In the first place, she's not here in the City. She's down in Palo Alto visiting some of her old school buddies from Stanford. In the second place, she's treating this outing just as she would if we were in Yosemite. She says, "Your job's not a nine to fiver, sometimes you have to work 'til the jobs done. I expect to see you when I see you and not a moment sooner.""

"Where do I find a wife like that?"

"In Alaska, where else?" And he told Mitch about Fern's adventures, all alone in the dead of winter in the wilds of Alaska. He concluded, "she's not a loner but she sure can take care of herself. A perfect policeman's wife."

Mitch turned serious. "We, that is, you, can't go to that restaurant. You can't confront the gang in broad daylight and have them believe you're part of the other gang. In case you haven't noticed, you're not Chinese."

"Okay, no confrontation, but let's take a look at them, maybe lightening will strike. Plus, I want to keep the pot boiling."

They parked Mitch's car on a side hill street about a half block from their target. Well concealed behind a large van, they had a clear view of anyone approaching or leaving the restaurant.

Mitch walked down to the empty restaurant, flashed his badge and found that the gang usually started dribbling in around noon. Usually just a couple or so at first then more later.

"Just in time to scare my lunch crowd away," the owner lamented. "They don't even buy much. Mostly they hang around the pin ball machines and drink a coke or two. And harass my customers. Can't you do something?"

"Maybe." Mitch replied. "I'm undercover investigating them. Be patient a little while longer, we'll see what we can do." He took a business card and left.

Back at the car he informed Josh, "A couple of them might come by any minute according to the owner. It might be a chance to get them away from the others if we work fast enough. The owner said these two are usually the first to arrive and are here alone for a while. You got any ideas?"

"Did the owner say how they get there?"

"Yeah, they have an old T-bird. Not the collectable ones, just an old sedan."

"Okay, I got an idea, let's wait 'til they drive up and see what happens."

A half-hour went by. "Maybe they're not coming today." from Mitch.

"Hang on, be patient."

Another half-hour disappeared before the old T-bird drove up. The two kids parked it in a delivery only spot about a half block from the store, took their time getting out and swaggered over to the lunch shop.

"Just the two of them, what'll we do?"

"You got the phone number of the store?"

"Yeah, in my pocket."

"Okay, call it and tell the owner that you have a message for the guys that have the T-bird outside. When you get them on the phone tell them that somebody just slashed all four of their tires. They'll be outa there in nothing flat. And we'll be behind their car waiting for them."

"Sure. And they'll be madder'n hell, holding guns, running right at us. Some plan!"

CHAPTER 66

"Okay, we'll hide behind one of the cars between the store and their car. Then when they pass us, we'll get them from behind. They're teens, just kids. They'll be off guard, untrained, easy to surprise. Better?"

"If you say so, like I always say, live dangerously. But don't forget, odds are these kids are carrying. We have to be fast and careful."

With that they drove down and parked near the teens car. Mitch made the phone call. They found a small van they could conceal themselves behind two cars behind the T-bird.

"Perfect," Josh said. "They can't see us and we can circle around the back of the van as they pass and rush them from behind. They'll be totally concentrated on their car. I'll trip them up, you jump on one and I'll do the other. In a moment we'll have them tied and gagged and outa here."

"How you going to trip them up?"

"With this" and Josh unwound a belt-like, long piece of fabric from his waist. It unrolled to be about twelve feet long and four inches wide. He knotted his throwing knife into the center of it.

"From behind I can sweep their legs out from under them with this. All we'll have to do is pick them up and cart them away."

The front door of the restaurant crashed open. The two teens burst into the street yelling obscenities and ran toward their car, carrying guns and elbowing pedestrians out of the way. In a moment they were opposite the van. Mitch and Josh quickly and quietly fell in behind them and in a few steps were right on their tail. Josh swung his improvised sling around his head one time and then crashed it across all four legs in front of him. The boys went down in a pile. Mitch and Josh pounced on the boys and forced their faces into the sidewalk, immobilizing them. Josh extracted his knife, cut the sash into several pieces and blindfolded and gagged the kids.

A half-dozen or so pedestrians had come to a halt and were watching the action. None of them said a word. Mitch pulled his badge from his pocket and flashed it. The crowd melted away.

Josh said, "Quick, load them into your car and we're outta here before any more of the gang shows up."

In a moment they had the two trussed up, gagged and blindfolded. Mitch had just started to pull out of the parking place when a pick-up truck crashed into his front fender and three teenagers poured out, waving guns. Mitch's car was pinned. In a moment guns were leveled at both Josh and Mitch. They were ordered out of the car and made to stand in the classic police pose, hands against the hood of the car with their feet spread wide apart.

One, a little older than the rest, boldly walked up behind them, kicked Josh's feet further apart and savagely hit him behind his ear with his gun butt. Josh sagged to the ground, out cold.

As the gags were being removed from the kids in the car, one called out, "Jeff, let me have a shot at the other one."

Jeff, the one that hit Josh, whirled on him and said, "shut the fuck up. If you wasn't so goddam fuckin' dumb, you wouldn't've got caught. I should be beatin the crap outa you." With that he clobbered Mitch on the side of his head. Mitch, with a groan, tried to turn and defend himself, but was immediately struck again and knocked unconscious.

Turning to the rest of the gang he asked, " Anybody know who the fuck these guys are?"

Nobody answered. Jeff started issuing orders. "Toss them in the back seat of their car and drive them to our place. And for Christ's sake keep a gun on 'em."

Josh gradually came to and slowly squinted his eyes open, only to be confronted with the business end of an automatic pointed squarely at his face. He was in the back seat of the car, half lying on top of the unconscious Mitch.

"Don't move, cocksucker," came from behind the gun. Outside of a spot above his ear where the gun had hit him, Josh felt okay. He could feel stickiness at the spot and assumed it was bleeding. He didn't move, but he could feel the car was going uphill and looking up at the skyline he could tell they were still in Chinatown. They drove a short distance and into a large enclosed area. Josh thought it was probably a parking garage.

Josh feigned weakness as he and Mitch were roughly dragged from the car and into a large room a few steps away. Mitch was still out, but groaning occasionally as they manhandled him over a doorstep and into the room. As they were pushed into the room, the teens were momentarily separated from each other coming through the doorway. Josh could have easily overpowered the two guarding them, but he had to wait because of Mitch.

The one called Jeff followed them in to the room and took charge. "Tie them up and stick 'em in the corner." Josh again feigned wooziness to the point of not being able to walk without help, but his senses were on full alert. He noticed that the room was underground, the windows were small and high on the walls, probably at sidewalk height. He deduced they were in a basement, probably under a commercial building like an apartment house, because of the size of the room. The room was largely open with an assortment of unmatched chairs and sofas scattered around.

Mitch and Josh were hauled across the room and dumped on the floor in front of a large gas furnace, big enough to heat an entire building. As one teen kept his gun aimed at them, another bound their hands behind their backs and propped them up against the cold steel of the furnace.

Jeff casually approached the two, "Did anybody search them yet?" he asked. No one had. He searched Josh first and found his wallet and Ranger Identification. Neither one seemed of any interest to him. When he searched Mitch he found his badge and let out a snort of derision.

"Is this what he flashed at the gawkers?" He showed it to the two that Josh and Mitch had caught.

"That's it. One glance and they all left," they replied.

"It's gotta be a fake. Real cops wouldn't try to hi-jack us like that."

"So, what're we gonna do with them? Rough 'em up and make 'em talk?"

"Not we, me! Hand me that baseball bat. I'm gonna start on the ribs and move up. They'll cave, and it won't take long."

CHAPTER 67

Josh's head was clearing. He heard what Jeff said and looking up at him, he saw a maniacal look in Jeff's eyes. At that moment he knew he was in the presence of a psychopath. He didn't doubt for a second that Jeff would do what he threatened to do. He glanced at Mitch.

Mitch was coming around and when Josh questioned him with raised eyebrows, he signaled he was okay with a wink.

Josh then immediately began to put himself into a yoga- like trance. A combination of Chinese and Japanese training that allowed him to take complete control of isolated parts of his body. Next he concentrated on his shoulders, hands and wrists. Gradually he could feel his shoulder muscles relaxing, his hands lengthening, his fingers stretching, his wrists diminishing in size. In tests his arm reach had extended over two inches by this self-hypnosis method. At the same time he conditioned his mind and body to take a beating.

The leader, the one that Mitch had warned was probably a psycho, took up the baseball bat and proceeded to swing it against Josh's left side, hard. Then, reversing it, he swung against Josh's right side. Instantly Josh was in pain. His mind flashed to the beating taken from the pool hall gang some weeks ago. His ribs weren't fully healed from that working over. He wasn't worried about taking the beating, unless this psycho started working on his head. He had to do something, and pretty soon.

Jeff talked to him. "That's just a sample, whitey. Who the fuck sent you after us?"

Josh moaned and again feigned more hurt than he felt. He needed just a little more time. He didn't answer.

This time Jeff hit him harder, once again on each side. Josh felt the pain, like a broken or cracked rib but at the same time, as if his wrists and hands were separated from his body, he felt the cord slip off. His hands were free. He had a plan.

He needed to make Jeff hit him once again. It was obvious that Jeff was a bully. One who enjoyed beating someone completely at his mercy. Josh counted on that. He cowered. Dropped his head to his chest. As expected, he took another blow to the ribs. This time, however, Josh whipped his hand around and grabbed Jeff's arm. Jeff was leaning forward, off balance. Josh used Jeff's momentum against him and pulled him forward. As he fell Josh pivoted on one foot and swept Jeff's feet out from under him. A swift chop to the neck and Jeff was unconscious before he hit the ground.

The action had been so fast the remaining four teens were momentarily frozen in place. Without thinking, Josh continued the attack, taking advantage of their confusion. The four were grouped close together, two sitting and two standing, relaxed, enjoying the show being put on by Jeff.

To Josh, everything seemed to move to slow motion. He continued his forward motion directly at the four teens and at the last moment, dropped to his left knee and swept his right leg across the legs of the two standing. Both fell to the ground. The remaining two, relaxing in their chairs were confused by what Josh had done, slowing their reaction time.

Josh spun in his tracks, delivered a roundhouse kick to one of the two sitting and a throat chop to the other. Both fell to the floor, partially dazed. Having bought some time, Josh whirled to the first two. They were struggling to their feet, one was digging for a gun.

To reach him quickly before the gun came into play, Josh initiated a flying kick. He leaped toward the boy, covering the distance between them in a flash. As he landed he kicked the head of the boy with his right foot, knocking him out. The gun was still in his pocket.

That left the remaining teen, standing behind him. Josh threw a reverse groin kick, disabling the boy and then whirled and followed with a wheel kick to the head. He fell, out cold.

Josh double-checked Jeff's condition; he was still out cold. Josh found and gathered up all the guns, then turned to Mitch. Mitch was barely conscious and still tied up. He weakly grinned at Josh and whispered, "some show."

Josh quickly examined Mitch's head. His brow was split open and bleeding and would need stitches. Josh staunched the bleeding with his handkerchief and returned to the teens before they recovered. He dragged the leader over to the other four and bound them together, back to back. He felt stabs of pain from his rib area as he pulled them.

Mitch gathered himself together and limped over to Josh and the teens, saying, "Holy shit, Josh. That didn't quite go the way we planned, did it? He beat the crap outta you, are you okay?"

"Yeah I'm okay, what about you? I think you're gonna need some stitches. And what's with the limp?"

"I feel okay, stitches'll wait. Leg's okay too, I think I wrenched my knee when the kid knocked me down. But what the hell do we do now?"

"First off, we gotta figure out where we are. I'm pretty sure we're in Chinatown and I think we're in an unused basement under an apartment house or something like that. There's a pretty large underground garage through that door. That's the way they brought us in."

Mitch limped over to the door. "Might be a good idea to lock this in case any more of the gang shows up."

"While you're there see if we can get out that way."

"In a moment Mitch answered. "You're not going to believe this, my car's here. One of them must have driven it up."

Quickly Josh suggested he check the car for keys. "I'll be damned, they're in the ignition," Mitch called back, then added. "Nobody's here, we've got the whole place to ourselves."

Back in the room, Mitch had a thought. "Didn't Mr. Chinn say the gang was probably a half dozen or more?"

Josh had been thinking the same. "Yeah, and we only have five. But I bet Jeff here's the leader."

"So what do we do? We can't stay here, and we don't have any place to take these guys. I think we should get the hell out of here before any more of the gang shows up."

"Hang on. Let's think this through. First off, I don't think we have worry about any more of the gang. There's only one door. If any show up, we'll just add them to our collection."

"We? Don't count on me for a little while, I'm kinda the walking wounded. You're on your own for a bit."

"A breeze. Second, we haven't finished our job yet. We agreed to break up the gangs for Mr. Chinn and we haven't found Leung. I'm gonna need some time with these guys and particularly Jeff to find out what they know about Leung. So what I'm thinking is, we stay here for the time being."

"And grab any more of the gang that shows up?"

"Yep. Nobody knows we're here, we've got control of the situation and we've got plenty of time." Josh walked over and checked their prisoners, one of them had come to and was looking around groggily. He checked their bindings and turned back to Mitch.

"Keep your voice low, the kids are beginning to come around. We need to decide how we're gonna scare these kids into talking."

"What about the other gang? Do you think we can still get them to take out each other?"

"I've been thinking about that. 'Trouble is, they all carry guns. We don't want to start a bloodbath, do we?"

"You're right. So where does that leave us?'

"I think we have to handle each gang by ourselves, like what we're doing with this group. We have to dismantle the gang and scare the hell out of them. So like I said before. We stay here, work on these kids and grab any more that show up. With any luck we'll have the whole gang by the end of the day."

"How we going to get them to talk? We can't really hurt them any more than what we've already done in self defense. After all they're still kids."

"Yeah, kids with guns. Kids that were willing to watch Jeff beat the life out of me. I'm not sure that Jeff is a kid. I bet he's more like twenty-two or three, besides I think he's a psychopath. He's the one I want to work on."

CHAPTER 68

"How do you scare a psycho?"

"First we make sure they're all securely tied and gagged. Then we separate them so that they can't see each other."

Just then they heard the squeal of tires and loud music from the garage. They quickly gagged the five prisoners and walked over to stand on either side of the garage door. The music stopped and a pair of car doors slammed. Two people, or maybe more?

They could hear talking. "That's Jeff's car, who owns the other one?"

"Shit, I dunno. C'mon let's go see what's happening. "

Mitch and Josh saw the door handle turn back and forth as the teens tried to come in.

"It's locked, what the fuck's going on?"

They started pounding on the door and yelling, "C'mon guys, open the door."

Josh, muffling his voice said, "just a sec," and quietly unlocked the door. "It's open," he continued.

The door crashed in and the first teen belligerently entered. He started to complain, "Who the----." Josh grabbed his arm, used the teens forward motion and pulled him into the room, simultaneously delivered a chop to his throat. The kid dropped to the floor, gagging and dazed.

The second kid reacted quickly and lunged forward toward Josh. Josh continued his own momentum into a twirl toward the teen. He wasn't where the teen expected him to be. As the teen rushed past him, Josh grabbed his hair and swung him around and into his knee, knocking him out.

Josh glanced at Mitch."Okay. Just two of them. They're both all right, just out of it for a while, lock the door again, I'll drag these two over and tie them up with the rest."

In a few minutes, they had the two gagged and tied up. When they searched the two new arrivals they confiscated two more guns.

Mitch seemed to be almost completely recovered. The bleeding had stopped, but he had dried blood all over his forehead. Josh said, "I hope you feel better than you look."

"I'm okay, I was ready to help you with these two, but you had it over before it started. Now what, you got an idea how to make them talk?"

"Yeah I do. Humiliation. In front of his gang. I'm going to bring him around, untie him and give him a decisive lesson in martial arts. While he's being humiliated, I'll question him. He'll be so mad, so frustrated, he'll talk."

"Here? You're going to do that here?"

"Sure, where better? He'll be totally humiliated on his own turf, in front of his own gang, what could be worse for him?"

Mitch hesitated and then said, "You know the department never did officially solve Charley Fong's murder, even with the signed confession. Too many loose ends. We hypothesized that it was a gang killing and it was related to his giving up information on your old friend, Leung. We're pretty sure it had to be someone he knew or felt comfortable with and it had to be more than one person. One he let wander around his office 'cause he was found sitting in his chair with a bullet hole in the back of his head, and the other one in front of his desk talking to him."

"Yeah, I remember. I felt a little bad about that. We forced Cho-Lai to give up that information. But he really was a bad guy, I'm sure he pulled the trigger."

Mitch interrupted him. "Cho-Lai's in jail, all kinds of charges against him, but the DA's holding off on the murder charge, trying to find his accomplice. They figure Charley would let the kids in, after all, he sees them around all the time. Remember how he hung out at the same pool hall where that other gang hung out? One of those kids'd be able to waltz right in to his office pretty easy. We think Charley cultivated those kids like runners for his business. A lot of those kids are young and dumb, but the bosses like Jeff here are usually smart and vicious and capable of anything, even murder. We think Jeff's a good candidate for that murder along with Cho-Lai. Like you said, he's a psychopath."

"Are you just guessing? Do you have any actual evidence?"

"Not really. We'd heard about him and this gang. We caught one of them, a fifteen year old kid, on a breaking and entering charge. While we were interrogating him he bragged that he'd be out right away, that Jeff'll have me out before night. They asked him who Jeff was and he blurted out, 'ask Charley Fong.' Then he clammed up.

"What happened?"

"Not much. He posted bond and later the merchant dropped the charge. Somebody got to him, I suppose."

"So you think our friend Jeff here might have been with Cho-Lai. Might have murdered Fong? Why would rival gang leaders cooperate like that?"

"Money and blackmail. Somebody's pulling their strings and supplying money. Do I think Jeff here was in on it? Personally I'd bet on it, maybe even it was him pulled the trigger. It's something we can use on him, if we can figure a way to do it. Maybe taunt him about being a coward and shooting people in the back? I dunno."

CHAPTER 69

Josh shot a look across the room at their captives. They were all awake by now. Their leader was glaring at Josh and struggling with his bonds.

He told Mitch, "first, I think we should give them each an old fashioned police pat down. Make sure they're not carrying concealed knives or razors in addition to the guns we found in their pockets."

One by one, Mitch and Josh did just that. They left the kids bound and gagged and rolled them over on the floor checking their whole bodies for anything. It was a good thing they did as they found two switchblades, a straight razor and a sap. The switchblades were inside their socks, easy to reach if they weren't bound and maybe reachable by one of the other kids. The razor and the sap were hanging from a loop inside one of their pant legs.

"Mitch exclaimed, "no wonder the merchants were afraid of these kids. They're a walking arsenal. I hope we got 'em all."

Under Josh's direction, they lined the kids sitting up against the wall, about a yard apart from each other, and told them to stay still or else. All except their leader, Jeff. Josh dragged him across the room, carefully concealing the pain his rib was causing him.

"So you're Jeff, the so-called gang boss. We know quite a bit about you. For one thing, you're mentally sick." Then he took a calculated risk. "You've been diagnosed with a personality disorder. In other words you're a psycho, probably a sociopath."

If Josh wanted a reaction, he got it. Jeff's eyes narrowed into slits and he quit struggling. Josh could feel the rage building within him.

"Also, you're a sniveling coward. Cowards beat up on people when they're helpless like you did to me. Cowards like you surround themselves with younger, weaker kids and try to dominate them. Something else, cowards shoot people from behind."

Jeff's eyes widened and his mouth fell open.

Josh leaned over and pulled the gag out from his mouth.

"Anything to say?"

Jeff snarled, "You son of a bitch, let me up and I'll show you who's a coward."

"A *sniveling* coward, that's what I called you. You want to take me on without a baseball bat? One on one? Right here in front of your gang?"

There was a slight pause before Jeff blustered, "sure as shit, you prick."

Without any hesitation, Josh picked him up off the ground, spun him around and sliced open his bonds. He gave him a shove forward and said, "okay, here's your chance. My partner'll stay over there by your gang and it's just you and me. Let's see how tough you really are."

Jeff tried surprise. He launched himself headfirst at Josh, trying to knock him to the ground. Josh easily sidestepped the attack and gave Jeff an eye flick as he went by. The eye flick was a delicately placed flick of the fingers across the eyes which momentarily made seeing difficult and could blind a person. Jeff recovered and stood rubbing his eyes. Josh made no move to capitalize on the situation.

"C'mon, coward. Here, I'll make it easy for you, I'll turn my back. I hear that you like to shoot people when they have their back to you."

Josh's intention was to inflict the "death of a million cuts." He baited Jeff time after time, both physically and mentally, until he blurted out the information Josh wanted. It began to work.

"Who said I ever shot anyone in their neck"

"That's your first slip, coward. I said the back, not the neck."

"Back, neck. What the fuck difference does it make." Jeff tried to mask another charge at Josh's back with his remark. Josh was in another world. He knew exactly where Jeff was at all times. Everything seemed to be in slow motion. Jeff's moves were so amateurish, it was almost embarrassing. He gracefully avoided Jeff's charge and threw a side fist to the solar plexus as Jeff stumbled by.

Jeff spun around, clutching his chest, suddenly winded and in pain. Josh continued to stand with his back to him. Jeff paused, trying to think of a way to get to Josh. Mitch thought it looked as if he had at least some training in the martial arts as he drew himself up and adopted a more fighting pose. He had evidently decided that roughhouse tactics weren't going to work.

Setting himself, he suddenly let out what he thought was a bloodcurdling, Chinese sounding yell and taking a running start, tried to throw a roundhouse kick at Josh's legs. Josh easily sidestepped the kick and simply tripped Jeff as he flew by him. Jeff fell face first to the floor, a tangle of legs and arms.

Josh had hardly moved except for turning his back on Jeff. Humiliating Jeff was turning out to be ridiculously easy. Almost a joke. He needed to needle Jeff and get him to spill information.

"What's Leung going to say when he finds out you admitted killing Fong?"

"I didn't admit killing anyone, and what the fuck's Leung got to do with it?"

Josh pounced on his slip. "So you admit you know Leung."

Jeff stretched his vocabulary, "Screw you, you prick." Then he circled Josh as if he was looking for an opening. Josh stood still. Suddenly Jeff planted his right foot, whirled and tried to make a kick jump at Josh. To Josh it was extremely amateurish. He easily parried the kick and planted a resounding and humiliating kick to Jeff's rear as he flew by. Once more Jeff ended up on the floor in a jumble.

Josh addressed the rest of the gang. "Is this the tough guy your gang follows? The coward that beats up defenseless shop owners and uses a baseball bat on a tied up prisoner? He doesn't look so tough to me."

Jeff was lying on the floor, his face bleeding from landing on his face. He gave the finger to Josh.

Josh laid a little more pressure on the gang. "You heard your leader pretty much confess he murdered Charley Fong. That means if you knew about it or helped him in any way, you may all end up in jail with him as a co-conspirators. Think about that."

He decided to egg Jeff on a little more.

"If you think your friend Jack Leung's going to help you with a murder charge, forget it. He'd have to admit that he ordered the hit if he was going to help you. Even if he did, he wouldn't admit it, not for you. You're expendable."

Jeff was groggy and not too smart. "Bullshit, he'll be there for me."

Josh thought he had Jeff right where he wanted him. He had inadvertently admitted being involved in the murder of Charley Fong and that Jack Leung was also involved. It was time to put Jeff out of his misery.

Jeff was standing, totally frustrated. He continued to glare at Josh. Josh wanted him conscious and able to talk. He decided to needle him into one more attack. "I think your gang's deserting you, what do you think? I think you're proving what I said, you're a sniveling coward. No guts. A couple of falls and you give up."

"I ain't giving up, you asshole." And with that he reached behind his neck and pulled out a twelve inch sharpened piece of flattened steel. Somehow Mitch had missed it when he searched Jeff. He lunged at Jeff, waiving the blade in front of him. He feinted at Josh with the knife in his right hand and at the last moment tossed the knife to his left hand and made a sweeping swipe at Josh's chest.

Once again it was easy for Josh to ward off the thrust. He grabbed the knife-wielding arm and using Jeff's forward motion, pulled him around his body, delivering a hand chop to the back of his neck as he slid by, knocking him to the floor, senseless. The knife slid out of his hand.

CHAPTER 70

Mitch walked over to Josh. "Jesus, you sure made that look easy."

"It was. He was big and strong, but had no training whatsoever. What about the kids? What was their reaction?"

"They're depressed and quiet. I think they're a bunch of easily led kids. I also think that a few of them are afraid of him. I wouldn't be surprised if a couple of them were glad to see him beat up."

"Great. Separate those two if you can and let's let the rest of them go."

"Go?"

"Yeah, let 'em go. I want to take Jeff and maybe the two that are afraid of him over to the On-Sing Tong. Let's keep him separated from the kids, okay? I think we can get a lot of information from Jeff, and maybe those two kids can help too. Tell the rest of them they'll never see Jeff again, he's going to jail for murder and they're damn lucky they're not going with him. Copy their ID's and then untie them and kick 'em out."

The four didn't believe they were being freed. Mitch cut their bonds, took the gags from their mouths, and booted them out the door with a warning.

"Don't forget we know who you are and where you live. And you better forget you ever knew Jeff, he's going to jail for murder." They piled into their car and split.

Josh decided what to do. "Mitch, you take those two in your car over to the Tong headquarters and I'll take Jeff over in his car when he comes to. Use the garage entrance so you won't be seen. I'll call Mr. Chinn and tell him we're coming over with the remnants of one of the gangs he wanted stopped."

"What'll I do with these two until you get there?"

"Have the Tong put them in a room somewhere, I don't want Jeff to know they're there. I may be slow getting there, I gotta call Fern and do some fence mending. I haven't talked to her since yesterday."

Mr. Chinn was suitably impressed when they presented Jeff to him and told him they could prove he had been in on the murder of Charley Fong and that they had totally broken up one of the gangs. Probably the more dangerous of the two.

Jeff was left bound and gagged with two guards while Josh and Mitch interrogated the two teen gang members. They were scared and the questioning went fast and easy.

Josh started. "What do you know about Jeff murdering Charley Fong?"

"Who's Charley Fong?"

"He's the difference between freedom and jail for you. We know Jeff shot and killed him. We know that you know that too. You can either add to the evidence we already have and testify to what you know, or you can go to jail with him, your choice."

It was no contest. "Okay, we know he did it. He swore he'd kill us if we ever told anyone. He even shared some of the money he got for the job with us."

"Why?"

"He made us stand at the end of the hall in case anybody came by. He just told us they was gonna beat up on the guy."

"They?"

"Yeah, he and the other guy."

"Who was the other guy?"

They looked questioningly at each other. Finally one of them shrugged and said, "some friend of Jeff's I guess."

"How much did he get?"

They looked at each other again. "We don't know but it must've been a lot, he gave us each five hundred. And he shared it with the other guy, too. Next your gonna ask us who gave him the money and honest to God, we don't know. We were afraid to ask."

Josh believed them. At least he had them as witnesses. He also had an idea. It was time to confront Jeff.

He and Mitch sat across a table from Jeff. Josh took charge.

"Jeff, you made lots of mistakes. You admitted you knew that Charley Fong had been shot in the neck. No one knew that except the police and us. We've got two witness that'll swear they heard you brag about killing him and how much money you got for the job. You like to think of yourself as a murder for hire pro when you're really a bungling amateur." Here Josh took a chance. "Then you made the biggest mistake of all. You bragged about it to too many people."

Jeff tried to bluff. "I want a lawyer."

Mitch chimed in. "First, you're not at a police station. I'm Sergeant Dan Mitchell of the San Francisco police, but we're just having a private conversation here." He flashed his badge. "We got you cold, kid. You're going to jail. Only question is, which jail and how long. That depends on your answers. We need to know who hired you."

Jeff was silent for a long time. Josh waited him out. Finally Jeff spoke. " In the movies they always offer a deal."

Josh kept the pressure on. "A deal? Why should we cut a deal with you? You murdered Fong, you pay the price !"

For the first time, Jeff showed some animation. He shouted, "It wasn't my idea to murder him. They made me do it. They said they'd make my gang number one in the city if I did it. Said if I didn't, my life wouldn't be worth a nickel."

"If that's true and you're willing to testify who made you kill Fong, we'll tell the D.A. you're a cooperating witness and he'll probably go easy on you. That's the best we can do. But we need to know who made you do it."

Jeff struggled with himself.

Finally he gave up. "But you gotta protect me. They'll kill me if they find out."

"We'll protect the hell out of you. You'll be our star witness. And don't worry about them, they'll be in jail or worse. So who are they?"

"The scary guy, they called him Jack something. He's the one gave me the gun and told me how to use it. He said he had a score to settle with this guy Fong. He told me to take someone with me who could sit in front of Fong and distract him while I wandered around the room.

So I got a guy that owes me and we went. He knew Fong and told him a crock while I pretended to just wander around the room. While he distracted Fong I shot him in the back. Right at the base of his neck. I never done nothin' like that before, but he said I had to if I wanted to be a real gang leader."

"Jack?" Josh didn't want to plant the last name into Jeff's memory. He wanted him to remember it by himself. "Jack what? It's important you remember."

"We called him 'spitball', 'cause his last name reminded us of a wad of spit. What the hell was it? Oh yeah, a lunger. His last name was Lunger or something."

Mitch asked him what he looked like and he described Jack Leung to a T.

"Okay." Josh said. I think we can work with that. All you need to do is write all this down and sign and date it while Mitch watches you and we'll do the best we can for you."

Mitch stayed with Jeff while Josh went to report to Mr. Chinn.

"The kid admitted killing the private detective? He and the other kid together? So from what you're saying that breaks up the gang too? And that's the gang that Lee's been using?"

"There's a couple of other gangs still around but they're just a bunch of kids. We know where they hang out and can neutralize them easily. Now we gotta catch Leung. But first I have to do some fence mending with my wife."

"In Yosemite?"

"Oh no, didn't we tell you? She's here in town, but she's been visiting friends at Stanford."

"Your wife is here in town? Well ! I want to meet her. Bring her over this evening and my wife and I'll take you out to dinner. It's the least I could do. And what about detective Mitchell, is he married? He should come too."

"That's awfully nice of you, but really not necessary at all."

"Nonsense. Of course it's necessary. Besides we still have work to do. I promised we'd help you find this Leung fellow. Also, I want to show off my Chinatown to you. Lastly, for your information, as president of On Sing I'm not accustomed to being argued with, so you go gather up your wife and I'll take care of everything else. We'll expect you and your wife and Mitch and his girlfriend for dinner. It's settled."

"Okay, I won't argue with you. Mitch isn't married, but I think he has a pretty successful dating life. I'll call Fern and tell her about tonight and I'm sure Mitch'd love it. All he has to do is scrounge up a date. One caveat. Don't tell Fern everything we've been doing."

"That should be easy. I don't know all the things you've done and I don't think I want to know."

CHAPTER 71

That evening, as directed, Josh and Fern together with Mitchell and his girlfriend met at Mr. Chinn's condominium for a pre-dinner cocktail. Situated near the top of a highrise apartment building, it was a four bedroom, very large and spacious dwelling with fantastic views of the bay. As they were ushered into the living room Mrs. Chinn told them that the building was owned by the Association.

As they introduced each other, Mrs. Chinn took both of Fern's hands in hers and said, "My dear, you're perfectly lovely. Dan tells me that your husband's been neglecting you lately while he's done some very important work for the Association. We're going to have to do something about that."

They had cocktails and admired the views from the huge windows that dominated the living room. Josh noticed that Mr. and Mrs. Chinn huddled together for a short time and then called in and dispatched several servants on errands. He wondered what was up, but decided they were just making last minute dinner reservations or something.

Sooner than Josh expected, Mrs. Chinn said, " I think we should be gathering our things and be on our way. We need to make a short stop and we'll just have enough time."

As a group they took the elevator to the basement of the building where a limousine was waiting. The liveried driver escorted them into their seats and took whispered directions from Mr. Chinn before exiting the garage.

After driving a short distance, they pulled up before a brightly lit but fairly small store. The sign over the door said, "DRAGON SEED BRIDAL AND PHOTO SHOP. " Nudging Mitch in the ribs, Josh whispered, "What's this?"

"Maybe he's going to have a commemorative photo made for you?" Mitch whispered back.

"Everybody out!" commanded Mr. Chinn. "Especially you, Fern!" Mrs. Chinn added.

Inside, except for clerks, the store was empty. The sign on the door said they closed at five. It became apparent that the store had stayed open late just for them. Beaming, Mr. Chinn, Turning to his wife, told her, "Okay, I got them here, the rest is up to you."

She took charge. "Josh, we'd like to make a little gift to your wife, commemorating her first visit to San Francisco Chinatown and thanking you for what your doing for us. Earlier, while you weren't paying attention, I had Mitch describe your wife to my Daniel. We both decided she would be a perfect candidate for what we had in mind, so follow me."

Fern glanced at Josh and raised her eyebrows. Josh shrugged his shoulders and then silently questioned Mitch, only to get the same shrug in reply.

Mrs. Chinn led the group to a section of the store that had a sign, "CHEONGSAM AND QUIPAO" over it.

She turned to Fern and said "We want you to have one of these," and held up a dress up to her. The dress was long, almost to her ankles, and had a high, closed collar. Mrs. Chinn said, isn't it beautiful?" Turning to Fern, she said, "you have the perfect build for the cheongsam, will you try it on for us? We have plenty of time. If it fits, you can wear it tonight!"

With the owner and three clerks in attendance, trying it on only took a few minutes. When she emerged from the dressing room, Josh was stunned. The dress fit her as if it had been made just for her. Then, when she took her first step in the dress, he was further impressed. It looked like the whole side of the dress opened up. Actually it was only up to her thigh, but it and Fern were perfect together.

"I love it!" Fern said.

Josh casually looked at the price tag on a similar dress and was shocked. Five hundred dollars! Mr. Chinn caught him turning green and said, "Not to worry, it's a gift. Besides, I'm a part owner and I'll give me a good price!"

"Then you must have it and wear it tonight." Mrs. Chinn said. "You'll be a walking advertisement for Chinatown and our store. We won't take no for an answer."

Fern was in a quandary. It seemed an outrageously overpriced gift to her and she wasn't aware of the developing relationship between Josh and the Chinese community. Mr. Chinn solved her dilemma.

"Fern, if the On Sing Association had hired detectives to do what these two have done for us it would have cost us several thousands of dollars. In view of their value to us, I'm almost embarrassed at the small value of our gift. Take it and wear it with our gratitude!"

Mrs. Chinn said, "I'm a Buddhist, but I'll say 'Amen' to that!"

They all had a good laugh at that and returned to the Limo, Fern in her new cheongsam dress. Fern snuggled up to Josh and whispered, "What in the world have you done for them?" Whispering back he said, "Later."

Mr. Chinn instructed the driver to go on to their next destination. Again it was a very short drive. Looking out the window Josh recognized the pyramid shape of the Transamerica Building as they came to a stop. The driver stopped in front of a tall office building and let them out. Mr. Chinn and his wife led the party to a ground floor entrance labeled, "Tommy Toys.".

Mitch said, "Wow! This is a famous restaurant, and expensive! I've never been here, too rich for a poor policeman. They say the natives love it but come for lunch because it's cheaper. At night it's usually tourists and expense accounts! I wonder where we come in?"

At the front door they were greeted by a young lady who obviously recognized their host.

"Good evening, Mr. Chinn, your room is ready."

Room? They were led a short distance through the bar to a private room, separated from the bar by a beautiful folding screen. The table was set for six, although it looked like it could accommodate up to maybe ten or more people. Before they had time to sit down, they were each served a melon flavored Cosmo. Icy cold, mild and a little sweet, it tasted vaguely Chinese and delicious. Mr. Chinn seated everyone where he wanted them. He ended up surrounded by Fern and Mitch's girl friend. " No fool he," Josh thought.

Josh noticed there were no menus on the table. After a toast to the future health of the Chinese Community of San Francisco, Mr. Chinn solved that little mystery. "I've taken the liberty of ordering our dinner off the special Chinese menu tonight. Most people order what's described as Chinese fusion cuisine, but they do have a Chinese menu also, if you ask for it. There'll be lots to choose from and plenty of time to enjoy it all. It's called the Emperor's Gourmet dinner and has about ten courses. Everything from abalone , shark fin soup, lobster and fish to Lamb Chop Wellington. My advice, don't fill up on hors d'eourves!"

Josh, on the way to the restroom, glanced at a menu on the hostess desk. The per person cost of the gourmet dinner was almost a hundred dollars! The only place he knew of that had comparable prices was Japan. There the prices were even higher.

At one point during the dinner the owner dropped by the table and chatted with Mr. and Mrs. Chinn. Needless to say, the dinner and the service were both exquisite.

After dinner and dessert, the limo returned Josh and Fern to their hotel after dropping everyone else off. It was going on eleven, neither of them was tired. They had a small brandy sent up to their room and found a way to continue the remarkable evening.

CHAPTER 72

Next morning Mitch was waiving the front page of the Chronicle at Josh when he arrived at the hotel restaurant. "GANG WARFARE BREAKS OUT IN CHINATOWN"

"Looks like your plan's working. Maybe they'll wipe each other out and do Mr. Chinn a big favor."

"Wouldn't that be great?" Josh responded. "Mostly I hope they get out of our hair. Did Mr. Chinn say anything about Leung's business interests?"

"He said he has a waterfront warehouse at the foot of Green-street, but Mr. Chinn doesn't know much about what he does there. He knows he can leave messages there for him and he'll hear back from Leung pretty quick. Mr. Chinn doesn't think that Leung's at his peninsula home very much. He's heard that the employees at the warehouse are a rough group and wouldn't be surprised if there were some borderline legal activities going on. That's all he knows."

"Great. Another gang? I wonder why he was using the teen gangs if he has his own warehouse gang? Maybe he drew the line at murder for his own guys. I wonder if the warehouse is part of the Chinese medicine chain."

"That would explain his investment in the Emeryville lab, wouldn't it So, what's next? Do we scout out the warehouse?"

"Yeah, but in the meantime, call your station and find out who owns the place and if they have any info on what's going on there."

"Cell phone time." Mitch said and called his station. While he was waiting, he asked Josh, "What'd Fern think about last night?"

"She was overwhelmed. Mrs. Chinn is squiring her around today. Something about a fortune cookie factory and a tour of the whole place. Now I don't know if I'm going to be able to get her to leave," he laughed.

"Here they are." Mitch said. A moment later he hung up and told Josh that all the info they have on that warehouse is old stuff.

"Over the years the place's been raided several times. Everything from illegal fireworks to counterfeit watches and other stuff. There's an awful lot of counterfeit high end women's purses and scarves along with the watches being sold. It looks like the spot changed ownership a number of times, but they don't know who owns it now or if it's being used or not. They've confiscated several shipments of stuff out of the warehouse in the past but haven't been able to legally connect anyone to it—yet."

"But Mr. Chinn says he can leave a message for Leung there and he gets it. Are you familiar with the place? Is there somewhere that we can do some surveillance on it?"

"I don't know. I know where it is and I can picture it, but we'll have to do a drive-by to find a place we can watch it from."

"I told Fern that I'd be gone for the day, so let's go."

They drove down Broadway to the Embarcadero and followed it to Green Street. Across from the warehouse were several possibilities. A restaurant, an apartment building and a three-story office building. They selected the office building. Mitch flashed his badge and got an empty second-story office space for as long as they needed it.

"What a great location for almost anything illegal!" Josh said. "One big door right on the Embarcadero, big enough to handle any size truck. The warehouse's on a pier and its got a deep water slip alongside it. A wide driveway along the other side so trucks could enter the warehouse and unload without being watched."

"There's more too, I think. Most of these warehouses have another bayside entrance. You can bring a small boat right under the building to an unloading place totally out of anyone's' sight."

"What your saying is that we're not going to learn much from here, right? So here's what we're going to do. We'll watch the place until we get a feeling for how many guys are in there and when they're there. Maybe we'll see Leung come in. I guess I'm going to have to go inside."

CHAPTER 73

"No way. The front door's huge and they only open it for a truck or something. The only door is on the side with a forty-foot narrow driveway in front of it. No windows except near the roof. Unless you plan to make a water entrance?"

"No water entrance. If they're dirty at all, they'll know that's their most vulnerable spot and have it well protected. No, I'll go in where they don't expect it. Probably the windows."

"Impossible without a ladder, they're at least thirty-five feet off the ground. And there's no way you can get away using a ladder anyway. All the windows are totally visible from the street. Didn't you notice the motion detectors and floodlights all around the building? Even at night, you'd be noticed!"

"Tell you what. At the right time, I'll go in. You wait across the street until you see me open the side door and call you in. Okay?"

"Josh, you're nuts! There's no way in!"

"Trust me, I know something you don't. Now let's keep an eye on the place and see how many guys are there."

They watched throughout the morning and decided there were at least a dozen guys working at the place, although there didn't seem to be much work going on. They looked like a bunch of stevedores. Big, husky and strong. A few cars driven in and out. No sign of Leung. Mr. Chinn had given them a description, they were sure they'd recognize him if he showed up.

Finally, around two in the afternoon, Josh said, "That's enough, we've wasted enough time, I'm going in"

"How?, for gods sake."

"With your help. You're going to provide a little diversion and I'm going in."

"Diversion? How can we do that without looking suspicious?"

"Simple, we'll blame it on a tourist. There's dozens of tourists' cars parked near here. You go borrow the plates from one of them and put them on your car. Just over your plates is all that's necessary. When I give you the signal you back into their metal door, doesn't have to be hard. The metal door will make a huge sound, especially inside the warehouse. That'll set off the motion detector so they won't notice me slipping in. While their attention is on you and the door, I'll make my move."

"I get it. I'll be the poor, apologetic tourist and talk my way out of the mess?"

"Sure. You're from Kansas or someplace and apologetic as hell. You won't do any damage to the door, they don't want police attention. And when you return the plate to the tourists' car, nobody gets hurt."

"Except maybe my car.

"It isn't yours, it's an unmarked police car and anyway, it's already dinged up"

"And we're going to do that now? You're going to sneak into the place in broad daylight? You're sure you can do that?"

"Piece o' cake!"

"Okay, if you say so. I guess I better take off and find an out of state license"

Forty-five minutes later, Mitch returned. "New Mexico okay?"

Josh was right. When Mitch rear-ended the metal door, It made a huge clanging, rattling sound and the motion detector alarm went off. As he tried to pull away from the door, it gradually rolled up, revealing a group of stevedores. Several of them ducked under the rising door and yelled at Mitch to stop. As soon as they had cleared the door, one of them, using a remote control, started the door back down again. It struck Mitch that they didn't want anyone to see what was going on inside.

"Gee, guys, I'm really sorry. I hope I didn't do any damage? I'm not used to driving in this much traffic." And he pointed to his license plate.

"Tourist? You're fuckin lucky this door's as strong as it is. I don't see any damage, so take off!"

Mitch, trying to look as incensed as he imagined a tourist might at the language the stevedore used, thanked them and drove off.

Meanwhile Josh had quickly run down the wharf side of the building to the far end. At the end he uncoiled a padded, three pronged grappling hook and threw it toward the rearmost window. Fortunately, the windows were wide open and had a steel casing. All he had to do was pitch the grappling hook through the open window and assume it would grab the casing when he pulled it tight. It did! Pulling it taut, he launched himself in a long arc and ended up behind the warehouse on the bay side, completely out of sight of anyone on the streets.

At the end of the arc, on the bay side of the building, he flipped a second grappling hook at the roof. The weight of the hook fell on the roof and caught.

CHAPTER 74

The next part was the hardest. He had to use every ounce of strength in his legs and arms to stay at the rear of the building. Underneath him he could see the boat entrance to the warehouse. An easy entrance, but he still thought it was too obvious. He didn't think anyone would imagine an entry from above. He had to hang on to the line and work his way up it to an upper window. It was an exercise he had done any number of times with other Ninja warriors, usually at night.

He carefully flipped the line so that he was directly below the chosen window, then started up. Using this technique over and over, he shortly reached one of the upper rear windows. There were a few sailboats and one ferry on the bay, but Josh wasn't worried about being spotted. They'd probably think he was a window washer.

The window was slightly open and Josh was able to straddle the sill. Just below his level were a lot of steel girders. There was nothing between him and the floor of the warehouse except those girders and a few pigeons. He left the grappling hooks in place, tying the lines tight to the window.

Lots of noise was his first impression. As he looked down, he immediately recognized the operation. It was a chop shop. At least a dozen cars in various stages of dismantling or being cut up. He realized what a good location it was for a chop shop. Among all the tourists cars going up and down the embarcadero, no one would notice a few fancy cars entering or leaving the warehouse. On top of that they could use either the hidden boat dock underneath the building or the wharf on the side to get car parts in or out.

The noise was an advantage. Josh worked his way down the girders and was able to noiselessly drop to the floor, out of sight, behind an empty car. On the way down, he counted eighteen workers, more than they'd estimated! His original thought was, coming at them from the rear of the shop, he should be able to take out most of the crew, one at a time. He could deal with three or four handily, even in a group. His only concern was firearms. Eighteen was a different matter.

Standing on the bumper of the car, he tried to locate every guy on the premises. Trouble was, nobody was standing still. Suddenly, out of the corner of his eye, he sensed movement. Whipping around he saw one of the stevedores standing in the doorway of a toilet holding a gun on him. He must have just come out and seen Josh. "Who the hell are you?" the guy yelled. It was loud enough that a couple of the other guys looked over and saw Josh also. All the previous plans immediately went out the window.

'Bluff or run?' ran through Josh's mind. Both! His instincts told him. He had to distract the gunman for an instant or two. Facing the front of the shop and at the top of his lungs he yelled, "Jack, guy here wants to know who I am, can you square him away?" He was taking the chance that either Jack Leung occasionally was here or there was someone else named Jack in the building. All three of the men stood up on their toes and looked toward the front of the shop. But the gunman kept his pistol pointed in Josh's direction.

Before the gunman could react, Josh leaped between two cars and took off running. The gunman was distracted just enough to give Josh time to get a car between him and the guy. A shot rang out.

Somebody yelled, "shoot high! Don't hit the cars! He's got nowhere to go. We'll pinch him off before he can get to the side door!"

Josh knew exactly what he was going to do. Leaping on to the hood of a car, he starting leaping from car to car, barely touching them. His speed kept increasing until he left his pursuers far behind. He headed toward the side door leading into the driveway. As they realized they weren't going to be able to catch him, the gang began firing more bullets. Josh, using another Ninja trick, changed direction lightning fast without losing speed. always one step ahead of them. He just wasn't where they expected him to be when they fired. A few steps away from the door he somersaulted to the floor. Landing with his legs flexed, he immediately went into a tuck and roll to minimize any damage to his legs. Out of the roll he was perfectly placed to wrench the door open, spin through it and crash it closed behind him. By the time the gang reached the door and pushed it open, Josh had reached the sidewalk, turned in front of the building and was out of their sight. Hurriedly, he crossed the street and ducked into the office building where Mitch was waiting for him.

"I thought you were going to casually wave me into the building?"

"I did, too. First of all, there's a lot more guys in there than we expected!" I counted eighteen I could see. Then there was one more in the can. He's the one that came out and saw me and started yelling. He also pulled a gun on me. That's when I decided to get out."

"Did I hear guns?"

"You sure as hell did. They wanted me dead as soon as I started running!"

"How'd you get out?"

"How dye think? I dodged their bullets and ran a hell of a lot faster than they could! I may have alerted them to the idea that I knew about Jack. I had to use his name to buy a little time. We may not have a second chance to get back in, but I learned that they're operating a chop shop in there, among other things."

"A chop shop? You mean you think that's what this place is all about?"

"How many chop-shops've you broken up? Ever see all the guys in the shop wearing guns? No, there's more here than just a chop shop. I don't think these guys got a good enough look to ID me, but we gotta be careful, those stevedore types are a rough bunch. One thing we got going for us. With the teen gangs destroying each other, we don't have to be worried about our backside."

"So how do we get to Leung?"

" I think he'll show up here. 'Specially now after the infiltration. We continue watching and go back in when he's there."

"We can't do that. There's no way in!"

"I know a way. All we have to do is watch the building and hope they take delivery of a hot car."

CHAPTER 75

By evening they'd watched two cars roll up to the front door of the warehouse, honk the Morse code signal for "H" and be let in. The Morse code for "H" was four dots and that was what each driver honked. Immediately the door was rolled up, just enough for the car to be driven in. The second car used the same signal and received the same treatment. No one even looked at the driver. They seemed to feel secure about the signal, opened the door just enough and waved the car through. No cars came out.

Josh suggested they could get in the same way. If they kept a crew working all night, chances were they'd be a much smaller group. They could overpower a small group and maybe learn something.

Mitch was concerned. "I don't know, Josh. We've had knives and guns pulled on us and you've been shot at, what are we doing? We seem to be a long way from solving your bear killings."

"I've thought about that too. It's like we're pulling on a string and the string gets longer and longer. But don't forget there've been several killings along the way, including one of our Rangers. I also feel somewhat responsible for Charley Fong's killing. If we hadn't turned him, he might still be alive."

Pausing for a moment, he added, "but after what the S.O.B. tried to do to me, I can't feel too much sympathy for him."

Mitch interjected, "I think this case is pretty much like other cases I've worked on. By the time you sort out all the people and the motives involved, they always turn out to be bigger and more involved than what you expected."

"This one sure is, are you having second thoughts about working with me?"

"No way. Plus I've been assigned to you. But I've been thinking that maybe you should check back in with the Chief and get her thinking before we get in any deeper."

"Maybe that's a good idea. Also, maybe we need more info about Jack Leung and how to get at him. Maybe the Chief will have some other ideas. Good idea, Mitch. Let's call it a night, and see if we can see the chief first thing in the morning. We'll bring her up to date and see what she thinks."

When Josh got the Chief on the phone, he wasn't so sure that calling her was such a good idea.

"What in hell have you two been up to?" She exploded. "I've got prisoners in my jail that say you've beaten them up and two murder cases to work on. Not to mention a hotel keeper that says you threatened him plus three or four teenagers with broken arms and legs, evidently caused by you two. You bet I want to see both of you first thing in the morning, here, in my office."

Josh had hoped that most of their activities had been under the radar and was surprised to find out what she knew. He didn't tell Mitch what she had said. Thought that Mitch might sleep better not knowing.

"She said she'll be expecting us first thing tomorrow. Can we meet for breakfast at seven-thirty? We can both get a good nights sleep and I can spend a little time with Fern.

Mitch headed for his room and Josh headed for the kitchen. He wanted to think over what the Chief had said and group his thinking before going to his room. He decided it would be a good idea to call Mr. Chinn and see if he could call the chief and explain things to her.

"I'd be delighted to. What you two have accomplished against our teen gangs is unbelievable. She needs to know that. I'll call her right now."

Somewhat relieved, Josh went on up to his room.

Next morning, the chief kept Mitch and Josh waiting for almost a half-hour. When they were finally called into her office, they were surprised to find Mr. Chinn sitting comfortably across from her.

"This won't take long," she said, somewhat icily. "Everything I said to you last night, Josh, is all too true. You've created a lot of mayhem by your rather unorthodox methods. And I don't appreciate in the least being called upon to clean up after you. The prisoners you've sent us should be off the streets, anyway. I've interviewed the shop owner and he witnessed to my satisfaction that you were protecting him when you beat up on the teen gang. Also Mr. Chinn has come to your defense. He says you've helped him and his organization begin to break up those hoodlums."

"On top of that, I understand you've uncovered a chop shop that we can raid. Is that true?"

"Yes Ma'am," Josh replied. He started to say more, but she cut him off.

"That's enough! Let me finish! Based on the results you're getting and Mr. Chinn's endorsements, I'm inclined to let you continue your investigation, your way, but with a couple of conditions!"

Learning quickly, Josh and Mitch replied together, "Yes Ma'am!"

"All right! Condition one. No firearms! If you can continue using your wits and wisdom and your demonstrated abilities at self-defense, okay! But no guns, Got it?"

Both nodded.

"Number two: You report to me every night by phone, ev—er—y —night! Got it? If I'm not here, you leave a report with the desk sergeant. No excuses!"

"Yes, Ma'am"

"Third condition. You work closely with Mr. Chinn. He's mature and sensible and knows the Chinese community inside and out."

"Fourth. You call your boss in Yosemite and bring him up to date on what you're doing and why I've given you a temporary lieutenant's badge."

"And fifth and final. You take good care of your wife. Don't let your enthusiasm for avenging the murders ruin your marriage. I've seen it happen too many times!"

"Now, you're dismissed. Mr. Chinn, thanks so much for helping, we really should have that dinner soon. I'm looking forward to meeting your wife and your meeting my husband."

Dismissed, they gathered together in the lobby. Mr. Chinn said, "I hope you take everything she said seriously, she's way out on a limb for you. It's a good thing you called me last night, she was about ready to cut you off."

Josh said, "I think everything she said was right on, and actually we need you, now more than ever."

Mitch spoke up, "If she knew all the things we've done that she doesn't know about, I bet we'd be out on our ears by now!"

Mr. Chinn said, "Chinatown has lots of secrets!"

They decided to have coffee somewhere and work out a plan. Mr. Chinn told them he wanted to snuff out the teen gangs and was at least sympathetic to helping track down the bear killers. Josh said he had been charged with solving the bear crimes and he needed to find out who was behind the bear problems in order to really stop them, plus he felt personally involved because of the murders. Mitch said that originally it had just been another assignment for him, but not anymore!

CHAPTER 76

Over coffee they tried to develop a plan. Mr. Chinn suggested they go back to the beginning. What was Josh's original assignment?

"Easy" said Josh. "Find out who was killing the bears and stop them. Then it became more complicated when my friend was killed."

"Is that still your main goal?" Mr. Chinn asked.

"Of course, at least as far as Yosemite is concerned, but I decided we had to get to the top of the organization, not just catch the truck drivers or whatever. Plus it's become personal to me now, after what Leung did to Fern.

"Okay. I think we can work together. I think our goals are the same. Now that you've brought the bear killing to my attention and told me how they treated Fern, they need to be dealt with. And it seems that the teen gangs and Jack Leung are tied into that operation as well as trying to undermine the Association."

Mitch questioned him. "So we continue after Leung, assuming he's either the big cheese in the bear operation or can lead us to the big cheese? And any damage we do to the teen gangs or Leung will be good for you?"

"That's about it. Plus, I think I can help. First, if I use all the assets available to me, I'm pretty sure we can locate Leung accurately and quickly. Second, I've got some other assets that may be of use to you in sort of a physical way, if you get my drift. You have to remember that the tongs have been in existence for hundreds of years. We have ways. But I have a question. How much are you actually going to tell the chief each day?"

"Probably about as much as we've been telling her. I'm thinking we'll tell her each day's results, but not much about how we got the results."

"Good, I can help you there. As I said before, Chinatown has lots of secrets. I think you should use On Sing Association as your headquarters. We've got space on the third floor, even a small workout room. That way we can work together and you will have a chance to meet some of my assets personally."

In Mr. Chinn's sedan on the way to the Association Building, Josh wondered what or who the assets would turn out to be. He could only wait and see.

Inside the building, Josh's curiosity was satisfied, quickly. The small workout room that Mr. Chinn had mentioned, was actually a small school. A training and workout room for martial arts. The assets turned out to be about a dozen teens and young adults in various stages of martial art training. A black belt teaching and several working toward their brown belts.

In the corner was a small office, to which Mr. Chinn led them. Josh was aware that Mr. Chinn knew he could speak Chinese fluently, but he was quite sure he didn't know of his martial art background. To his surprise, Mr. Chinn said, " I know who you are, I mean I know about your reputation in the martial arts. Our black belt over there immediately recognized your name. He told me you're a living legend. He said you were like a one-man army. When I told him about the gangs you and Mitch had whipped, he wasn't surprised. He begged me to get you to work out with him and his students at least once. I'm thinking I'll go him one better. He and his students are the asset I thought you could use. Particularly since your chief has forbidden the use of guns except in self-defense. Maybe you can use them and they'd be thrilled."

Josh said he would be happy to work out with them, but wasn't sure about using them, "It might be dangerous!"

Mr. Chinn said, "Let us see how it develops. In the meantime I've put out the word to locate Leung, let's develop a strategy. For example, how are going to handle our Chief of Police. And Josh, have you contacted your boss yet? I guess he's been in touch with the chief and you need to keep him off the chief's back. As far as your wife goes, between my wife and a planned ferry boat tour of the bay, I don't think she'll be complaining much, at least during the days. I'll leave the evenings up to you."

Mitch leered at Josh, "if you're too busy to entertain Fern at night, may I offer my services? I'm extremely well qualified! After all, what are partners for?"

"After what I plan to do to you in the sparring ring this afternoon, you'll probably be needing a nurse, not a date."

"Boys, boys" Mr. Chinn interjected. "Let's get back to business. Is there anything we should be doing that will help us locate Leung? What about the chop shop, can we get any information there that would help us?"

Josh replied, "I don't think so. The chief said they're going to stake out the place for a couple of days before they raid it. She doesn't want us anywhere near it before then. We could probably quiz some of the gang after they're arrested, but I bet none of them know anything valuable about Leung."

"What about your two cops that are trying to infiltrate the teen gangs?"

Mitch answered. "I've no idea. We could ask them."

"Why don't you do that," Mr. Chinn advised. "In the meantime, while we're waiting for info to come in, I'm going to talk to my elders. Josh, if you'd spend some time with the martial arts class? Let's plan on meeting here at four!"

Mitch took off to try and arrange a meet with the two undercover officers and Josh headed toward the Judo class.

CHAPTER 77

"Mr. Rogan? I'm Alan, Alan Chung. Class, this is a real honor. This is Josh Rogan, maybe the best Grand Karate Master in the history of the sport. On top of that, he's become a master in types of martial arts you've never even heard of. He's a living legend!"

Turning back to Josh he said, "When I heard that Mr. Chinn was meeting with you, I took the liberty of showing the class a DVD of you taken in Japan two years ago. They're really excited to meet you, can you talk to them a little?"

"I can do better than that. I just found out I've got the afternoon free. Why don't we all do a series of workouts and lessons together. Alan, you take charge and use me where you think best."

Alan was clearly somewhat intimidated by the world champion in his dojo. In the back of his mind he hoped he could spar with him, himself. He broke up the class into age and experience groups and put them through their paces.

Josh took the opportunity to size Alan up. It was immediately clear that the kids loved him and enjoyed the practice. It was also clear that he was more than just competent. The complete opposite of Josh, he was fairly short, about five foot four, and chunky. Maybe the kids liked and trusted him because he had an open and honest face and a quiet but effective way with them.

To Josh he said, "Can you watch them and step in whenever you want?"

After a half-hour of watching, Josh had an idea. He got Mitch on the phone and asked him how quickly he could get back to the Association building.

"Right now, if you need me. Can't see either of the undercover guys until this evening anyway, what's up?"

"We're going to get in a couple of hours of practice and put on a show for these kids."

While he was waiting for Mitch, Josh asked Alan if it would be okay to exercise the kids' imagination a little.

"Probably, what've you got in mind?"

"I'd like to talk about the limitless varieties of Martial Arts. How you're only limited by your imagination. Also about the mental and psychological aspects of the art. After that, Mitch and I, if it's okay with you, can demonstrate what we've talked about. Okay?"

"Perfect. Gang, gather around!"

To the kids' surprise, Josh addressed them in perfect Chinese. "Okay, first question. Why are you taking Judo?"

There was much hesitation before an older teen spoke up. He looked to be about nineteen to Josh. His answer? "To be able to defend myself."

"Good answer, goes to the roots of all martial arts programs!"

After that he got a number of answers.

"It's good exercise."

"My mom made me."

"I liked Mr. Chung." Etc.

"Okay, let me tell you why I like Karate. First off, it has a great spiritual side. In order to really good at it you must strengthen yourself through both physical and mental exercises. That's called Qigong. Secondly, you can keep improving your skills your entire life. Third, it's still evolving, it's a growing art."

He paused, "How many forms of Martial Arts do you think there are?"

"Several?" One of the younger teens asked.

"Dozens and dozens upon dozens!" Replied Josh. "That's what turns me on. There are new ideas coming out all the time. I'm trying my best to know and master them all. That's a part of what I'd like to show you guys this afternoon."

He spotted Mitch just coming in and said, "There's my partner now. If you guys will spread out along the walls, we're going to practice and demonstrate a few of the outer perimeters of Martial Art! Hopefully one of you guys'll catch the disease and take my place someday."

Alan had rustled up a couple of outfits for them and they started loosening up. Josh said, "To me, once I've learned the various moves, the most important thing in competition, is speed. You get to the point where you don't have to think about your next move, it just comes naturally. You'll be constantly ahead of your opponent, he'll be constantly off balance. In order to do that you need to practice, practice, practice. Something I'm sure Alan has mentioned a few times?"

A chuckle bounced around the room.

"At the same time, you must be able to think and plan. Use the element of surprise. First the basics, then the speed, then the surprise! Hard to beat! Okay, first the basics."

On the mats, Mitch and Josh went through a number of the basics and then on to some advanced moves. Mitch fought off a number of attacks by up to three of the students. Josh fought off an attack by Alan using a long pole only. Josh fought off an attack by seven of the students plus Alan, taking two or three out at a time by a series of flying kicks and moving so quickly the teens ended up in each others' way or knocking each other down. It was very impressive although quite easy for Josh.

"Okay, back to the walls everyone. Spread out so that there's two or three feet between each of you. I mentioned basics and speed, which I think you've just seen demonstrated. How about surprise? Let's see what Mitch and I can come up with."

With that, Mitch and Josh started a routine they'd practiced several times in the last few days. Taking off in different directions around the room, they raced faster and faster. As they approached each other, they sprang onto the wall and ran for several paces on the wall before dropping to the floor again. Josh went high on the wall and Mitch was below him. Their bodies were actually perpendicular to the wall as they ran. It looked like they were defying gravity. On the floor they continued the speed and repeated the maneuver when they met on the opposite side. Dropping to the floor, Josh asked, "Do you think it would be a surprise to your opponent if you could do that? The truth is, you can, with practice and the right mental attitude!"

He continued. "How about a double surprise for your opponent. Remember when I said to keep them off balance? Remember how I used your own momentum against you when seven of you attacked me at the same time? Okay, everybody stand up. Take a martial stance. I'm coming at you, one at a time, where you are. Keep an eye on me and try to anticipate where I'm going to be when I reach you. With that he built up speed around the room and coming to the first teen, passed him and ran at the second. Just before reaching him he ran up the wall, past the first teen and seemed to be aiming toward the second teen. The second teen squared off in a martial stance. Within a blink of an eye, Josh did a somersault off the wall and landed behind the first teen, who hadn't had time to turn. With a gentle sweep of his leg and using his hand to lower him gently, Josh laid the first teen on the floor.

"See what I mean? Basics, speed and surprise." With that, he pivoted his body around, launched a body kick and swept the legs out from under the second teen. "Surprise and maybe a little bit of diversion.

Watching you guys, I can see Alan's done a great job training you. All I can add is that if you want to be good, I mean **REAL** good, look beyond the physical part. Go on line, visit the library, read the history of martial arts and learn what the future is like. You need to develop the interior man as well as the exterior man."

As they left the loft Mitch was told he had a message.

"We may have a big problem. Somehow or other Jack Leung's found out about us."

CHAPTER 78

"Found out about us? What d'ya mean?"

"Word's out in Chinatown about two strangers, one Chinese and one Chinese speaking Caucasian. Nobody's supposed to help us and a reward's being offered for information about us."

"That helps us a hell of a lot!"

"It gets worse. Leung's supposedly gathered what remains of his stevedore gang and a bunch more to handle us. He's evidently going to war against the two of us! All because we wrecked his chop shop operation. From what I've heard, he's found out about the upcoming raid and closed down the operation. There may not be anything left for the department to raid."

"Okay! That means we have to move faster and smarter than he does. We need to push Mr. Chinn to move faster and we need to meet with your two undercover guys as soon as possible. Right now we better talk with Mr. Chinn and then with your two guys."

Mr. Chinn said he had heard the same thing. He thought Mitch and Josh should quit. The odds were just too great. He added that the word was out that Leung had as many as fifty ex-stevedores working for him. Josh disagreed.

"Like I was telling your martial arts students a little while ago, the best way to win a contest is with surprise. The last thing Leung would be expecting now would be a frontal attack. We need to find out where he is. If he's assembling a gang of that size, he should be easy to find. Haven't you heard anything?"

"Maybe, but I'm not sure I should tell you. I'm really worried about your safety."

"He's already after us, it won't do any good to hide. I'm going to hide Fern and then go after this guy, with or without your help. Mitch, are you with me?"

"Absolutely!"

Mr. Chinn deliberated for a few moments and then, "If you insist! I have heard he is gathering the gangs together tomorrow over in Emeryville, but I don't know exactly where. And as far as Fern is concerned, leave that up to my wife and me. She can move in with us for a few days. Adrien's been enjoying Fern's company so much and Fern's had so much fun, I'm sure she would jump at the offer!"

Josh, of course, immediately had a good idea where in Emeryville the gang was hanging out. He thanked Mr. Chinn for the offer for his wife, said he would talk to Fern immediately, and grabbing Mitch by his arm, left to try and meet with the two detectives.

Only one of them showed up at the rendezvous. He had heard the same info about Leung's gang but had even more to add.

"They're not just a gang of stevedores, much worse than that. Most of them are ex-cons. You should expect knives and guns. When something's too big for the teen gangs to handle, these guys take care of it. Rumor is that a lot of the businesses that Leung owns came to him because the previous owners died mysteriously. We've heard that he brings money to a troubled business, takes an ownership position and then the original owner has one of those mysterious deaths, leaving Leung the sole owner. At least on paper. He must have someone or something behind him with lots of money. Ten years ago he was a nobody. Now he's the owner behind the owner of a bunch of businesses and very dangerous. We're trying to find out where his money comes from, but very little luck so far!"

"Have you heard anything about them meeting in Emeryville?"

"Don't know about that. From what we've heard, they expect to find you in Chinatown, their home turf. They expect someone will turn you in and I wouldn't be surprised if they were right!"

"You may be right but I bet they're meeting in Emeryville because they lost the warehouse location. Do you have any idea if they know who we are?"

"All we've heard is what we told you. Two guys, one Chinese. The other a tall Caucasian that speaks Chinese fluently."

"Yeah, but Leung knows who we are. At least he knows who I am. He's organizing his gang in Emeryville to come after us in Chinatown. And you say the gang's a bunch of bloodthirsty ex-cons with guns and knives. They way I see it, we've still got the advantage."

Mitch chimed in. "You've got a strange way of looking at things! Last time you led me down this path, you convinced me that six to one odds were much better than twelve to two!"

'Worked out pretty well, didn't it?"

"Yeah but, fifty against two? Guns against hands? C'mon!"

"You left out brains! Think about it, what's the first thing they're going to do? Leung's not going to send fifty guys, in a bunch, up and down the streets of Chinatown to find us. They're going to split up in groups of twos and threes. They'll be questioning merchants and pounding on doors. You're not afraid of taking on two or three muscle-bound stevedores at a time are you?"

"I don't know what's scarier. Your Karate or your math. Okay, we can but try. So what's next?"

"Emeryville! We need to get over there by tomorrow morning and get a handle on the size of the gang. We can keep an eye on them until they start to move and then get ahead of 'em. The best thing would be getting long range snaps of the guys so we could ID them once they start showing up over here. Your department got any equipment like that we could borrow?"

"Sure, we've got telescopic lens cameras that'd pick up a flea on the perp's neck at two or three hundred yards, if that's what you want."

CHAPTER 79

In Emeryville, early the next morning, Josh debated meeting with the Emeryville police chief again. Chief Johnson had been helpful before, but in this case, Josh thought the less he knew the better. He assumed that the guys would only be in Emeryville part of the day at the most and then fan out to S.F. Chinatown. He also assumed they wouldn't be using the front door. He and Mitch had to find a way to keep the rear door watched and take as many pictures as possible.

As they drove around the block behind the Lab, they noticed a bunch of cars parked behind the lab and in the streets.

"Looks like the gang's all here" Mitch cheerfully opined.

After much searching, they found an elevated parking garage in the next street that had spaces in the rear of it that faced the Lab's back door. Mitch focused on the back door with the telescopic lenses and found he could almost read the name on the lock. Perfect!

"How we going to do this?" Mitch wanted to know.

"We'll start taking pictures when they leave. How about we take two-hour shifts until they leave. I'll take the first watch and you go get something to eat or take a nap or something. When you come back, bring me some water. We can pee in the bottle if necessary. I'll bet they're all gone by this afternoon. If they all leave at once, it's gonna be hard to get pictures of them all."

"Not to worry! This little baby can be set on continuous mode. It'll take a million pictures faster than you can blink! Maybe not quite a million, but lots!"

He showed Josh how to operate the camera and left. About an hour and a half later, the Lab door started to roll up. It was up only about three feet when the first guy ducked under it and walked to one of the cars. As he stood up, Josh started the camera rolling and got a perfect head-on picture. Shortly thereafter, more started leaving. As they exited the lab through the large delivery door, they were each facing Josh for a moment or two. The telescopic lens framed each face perfectly. Josh continued taking pictures until the door was finally closed. Just as he was finishing Mitch returned.

"Perfect timing! I think I got 'em all. Mr. Chinn was right. I counted about fifty guys, maybe a few more. I couldn't tell if they were carrying or not. Maybe they'll show up on the photos. They closed the overhead door so I guess they've all gone. How quickly can the police lab get these printed?"

"Quick!, maybe a half-hour?" and they took off.

"Terrific! Once we can identify these guys, we can start our operation. I was mulling over exactly what we'd do to these guys, and I've got it pretty well planned. Even got a name for it. Named for Julius Caesar's famous quote; 'Divide and Conquer!' It'll be fun! First we defang Leung and then we get him. Part of my plan involves using Leung's chop shop location. Do you know when the police intend to raid the place?"

"I think it was real early this morning, like maybe around five?"

"Couldn't be better. I've got plans for that building! Right now, though we head for the Chinatown police office and get those pictures developed as fast as possible and then on to the On Sing Association Building. I'm betting these guys'll break up into groups of threes, maybe fours and try to find us. We can use Alan's students to try to spot them before they find us. We get copies of the pictures for the kids and turn them loose. They don't need to get involved, just call us if they spot 'em. Think that'll work?"

"As good as anything, I guess. Just as long as the kids don't get hurt. Don't forget these guys probably have guns and know how to use them. They might not fire them in broad daylight but we can't take any chances."

"What about a gun? Can you get one if we need it?"

"Yeah, but the chief_____?"

"I know, she said no shooting. But she didn't say anything about threatening, did she? Let's have one, just in case, okay?"

Within the next hour, the pictures had been developed and a dozen copies of each made, Mitch had picked up his service gun and they were at the Association Building talking with Mr. Chinn.

"We've got pictures of all of Leung's gang. We think they're going to break up into groups of three or four and try to find us. We need Alan's students to fan out in Chinatown and spot these guys. Is that okay with you?"

"I don't think so. I want to help you but I can't put those kids in danger."

"Where are those kids right now? I bet they're walking in various parts of Chinatown, right? All they have to do is keep walking but keep their eyes open. When they spot one of these guys they use their cell phone and let us know where. That's it. No danger at all."

"So all you want them to do is spot one of the guys, call us and keep walking? If that's all, it should be okay. But we have to make sure the kids don't try any heroics. Alan can impress that on them!" He paused and Josh held his breath. Then, "And beyond that, what's your plan?"

"Divide and conquer! Actually they'll be dividing and we'll be conquering!"

"If you can impress upon the kids that they do absolutely no more than that, I think your plan's okay."

Josh and Mitch left to clue Alan into the plan to use his Judo students.

CHAPTER 80

Alan threw them a curve. "Okay, so you're going to divide and conquer them. Then what? What do you do with forty or fifty unhappy longshoremen?"

"Oh, hell, I hadn't thought about that," was Josh's response. Mitch came to the rescue.

. "Does Mr. Chinn have some longshoremen of his own? Big enough and tough enough to guard a few tied up stevedores for a few days?"

"We can probably do that. What d'ya have in mind?"

"I'm thinking we'll only have to overpower a few at a time, so we only have to get rid of a few at a time. Once they're tied up, it'll only take one or two guys to handle them in a small van. We just load 'em in the van and they're gone."

"Then what? They have to take them somewhere."

"How about Leung's chop shop warehouse. It's been raided and just sitting there empty with a lot of yellow ribbon. It's the last place they'd expect us to use. Isn't that what you had in mind when you said you had a use for the warehouse?"

"Sounds clumsy, but work it out," Josh suggested.

"We'll have to wait until three when the class starts, and you two better stay inside here so you're not spotted. I'll have some food sent up," Alan volunteered.

By three the whole class had assembled. Alan had told the boys to stay in their street clothes. Josh elected to speak to the class. First he thought he should make sure of their allegiance.

"Have any of you had a run in with any of the street gangs here in Chinatown?" They all nodded. One of them spoke up, "Sometimes they gang up on us on the way here and demand money!" Another said, "They're the main reason I'm here." The youngest one said, "They stole money from my Dad's store"

Josh was satisfied that this group was solidly against the teen gangs.

"We've put a dent in the teen gangs, but there's a much worse group out there that we're trying to break up. They're after Mitch and me because we're trying to help Mr. Chinn. Now we need your help! It's a simple thing but very important. We've got a bunch of pictures laid out on this table and want you guys to take a really good look at them. Some are Chinese, some are Caucasian, they're all big. And they're all dangerous. Many of them are ex-cons. We think these guys'll be wandering the streets, looking for Mitch and me in groups of threes or fours. We need you to spot them for us."

"How do we do that?" asked one of the older teens.

"How many of you have cell phones?" asked Josh.

Every hand went up. "Great!" said Josh. "Here's the plan Mr. Chinn's approved. Nobody pays any attention to teens wandering the streets after school. Particularly if they're either single or maybe a couple of guys. There're probably lots of them on the streets right now, right?"

They all agreed.

"That's simply what I want you to do. Break up into little groups of a couple of guys or less and wander around all the streets in Chinatown. If you spot any of the guys in the pictures here, call us and walk away. No heroics, no tailing, just keep walking as if you never saw them! Understand? Find them, phone us and leave. And that's it!! Can you do it?"

A few glanced at each other, and then one said, "Sure, sounds like fun!" and they all agreed.

Mr. Chinn said there is a little more to it than that. "First, we think there may be as many as fifty guys on the streets looking for Josh and Mitch. We also think they'll be in small groups of three or four. That means there might be a dozen or more of the small groups roaming around. Mitch and Josh are going to rely on your spotting a group so they can capture them, one small group at a time. So this might take all day and maybe into tomorrow! We need to get these guys off the streets so Josh and Mitch can go after a really bad guy."

Mitch added, "You'll have to keep wandering the streets and phoning in to us until we tell you to quit. You may spot the same guys or new ones over and over before we can take care of 'em. Just act normal, buy candy or something. Stop in at a doughnut shop, keep moving, whatever. They'll never notice you."

Alan took charge. "Okay guys, who'd rather go as a single, who wants a buddy." He got them all sorted out and reminded them as they were leaving, "don't bunch up. Everybody go in different directions. We'll try to cover all of Chinatown. And make sure at least one of each pair has a working cell phone!"

Josh and Mitch changed to street fighting clothes. Loose shirt and pants, sneaker type shoes and a couple of traditional weapons concealed in the shirt sleeves. Additionally, Mitch had his service gun tucked in the small of his back. They settled in to wait.

CHAPTER 81

"How're we gonna handle this?" Mitch wanted to know. "We can't beat up on them in broad daylight. How're we gonna capture them?"

"My first thought was for us to slip in behind them, pull your gun and arrest them. Kinda."

"What d'ya mean, kinda?"

"Well, we make them think they're being legitimately being arrested. You flash your badge and hold them at gunpoint and I'll cuff 'em. Then we need to get them off the street as quickly as possible and move on to the next group."

"You said that was your first thought, you had another?"

"Yeah. You said that we couldn't beat up on these guys in broad daylight? They probably would beat up on us if they had the chance, but I bet they wouldn't use their guns, except to scare us. My second thought was to let them think they were sneaking up on us and let them get the drop on us. Once we put up our hands, they let down their guard and we capture *them*! As far as any watchers would be concerned, we'd just thwarted a hold up! What d'ya think?"

"Strange as it may seem, I like the second idea. I think I'm itching for a fight. Specially when I think about what they're trying to do to us. One problem I see, how do we get rid of the guys we get?"

"Mr. Chinn came up with an idea for that. We call a number he gave me and before you know it, a delivery van'll show up and pile these guys in. If it gets too full, they'll make a run to the chop shop warehouse, and come back for more. He'll have a bunch of guys there to guard them. Pretty efficient, right?"

Within fifteen minutes they got their first two calls, almost at the same time. Four guys had been spotted on Jackson near Grant, about a block from the Association building. The second call was from a point farther away. They elected to go after the first group.

They raced down Grant, slowing as they neared Jackson. The boys had neglected to say if the guys were above or below Grant on Jackson.

Mitch scanned up the street and spotted them immediately. They were pretty obvious by size alone. Four big guys pushing pedestrians out of the way as they asked questions of them and the shopkeepers.

"Quick." Josh said. "A variation! I'll slip ahead of them and confront 'em. You come up behind 'em and we'll "arrest" 'em, okay?"

Walking slowly in order to let Josh get ahead of them, Mitch concentrated on keeping the four in sight. As he got within about forty feet of the guys, Josh suddenly materialized in front of them.

"You guys looking for me?" He said and stood there.

One of the guys whipped out a gun and said, "Hold it, don't move!" The four advanced on Josh.

Mitch was afraid that they might get on their cell phones right away and call for reinforcements, so he moved up in a hurry.

"Police," he called. "Hold it right where you are. Drop your guns or I'll shoot!"

The four hesitated for a moment, long enough for Josh to leap forward and with leg fully extended, make a karate sweep to knock the gun out of the leader's hands. They were then quickly subdued, hands tied behind their backs, ankles bound and stuffed into a doorway, waiting to be picked up.

To make it look all the more realistic, Mitch whipped out a notebook and asked for names and addresses of witnesses. Most of the passers by weren't interested.

"Only forty-six more to go!" Mitch said.

They weren't so lucky on the next group.

CHAPTER 82

"They've spotted three more groups!" Alan reported to Mitch.

"Which one's nearest?" Josh asked. "We'll get the closest ones."

Mitch picked the closest group and using his detailed knowledge of Chinatown was able to lead Josh through alleys and back lanes to arrive on the right street in just a few minutes. Again the four guys were easy to spot by their size alone. They were on a steep part of Washington just above Grant. Going door to door, shouldering pedestrians out of their way. There was no finesse in their plan. Just blanket the streets until somebody gave them some information about a tall, youngish, Chinese speaking round eye. As Mitch and Josh moved up behind the four they overheard pedestrians complaining to each other about the rudeness of the four. Josh thought that maybe they could pick a fight with the foursome and the pedestrians would applaud.

The gang of four was so intent on their mission, or so confidant in their bullying tactics, they paid no attention to what went on behind them. Josh and Mitch were able to walk right up behind them. Mitch stood back, revolver in hand, while Josh, from behind, tapped the nearest one on the shoulder.

"Looking for me?" All four whirled around only to be confronted by Mitch and his gun. Mitch announced himself. "Police!, you're under arrest!"

Belligerently, the biggest one said, "Oh yeah, what for? We haven't broken any laws!"

"Citizens complaint!" Mitch told him. "One of you knocked an old man to the ground. And unfortunately for you, we witnessed it. We'll book you for disorderly conduct and the attack on the elderly gentleman."

"Bullshit, there weren't no attack. This is a bunch of crap!"

"Cuff 'em, we're taking 'em in, Mitch said to Josh. Both Josh and Mitch had a pocketful of plastic ties to cuff the guys with. Josh was standing behind the biggest guy, securing his wrists, when he heard, "Drop it!"

Looking over the big guys shoulder, Josh saw another group of four guys standing behind Mitch, holding a gun pressed against his back. It looked like his teen spies had missed this group. He surmised that pure luck had brought this group around the corner to follow Josh and Mitch.

"Drop it, or I'll club you to the ground!"

Mitch caught Josh's eye and shrugged his shoulders. Josh winked at him and mouthed the words, "Divide and Conquer!"

The big guy, grinning, started to turn and force Josh to untie him. The other three moved to grab Josh. Josh, using the momentum of the big guys turn, grabbed his arm and helped him along in the same direction directly into the other three. On his way, Josh swept his legs out from under him so that he crashed into the three others. They went down cursing and yelling.

At the same time Mitch took advantage of a common mistake gunmen often make. The gunman was standing directly behind Mitch with his gun pressed into Mitch's spine. Possibly because he didn't know any better or perhaps he was trying to keep the gun hidden from pedestrians. Mitch whirled away from the gun and with a chopping motion knocked the gun out of the gunman's hand. Mitch didn't hold back. With guns in the picture, you don't hold back. The gunman's wrist was broken. Continuing the surprise attack, Mitch leaped toward the three remaining and picking one out as he was in mid-air, delivered a kick alongside his head and knocked him unconscious.

Josh, in the meantime had finished restraining the big guy and had dealt with his remaining three. One of the three had a attempted to pull a gun and Josh had been forced to dislocate his shoulder while taking the gun away. All of his four were on the ground, subdued.

Meanwhile Mitch was having a problem. Of his remaining two, one was running away. Mitch delivered a sweeping leg block to the one remaining and as he fell, managed a knee chop to his chin, knocking him out. He yelled to Josh.

"That one's getting away!"

Josh immediately sized up the situation. With his gun and badge Mitch could control the seven here on the ground and they did not want anyone to escape!

"Watch these guys, I'll get him!" and he took off.

The guy had run down Washington to the corner and was halfway across Washington, heading uptown on Grant. The sidewalks were full of pedestrians and the streets were full of cars. The guy had a half block lead on Josh. "Perfect," Josh thought.

Downhill, it was easy to build momentum. Within a few steps, Josh was moving with the necessary speed and launched himself onto the hood of a parked car. Barely touching the car he launched himself from it to the top of the next parked car and from there to the top of a moving car. His speed was so fast and his touch was so light, the cars' inhabitants were hardly aware of his passing. Washington was a one-way street going uphill. Josh was going downhill. Down the street cars were jamming to a stop as they watched this crazy man leap from car to car. He seemed to fly as he leaped from moving car to moving car. In no time he had traversed the street and was at the next corner.

When Josh reached Grant Street he was only a few feet behind the fleeing longshoreman. He continued leaping from car to car until he was past the gunman where he, at full speed, threw himself to the sidewalk before the startled runner, tucked himself into a ball as he landed and sprang onto his feet just in time to trip the guy as he ran by. The guy never saw Josh as he was looking back over his shoulder at where he thought Josh would be, behind him.

He had an audience. It had happened so quickly, the pedestrians hadn't had time to react. Before they could, Josh whipped open his badge case and displaying his San Francisco Lieutenant's badge said, "Police! He was trying to resist arrest!" He plastic-tied the guy's hands behind him and pushed him back up Washington.

Meanwhile, Mitch had done the same. He flashed his badge, calmed the bystanders and herded the group into a nearby doorway. Once there, he called for the meat wagon, confidant that Josh would catch the runner. While he was waiting, marveling at the sight of Josh leaping from car to car, he thought, "Twelve down, we're almost a quarter done"

What he said to Josh was, "not bad partner, you've given a whole new meaning to the definition of car-hopping."

CHAPTER 83

"Did you notice they had cell phones?" Mitch asked. Mitch had searched their pockets looking for guns and knives and found several. He also found several cell phones. He kept the phones but sent all the guns and knives along with the thugs in the meat wagon.

"Think we can use them?"

"Probably, this one's been vibrating."

"Answer it and see what we get"

Mitch pushed the talk button and whispered, "keep it down, we're tailing the guy now.". The phone displayed the number and area code of the call.

"Where the fuck you guys at? I been on the horn to you for five minutes," a belligerent voice echoed.

Thinking quickly Mitch, speaking in a deep whisper said, "for fucks sake we're following him right now. Get the hell off the phone.", and hung up.

"Must be somebody's holed up somewhere trying to keep track of the gangs. I wonder how long it'll be before they start missing some of their guys? Come to think of it, maybe there aren't fifty guys out looking for us. Maybe some of them, like you say, are holed up letting the other guys do all the work. There's some still out though, 'cause I'm still getting calls.

"Okay then. Change of strategy. We'll question the next group. We'll find out how many groups are working the streets and where they're reporting in to. But we gotta keep moving fast before they realize something's wrong. What'd you find out about any other groups?"

"They've reported on at least two more groups, but that was a half-hour ago, I'll check with them again." After a short conversation with Alan he said, "That's interesting. The two groups our kids have been reporting on stopped questioning people and headed towards each other. Now they've met and are talking together about three blocks from here."

"I bet someone's on to the news that they're missing some guys. Did the kids notice them using their cell phones a lot?"

"He didn't say, but I bet you're right. So what do we do?"

"Can you get us over there in a hurry? Is there some way we can sneak up on them without them seeing us?"

"Let's go!" Mitch responded. He led Josh across the street into and through a gift shop. Exiting the back door into an alley they quickly ran down it, crossed the next street and continued down the same alley. The alley was too narrow for a car but there were pedestrians and bicycles galore to deal with. Near the end of the second block, Mitch pushed a narrow wooden gate open and they ran down an even narrower alley. The only obstacles on it were garbage cans and a couple of cats. They emerged next to the front door of a restaurant and within sight of the group of eight or nine hoodlums gathered about a half block away.

"We can't stand here, they're bound to notice us." Josh said.

"Inside!" Mitch responded. "The owner'll let us watch from inside."

"Looks like they're arguing!" Josh said. "One of 'em's on a cell phone." Mitch observed and added, "Now what?"

"Wouldn't it be nice if we could make all nine of 'em disappear!" Josh suggested. "That'd make a permanent dent in Leung's operation!"

"Nine of them. I don't see how we can take them in the open, at least not just the two of us. I don't think we can pull the under arrest gag on them, there's too many. Maybe we should just follow them and see where they go."

"As long as they're not moving is there anyway we can get closer?"

"Hang on a sec." Mitch talked to the restaurant owner. "He says if we go out the kitchen door we can mingle with the bunch waiting for the signal light to change and cross with them. Probably won't be noticed. Then three doors down there's a skinny little alley that'll take us to the rear door of a cleaning shop. The owner's cousin owns it and he'll phone him to let us in. We'll be within ten or fifteen feet of the gang."

"Okay, let's go."

Trying not to be noticed, they did as the restaurant owner suggested. Joined the crowd waiting for the light to change and stayed with the crowd until they could veer to their right and out of sight of the nine guys. They found the alley. Calling it an alley gave it more of a title than it deserved. It was really just a two-foot wide space between two buildings. Behind the second building it widened to a respectable three feet and they quickly found the cleaning shop rear door. The owner was holding the door open for them.

In Chinese he asked Mitch if this was about "Those hoodlums loitering in front of my shop?" In impeccable Chinese, Josh told him, "that's exactly why we're here."

The owner did a double take and said, "You're the one they're asking about!"

Josh flashed his lieutenant's badge and said, "We're undercover and need to neutralize these guys."

"You want to use my phone and call for backup?"

CHAPTER 84

Mitch looked at Josh and shrugging his shoulders said, "Maybe it's time we call for help?"

"If we get your guys in, we'll lose control. Would we be able to question them and find out where Jack Leung is? I don't think so. They'd probably arrest them on something like disturbing the peace, they'd be out in twenty-four and we wouldn't learn anything."

"We got the other guys stashed in the chop shop, we could twist their arms for info."

"Yeah, but these guys seem to be in direct contact with their boss. The one you took the phone from was just taking orders. I'm for somehow or other taking these guys here. But as yet, I can't see how."

"Okay, I'm with you, but I don't see how we're going to do it either, and these guys aren't going to stand here forever."

"They must be waiting for someone. Maybe somebody's coming to pick 'em up?"

The shop owner asked, "Can't you make them move from in front of my store? I can see customers afraid to come in!"

Josh said, "That's it! To Mitch. To the shop owner he said, "Are you scared of them?"

"Not at all. In broad daylight? No, I'm not scared but some of my elderly customers are!"

"Would you be willing to go out your front door and tell them that you've called the police. That they're blocking the sidewalk and scaring your customers. That the police said they'd be coming up the street in a few minutes? Could you do that?"

"Sure. I can do that. Now?

"Give us a couple of minutes to use the alley and get up to the next corner. Be sure and tell them that the police will be coming up the street! Be sure and tell them they're coming UP the street. Okay?"

"Tell them police are coming up the street? Sure. Okay!"

As they rushed up the alley and then down the next street to the corner just above where the nine were standing, Mitch asked, "And then what?"

"Let's see what they do and then decide! I expect they'll head for this corner and try to get around it before the cops get here. If so, I may have a plan."

Peeking around the corner themselves, they saw the shop owner run out the door, yelling in pigeon English, "You go! Police coming! I call them! You see! Minute or so they come up street from station. You public nuisance, scare customers. Go away!"

The guys looked at him like he was crazy and for a moment Josh thought they were going to hit him. But after another moment, one of them broke uphill and motioned the rest to follow. Josh was thinking that they were either waiting for someone to pick them up or someone to meet them. Either way, they weren't going far, just around the next corner! Where Mitch and Josh were waiting.

Mitch saw them heading toward where he and Josh were waiting and said, with a hint of nervousness, "Wow, we got them right where they want us."

Josh said, "Might be easier than you think. Remember 'divide and conquer and surprise!' What we need is an equalizer or two, follow me."

Josh led Mitch back to the alley where he had noticed a bundle of bamboo poles behind one of the apartment houses. They looked to be between six and eight feet long and should be perfect for a pole fight. Mitch immediately grasped the value of the poles. They each picked one up and went back to the head of the alley and waited there.

In a few moments, the gang burst around the corner and stopped. The one that had made the decision for the gang to head up the hill seemed to be the leader. He motioned them all behind him and then cautiously peeked back around the corner.

Josh whispered, "Look at that, all in a bunch with their backs to us, what more could we ask? You ready? Follow my lead!" And he quietly took off. Mitch followed.

CHAPTER 85

As they ran quietly together towards the backs of the gang, Josh and Mitch automatically divided the group into two sections. Josh would attack the right flank and Mitch the left. This was one of the attack exercises they had practiced in the preceding days. They each felt they could take out at least two of the gang with the first strike, using their poles. The added advantage was that the strikes by the poles would be completely silent.

There were many ways that these fighting poles could be used. They could be used to hold off a group by holding one end and sweeping the pole in a large circle, threatening anyone that came close. Another way was to grasp it in the middle and use both ends to strike your opponent. The second method was what Mitch and Josh were planning on using.

They struck the rear of the group simultaneously. Each, using one end of their pole, swept the legs out from under one guy and then, immediately followed it with the other end, swept another pair of legs. As these four hit the ground, both Josh and Mitch delivered crushing blows with their elbows, knees or feet to an exposed and vulnerable part of the body. The four were effectively out of the picture, so quickly that the other five hadn't as yet reacted.

By the time Josh and Mitch stood up the five began to react. They were turning around, realizing something unexpected was happening behind them. Like many big, strong and muscular men they tended to think they could muscle their way out of almost any problem, which worked to Josh and Mitch's advantage. The gangs first reaction was to rush the two. They were bigger, more muscular than Josh and Mitch, plus they were five against two. No need for guns, they thought.

As they charged the two, Mitch and Josh sprang back a pace and away from each other. As they did, they grasped their poles by their ends and started swinging them in large circles. The gang stopped in their tracks and started reaching for guns. Exactly what Mitch and Josh had expected. They did what the gang did not expect, they charged. So fast that they were on the guys before they could draw their weapons.

Josh concentrated on the three before him. He feinted at one, wheeled in mid-air and delivered a blow to the head with his foot. At the same time he thrust the pole between the legs of the third thug. As he continued his move he jerked the pole up to the groin area and twisted it. Immediate testicle pain! Plus the pole twisting between his legs brought the guy down to the deck. Josh landed on his feet, leaped into a twirl in the opposite direction. On the way he knocked the gun out of the guy's hand and, in passing, elbowed the guy in his abdomen, knocking his breath out and bringing him to the ground.

He glanced around to see how Mitch was doing. Mitch had one down and one to go. To Josh, it looked like Mitch was playing with his guy. The guy was trying to pull his gun and Mitch kept knocking the guys hands away from it.

"Finish him," Josh said. "We gotta clean up this mess."

With one quick blow to the head, Mitch knocked his opponent out, and looking around at the nine guys laid out on the sidewalk, said, "How the hell did we do that?"

"Divide and conquer, surprise and practice. Besides we have right on our side. Now, call the meat wagon. Keep an eye on them, I'm going to check on the street to see if someone shows up for them. A few minutes later a Ford van slowly came up the street and stopped in front of the cleaning shop. It sat there for a couple of minutes, then the driver got out and went into the shop.

Josh jumped back to Mitch and said, "We better drag these guys into the alley quick or the van will find us." They had to drag four of the guys and force the other five, stumbling and occasionally falling, into the alley. With the aid of their poles and the guns they'd confiscated, they managed the group. They just barely dragged the last one into the alley and closed the wooden door behind them when the van slowly nosed around the corner. All the time the thug's cell phone was vibrating furiously.

Josh said, "I wonder what the shop owner told them?"

"He probably told them he didn't speak English! No way would they get anything out of that guy."

They watched from behind the wooden door as the van slowly circled the block three times and finally left.

"Did you call the meat wagon yet?"

"No. I thought it wouldn't be a good idea for it to show up at the same time their van was here. I'll call right now." Josh and Mitch spent the next few minutes making sure their prisoners were securely tied and gagged.

"I sure wish we could tail their van. Maybe it'd lead us to Leung!"

"They're gone by now. Besides my car's too far away."

"I know. Let's hook a ride with the meat wagon and see what we can get out of these guys."

"How're you going to make any of these guys talk? We can't torture them, even though they were willing to shoot us."

"Vell, I haff mein vays!" Josh told him. "Remember, divide, conquer and surprise!"

CHAPTER 86

At the warehouse, they found seven Chinese guarding twelve prisoners. All properly bound and gagged and furious. The Chinese were playing cards and generally lounging around, keeping an eye on their charges.

"Can you handle nine more?" Josh asked and was assured they were looking forward to it. Josh singled out the leader of the last group of nine and whispered to one of the guards that he wanted to question him, but only after he questioned any one of the others.

He and Mitch chose a closed-off room toward the back of the warehouse and had the first prisoner brought in. They opened the trap door leading to the open water and made sure he saw the bay beckoning below.

"Enough weights, a simple shove and a guy just disappears forever. Handy, isn't it?" Josh remarked to Mitch.

"We've never had anybody come back up!"

The guy blanched and looked like he wanted to say something. Mitch removed his gag after warning him about yelling or anything.

"What d'ya want? I'll tell you anything you want to know. We didn't mean to harm you none."

"That's a lot of bull. You're carrying guns and you didn't mean no harm? Frankly, that hole looks pretty usable to me. A little while ago you guys were ready to shoot us, so I don't really give a shit about you. What I do want is your boss's name and how to find him. And thereby hangs your salvation. We get his name and location and you avoid a watery grave, at least for the time being."

"Honest to God, I don't know nothin! They called me and told me to meet them under the old Key System building. They told us to scour Chinatown to find two guys. I guess it was you two?"

"Now that's a problem, you're already lying. How about your meeting in Emeryville yesterday?"

"Oh, shit."

"So how about the truth?"

"All right, all right,the big guy you just brought in. He organized us and kept track of us. But there was someone else at the meeting. He was sitting in a Rolls off to one side. I think he was really in charge because the big guy talked to him a couple of times."

"That's it? That's all you know? Hell, we knew that much already!" Josh told him." Turning to Mitch, he said, "Let's get rid of him. I'm sure one of the other guys'll be more helpful!"

"Wait! I can't tell you what I don't know! The only thing I can tell you for sure is that the big guy knows the guy in that car. I heard him say he'd worked for him before and he paid well."

"Well, that *might* help. Tell you what. You help us, maybe we'll help you. Let me see what my partner thinks."

Pulling Mitch aside, he whispered, "Get your gun out, we're gonna do a little bit of acting!"

"What d'ya call what you've been doing so far?"

"This time, he's joining in! Just follow my lead."

Josh strode over to where the guy was tied in a chair. He grabbed the guy by his hair, pulled his head back until the guy was forced to look straight up at Josh hovering over him and said: "Okay, my partner says we should give you one last chance. We're going to start asking you questions, louder and louder. You're going to answer them louder and louder. After a few minutes you'll be yelling as loud as you can. You're answer will always be, 'I don't know.' You got it?"

Trembling, the guy said: "Yeah, I can do that!"

"Not can. WILL, is the right answer!"

"Okay, Okay. I WILL do that!"

He whispered to Mitch. "Give me three or four minutes of yelling questions, Then when I yell, 'The Hell with you', you fire your gun into the water and I'll slap some duct tape over his mouth. We'll see how our little drama affects the next guy!"

Walking over to the tied prisoner, Josh raised his voice and said, "I'm getting sick and tired of your beating around the bush. Quit playing dumb! Who's your boss?"

"I don't know!"

Whispered, "Louder!"

"I DON'T KNOW!"

"BULLSHIT! WHAT'S THE GUYS NAME THAT PAID YOU?"

"I DON'T KNOW!"

"I'M SICK AND TIRED OF THIS. WHERE WERE YOU GOING TO MEET WHEN YOU CAUGHT ME?"

"I DON'T KNOW!"

A few more loud exchanges like that and Josh yelled. "THE HELL WITH YOU!" Mitch fired his gun into the water and Josh slapped duct tape over the guy's mouth.

CHAPTER 87

There was a loud pounding on the door accompanied with yelling. "What the hell? Wasn't supposed to be any killing!" It was a couple of the Chinese guards in a dither.

"Perfect." Said Josh. Yanking the door open he quickly pulled the two into the room, slamming the door shut behind them. He threw an arm around each of them and slapped a hand over their mouths. Mitch put a finger to his lips, telling them to keep mum, and then pointed at the live prisoner, still seating in his chair.

"I thought—?"

"That's what we wanted you to think! Did it work on the prisoners?"

"It worked on all of us. I gotta tell the other guys!"

"Stop! Don't do that! Not yet! We gotta keep our prisoners in the dark about this. You gotta go out there and cuss the hell out of us. Tell the other guards that the sons of bitches in there killed the guy. Be mad as hell about it and be loud enough for the prisoners hear you. Tell them we threatened you too."

"I don't know if I can make them believe it."

"Why not? You already said they heard us and thought we'd killed the guy. You're just confirming what they already know, right? Remind them that we've got all the guns in here! Then bring in the guy I pointed out to you earlier. Don't go soft on me. We need the next guy to be convinced his friends been killed and that he might be next. Bring him in." Mitch half carried and half dragged the prisoner into the next room, out of sight.

It wasn't that easy to bring him in. Even though his hands were duct-taped together behind his back and he was gagged, his brute strength made it difficult to manhandle him. And, he didn't cooperate. First he tried to run. Then he charged and tried to head-butt with no result. They finally duct taped his ankles together and with one on each side of him, were able to half drag, half duck-walk him into the interrogation room.

As he was seated and tied down, Josh and Mitch ignored him, except to instruct the two that brought him to tie him tightly. Mitch was peering into the opening to the waters below, making sure he was solidly in sight of the prisoner.

"Are you sure we used enough weights?" Josh asked. "Does everything look okay?"

"All I see are a few bubbles, no blood or anything like that in the water." Mitch replied. They both turned to their new prisoner.

"You're bluffing." The prisoner challenged, as soon as they removed his gag.

"You're entitled to think anything you want." Josh replied. "But, there's some info we want, there's over forty feet of water right below us, enough to hold you and several more of your guys. Eventually, one of your gang'll talk! The moment you guys pulled guns on us, your future was sealed. So-----talk and live, or clam up and die, which is it?"

"Are you cops? You flashed badges! If you're cops you're not going to kill me!"

Josh answered. "I'll tell you about me. First of all, I don't live in San Francisco or anywhere near it. Secondly, I was sent here by an organization much more powerful than your puny outfit and was told to handle a certain situation any way I could. You're in my way. I'm about ready to casually sweep you aside, got it? So, I repeat. Live or die? You got about thirty seconds. Who was in the Rolls and where's his headquarters?" Mitch dragged the guy and the chair over to the edge of the hole and pulled his gun.

"Is that the same gun?" Josh asked and Mitch replied. "Yeah, if I use the same gun, there's only one to get rid of."

"Okay, okay. I'll talk. I just work for him. I don't gotta die for him"

Josh glanced at his watch. "Ten seconds, that's all you had left. Okay, what's his name?"

"Jack. That's his name. That's all I know. Just Jack"

Josh said, "Bullshit," and glancing at his watch again, started counting. "Nine, eight, seven, six."

He got the message. "Leung, that's his last name. The guy in the Rolls. Name's Leung. He's Chinese"

"Better. Now, where's he live? And I don't mean his "down the peninsula" place either. I mean, where in San Francisco?"

"It's hard place to get to. Honest, I don't know the address. It's on Broadway near Kearny, upstairs over a strip joint."

CHAPTER 88

"Do we believe him?" Josh whispered to Mitch. "I think so," he whispered back. "We know that's where Leung used to live. I think this guy's telling us all he knows. He knows who was in the car, he's just guessing that he still lives over the strip joint." .

He walked back over to the goon, "We're going to check out what you said. For your sake, you better hope what you told us holds up."

To Mitch he whispered, "Let's keep up the fiasco a little longer. Have our guys take him out with the rest of the group and thank him for ratting on their boss. Make sure the rest of the gang knows he talked to save his life. In the meantime keep the first guy tied, gagged and separate from the rest of the group. Won't do any harm to let them continue to think we're a murderous crew and their lives are still in danger."

Mitch clued the guards on what was going on and noticed that they were looking a little apologetic. One of the guys said they'd called Mr. Chinn and told him that some of the captives were being shot.

"Oh, hell," was Josh's response. "We better call him right away and straighten him out."

"It's about time you called." Was the reply when they called Mr. Chinn. "I'm avoiding calls from your chief, your wife wants to know where you are and I got a call from one of my men that you murdered someone?"

"Don't worry about us murdering anyone. Your guys might *think* we did, but we didn't. What we wanted was that the guys we've caught *were sure* we did. By the way, it worked! We know where Leung's hiding out. We need to talk to you, how about right now?"

"It's four already. Your wife's at my home, you want me to get her over here?. She said to tell you and Mitch that you have to leave the house where you're staying. The owners unexpectedly returned."

"Oh, crap. Now what?"

"Don't worry about a place to stay. I've already called in some favors and have a double room for you and a single for Mitch reserved at one of the better hotels. You can use it as your headquarters. That's taken care of. You've got worse things than that to worry about. Your Chief's about ready to have a fit, she's expecting a call from me, and what'll I tell Fern?"

Josh had to pause a second and take all that in. He made some quick decisions. "Don't call Chief Anne, I'll call her as soon as I get to your place. I'll talk to Fern as soon as I can."

Mitch and Josh were in the association's offices by about four-fifteen and closeted with Mr. Chinn. To say he was unhappy with them would be a complete understatement.

"I do not like what's going on! I've always enjoyed a good relationship with Chief Anne and now she is accusing me of working with you behind her back. I need her good will to be effective and you're sabotaging me. You have a good many of our people upset, they claim you murdered someone. I've been getting citizen complaints about street fights and," looking directly at Josh, "your wife thinks I'm keeping you away from her!"

"Wow! That's a load! First of all, *nobody's* been murdered! Like I told you over the phone we made them think somebody had been shot, but it was all a show. We needed to convince their leader that we were deadly serious and it worked. We kept your guys in the dark to make sure it seemed real."

"Okay, I believe that part. One of they guys down there phoned me and confirmed what you said. But appearances are important. We can't sit on this too long, somebody's going to talk. And what about the other things?"

"I'll take care of Chief Anne. She's just miffed that we haven't reported in. When we tell her how close we are to getting Leung, she'll be okay," Josh hoped. We didn't start any street fights. We semi-arrested some gun carrying thugs on your streets. Some with the help of your own merchants. One of the merchants actually asked us to clear the sidewalk of the guys, they were scaring his customers. Yeah, the guys put up a fight, but no shots were fired, no civilians were hurt and your streets are safer."

"And Fern?"

"Where is she, at your home?"

"No, she went back to the hotel, and if I were you, I'd get over there right now. I think she's more worried than mad. Did you ever tell her anything about what you're doing? The Chinese have a saying, 'An open book sheds light, a closed book sheds distrust.' You need to open your book a little more with Fern! But before you go, call your chief!!"

Chief Anne was obviously perturbed again. Upset that they hadn't called in as previously arranged. But when Josh told her what they'd done, not all of it, and the progress they'd made, she was mollified. Fortunately for Josh and Mitch, none of the citizen complaints or the Association fears that they'd committed a murder had made their way out of Chinatown. She said that Josh's boss in Yosemite had called a few times and wanted to know when Josh was coming back. She told him that what Josh had uncovered so far was leading to a major bust and that she needed him a little longer. She also said that when he found out that San Francisco was picking up the tab for Josh's and Fern's lodging and meals, he wasn't nearly as concerned.

Josh called Fern and said he would be right over. To his surprise, her reply was a calm, "Good, I'll be waiting."

Josh used his room card and entered the room. He and Fern hadn't had a hard word between them since the day they were married. He didn't know what to expect. As he entered she walked across the room and slapped his face as hard as she could. "That's for scaring the hell out of me." and slapped him again. And that's for not trusting me enough to tell me what's going on." Then burst into tears and slumped into his arms.

Josh realized that Mr. Chinn's quote was correct. He needed to open his book more to Fern. He also realized that Fern was much stronger than he gave her credit for being. Not only physically, but emotionally and mentally as well. He could and should share his job with her. He held her and comforted her, promising to keep her in the picture from now on. Gradually she relaxed into his body and her anger melted away.

"You had me so worried. I kept overhearing things that you and Mitch were doing and they seemed so dangerous."

"It's my fault, I should have known better. Do you feel better now?"

"Much."

"How about we do a little celebrating, like maybe getting a massage?"

"A massage? What kind of a massage? And where?"

"I was thinking of an erotic massage right here in the room. Like by me?"

"How erotic?"

"Very!"

"Sounds lovely, how do we start?"

"Well, first you strip down to your scivvies."

"Scivvies?"

"I'm trying to be cool and professional. Then you lie down on the bed on your stomach and I'll try to find some good lotion in the bathroom."

"If I'm paying for an erotic massage, why am I leaving my scivvies on?"

"Because, my dear, I want the pleasure of uncovering that beautiful bottom of yours all to myself."

Josh started at Ferns' feet and using his memory of massages taken in Japan, soon had her totally relaxed. He alternately kissed and massaged his way up her legs and her back and then told her to turn over.

"Shouldn't I have a towel or something over me?"

"Ma'am, you paid for erotic, you get erotic. Lift your bottom so I can slip your panties, I mean scivvies, off."

Next he started at her feet again, kissing and massaging all of her, from feet to forehead.

"My god, that's erotic. I've never been kissed there before."

"Just part of the normal service, ma'am. Any special requests?"

"Uuuuuuh, yes. Can I give you an erotic massage? You know, with attention to all parts of your body?"

Of course, Josh complied with her request. They spent the rest of the evening in bed.

Later that night, almost midnight, they showered and dressed to go down for a late dinner in the hotel. The night clerk stopped them with a message to call Mitch. Josh placed the call to Mitch while Fern listened in.

"What's up?"

"Just wondering, what's up for tomorrow?"

Josh was in a frivolous mood.

"Tomorrow? Tomorrow I intend to beat the hell out of you."

"Oh really?"

"Yep. Meet me at the Association headquarters first thing, okay?" and hung up.

CHAPTER 89

Josh's plan the next morning was to get a good work out and at the same time contribute to Mitch's education. He arranged to use the sparring space at the Association headquarters. He thought that one of the most effective and unobtrusive weapons Mitch could learn to use effectively and pretty quickly was the stick. Mitch had already shown some prowess in its use. He would be a good student.

At the Dojo, he started with questions.

"Do you have to have a special stick to do bodily harm? The answer is no. A light stick, used properly and at the right place on the body can effectively neutralize an opponent."

"If you have a stick, is it your primary weapon? Again the answer is no. The stick is only effective if your mind and body are also weapons."

He put Mitch through his paces. "Look at me closely and tell me what I'm doing."

"You're watching me intently and leaning a little to the right as if you were about ready to charge me."

"Where're my feet and knees?"

"They're still straight below you."

"Good, now watch and learn." With that Josh leaned a little further to his right. Mitch turned with him. Suddenly Josh's upper body turned further to his right while simultaneously his legs propelled him to his left. Before Mitch could react, Josh had leaped towards Mitch's right side and with his stick delivered a stinging blow to his right wrist forcing Mitch to drop his weapon. Hitting the exact nerve spot, Josh had temporarily paralyzed Mitch's right hand. Continuing the sticks motion, Josh administered a stinging blow to Mitch's left wrist with the other end. Both of Mitch's wrists and hands were stinging and temporarily numb.

"If I'd used the full power of the stick, both of your wrists would be completely paralyzed now and you'd be disarmed. I leaned to the right to mislead you, using my mind and body. The stick became a more effective weapon because you were off balance. You need to practice that for the next hour because you need to hit that nerve with exactitude to fully paralyze the wrist! But if you miss a little you'll still do a lot of damage. So let's go! It takes a long time to control the stick so that you can hit the exact spot as I did and you're not going to get there in an hour, but you'll be ahead of now!"

As they sparred, Josh kept adding to Mitch's knowledge. "Remember, in a street fight anything goes. Use a garbage can lid, use the garbage! Use your belt, your shoes, a rock or maybe a piece of wood. Think, distract, attack and win. And keep moving! A great weapon is a short piece of chain! You don't have to beat an opponent to the ground to win, a man with two useless wrists and hands isn't going to win, right?"

CHAPTER 90

Back at their headquarters, Josh and Mitch discussed what they knew.

"The guy's story checks out. Leung must have moved his city hang-out back there. Question is; How do we know when he's there, how do we get in and what do we do with him?" Mitch wanted to know.

"Let's think about it. From the very beginning, everything's led to him. He was the secret investor in the Emeryville Lab. Charley Fong linked him to the teen gangs. The stevedore linked him to the chop shop and so did the roving gangs. Mr. Chinn voiced his suspicions about Leung wanting to take over the Tong. Either he's behind all this or someone's behind him, someone like Lee. The only way to find out is to make him talk or find evidence in his flats. We gotta get in when he's there, neutralize him and either make him talk or thoroughly toss the place, or maybe both."

"I wonder if he has body guards or an alarm system?" From Mitch.

"Probably both. So we need to bypass the alarm system and neutralize the body guards. Maybe we can use one to cancel the other. If he has an alarm system, it'll be completely internal. No police alarms in that place! Picture this. The alarm goes off, the natural assumption is that someone's trying to get in, right? All the guards rush to the alarmed doors and windows expecting to find a broken window or a jimmied door. Suppose we're already inside? Then they've got us right where we want them. We're behind them, they don't know we're there, should be a cinch to handle!"

"Breaking and entering, guns, kidnapping, somehow I'm not thinking your plan will thrill Chief Anne. Besides if all the windows and doors are alarmed how do we get inside?"

"Leave that up to me. Look, I know what we're doing isn't exactly police kosher, but it's the only way we're going to get anywhere! Look how long the police have had suspicions about Leung's place and couldn't do anything about it. I know you think I'm going too far too fast, but that's the way I work. What's the old saying, 'Rules are made to be broken?' The important thing is, we're not really hurting anybody, at least not so far. We're making progress. We made some arrests and the evidence's holding up. Nothing's has been tainted so far. We've got CHINN on our side and we're doing good!"

"I don't need a pep talk. Actually I'm enjoying every minute of it, so far. Besides, after we've both been canned, I figure you'll become a millionaire karate teacher somewhere and I'll be your associate. We'll both be rich! Soooo, what's your plan? We're going to teleport in to his place?"

"Not quite that dramatic. It's gotta be one of two ways. Usually there're some windows that aren't alarmed 'cause they think no one can reach them. I can probably surprise them there. And then there's the roof. We know he has the top two floors all to himself from the last time we broke in. I'll bet they never did figure out how we got in. Either way it's going to be a night operation and you're going to have to brush up on your Ninja prowess."

"Ninja? That's Japanese! "You're kidding, aren't you?" Then, kiddingly, "I don't got no Prowess there."

"You will have by tonight. I've booked a climbing tower for our private use this afternoon and I've got some gear waiting for us at an outfitter in Japan town. By tonight, you'll be able to scale the tallest building, just like Superman!"

"More probably, break my neck!"

The store in Japan town had complete Ninja outfits for sale. Even though they were really meant to be used as costumes, they'd work just fine for what Josh had in mind. Black suits, rubber-soled soft black shoes, hooded jackets and masks finished the outfit for Mitch.

From there they went south, almost to the San Francisco Airport, where the outdoor climbing tower was located.

"Have you done any climbing before?" Josh asked.

"Sure. Nothing professionally though. And nothing quite this tall either."

"Well, you know how they have notches and stuff to put your feet in when you're climbing?"

"Yeah, I like that part!"

"Well, We're not going to do that !"

CHAPTER 91

Josh had arranged a private session at the climbing tower. They had the place to themselves as far as other climbers were concerned, but the staff was there. They insisted their insurance company wouldn't allow anyone to use their mountain without the staff being present.

The tower was located at the rear of a huge lot behind an exercise facility and stood over seventy feet tall. The front had several climbing faces differing in their difficulty. From left to right the level ranged from beginner to expert.

"We'll start from the expert and work up from there." Josh said as he started removing several items from his duffel bag.

"Work up?"

"Yep. Around the sides and in the back are faces with no climbing aids at all. You're going to use some Ninja techniques to climb impossible walls. You're in great shape physically, you've got a good background in martial arts and you've got me.

Josh told Mitch to don his black Ninja outfit, all except the mask. Josh donned his, looped a coil of rope over his shoulder and was ready.

"Follow me." Josh commanded, and leaped on to the expert wall. If Josh had his way they would be all alone. He didn't like showing his expertise and abilities in public but the staff had to be here. Enjoying the opportunity to flex his muscles and talents, he literally flew up the mountain. The staff gasped. Josh had hardly appeared to use the climbing aids at all. Using his exceptional speed and balance, Josh had sprung from peg to peg almost faster than their eyes could follow. It looked like he had flown up the wall.

At the top, Josh looked down and beckoned to Mitch, "Your turn"

Mitch and the staff were speechless for several seconds.

"How the hell'd you do that?" Mitch asked. Then turning to the staff, he said, "How the hell'd he do that?"

"The manager said, "That's impossible. Nobody can do what he just did."

Josh answered them, "In a minute I'll do it again, but much slower so you can see what I do." With that, Josh uncoiled the loop of rope, fastened one end of it and rappelled quickly down to the floor. Part of Josh's strategy was to convince Mitch that he could do things he never dreamed he could be capable of doing.

This time he did it slow enough so that they could see that instead of laboriously inching his way up the vertical incline, Josh had picked his entire route before leaving the ground. Additionally, he *ran* at the target so that by the time he reached it he had velocity. He didn't cling to each handhold—he sprang off of them to the next and kept his velocity moving. Using the identical path used on the first climb but moving significantly slower, he still awed his audience.

Rappelling down again, he told Mitch to get ready to try the technique on the starter course.

"The first few times, we'll harness you with a safety line until you get the hang of it."

Mitch's' reply was: "Is there a stronger word than dubious? Good Lord, Josh, no way I can do that. Hell, I still can't believe *you* did it"

"Believe it or not, you can do it. I know it looks like your defying the laws of gravity. BUT, you know power and speed CAN defy gravity, at least temporarily. Forget the hill, how about just the first two pegs. Think you could reach the second peg?"

"Maybe."

"Okay. Get your harness on and let's try it. Give it your best try and I'll handle the safety rope so you don't fall. Take a good look at your path up the face, do you see it?"

"I guess. At least I think I see what should be the first three."

"Good. That's a beginning. Now back up far enough to get a running start at the wall and whatever you do, don't slow down. Try to go at least the first three posts. Don't even think about falling. You can't fall!! I've got your back.---------Ready?"

"The first three! I'm ready."

"Go!"

Mitch ran at the wall and leaped at the first peg. He barely slowed down as he grabbed it in both hands, thrust his body up so that he could next push off of the same peg with his foot on his way to the second peg. At the second peg he faltered and wasn't able to make the third. He didn't quite reach the third peg, his hand just slipping off and he fell.

Josh immediately took up the slack on his harness and Mitch was left swinging about fifteen feet off the floor.

"How'd that feel?"

"Easier than I expected. But I lost my concentration."

"Go again, try for four. Actually if you can get four today, I'll be surprised. Very, very few can."

The next three times Mitch tried, he couldn't get past the third peg, but on the fourth time he made it to the fourth peg and just barely missed making it to the fifth peg. He was thoroughly pooped.

"That's enough for today. Do you believe it can be done?"

"I believe it can be done, I'm not sure I can do it."

They decided to take the early evening off, Josh to his hotel and Mitch to the police station.

CHAPTER 92

Maybe she was napping in the bedroom? He tiptoed down the hall, past the open bathroom door and quietly opened the bedroom door. The bed was empty. Now worried , he began to notice some other disquieting things. A chair was overturned behind the bedroom door. The desk drawer in the living room was open and papers were strewn about on the desk. There was no way Fern would ever leave a room in that state. It wasn't much but Josh immediately jumped to the conclusion that Fern hadn't left voluntarily.

A cold chill ran up his spine. Fern might be in danger because of what he was doing? For a moment he felt weak with fear. Then something happened. He felt fear changing to anger. He felt a force within himself he recognized. His anger became a cold flame. He felt as if he was outside his body. He became calm, analytical and dangerous.

Rationally, he called down to the desk and asked if they had any idea of where his wife might be or if there were any messages for him. They gave him no help. Next he asked there was any record of visitors for her. They told him that a Mrs. Chinn had arranged to have tea with her in the hotel that afternoon and then left. That was all. He told them he thought his wife was missing and he was going to call the police. They told him there'd been a carpet cleaning crew on his floor that afternoon and they were sure they'd have noticed anything amiss.

Josh was immediately suspicious. Where'd the crew come from? Were they hotel employees or outside contractors? He ran down to the lobby. The clerk on duty thought they were outside contractors that came on a regular basis.

"They showed up in their white coveralls and equipment, checked in with me, told me which floor they were supposed to work and promised to not disturb any guests. All fairly routine"

"Fairly routine? What do you mean, fairly?"

"Well, I didn't recognize any of them. Usually a couple of them had been here before. These were all new guys, and they were all Chinese."

Josh got the name of the cleaning company and was just ready to call them when the young woman behind the desk called him.

"Mr. Rogan? There's a phone call for you. They said it's important. Can you take it here?"

He nodded and was handed the phone. "Who's this?" he barked.

The response was in Chinese. "Some time ago you were warned that white people disappear in Chinatown all the time. You ignored that warning. You didn't pay attention and your wife disappeared. You were lucky and got her back the last time we took her. You won't be that lucky this time. She's where you'll never find her. If you want your wife back in one piece you better go back to where you came from. You've got twenty-four hours to pack up and get out or it's too bad for your cute little Fern." There was a click and the line went dead.

Once more Josh felt as if he was standing outside of his body. Though he was in dreadful fear for Fern, he was coldly and analytically analyzing the problem. He knew Fern, she would be fearful but tough. He knew who the bad guys were and how bad they were. He knew they were capable of murder. He definitely was not going to let them control the next twenty-four hours. The worst thing he could do would be to bring in the police. First, they'd be playing catch-up to him and Mitch. Second, they'd have to play by the rules. But most of all, he didn't trust the kidnappers to just let Fern go if he quit.

He needed Mitch and they needed a plan. When he reached him, Mitch couldn't believe Fern had been abducted until Josh told him about the phone call.

"I'll be right there. Ten minutes."

Josh went back to his room. He needed privacy, time to think. He knew he wasn't going on the defensive, he was going on the offensive. They had to have taken her somewhere, but where. He had an idea and called Mr. Chinn at his home.

"Son of a bitch!" were the first words out of Mr. Chinn's mouth. "That God Damned Leung! What can I do?"

"Mitch and I have a plan, but I need your help. I think the most logical place he probably took Fern is his home down the Peninsula. I bet he thinks we don't know about it. Can your guys check out his Peninsula house for us? I think that's where they must've taken her. I guess I should also check out his flat, but I don't really think he'll be there. Unless you find that the Palo Alto property looks empty, I'll go in after Fern tonight!"

"I'll have something for you within the hour! Where'll you be?"

"Here, at the hotel. With Mitch. Waiting for your call."

Mitch opened the door without knocking and strode in. "What's the plan?"

"We're going to get her! I bet they've got her stashed at his home but we're going to check out his flat too. What do you think?"

"Makes sense to me. We've investigated the hell out of him, and those are the only place we've heard about. I think you're right, he has no idea we know about it. He'd be pretty damn sure she'd be safe there. So what do we do?"

"Unless Mr. Chinn comes up with a surprise, we'll move on his home tonight!"

"The two of us? How?"

"First off, I'll get inside without them knowing I'm there. Then I'll rescue Fern and capture Leung."

"Suuure."

"I mean it. That's exactly what I'm going to do!"

CHAPTER 93

Within an hour, Mr. Chinn had contacted Tong members in Palo Alto and they'd done a drive-by of Leung's address as well as talked surreptitiously to some of the neighbors. He got back to Josh at the hotel.

"It's good and bad news," Mr. Chinn informed them. "The good news is that it looks like that's where they've taken her. The place is heavily guarded and surrounded by a huge fence. It's pretty obvious that they're protecting something or someone there. It must be her. One of the neighbors said there was a big flurry of activity at the gate earlier when a van drove up. At first he had thought it was an ambulance but later he saw a sign on it about laundry cleaning. The bad news is that my man says there's no way anyone can get in. They've got men at the gates and lots of men inside."

"How do I get there?" was Josh's immediate response.

"Josh, let's think about this a minute. My men say there's no way to get into the place. What good can you do down there? Maybe we can negotiate something with Leung." Mr. Chinn advised.

"Tell me the address, Fern needs me and I'm going." He turned to Mitch, "Are you with me?"

"What're you planning?"

"What I'm planning is that they're going to have a surprise visit from a Ninja warrior that'll end up with Fern free and Leung captured. I'm sick and tired of playing by the rules, I'm going all out. Are you with me?"

Josh picked up his suitcase with the false bottom and headed for the door. Mitch followed.

Josh headed toward the rear of the hotel.

"Now what?" Mitch asked.

"Logic," Josh explained. "They're probably keeping an eye on the hotel to see if I leave, we're sneaking out."

Down the emergency stairs, through the kitchen, out the service door, they were able to get to Mitch's car unobserved. Mitch drove while Josh picked up his conversation with Mr. Chinn and coerced Leung's Palo Alto address out of him.

Mitch tried to find out what Josh's plan was. "I can't do what you do. I've got to play by police rules."

"This is going to be my operation. All I need you to do is wait outside and stop any outside re-enforcements from coming in. It's going to be a complete black operation. I'll attack them from the inside, they'll never know I'm there until it's too late."

"Mr. Chinn said they had guards at the gate and inside, on the grounds, how're you going to get in?"

"Watch me!"

A little after 9:30 they arrived within a block of the address. It was pitch black, perfect for Josh's plan.

"Park the car," Josh ordered. In the back seat of the car he prepared himself. Black Ninja suit and shoes. Black hooded jacket. Various throwing knives and stars plus hand claws designed for climbing trees and walls. In addition he carried a folding miniature crossbow and small darts. All was attached to a utility belt around his waist.

"We're going to get as close to the place as we can and you're going to climb a tree and stay out of trouble. If outside trouble shows up, figure out a way to stall them. Don't worry about me, worry about them."

With that they quietly slipped from tree to tree until they were next to Leung's property. It was indeed heavily guarded. It also had a tall, Mexican style wall built around it. The Oak tree that Mitch climbed enabled him to see over the wall and confirm that there were a number of men just sitting around the patio inside the gate, along with the two that were actually guarding it. There were pools of light and pools of shadow.

"Josh, the place is crawling with guys, and it looks like they're all armed. There's no way you can get by them."

"Watch me," was Josh's reply. "And be patient. It may take me an hour or even longer to get in place. I'm going to get in unseen, that takes time."

Mitch turned to watch him leave. Josh took a few steps away from the tree and -------disappeared. He just disappeared. Mitch couldn't believe his eyes. All he could do now was wait.

Josh had blackened his face and donned black form fitting gloves previously. Now he pulled a skin-tight, black hood over his head and face, leaving only a slit open for his eyes, and dropped to the ground. He was a black lump on the ground, invisible to Mitch.

Next he belly-crawled to the wall and lay against it for several minutes. He could hear the men walking and talking on the other side and feel the vibrations of their steps when the walked next to the wall. When he judged they were far enough away he leaped up, grabbed the top of the wall with his fingertips and hung there for a second. Hearing no response he quietly muscled his body up on top of the wall, quickly rolled over it and dropped flat to the ground. Now he was just another indistinguishable lump in the dark area behind some hedges, inside and next to the wall.

The men continued to talk among themselves, mostly in Chinese. Josh counted five of them talking, but felt that there were more, some not talking. The five were easy to track, Josh worried about the silent ones. Patience rewarded him. He lay there for more than twenty minutes, watching carefully and finally located two more men. One was sitting on a window sill and was faintly outlined by lights inside the house. The other was sitting quietly in a lounge chair next to a small pool. He had to assume that both were wide awake and keeping a sharp lookout. They never moved and the others didn't acknowledge them or try to speak to them. The other five took turns making a sweep around the back of the house. Josh had seven pairs of eyes to outmaneuver. He could track and slip by the five talkative ones easily, the other two would be more difficult. He wanted to get inside, unnoticed, at least for a short time.

While he was watching the grounds, he mulled over his plan. Mitch had been left outside purposely as Josh had decided that he would kill if necessary. Leung's gang had killed or been responsible for killing at least three he knew of, including Tim. They had threatened to put Fern's hand through a food disposer and now they were threatening her with death. These guys were armed and Josh didn't for a second believe they wouldn't shoot to kill if they spotted him. He decided he would meet fire with fire. He would kill anyone that got in the way of his rescuing Fern.

CHAPTER 94

Lifting himself off the ground and inch or so and using just his toes and fingertips, Josh snaked his way, ever so slowly, alongside the wall and behind the hedges until he was at a point midway between the two silent guards. Now he could see each of them clearly and more importantly he had a clear firing path at each. Neither of them had moved. The other guards continued to ignore the two.

Carefully, slowly and silently, Josh assembled his crossbow and fitted a dart into it. The darts were about ten inches long and were actually miniature arrows. Made of metal and razor sharp, they could penetrate and kill instantly. He took careful aim and pulled the trigger. A small thunk sound and a moment later the dart hit the man sitting in the chair, in his throat. There was no sound from the target other than a slight gurgle. As Josh had reasoned, he merely slumped a little further into the lounge and was out of the picture. No alarm.

Next was the man in the window. Josh was afraid he might fall and make some noise when he was hit, so kept him to last. Once again he used the crossbow. Again his aim was perfect. As Josh had expected, he fell out of his window seat, but he did so silently. He merely slid to the ground in a sitting position. Both were dead and of no concern to Josh any more. Based on the half-hour he had been watching them, and how little attention the others were paying to them, he didn't expect either of the two to be missed. Now to get inside.

The four remaining guards were moving around but as Josh watched them, he noticed they were predictable and lazy in their rounds. They were grouped in front and only looked at the sides and rear when one of them made a circle around the whole house. Josh worried that there might be alarms in the rear, maybe that was why they were careless on their rounds. He would be careful, but he had plenty of time, the sides and rear of the house were clear for fifteen minutes or more at a time.

Slowly, ever so carefully, he snaked his way, bush by bush, to the side of the house. His Ninja training took over. The patience to wait, immobile, until the right moment came was a basic trait of the Ninja. He never moved until he was sure that no-one was looking his way.

Lying on the ground, behind a row of bushes, he examined the side of the house. Made of brick, three stories tall, it had rows of windows on each story. Josh knew it would be folly to expect any of the ground level windows to be open and even more folly to enter that way. The roof was sloping away from him and had the usual exhaust pipes and chimneys sprouting from it. The nearest roof pipe was within throwing reach of his padded grappling hook.

He questioned himself. "Will I have enough time to throw the grappling hook, secure it and rappel to the roof before one of the guards makes his round?"

He was sure he did. In addition he felt that, having observed the guards making their rounds, they probably wouldn't notice a rope hanging loose from the roof if he was forced to abandon his climb. He waited.

The second the guard turned the corner and was out of his sight Josh was on his feet. His grappling hook and line was coiled and ready. Three strong swings and he let the hook fly. It reached the roof but slid ineffectively to the edge and fell to the ground. Quickly he coiled and threw again. This time he landed the hook behind the pipe and a little to its right. Immediately he leaped to his left and threw a huge curve into the line. The hook responded by sliding to the left and hooked the pipe. Josh glanced at his watch. Five minutes, he still had ten minutes to make it to the roof and haul in his line.

He tested the line, it was anchored solidly. Leaning back on the line he placed his feet on the wall and proceeded to swarm up to the roof in a matter of moments. There was no sign of any guards as yet. In a moment he retrieved his line and was invisible on the roof. It had been an hour and forty-five minutes since he had left Mitch in the tree, and a half-hour since he had shot the two guards. He was running out of time.

He had to get into the third floor, find Fern and neutralize everyone inside before the guards were discovered.

CHAPTER 95

Josh, keeping a low profile, crawled across the roof to check on the guards. Only three were in sight, he assumed the fourth was circumnavigating the building. In a few minutes the fourth appeared from the far side of the building and joined the others. Now Josh had approximately fifteen minutes to effect a surreptitious entrance to the third floor.

Leaning over the edge of the roof at the rear of the house, he saw three windows, all of them dark. All three appeared tightly closed and were the standard double hung type. They should be easily broached. Again the padded hook came into play. Choosing to enter through the center window, he securely fastened the hook to a pipe, it might be needed to get away. Again he used the Ninja gloves to give himself extra traction on the line. On his belly, he slid over the edge of the roof and lowered himself, hand over hand to the window sill.

The sill was barely wide enough to stand on, not wide enough to kneel. With his feet on the sill and the line wrapped securely about his left hand, he taped a small section of the window with duct tape. Carefully, he returned the tape to his pocket and extracted a glass cutter. Next he made a small circular incision on the duct tape and through the glass. Just enough to get his hand and forearm through.

He slowly peeled the duct tape away and the circular cut piece came with it. Reaching through the hole he easily unlocked the window and was able to drop the upper portion. Heavy drapes covered the windows.

Josh silently eeled his way through the window and dropped to the floor, behind the drapes. The whole operation had taken only a couple of minutes and been totally noiseless. He was inside and unnoticed.

The room was dark, but Josh's eyes were accustomed to the darkness and he could see well enough to navigate through the room. It was a bedroom, evidently unused. A large four-poster bed dominated the room, but there were no personal items around. Probably a guest room.

He slowly and carefully turned the knob on the door and inched the door open. It opened onto a hall. He could immediately smell incense and faintly hear voices. Opening the door a little more widely, he could see the hall was empty and the other doors off the hall were closed. He presumed one was a bedroom and the other a bath. He needed to be certain they were unoccupied.

He was just another shadow in the darkened hall as he quickly ghosted to each door and made sure the rooms were empty. They were. At the staircase, he could see the there was very little light on the second floor. What little light there was seemed to be coming from the first floor and up the staircase. Again he needed to be sure.

Stairs squeak. Josh couldn't afford to make any discernible sound, even though there was some noise coming from the first floor. Josh stepped over the stair railing and put his feet between the rungs and made his way to the second floor. No sound. At the bottom of the stairs he stopped and listened. The smell of incense was much stronger.

All the sounds he heard came from the first floor. His instincts told him there was no one on the second floor, but he made sure. Catlike he walked the hall and checked each room. Empty, all of them. Now to the first floor.

Again he bent low and descended the outside of the stairs. He moved quickly as all the voice were coming from a room toward the front of the house. Barely a shadow, he explored the rest of the main floor. Toward the rear of the house he gently pushed a swinging door open and found himself in the kitchen area. An Asian man and woman were sitting at the kitchen table drinking coffee and reading a Chinese edition newspaper. Neither noticed Josh.

Quickly, Josh confronted them, told them in Chinese they were in no danger, bound them to their chairs and then gagged them. He couldn't afford to have the help make an unannounced entrance with what he was planning.

He was sure that all the inhabitants of the house were congregated in that front room. He headed that way through the empty hall. At the open doorway he was able to peer through the crack and see three men sitting at a large dining table. At the head of the table lounged a middle-aged Asian man in a huge armchair. He was holding a cigarette between his thumb and forefinger, Chinese-style and had a glass of something in front of him. Obviously in charge of the group, he was dressed in slacks and open-necked sport shirt. Even though he radiated calmness, his words were high pitched and tense.

"Are the men still watching the hotel? Still no sign of movement? Maybe we should give him a little more encouragement. Maybe send him an ear or something?" He spoke in English.

Josh assumed the speaker was Leung. To Leung's left, one of the men spoke up. Josh shifted his attention to the new speaker. Upon inspection, Josh realized this man was not Chinese, he was Japanese.

"We gave him twenty-four hours, it's only been a few since he got the ultimatum. As long as you're sure he doesn't know about this place, we're okay. Relax, give him a little more time to realize the predicament he's in. If he doesn't move in a couple more hours we can send him her little finger, that'll make him move."

He spoke with a swaggering authority that made Josh take a second look at him. He was huge and muscular, thick necked, bald and covered with tattoos. Josh recognized the tattoos and immediately knew what he was up against.

The man had to be Yakuza, a member of the traditional organized crime syndicate of Japan. The Yakuza believe in violence and are very, very dangerous. How could he be here in America. He also had to be an illegal. Why was he allied with Leung? He must be just hired muscle. That altered Josh's plan. He needed be the first guy taken out in a fight.

Behind the Yakuza and just barely in his view, Josh could make out Fern, tied to an armchair. He couldn't see her face, but presumed she was gagged.

Leung was partially facing Josh's position, the other two mostly had their sides to him. As he was mulling over possible plans to capture the three and rescue Fern, a furious pounding and yelling erupted from the front of the house.

"Open up, open up, we're under attack !!." The Yakuza leaped to his feet and took a step toward the front door. Leung stopped him.

"Hang on a minute, it might be a trick."

Josh knew what had happened. They had discovered the dead guards. It had to happen sooner or later, he wished it'd been just a little later. Now he had to act.

Leung stood up and faced the other two, looking from one to the other and then at Fern, trying to assess the situation. As he swung his eyes from one side of the table to the other, Leung suddenly realized there was a third person standing at the foot of the table. A tall menacing figure all clad in black.

CHAPTER 96

A tall menacing black figure that hadn't been there a moment before. He was struck silent. No one else noticed Josh.

Josh stood there, in command for the moment, in total silence. Suddenly Leung lurched toward the Yakuza and pushed him around to face Josh. The moment the Yakuza saw Josh a gun appeared almost magically in his hand. Josh had expected an immediate and violent reaction from him and was ready. He pulled the trigger on the crossbow and a metal dart pierced the Yakuza's throat, killing him instantly. Mechanically, the Yakuza's finger tightened on the trigger and a shot rang out, hitting the ceiling harmlessly. Before anyone could move, Josh re-armed his crossbow and aimed it at Leung.

"You're next," he threatened.

Leung dodged to his right and yelled to the other man, "get him." Out of the corner of his eye, Josh saw the man swivel in his chair and then just sit there, harmlessly.

Suddenly, everything went into slow motion for Josh. He realized he had, with his superior speed and abilities, plenty of time to react to the guy in the chair. He needed to take care of Leung. In his haste Leung had tripped over a chair. As he rose from the floor he pulled a gun from his pocket and turning, snapped a shot at Josh and simultaneously lunged for the door into the hall. Josh calmly stood his ground, then tracked Leung with his crossbow and fired. The dart missed Leung's throat but pierced the left side of his neck and slammed into the wainscoting behind him, digging in several inches and pinning him to the wall, bleeding profusely. Josh thought his jugular might have been nicked.

Josh swiveled to his right to protect himself from the remaining man, and found him still sitting in his chair with his hands raised in surrender. He looked terrified.

The Yakuza was dead, Leung was pinned to the wall, barely struggling, still bleeding heavily and obviously not long for this earth.

Josh pushed the third guy back in his chair and said, "if you value your life, don't move!"

Josh ran to Fern and removed the gag from her mouth. "Are you okay, did they hurt you?"

"They threatened to cut one of my fingers off if you didn't leave town," was her response. "They were talking about making me talk to you and convince you to leave after they cut off my finger."

"The bastards," exclaimed Josh as he kept his eye on the group. "Well, one of them won't bother you anymore" and he nudged the Yakuza with his foot.

"He was the worst. He was the one that wanted to cut my finger off."

Josh walked over to Leung who was slumped, unconscious, hanging from the dart. "I don't think we'll have to worry about this guy much longer, he's just about bled out." Josh observed.

"Did you know that's Mr. Leung?"

"Yeah, I figured it out." He looked back at Fern, she was shivering. Then she started crying. " I thought I was going to be killed, these men are animals." Josh put his arm around her and murmured that everything was going to be okay. "You're safe and Mitch is outside to get us out of here."

"But," and she paused, "what's going to happen when the police get here, how can we explain this-------------mess?"

Josh extemporized, "Don't worry about it. Mr. Chinn's going to help us clean up the collateral damage. We'll never see the police and they'll never know we were here." Josh hoped he was right.

It was cell phone to Mitch time. He answered on the first ring. "Jesus Christ, where the hell you been? I heard a gun shot and lots of yelling and pounding. Are you okay, where's Fern?," tumbled out of Mitch before Josh could say anything.

"Everything is fine. I've got Fern and she's okay. I need to do some cleaning up in here, should take a half-hour or more. Can you see the four guards in the yard?"

"Yeah, they're milling around outside the front door. If I could hear the gun shot, they could too. I don't think they're too wild about going in. It's like they're waiting for something more to happen."

"Well, something is !. I'm going to open the door, tell them that Leung and his Chinese gangster friend have been killed and unless they want to be involved in a murder case they better split. I think they'll take off and take the gate guard with them."

"You got two dead in there? How're you gonna handle that?"

"I'm working on it. Also there're two dead outside. That's why your guys are in a panic. Call me back when the guys are gone."

CHAPTER 97

Josh had a number of problems to solve. One prisoner, four dead men, the darts, the padded hook on the roof, the tied up two in the kitchen, not to mention the four guys outside. Plus he had to get himself and Fern out of the house and away without leaving any signs they'd ever been there.

First he peeked through the front curtains and made sure the men outside were standing away from the door. Without pause, he threw the front door open and appeared in the doorway, still all in black.

He announced, "You can quit pounding on the door, everything's been taken care of."

One of them challenged him, "Who the hell are you?"

"Doesn't matter. I've got a message for you. One, Leung's dead. Two, the Yakuza outlaw's also dead. Three, the other guy wants you to go and four, the police are on the way. There's going to be kidnapping and murder charges filed and if you don't want to be included in what went on inside, you better get the hell out of here, ASAP !!"

His message was met with complete silence for several moments. Finally one of them spoke up. "What happened in there?"

"Believe me, you don't want to know. You just need to get out of here before the police arrive or you're gonna have a hell of a lot of explaining to do."

"What about the two dead guys out here, it looks like they were shot with a bow and arrow."

"They buddies of yours?"

"Never even talked to 'em"

"Then forget them. You don't want to be accused of their murders, do you?"

The guys talked it over for a short time, turned around and melted away. Josh called after them, "and take the gatekeeper with you."

Josh closed the door and started toward the kitchen. He was going to tell those two the same story.

In the kitchen he gently untied and removed the gags from the two elderly Chinese. "There's been a killing. Your boss and a guest have been killed and the police have been called. I'll testify that you weren't even in the room when it happened, so you can leave right now and avoid the police. As he suspected, they were more than happy to avoid the police. They probably were illegal immigrants. He had Fern accompany them to their room and oversee the packing of their meager belongings, while he returned to the third floor window where he had entered. Leaning out he flipped the line several times until the grappling hook was dislodged and then carefully retrieved it. He closed the window, pulled the drapes shut and reasoned that no one would notice that, maybe for years.

Back in the dining room, Fern told him the household help had taken off running.

He summarized to her. "Let's see, the outside guards are gone, the kitchen help is gone, my grappling hook is retrieved, I've been gloved and disguised all the time I've been here, all I need to explain now are four dead bodies and lots of blood and maybe your fingerprints? "

"They carried me in and tied me to the chair right away. The only things I touched were the chair arms."

"Good. We'll wash them off and be home free."

Looking at the carnage in the room, the first thought that came to him was that all the dead men were Asian. That could be an advantage. Maybe it could be made to look like Chinese gang warfare. He needed to get himself and Fern out along with the one surviving gang member.

He turned to Fern, "did anyone see you here besides these three?"

"Not a soul. I was in some sort of a van until the big ugly guy brought me in here."

"You sure? Because if nobody saw you except the guys here in the room and I was masked when I spoke to the kitchen help, then we're in the clear. Nobody knows we've been here. We have to keep it that way"

His phone vibrated, it was Mitch. "Everybody split, the yard's empty, the front gate's open and I'm still up the tree. So what now?"

"Can any of the neighbors see in through the gate?"

"Give me a minute, I'll see." In a minute he was back. "Nope. The way the houses are situated none of them can see into Leung's yard."

"Good. Grab your car and drive in. Come right on in to the front door. We're gonna get out of here and we've got an unexpected guest."

Josh returned to Fern and the remaining gangster. He was still sitting as instructed, but kept raising his hand as if he was in school and trying to get the teachers attention. He had also thrown up all over his shirt and pants.

"I think he's trying to tell us something," Fern said. Josh got him a glass of water. "What's so damn important?" he demanded.

"You go?" he croaked. "Take me with you, please." he spoke in Chinese.

"You're going with us okay. Tied up and gagged until we decide what to do with you."

The guy rolled over onto his knees and bowed to Josh. This time in pigeon English he said, "You came to save Lady? You come just in time. They were going to mutilate her hands."

"What do you mean, they? You were here and didn't let out a peep," Josh swung to Fern, "did he, Fern?"

"No, no, no." The man rasped out. "I didn't know anything about what was going on until the Japanese gangster started threatening to torture her. I had nothing to do with her being here."

"You didn't notice the lady was tied up?"

"No. I Swear by my Christian God ! I could only see the top of her head behind the Japanese. He was so tall."

"Then who the hell are you? And how come you're here."

"I am an accountant. I am, or was, Mr. Leung's accountant. I really should not be here at all. I only came here to tell him I was quitting."

CHAPTER 98

"You're his accountant and you came here to tell him you wanted to quit as his accountant?"

"That's right. And then he wouldn't let me leave."

"Where's your office, here in Palo Alto?"

"No, I'm in San Francisco."

"Do you still have any of Leung's papers?"

"Sure, I've got all of them. That's why I want to quit. He wanted me to keep double books for him. One for the IRS and another for him. He was much too dishonest for me."

Josh immediately thought this accountant didn't mind being involved in a little dishonesty, but not so much it became dangerous. Maybe he came down to get a bigger cut for himself. In any event, Leung's financial papers were something he could use.

"That settles it. If you're telling the truth you might have saved your life. You're going with us, but still tied up, like it or not."

Josh said he thought Mitch should be here by now, he went to the front door to check.

Mitch was waiting just outside the front door. Josh told him he better come in and see the mayhem.

"Holy H. Mackerel. What the hell went on here?"

"Looks like a rival Chinese gang forced their way in and killed these two. That's the way it looks to me, how about you?"

"A rival Chinese gang?"

"Sure, why not? If you'll notice, the guy on the floor is noticeably a Yakusa. They're Japanese. Leung and his gang were all Chinese. Chinese have no respect for the Yakusa. Leung must have gone outside the Chinese gangs and hired him when his gang got decimated. Some other gang got wind of it and decided to off him before he offed them. Makes sense, doesn't it?"

Mitch looked more closely at Leung still hanging on the wall. "How was he killed, looks like a small steel arrow."

"Maybe the cops'll figure it out. We need to call them."

"The police? Now?"

"After we're on our way. We're going to take this guy and stuff him in your car trunk. Then you're going to drive us back to Mr. Chinn's place and we'll talk to him. He'll be thrilled that we got Fern back and Leung's out of the way. With Leung gone, his nemesis Lee, won't have any backing and he'll get off of Mr. Chinn's back."

Mitch stood back and stared at Josh. Then he turned to Fern and asked again, "we just leave these two here? And the two outside? Josh, you killed them we gotta stay here and face the music. It'll probably end my career but it's the right thing to do. We can get Fern out but we should stay."

"Why? They were going to kill or mutilate Fern. I had to kill them to save her. Why should you or I or Fern pay for saving her life by getting rid of these vermin?"

"But."

"Don't but me. If I hadn't done what I did, I'd be dead now and maybe Fern too. How would you explain that? When the cops figure out that the big guy's an illegal Yakuza and that Leung's a wanted man for extortion and kidnapping, they'll figure it had to be some sort of Chinese gang retribution. Besides, everything that happened here tonight was set off by Leung."

Reluctantly, under Josh's reasoning and the onslaught of Fern's pleading eyes, Mitch gave in.

"Okay, up to a point. We leave everything just as it is here and go see Mr. Chinn. Let's see what he says."

"Agreed," said Josh. And on the way, we'll call the local police and tell them we're a neighbor and we want to report a ruckus going on. We even thought we heard a gun shot. In this part of Palo Alto they'll be here in a shot."

CHAPTER 99

Traffic was extremely heavy. It took over an hour for Mitch to make the drive from Palo Alto to downtown San Francisco and park. On the way and after anonymously calling the Palo Alto police, Josh called Mr. Chinn to bring him up to date. While he was dialing he was surprised to note the time, almost midnight. He reached the Association offices and eventually someone answered. It took a while and some persuading but he finally got Mr. Chinn on the phone at his home.

"Josh, is everything all right? What's going on? Is Fern okay?"

"Yes to everything. But there's some complications. We need to meet you at the Association offices as soon as possible. We should be there in about a half-hour, okay?"

Mr. Chinn was quick on his feet. "I'll be there. Who's with—?

Josh interrupted him. "See if you can pick up any local Palo Alto news, or better yet, do you have any way to listen in on the Palo Alto Police channel?"

"I'll try. I need to dress and make a few phone calls. I'll see you there." Short and succinct.

Mr. Chinn was waiting for them outside the offices, along with his wife. Mrs. Chinn gave Fern a big hug and said how worried she and Mr. Chinn had been for her. Fern had a hard time restraining the tears. She said she was just now experiencing the enormity of all that'd happened to her over the last 24 hours. Mrs. Chinn led her away to the ladies room to calm her down.

Mitch had been standing in the back along with their prisoner. Now he pushed him forward.

"Who's this?" Mr. Chinn asked, pointing at the prisoner.

"He'll keep," Josh answered. "First we need to bring you up to date on what happened. He proceeded to tell the whole story to Mr. Chinn, leaving out no details.

"So you see, I had no choice. It was my life or theirs. Worse, they probably would have killed Fern too. The moment the Yakuza drew his gun the die was cast."

Josh stopped and waited for a response from Mr. Chinn.

After a long silence, Mr. Chinn said he only had one question of Mitch.

"Yes?" was Mitch's response.

"You're a detective, you've investigated crime scenes, what do you think the Palo Alto detectives will make of this one?"

"Good question. I thought about it a lot on the drive up here. I'm inclined to think they'll be completely mystified. Four Chinese dead, shot with an exotic weapon out of the dark ages. No trace of the intruders. I think they'll come to the conclusion that there was a meeting of Chinese criminals that got out of hand. One faction came to the meeting prepared to exact vengeance against the other faction. Like Josh said, when they identify the Yakuza and find out about Leung's criminal history, they'll wrap it fairly quickly."

"You don't think they'll want to follow up on the supposed other gang?" Mr. Chinn wanted to know.

"Oh they'll go through the motions but they won't get anywhere, they never do dealing with Chinese gangs."

There was an even longer silence this time from Mr. Chinn.

Then, "Who's the little person you brought with you.?"

Josh explained. "A real catch. He was Leung's accountant and was trying to quit. Leung had forced him to stay while they had Fern tied up. I think he had an idea he was going to be done away with. He said that Leung had told him that 'nobody quits me and lives.' Anyway, he really wanted to get out of there and when I found out he was Leung's accountant and had a lot of records I decided to bring him along. I think he'll be really grateful."

Mr. Chinn came to a sudden decision. "Mitch, I think you're right. There are many, many things going on here in Chinatown that the Law doesn't know about. This can become one of those things. You, Josh, Fern, the accountant and I are the only ones that know what happened, we'll keep it that way. Chinatown can keep secrets. Is that a problem for you Mitch?"

"It's a stretch, after all, I am a policeman. But for the greater good and considering we saved Fern's life and these guys were all crooks, I can live with it. But what about the accountant?"

"Don't give him a second thought. He's an accountant. He just lost one of his biggest clients. He needs new business and there're lots of Chinese merchants that need accountants. Chinatown will simply swallow him up."

Josh had some additional thoughts.

"Nobody knew about Fern being kidnapped. Everything happened late yesterday afternoon and late last night and away from here. Fern and I can go back to the hotel and quiet everything down to normal. Then I think we should continue our gang busting activities and reporting to the police chief as if everything was going on as usual. After a day or so, when the news hits that Leung's been killed, we can throw in the towel. We'll say it looks like somebody did our job for us. What do you think?"

They agreed that the plan should work. Josh said he would clue Fern in and Mr. Chinn said his wife never talked to anyone about Association business.

Mitch said he needed a good nights sleep and would call Josh for breakfast. They could decide what they were going to tell the Chief of Police.

In spite of his stated belief that they shouldn't be found out, Josh went to bed worried about Fern and the consequences of their actions. She had been rescued but if somehow it came out that they were linked to the crimes it could still be dangerous for her. He didn't sleep well.

CHAPTER 100

Next morning the papers were full of the murders. "CHINESE GANG WARFARE??", "POLICE MYSTIFIED", "SLAUGHTER IN PALO ALTO", were typical headlines. The police were noncommittal officially, but a few items had leaked. One official who declined to be named said the police were operating on the theory that it was some sort of gang retaliation. Another said there was something about exotic weapons being used, something totally out of the ordinary, again off the record.

When asked, a police official said they'd been reacting to a called-in complaint about gunshots when they discovered the multiple murders, but they hadn't been able to locate the neighbor that had made the call.

The coroners office confirmed that all the dead were Asian, but refused any further information.

Mitch and Josh huddled together over breakfast and read the papers.

"No names yet. We can't go see the Chief until Leung's identified."

"Right, but we have to maintain appearances. How about we report in to your Chief and use a little misdirection. We'll tell her we've pretty well broken up a couple of the Chinese teen gangs and that Mr. Chinn's happy about that but we still haven't been able to track down Leung. Mr. Chinn will more than back us up."

He paused for a second, "then I'll add that I don't want to quit looking for Leung because I personally still hold him responsible for Tim's murder."

"And then we just wait until the police ID him publicly?"

"Shouldn't take long. And then we can leave gracefully with him dead and gone. As far as the Chief is concerned, I didn't catch him, but somebody did."

"I wonder if they'll be able to fix time of death accurately," Mitch asked.

"Should be about ten-thirty or so, maybe eleven? Where were you last night, about that time?"

"I was with you, remember?"

"Cute !" Josh gave a short laugh. "And where was I? Well, I was with Mr. Chinn in his office telling him about how we got rid of the gangs. Right? Which reminds me, I better call Mr. Chinn and jog his memory about that meeting."

Just then Fern walked in to the restaurant and announced she was famished.

Josh was very solicitous. "Are you sure you're okay. Slept well? No bad dreams?"

"No, I'm fine. Those winters I spent by myself in Alaska toughened me up to violence. Plus I've rationalized the hell out of the whole experience. You had to do what you had to do, otherwise they were at least going to cut off one of my fingers and probably kill me. I'm okay, really I am. And I'm hungry."

While Fern ordered and ate, Josh phoned Mr. Chinn.

"Do you remember what time it was when Mitch and I got to your office last night? Wasn't it about nine or so?"

No slouch at reading between the lines, Mr. Chinn immediately responded.

"I think that's about right. I think I got home about 11:30, so we were there over two hours. Why?"

"No reason. Mitch and I were just comparing notes. Did you read about the murders in Palo Alto?"

"I certainly did and it's strange. I had just been talking about that property a day or so ago with a fellow association member in Palo Alto. Anyway, I called him right away and he and I agreed it would be best to forget I ever was in touch with him."

"Probably wise. No telling who it was that got murdered yet. Are you available for a short time this morning? Mitch and I should report in about the teen gangs."

"Of course, come on by. Will Fern be with you?"

"I'll ask."

Before they could leave, Mitch's cell phone vibrated.

"That's either the Chief or my Lieutenant. It's crunch time."

It was his Lieutenant. "Where are you?"

"I'm having breakfast with Josh and his wife at their hotel."

"Where were you last night?"

"Last night? Here, mostly. Why?"

"Chief wants to know. What do you mean, mostly?"

"Well we were at the On Sing Association offices with Mr. Chinn for a couple of hours, why?"

"Which couple of hours?"

"I'm not sure, let me ask. Hey Josh, what time did we get to Mr. Chinn's offices last night?"

"Had to be about nine-thirty, maybe a little earlier. Why?"

"Chief wants to know where we were last night."

"Something happen with one of the teen gangs?"

"Lieutenant, could you hear what Josh asked? Did something go down with one of the teen gangs last night?"

"I'll talk with you later. Your detached duty's about to come to an end. I expect you in here bright and early tomorrow morning. In the meantime, stay close, got me?"

"Yes, sir, I'll be there, and if you need me today, Josh and Fern and I are heading over to Mr. Chinn's offices right now." He hung up.

"Whew" he said. "Good thing we were in town last night, sounds like they were trying to blame everything on us."

CHAPTER 101

"I just received a call from your lieutenant," was how Mr. Chinn greeting Mitch when he and Josh arrived at the Association offices. "He wanted to verify that you two had been here last night."

"Not a surprise," Josh said.

"Have you seen this?", Mr. Chinn asked, and shoved a newspaper across his desk to Josh.

It was a later edition than the morning papers they'd seen at breakfast and it identified Leung as one of the murdered men. The article went on to say that the murders occurred on Mr. Leung's property and they thought it might have been some sort of a home invasion. Possibly a Chinese gang. The other three men were as yet unidentified.

"Anyway, I was able to reassure him that you two were here and the time frame he was interested in was from about nine to eleven. He wanted to know if I was sure you were here to about eleven and I said I was because I had to lock up the offices, it was so late. Also, I remembered and mentioned to him, our Karate instructor was just leaving at the same time and we all left together. The instructor asked if Josh could give some more instructions to his class."

Somewhat dryly, Josh responded. "That's right, and I intend to do that if I can, thanks for reminding me."

"I also got a call from the Chief of Police asking that both of you report to her sometime this morning."

"Woops!, I think we're in for a reaming," said Mitch. "We better get over there PDQ."

Fern wanted to know if she should come along. Josh thought about it but decided she should not. "Nobody knows about your part in the whole mess, I think it'd be better if you weren't there. Let's keep that door closed."

Mr. Chinn reminded them that the Chinese Community and his Association were behind him and would support them all the way. "You were here last night and that's all there is to it, understood?"

Mitch and Josh nodded. Mr. Chinn and the Association had their backs and it was time to see the Chief.

This time they weren't kept waiting. They were escorted into the Chief's office the moment they arrived. The atmosphere was frosty, to say the least.

"What in the hell am I going to do with you two? Please tell me you weren't involved with that mess down in Palo Alto."

"We just saw the paper on the way over. Are they sure it's Leung and he's dead?"

"Oh it's Leung, no question. A messy death but he was easily identified. The coroner put the time of death between nine-thirty and eleven and there was no question he was killed there, in his own house. You didn't answer my question."

"Didn't Mr. Chinn tell you we were with him all last evening?"

"Yes, he did. Very convenient. The inscrutable Chinese, right? I guess I'm stuck with your answers, but I'm still mightily pissed at both of you."

She seemed to calm down a little. "Where's your wife, what's her name?"

"Fern. She's back where we're staying. She and Mrs. Chinn have become great friends."

Suddenly, as if a switch had been thrown, she was angry again.

"You two sneaked back into town and took a contract from the On Sing Association to get rid of the teen gangs and never saw fit to let me know you were even here. I didn't even know you were back until yesterday afternoon."

She turned to Mitch. " You. You're a San Francisco policemen. Your allegiance is to the City of San Francisco and to me, not Mr. Chinn or anyone else. I can't tell you how disappointed I am in you. You put me in such a position by your disregard for regulations that I should fire you. Can you give me one good reason why I shouldn't?"

Josh started to speak up in Mitch's defense but the chief put the flat of her hand in the air to silence him before he could say anything. "I want to hear it from my policeman."

Mitch stammered out the best excuse he could think of. "I was put on detached duty so I was taking the initiative whenever possible to find Leung and help with the teen gangs. Isn't that what a detached officer is supposed to do?"

"You see, that's the problem. I don't know what actions you've taken, but I'm responsible for them. Detached duty is not carte blanche, you must work within departmental rules. Lord knows what damage you've done to our reputation. I have to think about what to do about you. I may end up just demoting you. In the meantime, get the hell out of my sight. And as for you, Mr. Rogan, get out of my city. Go back to Yosemite with my blessings."

They left. "She's right and she's wrong. But she doesn't know the whole story, and it's a damn good thing she doesn't." Josh remarked.

"Boy, I'm sure glad Fern didn't come with us," was Mitch's reply.

"I guess I'm being run out of town. First the gang wants me to leave and threatens Fern, then the Chief of police also wants me out of town, and threatens you. It's probably time to leave, what dye think?"

"I think it's going to be awfully dull around here with you gone."

"You'll probably come up with something. A week ago Fern and I were happy and comfortable in Yosemite and then you showed up."

"Don't blame me, that was all Leung's fault. So what are you and Fern going to do? Just fold up your tent and go back to Yosemite?"

"Not right away. We still have a couple of vacation days left and I think that now there's no danger, Fern and I can explore San Francisco on our own. So we should be back in the valley by the end of the week."

CHAPTER 102

At the end of his vacation time Josh showed up at the Ranger headquarters office. The Superintendent had no idea of what Josh and Fern had been through the previous week.

"How was your vacation? Did you spend all your time in San Francisco?"

Josh and Fern had decided to keep their activities in San Francisco to themselves. The fewer people knew anything about the Chinese gangs, the better it would be for him and Fern.

"Yes, we did. A couple of side trips but mostly we stayed in town and visited some Chinese friends. I'm ready to get back to work."

"Fine. Remember Greg? I'm making him your partner at least for a while. Since poor Tim was killed, he's been patrolling on his own. That okay with you?"

Josh thought that would be fine. Greg had been one of the three he had worked with when they were planning to divide up and investigate several cities for illegal bear part activities.

Josh got involved again with the Indians, but with a difference. This time Fern went with him. They hiked with the Indians, hunted with them, ate with them, traveled with them and camped with them. Fern had done some research with the natives in Alaska and was just as intrigued with learning about the Yosemite Indians as Josh was.

Josh was specially interested in their abilities to survive and live off the forests along with their tracking abilities, their use of the bow and arrow and their horsemanship. In return he taught them secrets of the Oriental arts. Fern not only learned what Josh learned but became knowledgeable about Indian cooking and weaving and making clothes out of leather.

One evening, the resident elder of the tribe had a question for Josh and Fern. "If the two of you were turned loose in the woods with just a dress, a loin cloth, a knife and a bow and arrow, how long do you think you'd last?"

Josh looked at Fern and Fern looked at him. Josh paused for a moment and then with a nod from Fern laconically replied, "Long enough."

The elder replied, "We think so too."

In their quiet way, the Indians had just performed a graduation ceremony for Josh and Fern.

Several weeks had gone by with no word from either Mr. Chinn or Mitch. Josh had gone out of his way to see the San Francisco Chronicle every few days, but there had been very little about the murders in Palo Alto since the initial flurry.

One afternoon, returning from a routine sweep through the valley, Josh found a short "call me" phone message waiting for him from Mitch.

"It's about time," was the greeting he got.

"Just got in from my patrol," Josh informed him. "What's up, are you coming for a visit?"

"Wish I could but I'm still kinda in the doghouse around here. It'll be a while before I can get any time off. But that's not why I called."

"Something about the murders? I've been watching the papers and there hasn't been much there."

"Yes and no. The police are completely stymied about the murders and have no idea why a Yakuza was involved. What they have done is a complete investigation of Leung, his background, his associates, his business dealings, his real estate holdings, everything, and boy is it dynamite! On top of that, the Feds are getting involved.

"Tell me more."

"One thing that helped is that his ex-accountant somehow or other came out of the woods with lots and lots of records. At first the police were suspicious of him but he was able to show them that he had been working for a Chinese merchant in Chinatown the night that Leung was killed, so he's in the clear."

Josh cleared his throat and offered a dry "how fortunate for him," comment.

"It gets better. Would you believe that Leung was an Illegal?"

"You mean he was an illegal alien? How could that happen?"

"Don't know, but it's a fact. It looks like he crossed the border from Mexico maybe twenty years ago. The earliest records of him were in San Diego for a very short time and then directly to San Francisco. The police and several other agencies are particularly interested because he seemed to arrive in the States with lots of money. They're even talking about a huge plot that originated in China to take over the drug trade."

"Have they stumbled on to the bear part yet?"

"I think it's popped up but the Police and the Feds think that's small potatoes compared to the rest of the picture."

"So what's happening with Mr. Chinn and the teen gangs?"

"Mr. Chinn's going to be in touch with you soon, but he's really grateful. One of the things that showed up in the accountant's records was a detailed account of Leung's dealings with Mr. Lee. The gangs have been marginalized, they're still there, but leaderless and scared. Mr. Lee's probably on his way to jail, so the Tong is safe and Mr. Chinn's grateful as hell."

"I'll be damned," was all Josh could think to say except, "to quote the Bard, 'all's well that ends well.' Does that mean Fern and I'll be welcome in San Francisco?"

"Mostly. I think I'd steer clear of the Chief, if I were you. She's still suspicious of both of us. She's one smart lady. Fortunately for us, she's on our side. So yeah, come on down to my city, just don't get in any police trouble, not even a parking ticket !!"

"You're probably right."

"And when you do come or I get up there, you gotta explain to me what went on inside Leung's house. On top of that I have no idea how you got into the house in the first place, or how you eluded the guards."

"Later, I'll explain it all to you later, in the meantime we've got some good news for you. Fern and I?, We're going to be parents."

"You and Fern? Really? How'd that happen?"

"Jesus H. Christ, Mitch. Do I have to explain everything to you?"
END.

The Author

Mr. Wren started writing his first novel at age 82, after retiring from a successful Insurance career. His first novel took almost three years to write and publish. Profiting by all the mistakes he made in writing his first novel, he wrote and published this book in 7 months and is within about 4 months of publishing his 3rd.

In between he wrote KISS (Keep it Simple and Successful), a highly acclaimed, down to earth, practical and fact specific"How to" booklet on writing and publishing novels, that has been accepted as a teaching aid at University level writing and publishing courses.

Mr. Wren lives in Oakland, California with his very patient wife Betty. They have 4 daughters and 9 grandchildren. He is a 4th generation Californian, a sailor, traveler, gardener (at Betty's insistence) and tinkerer.

He wishes to thank the literally dozens of people who have contributed to this book. Some knowingly, some unknowingly.

Above and beyond the call of duty:

Nancy Blackman: Editorial comment, proof reading, back slapping, critiques, general encouragement. When I was down, she was up.

Jerry Williams!: Unfailing support, creativity, imagination, super-friendly criticism, and great neighborliness. A computer genius.

15883124R00161

Made in the USA
Lexington, KY
21 June 2012